Breaking the Alpha Council

Book two in the Alpha's Wars Series

S. E Dymek

Dedication

To Aaralyn, Ivy, and Caiden. My biggest inspirations for everything I do. To my husband, Aaron, who is my biggest support.

Acknowledgements

I'd like to thank my parents, close family, and all my inner, dearest friends who listened to me babble about ideas and were willing to read them. I love you all. Thank you to all my readers!

About the Author

S.E Dymek is an upcoming author who has published **The Star Saga:** Including The Morning Star, The Evening Star, and The North Star. **The Alpha War Series:** Book one Between the Alpha's War which are all available with Barnes and Noble, Amazon, Kindle, and other book selling sites. She is also published on several ebook platforms. She has a passion for writing romance novels including paranormal romance novels and fantasy. All of her works include twists and turns, keeping her readers on their toes. She is a mother of three and loving wife. When she is not writing; she is working as a veterinary technician. Born and raised in Rhode Island, she has found her second home in Texas.

Chapter One
Visitors

*A*s if she summoned them, a car pulled into the driveway of the pack house. Nora looked to Jace who was bloody and still very much naked. The long black town car stopped, its tires scratching across the gravel. The doors opened and Nora felt Jace stiffen beside her. She could feel the tension rolling off of him. A low growl rumbled from his chest as the doors of the black town car opened.The first thing she noticed was they were all wearing bright white shoes as they stepped out of the car. They had black suits on as they walked towards them. Nora reached out and ran her hand down Jace's forearm trying to calm him.

"Who are they?" Nora asked through mind link.

"The council." Jace replied, his voice bitter.

"Jace!" The man with short brown hair that was combed to the side called to him as he walked towards them.

"Bruce." Jace said nodding to him,

Bruce stopped just in front of the stairs, the two others following behind him. Nora studied them, it was the three of them together that she had sensed. Their auras weren't too much stronger than Jace's alone but together it was powerful. One man had spikey blonde hair and bright green eyes, the other was bald with chocolate brown eyes.

"I didn't know you had taken a mate! Congratulations! What's your name-" Bruce started to say.

"Are you an Alpha?" The one with the spiked blonde hair asked, cutting Bruce off as the attention turned to Nora.

She felt Jace trying to decide what to say. Nora cleared her throat as the three men gawked at her.

"Yes and No." Nora said hoping Jace wouldn't be upset with her.

"Jace, what does she mean?" The spiky blond hair man asked, the bald one shifted trying to get a better look at Nora.

"She means what she says; Lance." Jace said shortly.

Nora watched Lance grit his teeth and flex. Nora could tell these men were not talked to like this.

"I am acting Alpha of the Red Woods pack." Nora answered quickly.

"Interesting. And Kip?" The bald one said, crossing his arms across his chest.

"He's dead." Jace said, a growl coming through as his eyes glowed.

"Dead?" Bruce said quietly.

"Yes, he kidnapped my mate and was going to use her to help create more of his monsters." Jace said not letting them know that Kip was going to turn her into one; that way they wouldn't know she was once human.

"Monsters?" Lance said quietly.

"Don't act like you don't know." Jace growled and shifted, as if he was getting ready to fight.

Nora squeezed him tightly, she knew his body needed time to heal. He could not take on all three of them right now.

"What are you implying?" Lance growled back.

"I called and told you about them! You all sat idly by and let him cause havoc and chaos. Risking exposing us all." Jace said growling more.

Lance stepped towards Jace, his eyes glowing purple in color. Nora thought the color strange but stepped in between Jace and Lance. Nora's eyes glowed amber as she did. She placed a hand on Jace's chest and looked directly at Lance. She was intimidating and she had barely done anything. Lance was shocked, he simply just stared at her.

"Gentlemen, my mate is tired, naked, and wounded. Would it be all right to continue this conversation in the morning? You are welcome to stay." Nora said, trying to smooth the tension.

Lance stepped closer to Nora; it was half curiosity, half a threat. Jace growled, going to pull Nora out of the way and take on Lance. Nora wouldn't move, her eyes glowed a bright amber daring Lance to challenge her.

"Lance, that is enough. The female Alpha is right. We could all use some rest. I also don't want any more emotions out and about. Jace did just go to war over his mate. So let's not continue rocking the boat." Bruce smiled.

Lance stared at her steadily. He stepped an inch closer to her, closing the gap between them. His eyes fixated on her.

"You are very pretty." Lance said a smirk across his face.

Jace began growling fiercely again, going to tug Nora aside. Nora's eyes glowed brighter as she stepped to Lance. Her face soft but very serious.

"I suggest you listen to your friend before I move aside and you meet your fate." Nora said her eyes were vicious.

Lance's eyes flickered to Jace who was one breath away from shifting. Lance went to move towards Jace and Nora placed her hand on his chest, stopping him. Lance glanced down at her hand touching him, an intense chill vibrated through him.

"Choose your response wisely. I would listen to your friend." Nora said and let a wave of power roll off of her.

It wasn't just an aura of an alpha but something more. Lance stepped back feeling it, Jace felt it too but acted like he didn't. He didn't want anyone knowing how powerful Nora could be.

"Lance." Bruce warned.

"Jace and ?" Bruce continued but stopped asking Nora her name.

"Nora." She said shortly her eyes were not moving off of Lance.

"Lovely. Jace and Nora we all need rest. We can hash everything out in the morning. May we stay at your pack house?" Bruce asked with a polite smile, but it was more of a command.

Jace growled at the questions. Nora reached behind her and entwined her fingers into his hand. She didn't know who they were but she knew they were powerful. She smiled sweetly at Bruce who seemed to be the leader.

"We would love for you to stay here." Nora smiled back.

"Excellent." Bruce smiled.

"We weren't expecting company so you will have to do with what we have." Nora smiled and motioned for Jace to walk inside.

"You'll stay on the third floor. Last three rooms." Jace said before walking in.

Nora followed behind Jace. She felt movement close behind her. She glanced over her shoulder to see Lance following too closely to her. She stepped upwards and into Jace. He placed her arm around her and pulled her into him.

"This is the kitchen. Lori will be here shortly if you need anything she will get it to you or make it for you." He said not even pausing as he walked to the stairs.

Nora walked up the stairs with Jace. Lance, Bruce, and the other man followed them up the stairs. Nora could feel Lance's eyes burning into her. She felt Zara becoming angry inside of her. Jace stopped short and turned suddenly as they reached the second floor landing. He almost made Nora fall as quickly as he stopped. He turned and was face to face with Lance.

"If you keep disrespecting my mate with your eyes. My wolf will remove them for you. I don't care if you're a council member or not." Jace said his eyes glowing, his voice cold and deadly.

Lance stepped into Jace bowing up at him. Nora began to panic. Jace was wounded. Zara could feel Cole and he wasn't in the best shape either. Nora gritted her teeth as the two men stared each other down. Bruce was watching with a smirk waiting for someone to make a move. Nora was done with this.

"Bruce, could you reel in your man.." Nora said her voice was calm but holding authority.

Lance's eyes flickered to her as if no one had ever spoken to them like that. She was giving them an order. Jace was in his own category; he was one of the few that didn't mind standing up. The rest all fell inline. Who was this girl? Lance wondered. Bruce smiled politely and placed a hand on Lance's shoulder.

"Lance, let's not do this just yet." Bruce said a threat in his voice as he made sure to word his sentence just right.

"Jace, you need to remember who we are and your place." Bruce warned him, Nora watched Bruce's eyes glow purple.

She didn't feel anything but she looked at Jace and she saw him wince. Bruce sent his aura out there trying to make Jace buckle. He was fighting hard against it. She watched sweat bead across his forehead and his hands began to twitch. Nora took a deep breath and stepped between Bruce and Jace, trying to shield him.

"Mr. Bruce, if you go up this flight of stairs, the last three rooms are yours. If you don't mind, I am going to go take care of my mate. We hope everything is to your liking." Nora said, taking Jace by the hand.

She called us her mate… Again Cole said excited to Jace pointing it out but still having his guard up as he felt Bruce's aura leave him.

Bruce looked at her dumbfounded. How? The word echoed in his brain. How did she act like she didn't feel what he was doing? How did she not buckle and submit? He knew why Jace was the way he was. He was strong and his bloodline was powerful. He also was aware that Jace had trained himself to fight against the aura. Nora smiled pleasantly at him before walking up the stairs with Jace.

Nora felt them watching them as they continued up to the third floor. She was grateful when they finally made it into their room and she shut the door.

"Who the hell are they?" She asked Jace, still looking at the door.

"The council." Jace growled.

"The council?" Nora asked, confused.

"Yes three waste of space men who were appointed to uphold laws and make sure all packs were ran fairly. They let it go to their heads and do whatever they want." Jace growled as he began to pace.

"Lance, Bruce and what's the third one's name?" Nora asked.

"Douglas." Jace said, his eyes glossing over as he answered her.

"Council is here. Be cautious." Jace sent out to his pack.

Nora looked surprised when she heard his voice in her mind. She smiled a little bit, feeling included. He raised an eyebrow at her as his eyes went back to normal, asking about her smile. She shook her head slightly.

"I need to get you fixed up. Do all wolves just travel naked?" Nora said, pointing to the bathroom.

A smirk appeared across his lips and mischief flashed in his eyes as he began to stalk her. Nora's playful smile appeared as she tried to firm. She narrowed her eyes at him but stepped back against the wall.

"Bathroom. You have wounds." She tried to order him.

He pinned her against the wall, his arms on either side of her head. Her eyes glowed dimly at him as Zara pushed forward excitedly. In return Cole pushed outwards as well, Jace's eyes glowing bright blue.

"Say it again." He said his voice was seductive.

"Go to the bathroom." Nora said a small laugh escaping her.

"No. What am I to you?" He said his voice deep and made Nora's heart race.

"My mate." She said her eyes locked on his.

Jace pressed his forehead against hers as he closed his eyes.

"Again." Jace said his voice was soft but demanding.

"My mate." Nora said, no matter how she said it; it sent chills through him.

His mouth crashed down on hers claiming it. His kiss was hungry, wanting and demanding. His arm pulled her against him as he scooped her into his arms and with one swift motion carried her to the bed. Nora let out a small noise of protest but was quickly subdued by his tongue invading her mouth as she crashed onto the bed.

"I want her." Lance mind linked Bruce as they began making their way to their rooms.

"She's marked by Jace." Bruce linked back.

"And I will mark it over." Lance's mind linked back.

"You know it doesn't work that way. Wolf law says you are not to mark an already marked mate. You cannot lay claim to another, who is already claimed." Bruce linked back.

"It doesn't matter we are the council, we should be able to take who we want and when we want. We are supposed to be all powerful." Lance linked him back.

"Did you not just hear what happened? Jace went to war over his mate. Kip is dead." Bruce linked back.

"And ."Lance said, making a face as he looked at Bruce.

"And nothing we do not need any more trouble right now." Bruce said, turning and locking eyes with Lance.

Lance made a face and walked into his room.

"What was that?" Douglas asked Bruce.

"Lance being Lance." Bruce said but his voice had anger in it.

"He wants the Alpha's mate, doesn't he?" Douglas said his voice had no emotions to it.

"Yes." Bruce sighed.

"This might cause trouble." Douglas said.

"Yes. you're very observant." Bruce said sarcastically.

Douglas grunted and went to his room. He was the outsider among the three of them. The one who had joined but was elected due to his ability to uphold the law. Unlike Bruce who finagled his way to the top and Lance whose dad paved his path. Douglas was here originally for the right reasons. He sighed as he walked into the room. Jace just might be the Alpha who could turn things around he thought as he sat on the bed. He would have to play his cards carefully if he decided he wanted to push for this movement.

Lance slammed the door to his room, anger sitting in him. He walked to the bathroom throwing water on his face. That she-wolf and her honey-colored eyes was dancing in his head. She had a power about her, an aura he couldn't resist. He wanted her. He wanted her in every way. He wanted her perfect figure, thoughts of what he could do to her body ran through his head. She had a fire to her. A fire he wanted to put out. She needed someone strong to make her fall in line. It's like he found some new toy or trophy he needed to keep and put on his shelf. He was obsessing over her. He would get her. He just needed to wait. He told himself as he stared in the mirror. His wolf pushed forward, eyes glowing purple as he did.

Easy Hamilton, we will have her soon enough. Lance told his wolf.

Lance had found his mate once before. In a jealous rage Hamiliton killed her. Images of Eve reaching out and touching another man's arm flashed in his mind. Hamilton pushed forward before he knew what happened. He ripped both their throats out. He still sees Eve's face in his dreams. Her big sad brown eyes staring up at him, blood pouring from her throat as her eyes glossed over and went cold. Lance and Hamiltion both ached from their rash reaction. They walked around with this empty hole inside of them. They found that owning things helped fill the hole.

His newest obsession was Nora. Maybe she was the one who could tame Hamiliton. He felt Hamilton's rage stir in him as Lance thought about it. Maybe she wouldn't be so weak. All the others were weak. She had tamed Jace. Hamilton was worse than Cole. Cole was fierce, deadly, and dangerous but Cole had heart. Hamilton didn't.

We need to end him. Hamilton said.

"We will." Lance said out loud quietly.

Chapter Two
Playing Alpha

"Alpha." The word chirped in her brain, she sleepily tapped Jace. He rolled over and looked at her confused.

"Answer the phone call." She pointed to his head.

"Phone call?" Jace looked at her, his eyebrows frowned at her.

"Someone is saying Alpha." She groaned rolling away from him.

"Umm..Alpha, that's your phone call." Jace laughed, kissing her shoulder.

She looked at him confused and then she remembered. She made a face and sat up trying to concentrate. She wasn't sure who sent it.

"Alpha." Asher's voice flooded her mind.

"Oh I don't know how you do this. And you've done it your whole life." Nora groaned.

"Hello?" Nora responded to him.

"Sorry to bother you Alpha, I know it's early but we were wondering if you are coming by today. We have a few things that need to be addressed and titles to be given out. We also gathered all the information Kip had but I overheard Alpha Jace's Beta say the council had arrived so we didn't burn it. In case you need proof." Asher said quietly.

"Today." Nora said out loud and not in a mind link.

"Today?" Jace repeated.

"I didn't realize it was morning. I need to go play Alpha." Nora groaned a little bit.

"Asher, I will be there soon. I overslept." Nora mind linked back her yawn coming through the mind link as well.

"Thank you Alpha, see you soon." Asher replied back.

Nora stretched really big and then went to get out of bed. Jace wrapped his arms around her and pulled her back into him. His face nuzzled her neck. His lips grazed her mark and she felt intense tingles spread through her. She leaned back into him. She looked up at his bright blue eyes and ruffled hair. She smiled big. Her hand reaching up and brushing a lock of his hair out of his face. He moved his head kissing her wrist.

"So I thought you were against marking me?" Nora asked quietly.

"I was afraid I would hurt you." He said leaning into her open hand.

"So what changed your mind?" She asked, her voice quiet.

" I think it was the goddess but I am not sure. A voice screamed at me to mark you. That it could save you." Jace said, as he kissed her forehead.

" I would have done anything to save you." He said quietly, his eyes looking to the door as they narrowed.

"I think you did when you marked me. I felt it and my wolf showed herself to me." Nora said as she too looked to the door.

Jace sat up waiting for something. Nora looked at him strangely. She didn't feel anything. Maybe her body was still recovering.

"What is it?" She mind linked Jace.

Jace sighed and rolled his eyes at her. He glanced at her and she was wearing a t-shirt and a pair of his boxers. His eyes lingered on her for a moment loving the way she looked in his clothing. He sighed, shaking his head.

"All right losers you can knock and come in." Jace said loudly to the door.

The door opened that second and in stumbled Matt and Dante. They weren't in the room two seconds before they were rushing towards Nora. Nora looked confused as Matt crashed into her wrapping his arms around her in a bear hug. Dante laughed and captured her in a hug around Matt.

"Thank god you're alright Luna." Matt said, squeezing her.

"I knew you were kick ass but damn." Dante said, squeezing her once more and letting go.

"Matt let her go." Jace said again, rolling his eyes at them.

"Sorry Alpha. We are just happy she's ok. We love her." Matt said with a shrug.

Nora looked at him and laughed. "I love you weirdos too."

"Luna, Dante's right, you were unbelievable. You saved us all, not even just our pack… Kip's, the Black Sands pack. Even the Moonlight pack is grateful. They are all in debt to you." Matt explained enthusiastically.

" Matt, stop calling me Luna." Nora said, shaking her head.

"He may not." Jace growled slightly.

"And why not?" Nora asked, making a face as she did.

"Because you are his Luna now. My other half, my equal. By calling you anything else it is disrespectful." Jace is explained firmly.

" In private may he call me Nora?" Nora asked, annoyed.

Jace seems to plot it over in his mind as if deciding if it was ok. Nora's face was becoming more and more annoyed. Jace caught her face and sighed.

"Fine..only in private." Jace said his voice was full of authority.

" So…..Nora..-" Dante waited to see if Jace would react before continuing.

"How exactly did you do all that?" Dante continued asking.

"Well I -

" We need to keep all of that quiet. The council is here..I don't need them finding out about her…abilities." Jace said to him.

"I need to brief the pack." Jace said, talking out to himself.

"Jace I need to get over to the Red Woods pack." Nora said quietly.

Jace frowned, she was right she did need to go but he needed to prep his wolves before the council started asking too many questions. He sighed deeply, he couldn't let Nora go alone but he also couldn't delay her. He looked at Matt and Dante and made a face. He needed Dante here for appearance and if anything went down he would need his back up.

"Matt I am trusting you to take your Luna and my mate to the Red Woods. If anything and I mean anything happens to her I promise you, I will-

"Alpha, I promise nothing will happen to my Luna, I will die before I let anything touch her." Matt swore.

"We also have to plan her ceremony." Dante said hearing Matt swear loyalty to Nora.

"Let's take care of the council first." Jace said going over to Nora.

"Ceremony?" Nora asked, looking up at him as she sat on the bed.

"Yes, our pack needs to swear its loyalty to you like they did me. Normally this would be the moment I mark you but we have done that already." Jace said, as he leaned down and kissed her forehead.

"Get dressed and go get your pack in order. I will see you soon." He said to her standing up straight.

"My pack...Our pack." She repeated with disbelief and a smirk on her lips.

"Yes my Alpha Luna." Jace chuckled, starting to make his way to the bedroom door.

"Matt wait outside the door till she's ready. Dante with me. Send out an order for the pack to meet in the hall." Jace said, giving orders.

Matt and Dante bowed their heads to Nora as they walked out the door. Jace hestatied in the doorway. It was too soon after the battle, too soon after he had just lost her. He wanted to put her in a bubble. Wanted to lock her in these walls with him and keep the world out. She looked at him tilting her head asking what was wrong with the motion.

"Stay safe my little hunter." He smiled at her, the smile that set her heart on fire, throwing her a wink as he walked out the door.

Matt pulled the car into the Red Woods pack house driveway. Asher was waiting on the front steps anticipating his Alpha's return. His eyes glowed slightly as Nora stepped out of the car. Matt's eyes glowed seeing Asher's glowing. Ryker is ready to fight at any moment. The glow of Asher's wolf pushing to the surface causing him to be unsure of his intentions. Matt watched Nora walk towards him like royalty, like nothing was wrong. She ignored the eye glow and greeted him.

"Alpha." Asher said, bowing his head and baring his neck to her.

Matt's tension eased up a little seeing Asher submit to Nora. He was still wondering about his eyes. Matt was waiting for anything.

"Asher." Nora smiled brightly.

"I have gathered all the strong pack members and they are waiting inside to greet you. The rest of the pack will be by soon." Asher explained.

"Nora be careful I don't know why his eyes are glowing and I don't know if all members of Kip's pack were simply innocent. Please be careful." Matt mind linked her.

Nora reached back and squeezed Matt's arm as the mind link went through her mind. She wanted him to know it was ok. Asher tilted his head seeing the mind link happening and he did not hear it.

"Alpha, may I ask a question?" Asher asked.

"You may." Nora replied.

"You can mind link with both our pack and the Cross River pack?" He asked surprised.

"Yes, why is this not normal?" Nora asked, confused and glanced at Matt.

"Normally you have only one pack, you pledge loyalty too and then that pack becomes your world. You can only mind link with them." Matt explained looking at Nora.

"Well I haven't pledged loyalty to any pack." Nora shrugged.

"It's just not normally what happens." Asher said quietly.

"Well we all know nothing normal seems to happen to me. Let me go meet the pack, let's not keep them waiting any longer." Nora said, dismissing the comment.

Asher nodded and walked into the room. As Nora stepped in they all bowed their heads and bared their neck in submission. She scanned the pack, her eyes looking over them. She wanted to make the right decisions. She knew they were all waiting to see who she would pick as Delta and Gamma. She didn't know if this was something she could do in one sitting. She also noticed that these strong ones Asher had gathered were all males. A thought entered her head.

"Dante, is Sarah coming to our pack?" Nora said, mind linking him.

"Yes Luna, she wanted to change packs, if the Alpha and yourself would grant it." Dante said the mind link was quiet and unsure.

"I will speak to Jace regarding this. She's your mate. I don't see a problem with it." Nora mind linked back.

She looked to Asher who was lining people up. She looked at Matt from the corner of her eyes. Was she really about to meet the entire pack one by one? Matt shrugged he didn't know.

"Alpha, if you could have a seat right here, I will get things started." Asher said, tapping on a large red chair.

Nora looked at Matt who smiled weakly back at her before sitting down and taking a deep breath, this was going to take forever.

It was taking forever; minutes creeped by as each member came up and introduced themself. It was like small little job interviews. At first Nora was keeping up but as the endless line moved, names and faces began to blur. She couldn't tell who was loyal and who was not to be trusted. They all said the same thing, something along the lines of I swear by the moon goddess my loyalty to you Alpha Nora and will forever follow you. They stated their names and at the end each one's eyes would glow amber.

"Asher, I don't mean to be rude but how many more do we have?" Nora mind linked Asher as another one pledged themself to her.

Each time one member would pledge themself to her she felt a small spark or surge course through her like she was gaining power or status from it. It was strange. She wondered if this is how it felt for Jace. If this was normal.

"Alpha we have only four more of the male and warriors left." Asher mind linked her back.

"Would it be ok if we break for lunch before we start the remainder of the pack." Nora asked him, looking for a way out.

Matt looked over at her curiously, he could tell she was mind linking someone but he was not in on the conversation and made a face to her about being left in the dark. Matt was really growing on her and she looked at him like a brother now. She smiled and made a face back.

"Trying to find a way out for us, so hush." Nora mind linked him.

Matt smirked, shaking his head as he looked over the crowd.

"There's more in our pack." Matt mind linked her back teasing her.

"Of course Alpha I will have someone start preparing lunch so once we're done you can go eat." Asher mind linked her back.

"Thank you." Nora replied.

"There's more! Matt, I am not doing this back at home." Nora grumbled through mind link to Matt.

"Oh we don't do it this way, you get everyone in a room and they pledge all at once. Done simple and easy. Jace has no patience for things like this." Matt replied back.

"Oh Matt, I could hug you." Nora mind linked back excitedly, she may have found a way to move this along.

She would run this by Asher during lunch and hopefully he would agree since she met more than half of the pack. The second to last man walked up and muttered off the pledge, something about the way he was talking caught her ear. She looked up to him. As he said his pledge his eyes glowed but they were still red. She wondered if you could lie when you said your pledge. No one seemed to notice the small mishap but Nora did. She watched the man walk away, he was huge with a broad back. His hair was cut into a mohawk and he mumbled to himself as he left her sight.

"Asher, who was that?" Nora sent it to him.

"That was Roger, Alpha." Asher sent back.

"I would not choose him, Alpha." Asher added in the mind link.

"We will talk more about him later, thank you." Nora responded as she watched the last man leave.

"Food." Matt said, jumping up.

Nora smiled lightly as he held out his hand to help her out of her seat. She took it and began walking to Asher who was finishing things up.

"Asher, join us for lunch so we can talk a little in private." Nora orders.

"Of course Alpha." Asher said with a nod.

It was funny how his attitude had changed. When she woke up in the hospital room with him he was very cautious. He would answer a question with a question. He seemed guarded. Now he was willing to do anything she asked and was quick to answer. She knew he was grateful but she almost missed the sass.

Chapter Three
Meeting

  *J*ace called a secret meeting, the Alpha council was still asleep, his pack gathered in the hall. His eyes scanning them to make sure everyone was there. He had asked for only one family member from each family to come for the announcement. He wanted the people who went to war with him. They were the ones who saw what Nora was capable of. He still didn't understand Nora and how everything worked. So he knew his pack didn't either. He did not want to send a mind link out because he needed to see their faces, needed to make sure they understood the seriousness of this all. He nodded to make sure Dante who then locked the door to the hall.

  "I gathered you all here to talk about what happened during the battle with Kip's pack. Your Luna sacrificed herself to save us all. I don't understand the powers that the moon goddess has blessed her with. All I know is we are too keep them a secret. There is more to unfold with her and we as a pack will support her on this journey. If others find out about her powers, they may try to take our Luna. I will, we will not allow this." Jace's voice boomed through the room, the pack members nodding and agreeing. Jace didn't even need to use his Alpha aura to make them. Pride filled his heart.

  "The council is here and we do not need them to know anything about Nora. All they know is she is my mate and our Luna." Jace's voice changed in tone, sending out an order to make sure none of his pack members would tell the council anything about Nora.

His pack was loyal so he wasn't worried but there was an underlying fear in the pit of his gut. What if he wasn't sure about every member of his pack. What if there was one who wanted to ruin him. One who did not agree with Nora being Luna. The fear pitted in his stomach and laid a nest there. He was never afraid of anything or anyone but, now he had Nora and his stomach twisted thinking about losing her.

"We need to also discuss setting up a ceremony to confirm Nora as Luna-

Suddenly the door to the hall was kicked open. Dante began growling, bowing up at whoever dared interrupt their meeting. His eyes locked with Lance. Lance let out his aura trying to make Dante submit. He fought till the point he was breaking out in sweat and finally had to cave and bow his head. The room bowed their heads to all except Jace.

"Jace, having secret meetings?" Bruce asked, walking in from behind Lance.

"No, you and your men were sleeping so we didn't want to disturb you." Jace said, pushing away the annoying pain that Lance was trying to cause him to submit.

The room of his pack members dropped lower to the ground as Lance continued to send out his aura trying to make Jace submit to him. Jace locked eyes with him. His own eyes glowing as he felt another painful surge. He was strong and he could tolerate this but his pack members were suffering. His eyes flickered to Bruce and narrowed on him.

"Oh Lance, that's enough. I want to be able to talk to the man today, not tomorrow after he knocks out from trying forever to fight your aura." Bruce grumbled.

Lance lifted his aura and made a face at Jace. He would love to see Jace and his whole pack buckle to their knees, to beg, and grovel underneath his feet. His eyes went to Bruce clearly upset. Bruce waved him off as Douglas entered the room.

"So what's the meeting about?" Bruce smiled, walking to the front of the room and taking a seat.

Lance and Douglas began to spread out through the crowd. Trying to intimidate the pack. Jace watched them, his eyes glowing slightly. He wanted to attack Lance the most out of all of them. Lance was arrogant, entitled, never worked for anything, and didn't care about the rules or the role he was placed in. He just wanted whatever made him happy.

"Jace?" Bruce asked but his voice wasn't asking, it was a reminder that he was higher ranking than him and he wanted an answer now.

"We were talking about a ceremony for my mate becoming Luna." Jace answered shortly, eyes still locked on Lace.

"Oh excellent. That is a special occasion. We will attend. When is it?" Bruce asked.

"We were just going over the details." Jace said through his teeth.

Dante looked up at him, his eyes filled with worry. The tone Jace was using with the council was getting very close to being disrespectful. He was worried what they would do if they felt insulted. He was watching everyone the best he could. He would have Jace's back if needed.

"Ok then I will help! We will do it two days from now, at sunset. We should go out in the woods when the last ray of sunlight touches the earth and the moon starts peeking out. Your mate has a glow about her and I think it would be beautiful like that. We will be thrilled to honor you with our presence. It will be a blessing on your pack." Bruce announced.

Jace clenched his jaw, becoming angry. No one invited them, no one had planned anything yet. He could feel Cole wanting to come forward.

"That is a perfect idea, High Alpha Bruce. We will begin working on all the tiny details. Thank you for solving our problems. Luna will love it." Sarah spoke up seeing the rage that Dante and Jace were sending off.

She knew that it was better to work smart than emotional. Jace's eyes snapped to her, almost surprised. He watched her reach over and squeeze Dante's hand trying to calm him as well. The gesture made him miss Nora. If she were here she would tell him to agree, it was simple and they didn't need to cause ripples for no reason.

"What is your name, girl?" Bruce asked, looking over to Sarah.

"Sarah, High Alpha." Sarah said, bowing her head.

"Jace, is she new to your pack? I don't think I remember her." Bruce said, looking from Sarah to Jace.

"Yes, She recently joined. She is Dante's mate." Jace said quietly.

"Congratulations Beta. I wish that the moon goddess will bless the two of you." Bruce smiled brightly.

"Thank you for the perfect plan for the Luna's ceremony. We will begin working on all the extra pieces." Jace said, trying his hardest to be polite so they would leave.

"Oh you're most welcome. Jace, do you serve breakfast around here?" Bruce asked, his stomach growling.

"Yes, if you head to the pack house and go to the kitchen Lori will fix whatever you like or you can pick from the already made breakfast." Jace smiled.

Bruce nodded and then motioned for Douglas and Lance to follow him. Douglas did not show any interest in anything going on and was the first one out of the hall. Bruce lingered in the door waiting on Lance who continued to stare down Jace. Once they left Jace wanted to explode but he took a deep breath.

"You all can go back to your homes, spread the word about the Luna's ceremony as well as the other important thing." Jace order.

"Dante, I need you to take your mate and find me a white or gold gown for Nora. If it is white I want something that shimmers. Sarah it's your job to make sure it gets done. As well as setting up the area and making it beautiful. You can have whoever you want to get it done." Jace said giving orders but not even thinking about how sweet he sounded.

"I will do Alpha." Sarah smiled.

"I need to go check in with Nora. Dante, I need you to keep things in check around here and put someone on Alpha council duty. They don't have to officially go over and hang out but I want to know where they go and what they do." Jace ordered him.

"Of course Alpha." Dante nodded.

Dante pulled Sarah into him and he kissed her deeply before winking at her and heading out. Sarah, embarrassed by the display, bowed her head at Jace before heading out. He was going to go see his mate. He walked out the hall door, his eyes set on his car. He crossed the parking lot in no time. Reaching the car he flung open the door and as he was about to get in his car door was shut on him. Lance shut the door and leaned against the door of the car.

"Lance, I am trying to go see my mate. It's not wise to stop me." Jace said, warning him.

"I was just about to ask where your pretty little soon to be Luna is." Lance smirked.

"She is with her pack helping them build and start over." Jace said almost growling.

"Yes, that's right. She is an Alpha. How is that for you? No power struggles?" Lance chuckled.

"Its is fine. May I go?" Jace growled.

"I would like to see her later, have dinner with her." Lance smiled.

"When we get back we will see about dinner plans. We have had a busy day already and it's not even noon." Jace said to him.

"No you misunderstand. Not with you, me, and her. With just me and her. Of course it would be for business and for the investigation. Just food is always better when questioning a person." Lance smiled brightly

"I will talk to Nora and see." Jace said, trying to get into the car before Cole ripped him to pieces and he had another war on his hands.

"No seeing. It will happen ... Have a nice day, Jace." Lance said, commanding him before he left.

Chapter Four
Loyalty

"Asher would it be possible to have the rest of the pack gather in a group and pledge their loyalty." Nora asked, hoping she wasn't offending some tradition.

Asher was searching for the words to say, he was worried that she would not be able to get a good judge of the pack members. Nora studied his face. She watched different emotions flash across worried, unsure, and then as if he was trying to think of a plan.

"Asher if it's some type of tradition I understand but it's taking a lot out of me right now. I'm still recovering." Nora said, taking a bite out of her turkey sandwich.

"She really does need to get back and rest." Matt chimed in.

"No Alpha it's not that it's a tradition. I don't know where everyone's loyalty lies. I was hoping if you met them one on one you might be able to judge them." Asher explained.

"I have a plan for that." Nora smiled at them both popping a chip into her mouth.

"Well do tell." Matt said with a mouth full.

Nora patted him under the chin telling him to not talk with food in his mouth before looking back to Asher. She made a face before continuing.

"So that last person. Roger. When he pledged his loyalty to me his eyes glowed red. They didn't glow amber; Kip's color was red. So I have a theory that the ones that aren't really loyal to me will glow red and the rest will be amber. Then we just handle the ones with red eyes." Nora said with a smile.

"That is interesting. I wonder how he pledged himself but managed to keep loyalty to Kip, even though he is dead." Matt said out loud.

"There is a rumor that when a pack loses an Alpha that if no Alpha steps forward and they choose to stay with the pack and not go rogue. They can remain loyal to the previous Alpha." Asher said quietly, his voice unsure if he believed it.

"That would make sense." Nora said quietly.

"The plan sounds like it will work though. Where are we putting them? Jail? Dungeon? Nasty lab slash hospital?" Matt said, wiggling his eyebrows at Nora.

"I'm not sure about that part yet." Nora said, throwing people in jail just because they were loyal to someone seemed wrong to her.

"We also need you to appoint Delta and Gamma." Asher said quietly.

"Asher, who do you trust here?" Nora said, taking a sip of sweet tea.

Asher thought to himself quietly. Matt watched him like he was watching a tv show, popping chips in his mouth. He began to chew louder and open his mouth more waiting for Asher to make up his mind. He was doing it in part to be annoying. Nora narrowed her eyes at him and wacked him in the arm.

"Hey." Matt said, holding his arm like Nora had broken it.

"Oh stop! And chew right." Nora said, rolling her eyes at him.

She felt him before he was even in the room. Her body began to tingle like it knew before her mind did. His scent floated through the air, his scent alone gave her chills. She instantly wanted to curl into him. Zara inside of her began to freak out excitedly.

Cole. She purred, smelling him.

I know. Nora chuckled back to her. She was just as excited.

She contained herself pretending to not be jumping out of her seat to see him. He walked into the kitchen and she felt herself melt. He was always breathtaking. Her eyes lingered on his broad shoulders that she just wanted to cling to. She imagined how it felt to run her hand down his muscular back. Images of them together fluttered through her mind, her cheeks flushing at the sight of him. His charming smirk rolled across his face as his eyes caught hers. She knew immediately that he knew what she was thinking of. He crossed the room to her like nothing else was going on, nothing else mattered.

His anger at Lance melted away seeing her. Cole was begging to shred him to pieces, especially the way he kept looking at Nora. She was his. Thinking of Lance looking at her made his wolf and him possessive. Without thinking He went to her, lifting her out of her chair and pulling her against him. She let out a small squeak as she crashed into his chest. The noise she let out was quickly covered by his mouth. He pulled her into a passionate kiss. It was possessive and demanding. He showed her how much he wanted and needed her with just his lips. A small whimper escaped her lips as her body craved him.

Matt cleared his throat pretending to choke on his sandwich, breaking the moment. Jace pulled back from the intense kiss and gave Matt a look. Matt put his hands up as if to say no offense and pointed to the sandwich.

"What has my little hunter, I'm sorry Alpha accomplished today?" Jace smirked.

"That's right Alpha and you need to remember that." Nora said, poking his chest teasing.

Jace pulled her against his chest once more burying his face in her neck. He placed small kisses across it and reaching the spot where he marked her, he flicked his tongue over it. An intense chill went through her. It was the simplest touch but she felt her knees buckle. She grabbed onto his shoulder to balance herself and choked back a moan. He chuckled and then leaned towards her ear.

"I will show you later who's Alpha and I will make sure you always remember it." Jace whispered.

"So Alpha." Asher started to say.

"Yes-" Jace started to answer but realized they were not talking to him

"Yes." Nora asked, looking at Jace with a smirk.

"Did you want to me to just gather the rest of the pack and we can proceed with a group pledge?" Asher asked.

"Group pledge? How have you been doing it?" Jace asked.

"One at a freaking time." Matt said dramatically laying across the table, like he was going to pass out from exhaustion.

"One at a time." Jace said almost as dramatic as Matt.

"Hush you two." Nora said, waving her hand at them.

"You've been meeting an entire pack one at a time." Jace said, baffled.

"Well Asher wanted me to test each pack member by meeting them and seeing if I could sense if they were loyal or not." Nora explained.

"Love, that's not how you're going to find out if they are loyal to you or not. You have to work with them side by side. It takes time, not one meeting." Jace explained.

"Well lucky for you, I already figured out a way to weed out certain ones." Nora said, throwing him a wink.

"What am I missing?" Jace asked but looked at Matt.

"We think some of the ones that are still loyal to Kip when their wolves come forward their eyes will glow red, instead of amber." Matt explained.

"And why do you think this?" He asked Nora.

"Because it's already happened." She said sticking her tongue out at him.

A playful smile spread across his lips, his eyes glowed slightly as he stepped forward to her, daring her to continue. She stepped into him with a smirk on her lips, she let Zara come forward letting him know she will do what she wants. He growled slightly, his hands going to her hips. She let out a small growl as he picked her up.

"She's not meeting anyone, I'm taking her!" Jace said as he started to toss her over his shoulder.

"Jace!" Nora laughed, yelling at him.

"Nope you've tempted me too much." He said turning and heading towards the kitchen exit.

"Are they always like this?" Asher asked Matt.

"Maybe? Alpha….um Alphas can ya'll do that a little later ? We need to wrap things up here. I too would like to go home and toss a certain someone over my shoulder but we gotta do this." Matt called to them.

"See even Matt…..Matt is being more grown up than you right now." Nora laughed squirming in his grip.

"Matt doesn't know any better." Jace grumbled, turning around and bringing her back to the kitchen table.

"Matt, how are you and Lilly by the way?" Nora asked excitedly.

"Ahh she hates me but she loves me." Matt smirked.

"I understand the whole hunter-wolf thing." Nora said, throwing a wink at Jace.

"I'm not worried about it. Few can resist my charm." Matt's smirk spread into a grin.

"Don't you wink at me. You guys have her for another two hours." Jace said to Nora first and then Asher.

"Excuse you! I am not some piece of property! You don't get to delegate my time. I will be home when I'm home." Nora said, her eyes glowing as she looked at Jace.

Jace pulled her into him and nuzzled his face into her neck.

"You got two hours or I promise I am coming to get you." He said his voice was full of intent.

Nora shivered and moved away from him. She didn't trust herself to remain so close to him right now. She would love for him to take her home and do the things his voice promised. However, she needed to set up things here. That would have to wait.

"Asher, I think I'm ready...Let's do it outside. I could use some fresh air." Nora said walking to leave the kitchen.

"We could all use some fresh air." Matt said with a smug look on his face.

"Come on Matthew." Nora laughed at him.

"You know what. I'm going to stay." Jace announced, following after them.

Asher's eyes glossed over as he summoned the rest of the pack to the garden. Nora waited for him to come back to them before heading out. She paused in the doorway.

"Asher after we need to sit down and talk about who you trust here." Nora said to Asher.

"Jace, is there a way Sarah could get here? I want her opinion as well." Nora asked a thought coming into her mind.

Jace nodded understanding and his eyes glossed over.

"Sarah, your Luna is requesting your presence at the Red Woods pack. Come right away." Jace summoned her, adding Nora to the link.

"Yes, Alpha and Luna. I will be there in twenty minutes." Sarah responded.

"Alpha, we will be meeting in the garden. It's big enough and I would like you to see it." Asher said with a small smile.

"Lead the way." Nora smiled at him.

Jace came up behind her and wrapped his hand around hers . She smiled up at him, her fingers weaving into his as she began walking. She leaned against him as they followed Asher.

Chapter Five
Becoming Alpha

Nora walked into a stunning garden of green. There were vines flowing from archways and wrapping up light posts. A beautiful fountain in the middle of everything. She was surprised that Kip would have something so beautiful.

"This is stunning." Nora whispered as she looked around, the pack members began to join them.

"Wait, it's about to become magical." Asher said to her.

"What do you mean?" Nora asked, looking quickly about.

"You'll see seconds after the sun sets." Asher smiled back.

The sun was setting and the moon was slowly coming out as they waited for the last bit of pack members to gather. Then as if someone pressed a button flowers began to bloom. The archways and vines that wrapped around the lamp post all sprouted white flowers. Along the fountain bloomed blue moon wisterias and moon flowers. Nora looked around in amazement. It was breathtaking. She saw a few of the pack members smile up at her as they saw her expression.

"We need one of these at home." She whispered to Jace.

Jace was not watching the flowers bloom but he was watching her face light up. He squeezed her hand lightly as the words "at home" tugged at his heart. A small smile came to his lips as he realized she thought of his pack as her home.

Asher looked over the pack and nodded his head to Nora, letting her know it was time. She inhaled deeply and all of a sudden felt super nervous. She knew she was going to have to address them but she didn't think she would feel like this. She also had no clue what to say.

"You got this." Jace and Asher's voices echoed in her mind.

She chuckled lightly that they both said the same thing.

"Hello all. Thank you all for coming out to meet me. I am sorry we are having to do it like this. Your home here is absolutely beautiful. I am going to do my best as your Alpha to help lead you out of this hard time. Shortly we will be assigning roles. You all know Asher is my Beta. We will soon find Delta and Gamma. I would like to get to know each one of you as time goes on. I hope to grow this pack closer and stronger." Nora smiled.

She saw several head nods throughout the crowd, she didn't want to get into how Kip was a horrible leader and that the way things were run under him would not be continuing. She wanted to keep this short and sweet.

"At this time we all pledge loyalty to Alpha Nora. Alpha Nora has requested that when you pledge you look up." Asher said, stepping forward.

"Look for red eyes." Nora reminded Matt, Jace, and Asher.

They nodded hearing her mind link. The crowd nodded to her and then they all waited for someone to start so they could follow. Asher stepped forward. He then turned to face Nora and kneeled down.

"I Asher of the Red Woods pack, pledge my loyalty to Alpha Nora." Asher said as a guide for the rest to follow; as he pledged his eyes glowed amber.

Behind him they all kneeled and then a chatter rose all in unisom, pledging their loyalty to Nora. A surge coursed through Nora as the rest of the pack pledged to her. A sea of glowing amber eyes looked up at her. Then she spotted them, the red glowing eyes she knew would be there. Three of them in the very back. She wondered if they were Kip's Delta and Gamma. That would be a total of four, counting Roger. She felt Jace stiffen behind him, his eyes glowing ice blue as Cole pushed forward spotting the threats. Nora rubbed his arms slightly trying to calm him.

"I don't want them to know, we know." She mind linked Jace.

"What do we do now Alpha?" Asher asked her through mindlink.

"I'm not sure, I guess we'll watch them. I don't want to push this issue right now, maybe I can win them over and if not then we will cast them out." She replied through mind link adding Jace into it so he would know her thoughts.

"We should just get rid of them." Jace's mind linked her back, Cole begging to be let out.

"I actually agree with Jace. We don't need anyone else ruining this already damaged pack." Asher mind linked back.

"What if they are just still loyal to Kip because they don't know change, what if they never had a choice. Let's give them a chance." Nora urged through mind link.

The pack's eyes faded back to normal colors as their wolves receded. They sat quietly waiting for Nora to address them. Nora realized they were waiting on her, she was too wrapped up in the conversation between her, Asher, and Jace.

"Thank you all so much for your pledges. I hope I am worthy enough to lead you all in the right direction. We shall hold a banquet in two days time to celebrate. In that time we will come up with your leadership team and announce titles. Thank you all for coming and I can't wait to meet each of you individually." Nora smiled at them all.

They bowed their heads and then began leaving. A young woman came up to her. She seemed bold but timid at the same time. She caught Nora's attention as she slowly made her way to her.

"Alpha?" She said so softly that Nora barely caught it.

"Yes?" Nora smiled at her.

"I am sorry to speak out of turn-

"Speak out of turn?" Nora asked, looking from her to Asher.

The girl dropped her head when she asked and went silent. Nora looked to Asher to explain what this was about.

"Kip made sure the women were seen and not heard. They had no rights." Asher explained shortly.

"What's your name?" Nora asked her softly.

"Lyla. Alpha." The girl replied, keeping her eyes downward.

"Lyla, how can I help you? You may look at me." Nora said softly again.

"I ..I wanted to talk to you about the conditions of the pack and how they treat the women." Lyla said, her voice getting stronger as she spoke.

Nora could tell it took a lot out of her to gather the strength and come to ask her. She saw her nervously playing with one of her fingers as she spoke to her. She kept glancing down and then as if she remembered it was ok to look up, she would tear her eyes from the ground and look at Nora. Nora reached forward and took the girl's hand in hers.

"Lyla I actually have Sarah coming here shortly. We were going to be discussing several things and this will be one of them. I promise you no one is going to hurt anyone, anymore. You're welcome to join Sarah and I to discuss this matter." Nora smiled at her.

"Thank you Alpha. I would really like to be part of that. Please send for me when you meet with Sarah." Lyla said, bowing her head.

As Lyla bowed her head, Nora noticed a scar in her hair line that ran down to her ear. Without think Nora reached out and touched it. Lyla winced slightly and looked scared.

"What happened?" Nora asked.

"I…I made Alpha…Kip upset." Lyla whispered.

"Why was he upset?" Nora asked, anger beginning to course through her veins.

"I looked up when he was speaking to me." Lyla said quietly.

"You looked up?!" Nora nearly yelled, becoming angry.

"Sorry Alpha." Lyla said, shrinking away.

"No you don't need to be sorry. I am sorry I didn't get here sooner." Nora said, trying to force her anger down; she didn't want to scare Lyla.

"Lyla, go get something to eat and some rest. I will summon you once Sarah has arrived." Nora smiled, patting her hand gently.

Jace could feel the tension rolling off Nora. He squeezed her hand gently letting her know he was still there for her. She leaned back against him as she watched Lyla walk away. His woodsy scent invaded her nose and she felt herself instantly relax. His warm body almost made her forget why she was outraged.

"This pack is so damaged." She whispered to him

"We will fix it in time." Jace whispered to her, rubbing her arm.

Nora nodded, she had thought to quickly pass the pack onto Asher but as things were starting to unravel more and more. She felt obligated to stay and make sure this pack turned around for the better. She knew there were others who still felt the way Kip did and she needed to make sure that his reign of terror did not continue.

"Asher, we need to start setting things up. Let's go back to the pack house. Sarah will be here shortly." Nora said knowing she needed to start making decisions.

"My first order as Alpha is that all women in this pack are equal. You are not to belittle, harm or abuse any female of this pack. Women are to hold their own opinions and are no longer to be seen and not heard. If anyone has any concerns about this new order they can speak to me directly." Nora sent out a mind link to all of the Red Woods pack.

She was prepared for backlash and welcomed it.

Chapter Six
Planning

*A*n influx of multiple thank yous flooded Nora's mind. An overwhelming surge of gratefulness and overjoyed feeling made her stagger in her steps. She grabbed ahold of Jace's arm to steady herself. Jace looked at her quickly, her eyes tearful as she got through the emotions. Then it happened, a small tinge of anger and upset hit her. She knew there would be upset somewhere in the pack.

"Nora what's happening?" Jace asked, Nora was squeezing him so hard she was leaving finger indentations on his arm.

"How do you deal with this?" She whispered as the emotions subsided.

"What?" He didn't notice anything.

"The mind links. You can feel everyone's emotions when they do it." Nora said, releasing him.

"It's hard at first but we grow up with it. You will get used to it." He said, kissing her forehead.

"I hope so. That was a lot." She said letting out a breath.

"What did you do?" Jace asked, confused.

"She set all the women free." Asher said with a grateful face.

"You have no idea what you just did for the women in the pack. Thank you." Asher said, bowing his head.

Jace smiled proudly and squeezed Nora against him. She was turning into an Alpha more and more. He glanced at the sky and thanked the moon goddess for picking her for his mate.

"You're doing great Luna Alpha." Matt mind linked her as they got back to the Red Woods pack house.

She smiled at him and nodded her thanks. Nora spotted Dante's car. She watched Jace's expression change but then it faded when he saw just Sarah sitting on the front steps.

"Worried Dante left to come here?" Nora sent him.

"Yes I need some to watch the roaches." Jace replied back.

As they reached Sarah she stood up and bowed her head to them.

"Alpha, Luna." She greeted them respectfully.

"Sarah, I'm so happy you came. I have a lot to ask you. Come inside we will get settled." Nora smiled brightly at her.

"Of course Luna." Sarah nodded.

Asher led the way into the pack house, he started towards the office. Nora followed him but didn't really want to do this in such a close and confined area. She could feel Zara clawing inside of her. She didn't understand what she wanted but being outside had made her settle a bit.

"Asher, is there a back patio or someplace like that?" Nora said, stopping half way there.

"Of course Alpha." Asher said shifting gears and walking towards the back of the house.

"You ok?" Matt asked Nora.

"I don't know but being outside makes me feel better." She said as Jace glanced at her.

Our Little wolf wants out of our little hunter. Cole said to Jace.

Jace nodded understanding now. Nora was a new wolf and didn't understand all the signs yet. She hadn't even shifted yet. If her wolf kept pushing her and gnawing at her, she might shift and it would be dangerous to do that here. He needed to help her transition and he needed to start teaching her soon.

"Jace?" Nora asked, looking at him as she patted the seat next to her.

Jace didn't even realize they had walked outside onto a small little patio. Jace smiled at her letting her know he was fine and sat down next to her.

"Asher and Sarah I want a list of names of people who you think would be best for the roles as Delta and Gamma. Sarah if you weren't coming over to Cross River I would say one of those spots are yours. I want a woman in one of the roles." Nora said, shifting slightly in her chair.

Asher looked at her at the mention of a woman holding the position. He cleared his throat trying to find the words to question her.

"Alpha not that I am against it but a woman has not held a position before." Asher said, a little nervous.

"And I'm pretty sure an Alpha being a female is a first." Nora said, making a face at him.

"Well yes." Asher said but Nora cut him off before he could continue.

"Perfect, now I need names. For females I was wondering what you thought of Lyla?" Nora said and then finished looking at Sarah.

Sarah looked down as she thought, she made a few faces. Asher watched Sarah and then looked to Nora who was waiting for a response.

"Lyla is quiet." Asher said, filling the silence.

"Well duh she's quiet to you, you're a man. She wasn't even allowed to look at you and never mind speak to you." Sarah said with anger in her voice.

Asher sighed deeply at her anger and Sarah narrowed her eyes at him. Jace let out a low growl letting them know he was becoming upset. Asher eyes flickered to him, a tinge of amber in his eyes. Sarah bowed her head respectfully. Nora gave Asher a look and he stopped.

"Lyla is…quiet. She kept to herself for the most part. She has no family. Kip murdered her mother; her father lost it over her mother's death. He confronted Kip and Kip killed him. After that Lyla shut down. Stayed to the side lines and the background didn't want any trouble from anyone." Sarah said softly.

"What happened to her mother?" Nora asked.

"Kip had always wanted an army. Before he thought about creating them he was wanting to….make them." Sarah said awkwardly.

"Meaning?" Nora asked, confused.

"Kip was trying to impregnate all women of the pack. He started with the woman who were already mated. Trying to force more control over his pack. Lyla's mother was the first. She fought back hard and fiercely. Kip killed her and when the mate bond was broken it collapsed her father. Rage took over and he attacked Kip. After several attempts they killed him. Lyla's mother was the first but she wasn't the last. Kip tried again with another already mated female and the same thing happened. After the third attempt went wrong. He found a way to start creating his monsters. The pack was going to go against him and his chaos but once he started spawning those things, they cowered in fear." Asher explained.

Nora looked horrified. Why hadn't anyone stopped him before it went this bad? She glanced over to Sarah who shifted uncomfortably. Part of Nora wanted to ask if she had anything like that happened to her but she wouldn't right now. Not in front of Jace and Asher.

"I was supposed to summon Lyla but I am glad I have not yet." Nora whispered.

"What I can tell you about the women Luna, is most are broken or scared. There are few that held it together but now you're here and making changes more might step forward to be part of the change. Do not blame the ones that will fall into familiar patterns. They might still be too of the men or that this isn't real. There are some that are very, very damaged. Jaime is someone who is strong. Who always fought. I would suggest talking with Lyla more as well. She might have it in her, but meet with Jaime too." Sarah explained while she thought out loud.

Nora let out a sigh and brought her leg up to her chest cradling it as she listened to Sarah talk. Her chin rested on her knee. She wished Kip had died slower. Nora's eyes began to glow as she felt anger bubble in her. Jace looked at her as he felt the anger roll off of her. Cole pushed forward trying to connect with Zara; hoping he could calm her before she forced Nora to shift.

Little wolf Nora isn't ready for that yet. Cole said softly to Zara.

She needs to be. I need out. Zara growled.

She will in time, give her time. Cole said to her, sending out his aura trying to calm her.

Jace watched Nora shut her eyes as Cole and Zara communicated. The fact that Zara was allowing Cole in was amazing. He was grateful. Nora wasn't sure what was going on, she could feel Zara becoming angry and restless. She then felt Cole but didn't know what was going on. She felt a calming aura rush over her and she felt Zara settle down.

"Asher. Names?" Nora said her eyes still shut as she tried to focus on anything else.

"Jordan is someone you need to meet, he would be a strong leader and wants equal rights for both males and females. He has two young daughters and was strongly thinking about leaving. Gabbit is another. Then there's Chance. I don't know much about Chance but there was always talk about him being a good guy. I second Jaime and also I think Iris." Asher said, watching Nora closely.

"Gabbit is a pig and Iris broke all the rules but not because she was being a rebel and going against Kip; because her mind is shattered." Sarah said softly.

"Ok so I will meet with Jaime, Jordan and Chance tomorrow morning. I need to appoint someone to oversee the pack's medicine. Who is your medical person?" Nora said quietly now, holding her head.

Zara became enraged again hearing Sarah talk about Iris. She could only assume her mind was shattered because of unspeakable things that were forced on her. Jace reached out and touched Nora's shoulder trying to help her.

"Jordan is actually a doctor." Asher said keep his tone calm.

"*Sarah no more talk about anything that can upset your Luna. She hasn't shifted before and with the rush of emotions her wolf is trying to force her. We need her to calm down.*" Jace said, linking Sarah.

Sarah nodded quickly to him letting him know she heard him and would follow his instructions.

"Perfect." Nora said softly, feeling a headache starting to make its way from the back of her neck up into her head.

"Alpha, did you want to talk about the feast following your appointing the members to their new titles?" Asher asked, Jace shot him a look of anger.

"Asher, I think you and Sarah can handle this. Jace, can we go home? I'm not feeling well." Nora said going to stand up but wobbled.

Jace pulled her into him and scooped her into his arms. Nora grunted her response in protest but then quickly realized how much better she felt being close to him. Nora sighed, giving in and rested her head on his chest.

"We will take care of everything Luna." Sarah said her voice with a smile in it.

"Alpha, get some rest." Asher said standing up in respect as Jace began to carry her out.

Chapter Seven
Heat

Nora curled into herself in the front seat of Jace's car. The pack house wasn't far but she felt like she was on fire. Like her skin was burning, even the air around her was hurting her flesh.

"Jace." She whimpered.

Jace slammed on the brakes and glanced over to Nora as her scent hit his nose. He squeezed the steering wheel tightly in his hands. He didn't expect this. He couldn't go home because the council was there and the way Lance was looking at her before. He would definitely try something. Jace would let Cole kill him. His cabin.

"Dante, I have to leave. Nora is going into heat. I don't trust anyone from the Red Woods and I will slaughter the council if they look at her the wrong way. Do you have this?" Jace's mind linked as he slammed the car into reverse.

"I got it Alpha. The council has been nosing around, moving like roaches. I caught Bruce in your office. They were wondering when you were coming back. They want to question you. I will let them know you have business you need to take care of and then you will be back." Dante mind linked him back.

"Keep me updated." Jace replied.

"Sarah, Luna has gone into heat. I'm taking her away. I need you to help Dante and Asher both as much as you can. I cannot mind link Asher, so let him know. He's in charger and if he fucks anything up, I will have his head." Jace said firmly.

"I will Alpha, take care of my Luna." Sarah replied back.

Nora let out a yell as she slammed back into the seat. Sweat was pouring across her head, her body aching everywhere.

"Jace. What is going on?" She yelled as an intense wave rushed over her.

"You're going into heat." Jace said, taking a sharp turn.

"What, like an animal?" Nora groaned, pushing back into the seat.

Jace ignored the comment, the cabin was forty five minutes away, he had the gas pedal slammed down to the floor trying to go as fast as he could.

Suddenly the burning heat turned into a burning need. Nora's eyes looked over Jace and she wanted him desperately. Jace felt the shift and he gritted his teeth fighting his own urges to stop the car and take her.

"Stop the car." Nora arched herself and then when he did not respond, Nora reached over and rubbed Jace's arm, he clenched his jaw harder.

Jace tried to focus on anything but Nora. She was becoming upset the more he ignored her. She reached across the center console so she could touch his thigh. She began rubbing the inside of his leg. Purposely brushing her finger tips over his area. Jace let out a low growl as he squeezed the steering wheel tighter.

"Nora. You're going to make me crash the damn car." Jace growled as her hand lingered over his member, rubbing it through the outside of his pants.

"I want you." She growled back her eyes glowing.

"Sit down." Jace order trying to use his Alpha tone on her to see if it would have an effect on her.

"It hurts. I need you." She moaned.

"I know we need to get you to the cabin." Jace said trying to suppress the urges, that kept coming in waves each time she moved or made a sound.

Nora let out another small sound and her fingers began undoing his pants. Jace tried shifting away from her but her fingers held on to his pants tightly. She growled as he tried to move away from her as he continued to drive.

"Stay still." Nora yelled her eyes glowing and she pushed her alpha aura on to him.

Jace went to comply to her command of staying still. He was confused at how powerful she was but was quickly able to gain control of himself. In the short seconds he was taken back Nora had undid his pants exposing him. She wrapped her hand around Jace's enlarged member and began moving it up and down. Jace groaned as he fought hard against the urge to give into her. She began to lean forward like she was going to take him into her mouth. He felt his body twitch. His whole body wanted to arch into her warm moist mouth. If her lips touched his head he was going to cave. He turned into the driveway of the cabin. The tires of the car kicking up the white rocks from the driveway as he came to a hard stop. Jace turned the car off and went to grab the door handle to get out. Nora grabbed him by the shoulder trying to pull him back to her. Jace took her hands off of him gently and got out of the car. He fixed himself as he got out and zipped his pants back up. He took a deep breath and began walking to Nora's side of the car.

"It's so hot." Nora complained as she tugged on her shirt in the car.

She then noticed Jace was out of the car. She couldn't think straight, her body telling her to go after him, the rest of her feeling like she was burning up from the inside. She struggled to get cool and tore her shirt. She looked around, seeing him in front of the car. Nora flung open the door to the car. Jace tensed up seeing her. Her shirt hung off her in pieces. Her dark blue lace bra was exposed. Her chest was raising and falling, causing her breasts to move with each fast paced breath she took. Her scent was driving him insane. Her eyes looked at him like she was hunting him and he was her prey. His eyes darkened as he looked at her, a smile rolling across his lips.

"Come get me, little hunter." His voice was deep and gravelly.

Nora didn't even hestatied. She rushed towards him crashing into him. Her arms wrapped around his neck. His arms captured her and pulled her against him. His mouth smashing into hers as he kissed her. Her legs wrapped around him as he began carrying her towards the cabin. He climbed the steps in two long strides trying to get into the cabin as quickly as possible. Nora's mouth moved from his lips to his jaw and then his neck. She was kissing and nipping his neck as Jace kicked the door open; the loud slam echoing in the dark cabin as he blindly started making his way to his bed. Nora's hands had already found their way to his pants as she undid them frantically. She growled slightly as she tugged on them, she couldn't wait. She needed him now.

"Now." Nora growled impatiently.

Jace growled back as he tossed her back onto the bed, getting on top of her. He leaned down and kissed her softly. She arched into him, her mouth meeting his. He kissed down her neck and let his fangs scratch over her mark. An intense chill was sent through her as a moan escaped her mouth as she moved against him. She arched her pelvis up towards him, wanting and needing him. His mouth traveled down the length of her neck and then shoulder. Warm against her skin, Jace's mouth kissed, bit, and sucked his way down to her stomach. Each touch of his lips, tongue, and graze of his teeth set her even more on fire. She was becoming restless. Her body quivered and ached so badly it hurt. She pulled him down against her, his face landing neatly on her stomach. Her next move was to flip him over onto the bed, so she would be on top and take control.

Jace smirked seeing her plan and pinned her down by her hips, his fingers entwining into her pants. Nora lifted her hips. He yanked downward on them and in one fierce motion they were off. He grabbed a hold of blue lace underwear and ripped. The underwear turned to pieces in his hands. He pushed her thighs apart and placed his face between them.

Nora moaned, arching her hips to meet him. He ran his tongue over her crease before venturing between her lips. His tongue teased her bud moving in circles. Nora cried out in pleasure, her hand weaving into his hair. He pulled her bud in between his teeth sucking on it gently. An overwhelming intensity rushed through her causing her body to flush. Her body began to twitch fiercely from the pleasure and the nagging, gnawing feeling of needing him in her was overwhelming.

"Please." She moaned desperately.

She tugged on his hair begging him. He ignored her, playing with her as he continued to torment her. A small growl came from her in between noises of pleasure. She pulled hard on his hair this time.

"Fuck me." She said a growl came out as she tugged on his hair.

She felt him chuckle as he moved his face away. He ran his finger down her crease inserting two of them in her and began to move them. She arched into him, it was some release but not what she wanted.

"Jace…Please." She whispered.

The small plea of need from her and he couldn't torture her anymore. He needed her just as badly. She felt him move away and a rush of anger spread through her. Why was he making her wait? She went to sit up and yell at him but Jace was back straddling her. He pressed his member against her core and slowly eased in. She let out a sigh of satisfaction as the pulsing ache began to ease. . She moved against Jace trying to make him move harder and faster but he was still toying with her.

"Jace.. I swear-" She yelled at him but then he began to move with her.

His mouth captured her to silence her as he began to move at the pace and speed she wanted. She felt amazing and she had been beyond ready for him. Nora shivered with pleasure. She moved away from his mouth and began kissing his neck and shoulder. Suddenly she felt fangs. She was shocked but the feeling soon went away the more Jace moved. She felt an urge to bite down the intense pressure building in her core. The words mark him echoing in her mind. Jace felt her fangs against his skin and knew what she was feeling. He had felt it every time they were together until he had marked her. He moved his head to the side letting her have more access to his neck.

She felt her release finally coming as her fangs descended more. Her mouth on the skin of his neck, she bit down, sinking her fangs into him. She felt herself shudder around him and Jace released as she marked him. He felt his whole body tingle and vibrate as it never did before. He felt the connection to Nora become stronger than ever. Bliss overwhelmed him as his feelings mixed with Nora's emotions. He could feel her now. She pulled away from him, her eyes glowing bright amber and knew his eyes were ice blue. He rested his forehead against hers breathing heavily. Nora closed her eyes trying to calm herself but she was exhausted. Her body still twitching from the aftermath of pure bliss. Jace rolled to the side of her pulling her against him. She didn't know what just happened but she felt like she had been hit by a truck. She closed her eyes and instantly slept.

Chapter Eight
Option Two

Nora slept like the dead. Jace had gotten up and checked the perimeter several times. He had the area laced with mistletoe so it should ward off wolves that may smell her scent but he was still worried. A female in heat can draw unmarked males to them and in a craze. Right now she was safe but he didn't know how long her heat would last or how many episodes she would have. He felt something in him stir and right away he knew she was awake.

"Where did you go?" She sent him through a mind link.

"Coming back now, checking the perimeter." *Jace responded as he got to the cabin stairs.*

Opening the cabin door, he saw her sitting up on the bed, her knees pulled up to her chest and the white blanket wrapped around her. He felt her intense confusion and embarrassment. He felt it like it was his own. He walked over to the bed slowly and sat down. He pulled her against him. She curled into him, putting her head against his chest. She had so many questions but didn't want to ask them. She looked up at his face and when she did he leaned down and kissed her nose, making her smile.

Her eyes then fell on to his neck and they grew wide seeing the two small puncture holes that had almost healed. She thought she had dreamt of biting him. She pulled back from him her fingers going to her teeth as she got off the bed quickly.

"Nora?" Jace said, watching her look around.

He could feel her intense panic and was unsure what she was looking for. She spotted the bathroom and rushed to it, flicking on the light and leaning into the mirror. She stared at her teeth, running her fingers over them confused. Jace sighed getting up off the bed. He walked into the bathroom coming up behind her and wrapped his arms around her. She looked at him in the mirror.

"I..I had fangs?" Nora asked, confused.

Jace smiled softly and nodded. She looked at herself again and then him in the mirror, her eyes falling on the fang marks. She turned in his arms and ran her finger over the freshly made mark. Jace's skin goosebumps under her touch.

'I..I..I freaking bit you." She said, confused.

"I bit you too." He laughed and then ran his finger over her mark, a chill went through her.

"I know but…are you ok?" She whispered.

Of course he's ok and he liked it! Zara purred in Nora's mind.

Nora frowned, everything was happening so fast. She ignored Zara and looked at Jace waiting for his answer, her stomach twisting inside of her.

"Nora, look at me, I am fine. It's what wolves do." He said taking her chin in his hand and pushing her face upwards towards him.

"So explain things to me. I'm new remember. Why am I doing this? This is a heat thing. Explain why I marked you? Do females mark males? This is a lot and why am I sharing my head and thoughts randomly with Zara? I can hear her in my head." Nora said, taking her chin out of his hand and rubbing her forehead.

"Ok well females go into heat twice a year. Unless you become pregnant. The overload of hormones will pull unmated males to you…and yes before you say it. Just like in animals. You are part animal now. We are wolves. It will cloud your mind and you will do things, say things you never thought you would. Don't stress about it." Jace started explaining.

"Are you freaking kidding me?" Nora said, embarrassed and angry.

"Nora it's fine, I will make sure you're safe." Jace said to her, since she marked him he could feel her emotions more intensely.

He was trying to fight back the anger that he was feeling as it overcame Nora. He took a deep breath and tried to remind himself that it was her anger not his.

"Safe? Safe? Why is this deadly?" Nora chuckled.

"What am I going to die if I don't have sex?" Nora laughed.

"Well your body temperature can rise to dangerous points during your heat and it can be deadly." Jace answered softly.

"Wonderful." Nora groans, flopping back onto the pillow.

"As far as Zara, she is a part of you. She lives in you so you can communicate with her and vice versa." Jace explained.

"So Cole talks to you too?" Nora asked, feeling a little less crazy.

"He's quiet most of the time but when he does he's usually demanding something." Jace smirked.

"And the marking?" Nora said, smiling at the comment he made about Cole.

"No it's not normal for a female to mark her male. I didn't mind. I actually feel closer to you now. Like your feelings are my own. I knew we would be connected in ways that normal "human" relationships aren't but since you marked me the pull and connection is stronger." Jace smiled and leaned down and brushed hair out of her face.

Why did we mark him? Nora said to Zara.

Because he's ours. Zara growled, anger and desire radiating through her.

Great so you're possessive. Nora rolled her eyes.

No, I just want what's ours. Zara snickered.

"Great, my wolf is possessive and probably jealous so we're gonna have to deal with that." Nora said to Jace.

He laughed and kissed her forehead. " Most wolves are."

"Hmm?" Nora asked, her skin tingling under his lips.

"Well Cole wanted to kill Joel and then Logan. He wants to rip apart Lance if he looks at you one more time." Jace said, touching her cheek lightly with his hand.

"Well I guess Zara is a good match for him then." Nora smiled, shutting her eyes, loving the way his fingertips felt against her skin.

Her body temperature began to rise and she felt a rush of intense need building. Her eyes shot open as she realized it was about to happen again.

"Jace, how long does this last?" She whined.

"Three to five days, Love." Jace said with a small smile.

She whimpered but moved closer to him. His presence, his touch was calming to her. He pulled her against him holding her, her temperature still increasing. Jace glanced at the bathroom and an idea hit him.

"Come on." He said getting off the bed and taking her hand.

"I don't know if I can move, each slight movement makes everything feel overwhelming." She said curling into herself.

Jace reached over and scooped her. He carried her into the bathroom and she clung to him. He was her only saving point right now. A large clawfoot tub was in the center of the cabin. Jace while still holding her turned the tub on. He let the cold water run into the tub filling in. He let Nora's feet drop to the floor. She whined as he put her down, she didn't want to be away from him. She needed him. The throbbing feeling of wanting him increased as she looked at him. Her eyes watched every move he made.

Jace pulled off his shirt and that sent her over the edge. Her eyes rolled down his absolutely perfectly ripped chest and abs. He was trying to prepare himself for the next step. Nora stepped into him. Her hands running over his chest and down his abs. She stood on her tippy toes placing kisses along his collarbone and down his chest. The rush of hormones she was sending out hit him in a wave and he grabbed a hold of the tub. Before he could recover Nora's mouth had made it to his belt line. Her fingers undoing it as she kneeled in front of him. Jace groaned, fighting with himself. He held his breath and bent forward scooping Nora up into his arms. She wrapped her legs around his waist, her mouth kissing him fiercely.

"I need you." She whispered to him as she moved to kiss his mark.

Jace stepped backwards into the tub, submerging them both. Nora let out a small yelp as her hot flesh felt like it sizzled in the cold water.

"Holy fuck!" She yelled as the cold water felt like it was burning her skin.

"Shhh. it's ok." Jace said, pulling her into him.

"It's freaking freezing, it burns." She whispered, trying to get out.

"Give it a minute. It will help." Jace said, locking his arms around her.

Nora struggled trying to get away from him but just like he said the nagging ache slowly back away and the fire dulled.

"See." Jace whispered, sensing everything she was feeling.

"So what, we're just going to carry around ice water and dunk me in?" Nora said through chattering teeth.

"Well no it will only last for so long but for now it will do." Jace said, kissing her forehead.

"Well if you don't want me to attack you again. I suggest you keep your hands and lips to yourself." Nora said, trying to get out of his arms.

"Well honestly Love, we have two options we can keep chucking you in ice water or…" Jace smirked, running his hand down her arm teasingly.

She shivered against him but not from the cold. His touch drives her insane.

"Or?" She whispered breathily.

"Or we can enjoy this." Jace said, nipping her shoulder lightly.

Nora leaned back into him as he slowly began kissing her neck. She reached up, running her fingers lightly through his hair.

"Option two." She said turning in his arms to face him.

Chapter Nine
Problems

The door to the office flung open with so much force it hit the wall behind it and bounced back. Dante straightened up his eyes glowing ice blue ready for whoever dared to walk into the Alpha's office in such a manner.

Lance came strolling in. His chest rising and falling rapidly. Eyes glowing purple as he entered. Dante looked at him confused. The anger rolling off of him was making Noah upset. He was on the verge of wanting to attack but at the same time due to ranking he wanted to back away.

"Can I help you?" Dante said quietly, he was internally trying to talk Noah down.

"Where the hell is your Alpha!" Lance yelled.

"Taking care of some business with his mate." Dante said ignoring the voice and volume level Lance was using with him.

"When is he coming back!" Lance demanded to Dante,clenching his fist in at his sides.

"Alpha will be returning when he is done handling his important business." Dante said firmly, trying to hold himself together.

Let's just go for the throat, Alpha would thank us. Noah chimed in.

We can't kill a member of the council, that would bring war. Dante said although he liked the idea.

"What exactly was this important business? He didn't even get permission to leave." Lance growled, stepping towards him.

"Alpha Jace didn't let me know which business he had." Dante said, staring at a spot on the wall behind Lance's head.

"Well that's complete bullshit." Lance growled.

Maybe if he focused on an actual object he would feel better. Dante took a deep breath as he fought with Noah not to push forward. Dante knew if he did Lance would take it as a threat and there would be a fight.

"I'm sure my Alpha will return any day now. He wouldn't leave his guests too long if he didn't have to." Dante smiled.

Permission, Alpha doesn't need permission. We should get permission to - Noah began ranting inside of him.

Noah! Dante yelled at him.

"The minute he returns I want to be informed." Lance growled.

Dante just nodded his head in agreement and waited for Lance to leave. He was so angry he was shaking.

"Dante? You ok?" Sarah's worried voice chimed in his head.

Sarah, he had missed her. He never expected to find his mate. He thought he was going to move through this life alone.

"The Council is bothering me, wanting information on Alpha. How are you hanging in there?" He asked letting her know he missed her by the tone of his voice.

"Talking to your Alpha?" Lance said, still lingering like a fly.

"No my mate. Is there anything else I can do for you?" Dante asked, annoyed.

"Inform us once he arrives. Exactly when he arrives." Lance growled, walking out of the office and slamming the door.

Dante exhaled, releasing his clenched fist. He hoped Jace would be back soon because if Lance didn't back off and mind his own business soon he was seriously thinking about letting Noah at him.

"I'm struggling. Jaime is a quick learner and has the strength but there's something about Lyla. The women here are still so fearful and I get it. I've lived it. With Nora gone it's hard to encourage them and keep them going. There's a handful of men who are still being assholes. Asher is doing a great job though. How long is the council staying? That can't be good." Sarah replied back through mind link.

"Do I need to come over there and knock a few of them down a peg? Honestly they haven't said and I agree they never stay anywhere too long. They are plotting something I just can't tell what." Dante responded.

"I miss you." Sarah answered back, she felt her stomach tighten as she said it.

They hadn't been together long and she had never been with anyone before but she couldn't help feeling a little lost without him. She was afraid of what he would say back. She began fidgeting with her pinky finger.

"I miss you too. Once Nora and Jace are back, you won't even have to start making your way this way. I will be there to get you." Dante sent back.

Hearing him say it back she relaxed. She didn't know why she would question it but the fear of him not wanting her was scary.

"Sarah." Jaime's voice shook her from her thoughts.

"Sorry, yes Jaime?" Sarah said, closing the mind link to Dante.

"I feel like we're going to have a problem soon if Alpha does not return." Jaime said fidgeting.

"Problem?" Sarah asked.

"Go ahead, Lyla show her." Jaime said, nudging Lyla.

Lyla handed Sarah a folded up piece of paper. She was biting her lip nervously as she held it out to Sarah. Sarah took the folded up piece of paper in her hand and began unfolding it. She looked down at the chicken scratch handwriting, her brows formed a frown as she read it.

Death to any woman who wants to step up and take a man's place. Step up and be prepared to fight like a man. This is the only warning you will get. Know your place.

"Where did this come from?" Sarah growled.

"It was left on the woman's pack house door." Lyla said softly.

"When?" Sarah asked shortly.

"It was there this morning when I left. I am not sure exactly when it was put there. Could even be the middle of the night. It wasn't there when I got in last night but there when I woke up and left." Lyla said, rambling a little bit.

"Do either of you recognize the handwriting?" Sarah asked them.

"No." They both said in unisom.

"Does Asher know?" Sarah said, gritting her teeth.

"No, the Beta does not know we came to you first." Jaime answered.

"Alright, well, let's go tell him." Sarah said getting up, as she did the chair fell over behind her.

She stood up so quickly and with such anger. She was ready to fight anyone and anything that would set these women back. They deserved more than what they had to live with all these years under Kip. They were not going back.

"Jaime mind link Asher and find out where he is."Sarah said to her trying to bite back the anger in her voice.

Jaime nodded her eyes glossing over.

"Beta Asher, Sarah would like to know where you are?" Jaime sent out.

Asher was in the middle of going over new plans for housing for the pack.The mind link came through he paused looking at the blue prints he had rolled out on his desk.

"My office. Is everything ok?" Asher was sent back.

"Sarah would like to come meet with you and show you something. It's important." Jaime sent back.

"I am in the men's pack house in the front office. Tell her she can come here." Asher sent back, he was anxious to see what Sarah had.

Dante walked out of the office and found Douglas leaning up against the wall. He looked up at Dante like he had been waiting for him. Dante sighed loudly. He needed to go meet up with his pack to go over training exercises.

"I just told Alpha Lance, I don't know when my Alpha is coming back. You'll know when he gets here." Dante said shutting the office door and locking it.

"I actually wanted to speak with you." Douglas said.

"Ok." Dante said, waiting for him to continue.

"Not here. It's private and I don't want others hearing." Douglas said, looking around and then motioned to the floors above them.

"Ok." Dante said as he looked at him confused. Was he talking about the other council members?

Seeing Dante's questioning look and then confused by his motion he nodded yes. Dante still didn't know if they were on the same page. There was no way he would want to keep a secret from the rest of them? Or would he?

"You're not very bright are you." Douglas muttered.

Yes, I am talking about the other council members. Douglas mouthed to him rolling his eyes as he did.

"I'm about to go check on my pack members now. They are running some new training exercises." Dante said, still confused.

"Oh how exciting. I love new training exercises. Lead the way." Douglas said,flashing a smile.

Don't trust him. Noah growled.

I know, we will be careful. Dante responded.

Douglas walked out the door in front of him, he kept a steady pace until they were towards the cars in the driveway.

"Red one." Dante said shortly.

"Nice color." Douglas said mostly to himself.

Getting to the car Dante unlocked the doors and they both got in. Dante started the car and pulled out of the driveway. Douglas was silent as they drove towards the training area. Dante kept glancing over at him waiting for some type of announcement. This whole thing was suspicious. Dante sighed, getting annoyed as they turned down the road to the training area.

"I want to get rid of Lance and Bruce." Douglas said quietly.

Chapter Ten
Return

Dante pulled the car over to the side of the road. He gripped the steering wheel slightly tighter. Was this a trap? What was he after? Dante looked at him, his eyes narrowed, Noah begged to be let out.

"Explain." Dante said, trying to find the safest answer to reply with.

"Bruce is trying to dabble into something dangerous. He was working with Kip. Lance and I turned a blind eye because we never thought it would take off. We didn't think Kip had the brains or resources to even do such things. Bruce is a more collected Kip. He is a calm, charismatic, and charming person on the outside, but underneath all that he's power hungry. The council position isn't enough for him. He wants to be like a king. He was using Kip to start all of this for him. He had the same ideas. Get an indestructible army to rule all wolves and humans. Lance, well Lance is just in it for himself. He doesn't care what happens as long as he leads his life doing what he wants. He will back Bruce no matter what. Right or wrong doesn't matter. As long as he gets what he wants. Right now he wants your Luna. " Douglas explained.

Dante felt the bones in his jaw pop from how hard he was clenching it shut. His eyes glowed ice blue. Noah howled like crazy in his mind. It was deafening, he was having trouble trying to think or process anything. His wolf side begging him to react. Dante took a long deep breath. He thought of something to calm him. He shut his eyes and Sarah's voice filtered into his head. Her telling him she missed him, put Noah at ease.

"And what do you want?" Dante asked through his teeth.

"Honestly….I haven't figured that out yet." Douglas said quietly.

"Then why tell me all this?" Dante asked, suppressing a growl.

"Because I know what I don't want." Douglas said with a shrug.

Nora woke up in a haze. She rolled over landing neatly against Jace's chest. She sighed happily curling into him. His arm reached around her and pulled her into him. He mimicked her happy sigh as he rubbed her arm softly.

"Morning." Nora smiled at him.

"Morning, how are you feeling?" Jace asked not opening his eyes.

"Hmm..Better. How long has it been? Am I done? Can we go back? I need to check on the Red Woods pack. I need to check in with Asher." Nora said, getting up quickly and to her feet.

A smile came to Jace's face as he watched Nora wander around trying to find her clothing. Nora stopped finding the shirt had been wearing and picked it up. Her eyes caughtJace's. A small confused playful smile came to her lips.

"What?" She asked him.

"You are just so..so perfect." Jace said getting up.

"Hush." Nora chuckled.

She began searching for her under garments and pants. She didn't even hear him move and suddenly he was behind her. He grabbed her around her waist and pulled her back against him.

"And sexy." He said, kissing her shoulder.

"Jace." Nora said, trying to protest but she had trouble resisting him.

"And gorgeous." He said, kissing his way up to her neck.

"Jace, we need to get back." Nora whispered as she shut her eyes, enjoying the feeling of his lips.

"And smart." he said, spinning her around towards him.

Nora smiled at that compliment. She brushed her nose against his, as he cupped her face with his hand. He just looked at her.

"You are amazing in every aspect. You are handling all of this so well." He said, kissing her forehead.

"Thank you. I am about to start panicking so be ready." Nora laughed.

"I will help you with whatever you need Love. Dante will help, Sarah is a perfect match for him and I think will be a strong person to help you. Matt and his goofy ass will always help. Our pack loves you and will be there. If you want to even ask the hunters for assistance I think they will. We should start building a better relationship with them anyways." Jace said starting to go back into Alpha mode.

"You're right we can do this. Have you heard from anyone?" Nora asked, stepping out of his arms and spotting her bra.

"No but I keep getting angry vibes from Dante. Something has been going on but not enough where he has alerted me." Jace answered, finding his clothing.

"Ok well we should head back. I'll link up with the Red Woods and you with Cross River. We will see who needs what quicker and decide where to go." Nora said, slipping her shirt on, she frowned realizing it was ripped down the middle.

"Sounds like a plan." Jace said, throwing a wink at her and then chuckled remembering what she did to her shirt.

He pulled his shirt up over his head and tossed it to her, with another laugh. She quickly pulled it on, making a silly face at him. She was about to mind link Asher when worry began to set in.

"Are you sure I'm…you know, all done?" Nora asked Jace, a little worried.

"The fact that you're thinking about the packs and what needs to be done is sign enough." Jace smirked

"What's that supposed to mean?" Nora asked, making a face.

"Well for one I'm not beating you off of me with a stick." Jace said, making a face at her.

"Like you minded." Nora said, narrowing her eyes at him.

"Two, I can tell your hormones have returned to normal. Your scent has shifted." Jace smirked.

"Good." Nora said, walking to the door of the cabin.

"How's Zara?" Jace asked.

She sighed going to open the door, she had so many questions about her wolf side and not many answers. She searched herself as Jace asked.

"I think she's…she's asleep." Nora said it sounded silly coming out.

"She probably will be for a little bit. Heat is exhausting most of the time, it's more for your wolf side." Jace explained.

Nora nodded, opening the door. Stepping out onto the small porch of the cabin, she shielded her eyes. The sun was so bright.

"What day is it?" She asked looking for the car.

Jace found his phone in his pants pocket and pulled it out looking down at the date and time.

"Thursday." Jace said, waiting for Nora's response.

"It's been four days." Nora said, turning to him.

"It could have been longer." Jace shrugged.

Nora groaned getting to the car. Jace unlocked it and she sat down inside. She looked around the inside of his once neat car. Things he had in the cup holders and underneath his radio were moved all around and knocked over. She made a face wondering what happened.

"You." Jace laughed while starting the car.

"Hush." Nora laughed, small memories of climbing over the center console to get to Jace flashed in her mind, her cheeks burned red thinking of it.

"It's fine, I know I'm irresistible." Jace smirked leaving the cabin driveway.

"Mhmm." Nora said, grabbing his hand that was resting on the stick shift.

"Why did we come here?" Nora asked as she watched the cabin fade into the background.

"Because others would have wanted you. And I didn't feel like killing a bunch of crazed wolves." Jace said with a shrug.

"So we have to come here every time?" Nora asked.

"No, once the council is out of my freaking territory then we will just stay home. I will give orders for all unmarked males to stay away from the pack house." Jace answered.

"So it doesn't affect marked males?" Nora asked.

"It does but because they are bonded to their mate they can resist it. Where unmarked are blinded and overwhelmed." Jace explained.

"How long is the council here for?" Nora asked.

"I'm about to find out." Jace said annoyance in his voice.

"Dante. I'm heading back now. How have things been?" Jace mind linked Dante.

"Alpha. The pack is fine, everything has been running smoothly." Dante replied back.

Jace could hear a but in Dante's voice. What was he holding back?

Nora watched Jace's eyes gloss over and decided she should check into her pack as well.

"Asher, Sarah, how are things?" Nora sent the mind link to both of them.

"Luna, it's so great to hear from you. Are you ok?" Sarah mind linked back quickly.

Nora could tell she was excited to hear from her.

"Alpha everything with the pack has been alright. The transitioning is a little rocky but we have been managing. I agree it is good to hear from." Asher replied more professionally.

"Rocky?" Nora asked.

"The men- Asher starts but Sarah's mind link pushes through.

"The men are threatening the women. There is a group here who want it to be the way it was under Kip. Asher and I were just about to meet regarding it." Sarah mind linked.

"Threatening?" Nora said, becoming angry.

"Alpha, we have not validated anything yet. We know that they like to bully. We are working through it. When you arrive we will show you. Just take it easy and we will see you as soon as you can be here." Asher replied.

"I am coming now." Nora sent back.

Nora ended the mind link. She already had her suspicion as to who was behind the threats. She felt anger shudder through her. She glanced over to Jace who was also squeezing the steering wheel a little too tight.

"Jace?" Nora asked as she felt his anger as if it was her own.

"What's happening?" Nora said, reaching out and touching his arms.

"I need to get to the pack house. Apparently I need to talk to council member Douglas. He knows secrets and wants to have us bring down Lance and Bruce." Jace growled at Lance's and Bruce's names.

"Jace, I need to go to Red Woods. There are threats going around towards the women. I know the select few that might be behind them. I need to nip this all in the butt before it explodes." Nora frowned.

"That's fine. I need you to stay away from Lance anyways." Jace growled.

"Why?" Nora asked.

"Apparently Lance thinks that you're available for him." Jace said he began to shake from the anger.

"I am not." Nora growled.

Jace was quiet as Cole stirred inside of him. He had been asleep this whole time coming alive at the statement.

"I am marked by you. Why does he think he even has a chance? You are…you are my one." Nora said softly, the vulnerability of what she said made her nervous.

"And you are my one." Jace said softly, hearing the vulnerability in her voice.

"He just thinks because he's part of the council he can have whatever he wants. Rules or no rules." Jace said, taking Nora's hand as she entwined her fingers into his.

"We will kill him, if he tries." Jace said his voice was a little different as his eyes burned bright, Cole coming through at that moment.

"Jace be careful I wouldn't do anything until you have everything figured out." Nora said, rubbing his hand in hers.

"I'm going to drop you off at the Red Woods pack. That way you can take care of them and be away from Lance all at once. Let me know if you need help with the problematic people. I will send help or come myself." Jace said thinking out loud.

"Ok but promise me you won't do anything risky without talking to me. You or Cole." Nora said, a little nervous.

"Fine." Jace said, nodding his head.

Chapter Eleven
Red Woods

*J*ace pulled the car into the pack house driveway at Red Woods. Asher and Sarah came out the front door eager to see Nora. Nora gritted her teeth. There was something deep in her stomach telling her something was wrong. She couldn't tell if it was the chaos going in the Red Woods pack or something more. Her stomach knotted as he looked at Jace. She didn't want to leave him, she felt unsure of what her body was trying to tell her.

Jace looked over studying her, he could feel the rollercoaster of emotions she was on. He reached over taking his hand in hers and squeezed it. He brought her hand to his lips kissing the back of her hand softly.

"As soon as you're done, I will be back to get you, promise. I would stay if I didn't need to get back to our pack." Jace said his lips brushing against the back of her hand as he talked.

"I know. I ..I just feel like something is coming. Something bad." Nora said worriedly.

"Whatever it is, we will face it together." Jace said, pressing his lips to her hand again.

"Please be careful." She whispered.

"Always Love." He smiled at her and then nodded to the passenger side window.

Nora took a deep breath and glanced to the side of her. Sarah and Asher were waiting for her. She let out the breath she was holding. She looked at Jace touching his face with her hand. He leaned into it.

"Well I guess I gotta go play Alpha." She smiled weakly.

"You don't play Alpha. You are the Alpha. You got this." Jace said to her, kissing her forehead.

Nora shut her eyes as his lips pressed against her forehead sending warmth through her.

"Go get them, my little hunter." Jace smirked and nudged her.

Nora leaned over and kissed his lips, she didn't understand why she was having so much trouble getting out of the car. She pushed the feeling down before opening the car door.

"See you soon." Jace said to her.

"Better be soon." Nora smiled.

Nora got out of the car and put her brave face on. Sarah looked like she was going to burst from anticipation and anger. Asher was calm and composed but still something seemed off. She greeted them with a smile and prepared herself for the overload of information she was about to get. She could see it oozing out of Sarah.

"Before we start, how about we go inside?" Nora smiled.

Sarah nodded and Asher held the door for them. Nora walked in and made her way to the office. Walking in she saw Asher had been hard at work with new designs and plans to make the pack better. She looked over the blueprints he had and smiled. He had so much hope for his pack, she knew in the end he was going to be perfect as Alpha. She read over the notes on the side. Talking about building a school. Asher walked in and let her finish reading.

"The children don't have a school?" Nora asked.

"No." Asher said sadly.

"Do they go to public school then?" Nora asked, her face frowning.

"No Alpha, a handful of parents hold class and take turns teaching." Asher said quietly.

"The girls only get taught up to reading and writing." Sarah said with anger in her voice.

"Ok so priority number one is get the older girls up to speed and this school should be our first project." Nora announced.

"Sounds great Alpha." Asher smiled.

"How has it been going with find our new Delta and Gamma?" Nora asked, taking her eyes from the blueprint and looking at them both.

"I really like Jordan but I feel it will be giving him too much. He is going to be in charge of the hospital and medical staff, adding another position might be overwhelming. I think Chance will be the better fit." Asher said debating as he talked.

"Ok then and Sarah?" Nora asked, looking at Sarah.

"I am torn. Jaime has this natural born leader ability. She is quick, she's smart but she can be narrow minded. Llya is quiet and thinks things through, it is like pulling teeth to get her to feel like she has a voice but when she talks a leader comes out." Sarah sighed.

"Ok I would like to meet with both sets of candidates and get a feel for them myself. Now you said there was a problem with some of the men?" Nora asked, looking at Sarah.

Sarah nodded and pulled a folded up piece of paper out of her pocket. She handed it over to Nora and stood silently as she read it.

"It was taped to the women's pack house door." Sarah said quietly.

"Asher, have you seen this yet?" Nora said, holding the paper out to him.

"No, Sarah informed me about it but I have yet to see it. She wanted to wait until you were here." Asher explained.

Nora watched him read it. As he did a frown set in his brows and his eyes narrowed. She felt a small wave of anger roll off of him. Nora felt better knowing he was upset as well.

"I don't know anyone's handwriting." Asher said thinking out loud.

"That was my next question." Nora said, frowning.

"I don't think we necessarily need to know everyone's writing." Sarah said with a smile.

"Oh you know what you're right!" Nora smirked.

"Hmm?" Asher said, still staring at the paper as if it was going to tell him who wrote it.

"Asher, we already have four people who still hold loyalty with Kip. I think we should start there." Nora smiled at him.

"Oh yes, right. Sorry." He smiled while looking at the paper.

"So we just need a way to get everyone to write something on a piece of paper to compare it." Sarah said thinking out loud.

Nora made a face trying to think as well. She looked to Asher who seemed lost in thought. She wondered what was going on with him. He then suddenly seemed to snap out of it as he looked at her and Sarah.

"The gathering in your honor is tonight, well it's been on standby ready to go the minute you got back. My point is we can use it to get people's writing. Have a sign in sheet or card thanking and welcoming the new Alpha. Make everyone write a small little message." Asher said coming up with an idea.

"I think that will work." Sarah smiled at Asher.

"So it's tonight?" Nora asked, feeling a little drained.

"Yeah the quicker we get this done, the quicker we will know who it is and we can put an end to it." Sarah smiled brightly.

"Ok." Nora forced a smile.

"I am going to need a dress or something to wear." Nora said thinking out loud.

"Of course Luna." Sarah smiled going to open her phone.

"The traditional color for the Alpha to wear at the first gathering is Red." Asher said to Sarah.

Red like blood. Nora had no clue why that thought entered her head. She was taken back by it.

Because you know something bad is going to happen. Zara yawned.

Do you feel it too? Nora anxiously asked Zara.

Mmhmm. Zara said a little sassy.

Are you not worried? Nora asked Zara.

No matter what it is, we got it. Have faith in us. Zara said.

"Alpha?" Asher said to her.

"Sorry I..I'm still getting used to having another voice in my head. Zara woke up and we were talking. What were you all saying?" Nora asked, letting out a deep breath.

"Did you want us to send over Jacob, Chance, Lyla, and Jaime?" Asher asked again.

"Yes, let's do that. Once I can talk to them and get a feel; I will know where we are. Also be able to announce titles tonight." Nora said out loud while she planned.

"Excellent, I will have them sent right over." Asher announced getting up.

"Wonderful." Nora smiled.

Nora watched Asher leave and looked at Sarah who seemed to be thinking. She took the moment to reach out to Jace.

"Hey."

"Hi Love." His voice buzzed in her head making her smile instantly.

"So they're holding a gathering tonight here for me. I have to announce the titles and greet everyone again. I guess it's more formal. I'm assuming it's going to be like a dinner or something. Will you be here for that part?" Nora asked him through a mind link.

"I might be able to make it. I will try really hard. There's a few little hiccups over here that I'm smoothing over and then I will try to be there." Jace replied back.

Nora winced, she felt pain. She couldn't tell if it was her pain. Something was telling her it wasn't hers. Something was telling her there was something wrong with Jace.

"Jace, is everything ok?" Nora asked, her heart panicking a little.

Zara can you feel Cole? Nora asked her.

"Everything's fine. Just a little stressed. I'll see you soon Love. Stay there till I come get you." Jace cut the mind link short.

Zara! Nora asked again, demanding her answer.

No, he shut himself out from me. Something is wrong. Zara said, angry.

"Jace." Nora tried reaching him again but like a phone call that didn't get picked up there was emptiness there.

"Alpha this is Jordan, Chance and Jaime. You've already met Ms. Lyla." Asher's voice interrupted her mindlink.

Nora looked at them standing in front of her. She was freaking out. Everything in her was telling her to go to Jace but now she had this.

"Hello, nice to meet you all. Can I have a moment?" Nora said, not asking and stepping aside.
"Matt." Nora sent a panicked mind link to him.
"Luna?" Matt answered.
"Where's Jace, is he ok?" Nora linked back rapidly.
"He is fine, I promise my Luna. He is just stressed and in the middle of meeting with the council. I promise nothing he can't handle." Matt replied back.
The words he said put Nora at ease but she could sense hesitation in his voice.
"You promise me Matt?" Nora asked him.
"Yes, my Luna. Nothing he can't handle." Matt replied.
"Tell me right away if he is not ok." Nora ordered him.
"Will do my Luna." Matt replied back, ending the mind link.
Nora clenched her jaw, what the hell was everyone hanging up on her for. She glanced back at the four eager candidates and took a deep breath. She needed to get this over with. If Matt said he was ok, then he should be ok. She told herself walking back to them.

Chapter Twelve
Cross River

*J*ace hated leaving her, it felt like leaving a part of himself. He told himself it would be for only a short while as he put the car into park. Getting out of the car he could already see his blond spiky hair waiting for him. Each passing minute he hated Lance more and more.

"So kind of you to greet me at the door." Jace said to Lance, stopping in front of the stairs waiting for him to move out of his way.

"Where exactly have you been?" Lance growled.

Jace smirked; he couldn't help it. It was like he was coming home to an angry wife.

"Honey! I'm sorry, am I late for dinner?" Jace smirked.

Without a word; Lance cranked back and landed a closed fist punch on Jace's jaw. Jace's head whipped to the side on impact. He winced, feeling his tooth scrap the inside of his cheek ripping through the flesh. He ran his tongue over it looking at Lance. Jace's eyes glowed ice blue as he turned his head to the side and spit blood at Lance's feet. Lance 's eyes glowed purple.

"You want to go?" Lance said bowing up at Jace.

Jace smirked, " I thought we were having dinner?"

Lance cranked back to hit him again and Jace was done. High Alpha or not he wasn't going to get hit again. Lance's fist headed for Jace's nose. Jace moved out of the way and caught Lance's fist. Jace squeezed it and shoved it back at him. Jace was strong for an Alpha, strength came from blood lines and if Jace had followed the path laid out for him. The path his father had wanted; he would have been one of them. Seeing his father go through power hunger, he stepped away from it the moment he became Alpha. He had no interest in being part of the High Alpha Council.

Lance flinched, stumbling backwards. He seemed a bit surprised at Jace's abilities. Jace knew he couldn't allow himself to win this fight, if he did it would be worse. He needed to just play defense, if he was going to do this. He wouldn't grovel or show Lance he was beneath but he couldn't win. Cole pushed against him fighting for control. He wanted out, he wanted to rip Lance's throat out.

Cole back down, you know it will mean war if we shift. Jace growled at him.

War wouldn't be bad. Cole said back.

Not now. We have too much going on. Another war is not what we need. Jace said to him.

Lance regained himself and charged at Jace, catching him football style around the waist and driving him backwards into the ground. Lance landed on top of him. Jace began blocking blows from Lance's angry fist. Cole scratched on the inside of him wanting him to shift. He couldn't shift it would drive the fight into something much more than what it was. Jace had enough of Lance hitting him. He reached up and grabbed ahold of his shoulders pushing him to the side. Using his weight Jace managed to toss Lance off of him. They rolled on to the ground away from each other.

"What? Does your wolf want out?" Lance instigated.

"Why? Do you want to see the outcome of that?" Jace growled.

Let me just kill him. Cole growled.

Lance bowed up again and was about to come at him again when the noise of someone clearing their throat stopped him. Bruce stood in the doorway along with Dante and Matt who stood directly behind. Matt and Dante are both torn between helping and not wanting to add to the chaos. Their eyes flickering ice blue waiting on their Alpha's command. Jace sighed they would go to their deaths for him. He didn't want that. Jace shut his eyes forcing Cole back and his eyes stopped glowing.

"What's going on here?" Bruce asked with a smile on his face.

"I'm late for dinner?" Jace couldn't help it, it fell out of his mouth.

Lance growled and charged at him. Lance slammed into Jace once more slamming him back into the ground. Laughing Jace blocked his blows. He heard footsteps coming towards them. A hand grabbed ahold of Lance's shoulder and yanked him back. Lance spun around ready to fight but stopped seeing Bruce.

"That's enough." Bruce growled, sending out his Alpha aura.

Dante and Matt buckled to their knees as Bruce's aura hit them. Jace felt the wave and winced slightly. Bruce narrowed his eyes at Lance who stopped.

"Go back inside." Bruce said through gritted teeth at Lance.

"But I-" Lance started to protest but he stopped seeing Bruce's face.

Lance kicked the ground and walked back towards the house. Walking up the steps he shoved past Matt and Dante purposely knocking them over as he did. Bruce walked over to Jace standing above him looking down on him.

"Jace, what in the world were you thinking?" Bruce asked, shaking his head.

"Alpha. Jace, please shut up." Dante's voice came through begging him.

Jace shrugged if he opened his mouth another smart ass comment may fall out and he didn't want to go rounds with Bruce next.

"Well whatever it was, you know the punishment for disrespecting a High Alpha." Bruce said softly.

Jace did not respond. He knew and he didn't care. It was nothing he couldn't handle. His only thought was he was glad Nora wasn't there.

"High Alpha Bruce, I will take Alpha Jace's place in the punishment." Dante called out from his knees.

Jace sat up narrowing his eyes at Dante. "No he fucking won't." Jace yelled.

"Oh this is interesting." Bruce smirked looking at them both.

"It might hurt more to see someone you care about hurt." Bruce proceeded with his thoughts.

"It won't show the pack anything though." Jace said, getting to his feet.

"Come again?" Bruce asked.

"You don't think it's not known that I could care less about your titles. Your rules. The way you parade yourself around like you're better than the rest of us. It's known that I could care less who you all are.-

"Watch yourself Jace." Bruce growled, stepping towards him, cutting him off.

"Alpha stop." Matt pleaded in a mind link to him

"Hurting a member of my pack will just continue to show the rest of the world that once again you have no leadership or authority." Jace said squaring off to Bruce.

"That my disrespect is valid." Jace whispered.

Bruce almost came unglued but then composed himself. He stepped into Jace squeezing his shoulder under his hand.

"I know what you're doing and I will play along just because I more than ever want to rip you limb from limb. So punishing you is worth it. Be lucky I don't kill one of your beloved members just because you pissed me off. Remember your place." Bruce growled pushing downwards on Jace's shoulder.

As he pushed down on his shoulder he used every ounce of Alpha aura he had to force Jace on to his knees. Jace's head slunk forward as pain crept through his body. Bruce smiled and then looked at Douglas.

"Get the whip and wolfsbane." Bruce ordered him.

Douglas sighed and went to the car. Jace rolled his eyes at the fact that they carried that stuff around with them.

"You two get over here and string your Alpha up to that tree." Bruce smiled.

Dante and Matt's eyes both glowed as their wolf fought to disobey the order but couldn't help but follow it. Douglas returned with ropes, whip, and a jar of powder Wolfsbane. Jace shook his head, they were very dramatic. Bruce nodded to Matt and Dante to get Jace, they both hesitated and Bruce was becoming upset.

"Dante and Matt let's go, we don't have all day for this." Jace said getting up and walking to the tree.

Dante clenched his jaw as he followed Jace with Matt behind him. Jace pulled his shirt up over his head and dropped it on the ground. He then held his wrist out to Dante. Dante growled as he began weaving the rope around them.

"Stop. Follow orders. This is a rule, it will be over and done with but if you continue to upset him. He's going to set his sights on you two. I will hurt you both if he tries to hurt you." Jace said, threatening them.

Matt and Dante hung their heads as they nodded.

"You…Matt toss the rope over the limb and hold the other side of it." Bruce said.

Matt did as he said. Dante stepped back watching Bruce unravel the whip. He looked at the wolfsbane wondering what he was going to do with it. Bruce saw him looking and smiled.

"You'll see." Bruce said to Dante walking over to Jace and lining up.

A loud crack went through the air and then a sizzling noise as the whip slashed into Jace's back. As the whip hit his skin it peeled away leaving a thin perfect red line. Jace gritted his teeth as he heard Bruce go to hit him again. Bruce's eyes flickered to Dante.

"You count. He gets ten." Bruce ordered.

The whip crack rang out hitting Jace's flesh. He gritted his teeth through the pain, not letting any noise out. He would not give him that satisfaction.

"Two." Dante yelled.

"You don't count it, I won't count it." Bruce said looking at Dante when he took a long time to say two.

"Three." Dante yelled as another line appeared across Jace's back.

Bruce smiled brightly and he could see Jace started to shake from pain.

"Four."

Jace was now leaning against his hands. Any second Bruce thought and he would for sure get a cry out of pain out of Jace.

"Five."

"Hey." Nora's voice fluttered in his head, at first *he thought he was making it up.*

"Hi Love." He said back hiding his pain.

"Six."

"So they're holding a gathering tonight here for me. I have to announce the titles and greet everyone again. I guess it's more formal. I'm assuming it's going to be like a dinner or something. Will you be here for that part?" Nora asked him through mindlink.

"Seven."

"I might be able to make it. I will try really hard. There's a few little hiccups over here that I'm smoothing over and then I will try to be there. Jace replied back.

He could feel his flesh separating and he was having trouble masking his pain through the mind link. He needed to end it so she wouldn't know.

"Eight"

"Jace, is everything ok?" Nora asked, her heart panicking a little.

"Everything's fine. Just a little stressed. I'll see you soon Love. Stay there till I come get you." Jace cut the mind link short.

"Nine"

"If Nora asks anyone, you tell her I am fine." Jace sent it to Matt and Dante.

He saw Dante nod and then watched Matt's eyes gloss over.

"Matt you tell her I am fucking fine now!" Jace growled.

"Ten."

The last whip felt like his back had shattered open. Bruce smiled triumphantly thinking the growl was for him. He grabbed the jar of wolfsbane and approached Jace. He then dumped it on his back. Jace crashed to his knees as his back began to burn.

"Wolfsbane so you don't heal so quickly." Bruce laughed walking away.

Chapter Thirteen
Be Merry

"*L*et him hang there for a second." Bruce snickered as he began walking to the pack house.

Bruce walked into the pack house like he had just accomplished something grand. Matt was still holding the rope. The only thing holding Jace up at this point. Douglas sighed and shook his head as he walked inside as well. Dante came to Jace's side. He grabbed a hold of his hands and looped them around his neck. He then nodded to Matt to let go of the rope. Matt did and Jace crashed onto Dante.

"Just let me fall." Jace groaned.

"Shut up." Dante grumbled back to him.

"Matt, we need to get the wolfsbane off of him so he can start healing. It's what's making him feel so bad." Dante said, supporting Jace's weight.

"Tell me to shut up again." Jace growled.

Dante's forearm skin grazed Jace's back, the wolfbane burning into his flesh. He winced heavily trying not to drop Jace as the pain shot through him. Matt rushed over and undid his hands.

"Just let me go." Jace growled again, becoming angry the worse he felt.

"We need water." Dante said, holding Jace up.

"I said put me down." Jace growled trying to send out his alpha aurora but the wolfbane was affecting him.

"I'll go get the hose." Matt nodded.

"Once we get the wolfsbane off you will start healing." Dante said ignoring Jace's comments.

Matt grabbed the hose and rushed back over to them. He looked at Dante who locked his arms around Jace's torso.

"Ready?" Matt asked Dante.

Dante nodded and braced Jace. The powdered wolfbans clung to his opened wounds. The only way to get the powder off of him was to blast it with the hose. The water hit Jace's back and he let out a loud growl as he tensed up in Dante's arms. Matt winced seeing his Alpha's pain. He tried to hurry but the powder was stubborn and took some effort to get off. Finally after several long seconds Jace's back was powder free. Jace slunk forward into Dante for a minute catching his breath back.

"Let me go." Jace order.

"Fine stubborn ass." Dante whispered to him before letting him go.

Jace dropped to his knees, taking several deep breaths. He felt his body kick in and it began working on healing itself. The wolfbane did some damage so it would take longer than normal but he would heal.

Nora stepped into the long red gown and pulled it up over her stomach. It was tightly fit to her torso and then flared out from her hips down. It had gems hugging a heart sharp neckline, a long slit on the side so when she walked you could peek and see part of her legs. She stared at herself in the mirror, taken back a bit she had not been this dressed up in years. Her hair was pulled back from her face and she wore a simple sleek ponytail. She took a deep breath wondering what Jace was doing.

"Alpha, we are ready." Asher's voice came through the bathroom door.

She took a deep breath and nodded to herself before opening the door. She stood in the doorway feeling awkward as she adjusted the dress. Asher looked at her stunned, his look of shock was soon replaced with a smile.

"You look stunning, Alpha." Asher smiled at her.

"Thank you ... .I feel out of place." Nora said, fidgeting slightly.

"You don't look like it." Asher said, offering her his arm.

"Thank you." She smiled, taking his arm in hers.

"So how does this go?" Nora said as they started to open the door.

"Simple. You're announced, we go in. You greet everyone. We eat, drink and be merry." Asher nudged her as he said merry.

"Ok. I can do that." She chuckled.

"Alpha, I believe you can do anything." Asher said to her, his soft but strong voice.

"Thank you, it means alot." She smiled, squeezing his forearm.

"Well let's get this over with." Nora smiled walking out.

They walked down a long hallway, Nora followed Asher's lead. They came upon two large wooden doors. Asher clicked his foot on the wooden floor and they began to open. Nora squeezed tightly on his arm, nerves setting in. Asher's warm hand covered hers as he rubbed her hand slightly trying to bring her comfort. She didn't know why she was so nervous. She took a deep breath and looked to Asher as he was waiting for her to let him know she was ready. She nodded and he stepped forward to bring her with him. As they crossed the threshold of the doorway, a man standing on the side of the door slammed his foot twice into the ground. All gathered turned and looked in the direction of the doorway. Seeing Nora they bowed their heads, bared their necks and kneeled.

She inhaled being overwhelmed for a minute. As Asher began leading her down the walkway. The room was dark and set with warm fall colors. The hall had trees drawn on the wall and leaves lining them. It looked like they were outside in a fall forest. The wood of all the tables and chairs were dark and rich in color. Asher led her up to a small stage. Two seats were up there. Nora knew it was meant for her. The throne was made out of the same deep dark wood and stretched upwards into a tree as well. It was outlined with red leaves that dangled over the throne area. Nora smiled at the detail. Asher let go of her hand and stepped off the stage.

Nora turned facing the crowd, her eyes scanning the crowd of bowed heads. She didn't see one that wasn't. She was looking for him but she knew he wasn't there. If Jace had been there he wouldn't have been waiting in the hall to see her anyways. Nora cleared her throat, her stomach turning on itself. She knew something was wrong. Jace would be here if something wasn't. She regained her composure and knew she had to address them.

"Hello all, you may rise. Thank you so much for joining me in celebrating. I know normally this to celebrate your new Alpha but tonight we are celebrating our pack." Nora's voice spread over the crowd.

The crowd carefully looked up to her confused about why the Alpha would want them to look at them. Nora watched the women in the pack struggle to follow the command. They were still so afraid.

"Eyes up everyone!" Nora commanded drawing on this power she felt in the pit of her stomach.

Immediately everyone's head popped up, as if some invisible force made them. Nora smiled a little bit at herself.

"Great. As I was saying we are celebrating our pack and the new things to come. Change is scary but change is good. We need change in order to grow and grow." Nora said as she watched several members nod in agreement.

"Tonight I am announcing our new title holders." Nora smiled and a cheer rose up.

"As you know, Asher is my Beta, he has shown great strength and guidance in this whole process." Nora motioned to Asher as she spoked.

Asher bowed his head in gratitude. She then scanned the crowd looking for someone. Her eyes landed on Jordan. She smiled at him.

"Jordan please come up here." Nora said, motioning to the stage.

Jordan bowed his head and walked to the stage, he didn't step up but stood in front of Nora. She wondered about this stage and why no one but her seemed to be allowed on it.

"Jordan, you have courage and the ability to make decisions in critical moments. I would like to appoint you head medical doctor of the pack. I need someone like you who will be able to make life saving decisions when it matters the most." Nora said, smiling at him.

"Thank you my Alpha. I accept this honor." Jordan said, bowing his head.

"Chance please come up here." Nora said as Chance smiled brightly coming up to the stage.

"Chance I would like to appoint you Gamma of the Red Woods pack." Nora said with a smile.

There were a few grumbles in the crowd. Nora looked over the crowd and saw the four she knew were behind the disturbance. She knew it was because Gamma was the last rank in the order and they wondered why she was going out of order.

"Thank you my Alpha. I am so honored." Chance said, bowing his head.

"Lyla please come forward." Nora said her voice was strong and powerful as she said.

Hush fell over the crowd as she heard a low growl. This is what she was waiting for and she was ready for it. Lyla stood up from her table and began walking toward the stage. One of the four men stepped out from his table and stepped into the aisle blocking the way for Lyla. Nora's eyes locked with Roger as a small smile curled onto his lips.

"Are you trying to disrespect the Alpha?" Lyla growled as he blocked her way.

Nora went to intervene but wanted to see how this played out. She watched Asher's eyes begin to glow. Lyla began to growl slightly at the man.

"Clay." Asher bellowed towards him.

Clay's eyes flickered to Asher challenging him. Lyla began to growl deeper, her eyes glowing bright amber. Nora's eyes flickered to some movement in the back. She watched another man stand up. This was enough. Nora stepped off the stage and began walking toward them. The power radiating off her was making the people she passed bow their heads. She walked up behind Clay and stared at his back. If she could she would have burned a hole in his back with her eyes. Reaching him she touched his shoulder and pressed down. A surge of energy went through her and she pushed it into his shoulder. At the same time she let out her Alpha aura, using her Alpha aura to conceal her powers. No one knew she was doing what she was doing. Her eyes glowed fiercely.

"Kneel." She growled and he buckled to his knees.

The man groaned and collapsed hard onto the floor. The pack around them bowed their heads and lowered themselves. Nora let her Alpha aura creep out to the ones she knew was behind everything.

"If anyone has a problem with these changes you have one option and that is to leave. You either kneel to me and my changes or I will make you. If you continue to cause havoc and attempt to harm any members of this pack, I will show you how to leave. There will be severe consequences if these new rules are broken." Nora said, looking out.

The three remaining men buckled to their knees as well. Nora looked at them, forcing all four men further to the ground.

"This will be my last show of mercy. If you want to still follow Kip's pack laws leave tonight." Nora said, pulling back her power and aura.

She then looked to Lyla and offered her hand. Lyla slowly took it and Nora walked her up to the stages with Chance and Jordan. She then looked out over the crowd.

"I have one last announcement. I know all the titles have been filled but I am making a new one. Jaime will be my administrator assistant." Nora said, making up a title.

"She is respected like she is a delta as well." Nora announced and motioned for Jaime to come forward.

She looked over to Asher who had a small smile on his face. She raised her eyebrow at him but his smile just continued to grow. She found herself smiling as well.

"Ok well here are your high ranking wolves. Now let's eat, drink and be merry." Nora said, repeating what Asher had said to her earlier.

Chapter Fourteen
Pain

*N*ora went up to the stage, they all bowed to her and thanked her. She smiled softly at them taking a seat. Her eyes scanned the crowd, she didn't know why she was looking. She would feel him if he was here. She wondered what he had been taking care of.

"Alpha." Asher's voice came up on the side of her, while she was scanning the room for Jace.

"Asher..Sit with me?" Nora asked, patting the seat next to her.

"It's usually a spot for the Alpha's Luna." Asher said quietly.

"Well I am not going to have a Luna. You're second in command. Sit. Keep me company." Nora smiled at him.

"If it will make my Alpha happy." Asher smiled at her sitting down next to her.

"Very." Nora chuckled.

A few pack members glanced up seeing Asher sit down in the Luna's seat but no one said anything. Asher motioned for someone serving drinks to bring two up. The server came up, dropping her head every low and handing the two glasses to Asher. He nodded to her and she left. He looked at the two glasses handing one to Nora.

"What is it?" She asked looking down into the red substance in the glass.

"Wine, it's made here in the pack." Asher smiled.

Nora smiled and went to put the glass to her lips. Asher grabbed it from her suddenly. Nora looked shocked at him.

"What?" Nora said, a little startled.

"I didn't think about this before but we should have all your drinks and food tested before you eat or drink them. Right now with tension being high." Asher said looking down at the drink.

"You're not allowed to drink that." Nora said in her alpha tone commanding him quickly.

If it was poisoned she was not having Asher die on the account of her.

"Well there goes that idea." Asher tried to fight the command but was not able to.

His eyes scanned the crowd and then he got a small smile on his face.

"I have an idea." Asher said to her.

"Roger." Asher called out into the room summoning him.

Nora looked at him intrigued as Roger began to approach the stage.

"Yes Beta." Roger said to him his tone showing he was not interested.

"Drink this." Asher held the cup out to him.

Roger looked at him suspiciously and took the cup from his hand looking into it. Roger was debating with himself.

"Drink." Asher said, commanding him.

Roger slowly put the drink to his lips and took a sip before handing it back to him. Asher smiled and waved him away.

"Ok?" Nora said as Asher took the cup back and Roger walked away.

"Well if he falls over and dies, we will have eliminated two problems." Asher chuckled.

"That's a little cruel." Nora smirked, shaking her head.

"Well if anyone is going to attempt to poison you it's him and why not have the one person who is most likely to do it be your tester." Asher laughed, still holding on to the drink.

"Ten minutes tops and then you can have it." Asher said, winking at her.

They watched Roger fidget a few times like he was nervous. Nora wondered if he would really attempt to poison her or if someone there would. It would be the quickest and easy way to get rid of her. Asher did have a point. After ten minutes passed and Roger was still fine he handed Nora the cup.

"Ok now try it, it's going to be the best wine you have ever tasted." Asher said proudly.

Nora smiled and brought the cup to her lips taking a big sip. Asher watched her face fill with surprise and enjoyment. The wine hit her tongue and her taste buds exploded. There was a sweetness to it but something deep and warm. She moved the liquid around her mouth trying to figure it out. She picked up a note of honey but that wasn't it. She looked at Asher questioning.

"Not telling." He laughed, taking a sip of his own.

"Fine." Nora said, making a face at him and taking another sip.

"It is really the best wine or drink I have ever tasted." Nora smiled.

"Told you." Asher laughed.

She looked over the pack, taking another sip. She wished Jace had been there. She wished she knew what was going on over there. She sighed deeply, maybe she could head there tonight after this was all done. She was trying to figure out the appropriate time to leave.

Suddenly her back felt like it was on fire. She looked down at the cup and then to Roger. He hasn't moved, he showed no signs of pain or distress. The pain kept increasing. Nora winced moving forward trying to get her back away from the seat. She leaned forward into herself as another wave hit.

"Alpha?" Asher asked, standing up and going to her.

Nora stood shaking, her fist balling up as she clenched them. She leaned forward and Asher came forward grabbing a hold of her to steady her. Her skin was clammy.

"My back, it hurts. It burns." Nora whimpered.

Asher looked over at Roger and he wasn't feeling anything. It couldn't be poison…could it? Nora had another rush of pain and she fell into Asher. Sarah, who was in the back of the room rushed forward.

"What's going on?" Sarah said, trying to figure out why her Luna was in pain.

"She's saying her back is burning." Asher said to Sarah.

"Bathroom." Sarah said, looking at Asher.

Nora couldn't move, each movement she made the fabric of her dress press against her back and the pain seared into her. Asher scooped her off her feet and carried her off stage. He went through the side hall and into the bathroom. Sarah follows close behind. Asher set Nora down as she let out a soft yell.

"Hang on, Hang on." He said not knowing what to do for her.

She let out another cry and Asher grabbed the sides of her dress and pulled. The fabric ripped perfectly down the center, exposing her back. Nora winced, leaning forward as the pain continued to burn. Sarah came around the front of her bracing her so she wouldn't fall forward.

"What is it?" Sarah panicked.

"Nothing. There's nothing on her back, it's fine, it's perfect." Asher said, now panicking more.

Nora winced as her neck where Jace marked her started to burn. Her hand went to her mark covering it as she winced. She then connected the dots.

"Jace." Nora said out loud.

"What?" Sarah said, confused.

"The pain. It's not mine. It's his. I need to go, he's hurt. I knew he wasn't here for a reason." Nora said, straightening up.

She closed her eyes, focusing the pain out of her mind. She knew that after Jace marked her she would feel his feelings like they were her own but she didn't know she could feel his pain.

"Shit." Asher whispered, realizing that there was trouble.

"Sarah, give me your dress." Nora ordered her.

"What are you going to do? You could be going back into a trap or something." Sarah said, starting to undress.

Asher turned around to not see Sarah undressing. Nora pushed the red dress to the floor and grabbed Sarah's black dress. She slipped it on. The dress was black but shimmered red. Sarah wanted to honor her old pack at the ceremony. It fell just above her knee. Nora nodded to her, giving her the red dress.

"What are you going to do?" Sarah asked as Nora gave her the dress.

"I'm going to go save my mate and hurt whoever hurt him." Nora said, her eyes narrowing and glowing at the same time.

"What if it's not safe?" Sarah said, worrying for her.

"If Jace is hurt, then it's not going to be safe for anyone." Nora growled.

"Let me see what Dante says, please wait." Sarah said, trying to get Nora not to rush into anything.

Nora realized Sarah was going to do everything she could to make sure she was safe. She sighed.

"You have five seconds." Nora said, annoyed.

Sarah nodded and her eyes glossed over as she mindlinked Dante.

"Asher, go back out there and make sure everything is going smoothly. That was a little bit of a scene." Nora commanded him.

She could see that he wanted to protest but he wasn't going to go against her command. He sighed, nodded and then left the bathroom. Nora waited impatiently. The random stinging on her back reminded her that Jace was hurting. Nora's eyes went back to normal.

"Dante said that Jace said he is fine and to not worry. He will come get you soon." Sarah said with a weak smile.

"Ok good." Nora said, trying to hide that she didn't believe them.

"Did he say how long till he came for me?" Nora asked, forming a plan in her head.

"He told Dante within the hour." Sarah said, but there was something in the way she said it that Nora didn't trust.

"Jace." Nora sent to him through mind link.

She didn't get any response. She shut her eyes seeing if she could feel him. She felt emptiness there. He had either blocked himself from her or he was asleep? Nora thought to herself.

"Ok. Well I've had enough excitement for one night. I'll be in my room when he comes for me." Nora said, walking out before Sarah asked or said anything else.

Chapter Fifteen
Shifting

Nora walked out of the bathroom and down the hall. She walked fast and quickly through the hall. She had forgotten for a second that she was in charge and had power. She didn't need to sneak out. She was just going to leave. She walked into the hall, the pack members standing as she entered. Asher looked concerned. She smiled at him as she began walking to the front door.

"Alpha." Asher called after her.

"I have something I need to attend to. Everyone eat, drink and enjoy themselves." Nora said walking to the door sending out her alpha aura letting them know it was a command.

Asher had started to follow her but like a wave was hit by her aura and was forced to follow it. She walked to the door pulling it open. The night air hit her and she looked around. She needed a car. She needed to get to Jace now. She was starting to panic. She wanted to be at Cross River now. She felt Zara press against her skin. Nora felt funny, her wolf had never wanted to take control before.

"I could get us there fast." Zara said to Nora.

"I don't know how to shift and I wouldn't know how to change back." Nora said debating.

"Just give me control and I will make sure you turn back." Zara said.

"I don't know." Nora said.

"Our mate is hurt, we need to be there now. Trust me this is the only way this is going to work." Zara growled.

"Fine." Nora yelled.

Nora began walking towards the woods as Zara kept pressing for control. Nora growled at Zara as she ducked into the woods.

"You're wasting time." Zara growled back.

"Fucking give me a minute." Nora growled.

Nora shut her eyes trying to let go. She was never taught this and it wasn't coming naturally. She let out a huge sigh.

"Do you know how we do this?" Nora asked, annoyed.

"You need to trust me. When you feel me push give into it." Zara instructed her.

"I don't trust you. I don't know you. Promise me you will let me shift back when we get to the pack house." Nora said, pacing back and forth worried.

"You need to trust me. I am part of you and want what's best for us. Right now we need to go save our mate." Zara said to her.

"Fine, let's do this.' Nora said, closing her eyes.

Zara fought for control and instead of fighting it Nora gave in. She felt like she had taken a step back in her own mind and allowed Zara to come forward. She was now watching herself. She felt her body begin to crack and her bones pop. She crashed to her knees and let out a yell as the pain overwhelmed her.

"It's going to only hurt for a moment, don't fight it or it will last longer. " Zara said.

Nora let out another yell as her bones shifted again aligning themselves. She was just about to say she couldn't do this when everything stopped. She was seeing everything sharper and clear. The world felt different. She realized that she was now just a passenger and Zara was in control. She felt her stretch and shake. She felt Zara excitement about actually being out and happiness flooded her.

"Are you ready?" Zara said she was kind of cocky about it.

"Get us to our mate." Nora said to her.

Zara dug her paws into the earth and took off running. She was fast and took off like nothing was going to stop her. Everything was passing by so quickly. Zara had one goal in mind and it was getting to her mate. Chunks of dirt were being kicked up as she ran. A fallen tree was in their way Nora winced worried about crashing into and Zara jumped it like it wasn't even there. They would be there in no time. Nora relaxed, enjoying the ride. She knew she had to embrace this side of herself but she didn't know Zara. She now knew she needed to spend more time with her. Her wolf side was incredible.

---

*J*ace kneeled on the grass trying to catch his breath from the pain. He decided he was going to just lay there. He glanced up at the sky, it was night. Nora, he thought. He just needed to rest a moment before he met her. He laid on his stomach and then suddenly the world went black.

"Shit." Dante groaned.

"What?" Matt said, dropping the hose.

"He passed out." Dante said, looking at how far they were from the pack house.

"He didn't even attempt to make it easy." Matt chuckled.

"Let's get him to his room." Dante said with a sigh, kneeling down trying to get the best way to carry him.

Dante wrapped his arms under his shoulders and motioned for Matt to get his legs. Matt walked over to Jace's legs squatting down.

"Did you call for Wyatt?" Matt asked, still not picking up Jace's legs.

"I will. Hurry up." Dante rushed him.

"We're taking him all the way up to the third floor?" Matt asked

"That's where his room is." Dante growled.

"He's such a big bastard." Matt groaned.

"Pick up your Alpha's legs or I'm going to break yours." Dante growled.

"I will. I was just saying there's bedrooms on the first floor." Matt said going to grab his legs.

"Matt!" Dante yelled.

"What I'm going to." Matt said annoyed.

"Matt. Put the legs down and move away." Dante said quietly motioning behind him.

"What? You just said-" Matt said, dropping Jace's foot and looking behind him.

A large white wolf was standing behind him hackles up and teeth bared. The wolf was incredible, she looked like she was glowing. Her eyes were the brightest amber color he had ever seen. Even the wolf's fur seemed to shimmer in the moonlight, like she herself had a glow about her. She was growling as she walked towards Matt.

"Dante, do you know this wolf?" Matt said, putting his hands up defensively and moving to the side.

"No. I don't think so." Dante whispered.

The wolf spotted Jace and rushed over to him. Seeing Jace the wolf began to whimper. The wolf nuzzled her snout into Jace's arm whimpering. Dante looked down at the wolf and it hit him.

"Nora?" Dante whispered.

The wolf's eyes shot up meeting Dante's. A low growl came from the white wolf, as she protectively stood over Jace.

Zara, that's Dante and Matt, they are friends. Nora told Zara.

Zara looked at them studying them and then went back to Jace.

Who did this? Zara demanded to Nora.

I don't know but it wasn't them. They could never hurt him. Nora explained to her.

Zara whimpered more as she looked over Jace's bloody back.

"He's going to be ok. We need to get him help." Dante said to the wolf quietly.

"Nora?" Matt said, crouching down to look at her.

Zara ignored them and then Nora felt something, Zara began to pull on her energy.

What are you doing? Nora asked her.

Trust me, I think we can help him heal. I've felt you do this several times when in human form. I think it might be more powerful if we try in wolf form. Zara said.

Be careful; too much can hurt us. Nora told her.

Zara pulled on her and Nora's energy and she felt the surge coming together. She moved closer to Jace looking over her wounds. She then ran her tongue over his bloody back. Running it up so it touched each wound. As she did she released the energy she had built up. As her tongue hit them it was like Jace's skin responded. He began healing quickly. His wounds had been trying to heal but the wolfbane had slowed down his healing abilities. The new energy Zara placed in him helped kick start his wolf healing and sent it into hyperdrive.

"Woah." Dante whispered, letting Jace shoulders down so he was laying flat.

"Do you see this?" Matt asked.

"That's incredible." Dante whispered.

Dante looked down at his Luna who had basically just healed his Alpha. They knew mates could transfer pain to each other but he had never seen one heal another. He knew Nora had powers but he didn't know she could find a way to use it to heal.

"Matt, we can't let the council see her wolf." Dante said quickly.

"Yeah she definitely is different." Matt said, looking at the white wolf

"Hey..umm Nora's wolf. Umm can you let Nora come back now?" Matt asked the wolf in a sweet unsure voice.

The wolf's eyes snapped to Matt unsure of him. Dante went to stand next to her. Zara didn't know if she trusted them yet. She moved away from Dante.

Zara it's ok, let me back. Nora said going to push like Zara always did for control.

No, we have to make those pay that did this. Zara growled.

Zara, we don't know what happened. We need to make sure Jace is ok and when he wakes up we will handle it.

"Nora, if you're in there, we need you back. Your wolf.. She doesn't look like a normal wolf. If the council sees you. It's going to be bad." Matt said softly to the wolf.

Zara walked over to Jace's head and nudged it, wanting him to wake up. His eyes fluttered open as he squinted trying to make out what was in front of him. Zara whimpered trying to reach out to Cole.

Zara listen to them. I trust them. You said for me to trust you now trust me. Nora said to her trying to not be angry with her.

Fine Zara growled.

Thank you Nora said to her.

How do we do this? Nora asked her.

It's the opposite: I let go, you take over. Zara said kind of snotty to her.

Ok so freaking let go then. Nora said back to her.

You need to take control first. Zara groaned.

Nora pushed forward in her mind and she then felt Zara slip back. It was like she was moving from the passenger seat in the car to now driving it. Nora felt the bone crunching feeling of her bones popping out of place. She let out a painful yell as they moved and rearranged.

"Nora?" Jace said foggy trying to roll over to sit up.

A final surge went through her of pain as her bones finally realigned and popped all back into place. She let out a final yell curling into herself kneeling hugging her knees. Breathing heavily as she shook from the experience.

"Nora!" Jace said his vision cleared up as he saw a naked Nora hugging her knees.

He shot up angry and not sure what was going on. All he knew was Nora was naked and screaming. He was going to kill whoever did something to her. Jace kneeled in front of her searching for a wound or anything.

"Hey. Hey, what's going on?" Jace asked, looking at her anger and fear rushing through him.

His eyes found Dante and Matt. Jace's face is full of questions and anger. He just needed to be told who hurt her and they were dead.

"Jace calm down, she shifted." Dante said calmly.

"She shifted?" Jace repeated.

"Her wolf is amazing." Matt said behind her.

"Who taught her how? Who taught you how? Are you ok?" Jace asked, touching her cheek

"I'm fine. I figured it out myself." Nora said her eyes locked with his.

Now that he wasn't hurt anymore she was angry. Angry at him for lying. Her eyes looked at Dante and Matt, she was also pissed at them. Jace was confused at why she was angry. He then realized he was still outside. He looked over to Nora who looked like he betrayed her. He then realized she was completely naked.

"Shirt!" Jace yelled at Dante and Matt.

Matt and Dante both pulled their shirts up over their heads and handed them to Jace. Jace grabbed Matt's because Dante's had blood on it from him. He pulled the shirt over Nora's head and she slipped her arms through it. As her head popped out she was glaring at him.

"You lied." Nora growled at him.

"What?" Jace said, confused.

"You lied to me. You said you were fine and you weren't!" Nora yelled into his face.

She stood up quickly and glared at Dante and Matt who quickly bowed their heads.

"Even worse, you made them lie. I know I can't be mad at you two for lying. But I am." Nora said, looking from Jace to Dante and Matt.

She looked back at the house and then down at Jace, he was still confused. She was mad at him for lying. She apparently had shifted with no one telling her how or guiding her. She also managed to shift back without help. She now was very angry with him. She let out a low growl and stomped up the stairs into the house. She slammed the door behind her

Jace let out a long sigh as he was still on his knee in the front yard of the pack house. He looked at Matt and Dante.

"Explain." Jace said, trying not to growl.

"Um well we're not sure exactly how or-" Matt started to say as a deep chocolate brown wolf came running out of the woods.

Matt tensed up his eyes glowing but Dante smiled, he knew who it was before she even shifted back. Sarah stood where the deep chocolate brown wolf once was. She bowed her head.

"My Alpha, I am so sorry. The Luna told me she was going to wait for you to come for her and by the time I realized she was gone. She was so fast in wolf form. I couldn't catch up." Sarah said quietly.

"What happened, why did she come?" Jace asked, confused.

"I don't know. She started saying her back was burning and she was in alot of pain. She then knew it was from you." Sarah said her head still bowed.

Jace let out a sigh. He had tried his best to block the mate bond but he clearly didn't do it right. It had to be when he got weak or passed out. He looked at Dante and Matt confused his back no longer hurt. It should still hurt. He shouldn't have healed this fast.

"My back?" Jace said standing.

"Nora." They both answered.

"How?" Jace asked, starting to make his way to the front door.

"I dont know." Dante answered with a shrug going to Sarah.

"Same here." Matt answered.

Jace rubbed his forehead slightly, taking a deep breath and then going to follow Nora inside. He was tired but not hurting. It was a different tired. He was drained and now he felt horrible because Nora was upset with him.

Chapter Sixteen
Liar

*N*ora stormed into the house in nothing but Matt's t-shirt. She was so angry she didn't know what she wanted to do. She threw the door back slamming it. The slammed echoed in the pack house. Her mind was shouting over and over again that he lied to her. She was so angry she was shaking. She began marching up the stairs. Making huffing and growling noises as she did. She gripped the railing to the stairs so tightly she felt the metal bend beneath her grip. She ignored it, stomping her way up the stairs.

You're not wrong to be mad. Zara chimed in.

I know. Nora growled getting to the second landing.

Lance was leaning against the second landing, railing a smug look on his face, as he was trying to figure out what all the noise was. His eyes then spotted Nora and the smug look turned into a charming charismatic one. His eyes wandered over her body, a smile on his face as he realized she was in nothing but a t-shirt that barely covered her bottom. His eyes looked her up and down as they seemed to sparkle with lust.

"Evening Luna. What's causing you such distress?" Lance said, acting like he cared.

"Nothing, excuse me." Nora said, trying to step around him but he just stepped further into her way.

"Luna, talk to me. I am pretty capable of solving every problem that comes across me. I would be a great ally to you." Lance said, touching her shoulder.

Nora went to step back but Lance's other hand went to her waist holding her in place. As he stepped closer to her. He was making her even more annoyed. She kept reminding herself that he was some high ranking wolf and she needed to be respectful in denying him. Right now she wanted to fight someone but she tried to choke that feeling back.

"You just need to ask and I will help you in any way you want." Lance said low and seductively.

"Thank you for the offer but I am quite capable of helping myself." Nora said with a smile, trying to step back away from him.

"Everyone could use a little help." Lance said ignoring her saying no.

A loud growl erupted from the bottom of the stairs. Nora didn't even have to look to know who it was. She knew that Jace was on his way up to tear into Lace. She needed him to not do that. He just got hurt from god knows what. She needed him to be calm. She went to turn but Lance was still holding on to her. She pushed on his hand.

"Lance, get your hands away from my mate and move aside." Jace growled as he nearly ran up the rest of the stairs.

Lance wouldn't let go. Nora let out a little energy and where Lance was touching her, he felt a zap. He pulled his hand quickly away shaking it, confused about what happened. Nora stepped back, getting free from him.

"We must have a spark." Lance said to Nora shaking his hand as he ignored Jace.

"I don't think you're right. Now excuse me." Nora said once again to Lance.

Jace reached the landing at this point he was growling fiercely, eyes glowing as he was on the verge of letting Cole rip Lance to shreds. Nora was still angry and ignored Jace. Trying to focus on Lance.

"Ahh Jace, me and your mate were just having a conversation. It didn't include you." Lance smiled provokingly.

"Nora what I wanted to ask you was to have dinn-"

Jace growled, stepping towards them, cutting Lace off mid sentence. Nora could feel Jace behind her and the anger rolling off of him.

He's going to let Cole out. Zara said to Nora.

"Do we need a round two Jace?" Lance said, narrowing his eyes.

Nora stepped back looking at Lance wondering what exactly he was talking about. She looked back at Jace as a deadly looking smile rolled across his lips. His eyes glowing bright. Nora stepped towards Jace touching his shoulder softly, trying to calm him. She didn't need him killing Lance right now. Nora touched his face trying to get his attention. She saw his eyes dim at her touch and a small flicker of hope came to her. She might be able to stop Cole.

"Back feels good now, I could go again but not after I get to you first." Jace said dangerously.

"Your back isn't even healed." Lance laughed.

"It is, I'm a quick healer. Want to play your odds?" Jace said, touching Nora's hand gently, moving it off his face as he went to step towards Lance.

His back! Zara growled.

It clicked as Zara became angry in her mind. Lance was the reason for Jace's back. How did he even get a chance to do that? How did Jace allow that to happen to himself? Images of Jace passed out on the ground, his flesh tore open and bleeding flashed in her mind. Nora began to shake.

"You! You did that to his back!" Nora growled.

Jace looked to Nora, the anger and growl that came out of her was frightening. Nora stepped forward to Lance, her eyes glowing amber as Zara pushed forward. Jace watched as claws descended from her fingers. The power radiating off of her was incredible and took Jace by surprise.

"I..I-" Lance began to say, confused at what was happening.

Nora grabbed him by the shirt, her fangs descending as Zara was taking control. She wanted to rip his back apart like they did to Jace. Slice her claws through his flesh.

"Who do you think you are to touch him?" Nora growled his shirt beginning to shred in her hands.

Jace came up behind her and grabbed her around her midsection pulling her back into him. She struggled but realized it was Jace and didn't want to hurt him.

"I am going to-

"Lance go." Jace said to him as he cut Nora off and she began to shake more, her body almost vibrating in his arms.

"I-" Lance said, still not sure what was happening, the power he was feeling from Nora was confusing him, he never felt strength like that.

"Fucking move now." Jace yelled as he tightened his grip on Nora.

The front of Lance's shirt ripped off of him as Nora struggled in Jace's arms trying to get at him. As his shirt fell away from him in pieces as Lance finally stepped aside. His mouth was hanging open as Jace picked Nora up and hurried up the stairs.

"You don't ever touch him again!" She yelled as tried to reach out and grab him as they passed Lance.

Jace turned in one quick motion and used her own momentum to flip her over his shoulder. Jace scaled the stairs in no time carrying her over his shoulder. Nora was growling fiercely, her eyes locked on Lance.

Jace kicked open his bedroom door walking over to the bed and flopped Nora down on it. She was still enraged. She went to get up but Jace shoved her back down.

"Stop." Jace said firmly.

"I'm going to kill him." Nora growled.

A small smirk curled at the end of his lip as Nora threatened to kill Lance. She ignored his smirk and went to get up. Jace caught her again. He pulled her against his chest and held her in a hug. After several seconds he felt her starting to slowly relax. Her claws receded back into her hands. Jace kissed the top of her head. She moved her head back looking at him. She was still shaking slightly from all the rage she felt. She had never felt anything like that before. She had been mad before but never to the point of wanting to rip someone apart. She actually pictured herself mauling Lance. Jace kissed her cheek and then began kissing her neck. Trying to distract her. He kissed her mark and he felt her shiver.

"Better?" He asked in a whisper.

"A little." Nora said quietly.

"I have questions." Nora said after taking a breath.

"I probably have answers." Jace smirked against her shoulder.

"One, what the hell happened to you? Two I was going to kill him. Like really kill him. I could see myself doing it. I still want to but ugh I don't even know what my question is." Nora said, frustrated.

"Well one is simple, your mate is a smart ass and has a bit of a hot temper that got me in trouble. So insulting a high alpha, which is what those low life roaches are; results in a punishment like being whipped. I would have been healed by now but they rubbed wolfsbane into the wounds." Jace said like it was a normal thing.

"Punishment with a whip like a whip, whip." Nora growled, her anger starting to rise up.

"Kinda of in the name love." Jace said with a silly smile.

"This isn't fucking funny. They whipped you. I swear to-"

Jace's mouth crashed over hers capturing it into a kiss. She was so angry but it melted as he kissed her. He ran his hand down her back, his fingertips grazing her skin. Each touch of his flesh against hers distracted her. She pulled away quickly trying to get a hold of the situation before it turned into something else.

"Jace, this is serious." Nora said, stepping back from him.

"Fine, then I have questions." Jace said, sitting down on the bed.

"Fine, go ahead." Nora said, annoyed.

"Dante said you healed me…how?" Jace asked, keeping his voice low.

"I didn't heal you. I used energy. I took some of my energy and gave it to you. To help speed up your own healing process." Nora said, matching his voice.

"How did you think to do that?" Jace asked.

"It wasn't my idea it was Zara's. I'm just glad it worked." Nora said looking over to the door, she was anticipating Lance to come busting in there.

"Shifting?" Jace asked.

"Same." Nora said walking over to the bed and sitting down next to him.

"So Zara walked you through it." Jace said quietly.

"Yeah. It hurt. Are you ok?" Nora asked, wondering about the change in mood.

"Yeah. I'm sorry I wasn't there for your first shift. It's painful at first but it goes away the more you get use to it." Jace explained.

"Jace I didn't plan on shifting without you. The rush of not knowing if you were ok or what was going on caused me and Zara to panic. I felt it, your pain like it was happening to me. I couldn't get a hold of you. There was no way of getting here. Zara stepped up and got us here. " Nora explained.

Jace frowned; he didn't realize what he had put her through. He went to say something but Nora put a finger to his lips.

"You lied to me. You had others lie to me. I understand that you probably thought you were protecting me but that is not a reason to lie." Nora said still very angry about it.

"I didn't want you to see that. I didn't know how you would react and seeing how you just ripped Lance's shirt off in the hall because you found out. I am willing to bet you would have shifted and tried killing them." Jace said with a small smile on his face.

Nora was silent; she knew he was right. She probably would have torn everyone who tried touching him to shreds. She sighed.

"There's another thing Matt and Dante said your wolf looks different. I don't know what that means. I didn't see Zara but we don't need the council seeing you in wolf form. I need them to hurry up and leave. Then things will go back to normal. I promise." Jace said, catching her hand.

"Normal…what is normal? We haven't had normal." Nora laughed, dropping his hand, as she became overwhelmed.

"Jace, I can't even begin to understand what's going on with me and now I have to worry about whether you're going to lie or hide stuff from me because you're worried about protecting me. Which by the way I was on my own before I met you. I also have proven myself more than capable in both forms. I would also like to add that'swith out knowing anything about my wolf side or my hunter side or Alpha or Luna whatever the fuck else I am." Nora growled at him, becoming mad again.

Jace walked over to her not saying anything. He knew she had been through alot and had way too much going on. She had been amazingly strong through all of it. He grabbed her hand, taking it in his.

"Hey." He whispered to her trying to get her attention.

"What?" Nora said, her eyes glowing at them.

"Why don't we just go kill them all and take them out of the equation." The words fell out of her mouth, Nora's hand flew up to her mouth as if trying to stop them.

"So as much as I would love that, we would have another war on our hands." Jace laughed.

"Explain the rage and the wanting to kill." Nora was shocked that she had said that.

"Well your wolf, wolves are emotional creatures. All your feelings are from you but they are heightened because of your wolf. So when a threat arises like in the wild your wolf side wants to destroy it. You have to learn to navigate around it. It takes time but you will be able to do it." Jace said, pulling her into him.

"Ok, that makes sense. I don't enjoy it but it makes sense." Nora sighed and then cuddled into his chest even though she was still mad.

"Nora, I promise I won't ever lie to you no matter what. Even if I think I'm doing it to protect you." Jace said to the top of her head as he held her tightly.

"If you promise, I forgive you." Nora said, shutting her eyes and inhaling him.

"Do you think I am going to get in trouble for ripping his shirt off?" Nora asked.

"I don't think he will be telling anyone. I do think however that he is now going to become much more interested in you." Jace said his tone changed to being upset.

"More interested?" Nora asked, pulling back to look at his face.

"Yes Lance has a habit of thinking he can have whatever he wants or whoever. He said to someone that he wants you." Jace said growling.

"Well he can't and secondly no thank you." Nora said half laughing at the thought.

"That's the problem with the council; they think they own everything and everyone." Jace grumbled.

"Why?" Nora asked.

"They are the most powerful, they have huge armies and power that's been handed down to them. Their ancestors treated the position right. Lance and Bruce are power tripping teenagers that use it to benefit only themselves. Hence why I could care less about them." Jace said annoyed.

"But yet they were still able to punish you." Nora growled.

"Because I let them." He smirked teasingly.

"Someone needs to take them down." Nora muttered.

"I think we might have to make them go away." Jace whispered to her.

"What do you mean?" Nora asked.

"We'll talk more about that later. Let's get you settled. I'm sure you need to check in with Asher seeing how you ditched your party." Jace smiled.

"Yeah you're right." Nora muttered.

Chapter Seventeen
Reunited

"So you're going to tell me what happened?" Sarah sighed as Dante wrapped his arms around her.

"Alpha likes to push his limits by doing so he insulted a higher Alpha. They punished him. He didn't want Nora finding out because he was unsure how that would go." Dante said, kissing the top of her head.

"I'm glad you're back." He said,and leaned down to nuzzle into her neck.

"Yeah well things are rocky over there. Nora just announced titles, commanded everyone to deal with it and took off." Sarah said, summarizing everything.

"Ok.."Dante said quietly.

"There are a few men in the pack that don't want change. Nora made an example out of one of them tonight but I think that will only keep them at bay for so long..I think something big might happen. Nora is doing good at keeping everyone in line when she is there. Asher is doing a great job but he doesn't have the power of an Alpha." Sarah explained trying to ignore the tiny tingles Dante's touch was giving her.

"How about here? What's the deal with the council?" Sarah asked him, Dante's hand snuck under her shirt as he pulled her against him more

Sarah shivered against him as his finger tips grazed the small of her back. She pulled away but it wasn't a real pull. She wanted to be there but at the same time she wanted to have a conversation about what was going on. Dante smirked and let her go. She was surprised and a small frown came over her face. He took a step back away from her, she knew he was teasing her.

"Well if that's how you want to play. I will just go back to Red Wood. See you around." Sarah smiled and started walking away.

She heard a growl and that was all. Before she knew it Dante scooped her up and was carrying her over his shoulder. She let out a small squeak laughing as he carried her away.

"Where are you taking me!" She yelled laughing.

"Home." Dante smirked, hitting her on the butt playfully.

"Dante! I don't know if that's where I'm needed right now." Sarah protested.

"Oh it's where you're needed all right." Dante smirked, holding on to her tightly.

"You know you're very annoying." Lilly said, leaning against Matt's car.

"Just one of my most charming qualities, gorgeous." Matt grinned.

Yes he did annoy her but she couldn't help the fact that she enjoyed it and he knew she did. She was a hunter and he was a wolf. It was an impossible relationship but she was his mate and he was going to move mountains if he had to make this work.

"Charming, funny choice of words." Lilly said, rolling her eyes.

"I know sexy and irresistible seemed better fitting but I was waiting for you to say them first." Matt said a coy smile dancing on his lips.

"Why are you here?" Lilly groaned asking him.

"To see you gorgeous." Matt winked.

"I told you we won't work." Lilly sighed.

"And I told you I don't give up, so I think you should just give in." Matt smiled brightly.

Lilly remained silent, glancing back up at the stone building. Societatea Vânătorului the words hung above it. It had been her home since she can remember. She hated wolves since she was old enough to know. She glanced at Matt, she didn't hate him.

"Besides me being a wolf what's really the problem? Daddy issues? Trust issues?" Matt smirked, still being playful.

"Redhead issues." Lilly smirked.

"I know we are irresistible." Matt grinned bigger.

"No, I don't do redheads. Sorry." Lilly's smirk deepened.

"Don't do or never have?" Matt said turning the conversation sexual, his voice getting low as he stepped closer to her.

"I..I um. Stop it, never mind. Why are you really here?" Lilly said becoming flustered as she tried to chase away the thought of what it would be like to feel Matt's skin against hers, to touch, to kiss. She shook her head trying to focus.

Matt chuckled seeing the bridge of her nose turn a shade of red and her ears following suit. She was adorable when embarrassed.

"Besides seeing you, Alpha Jace asked me to come speak with Logan. We might have another situation arising. We might need assistance again." Matt said trying to be professional.

"Situation? Assistance?" Lilly repeated trying to get more information.

"I know the sound of my voice is enchanting but it would be great to tell both you and Logan at the same time." Matt said quietly.

"Ugh, fine, come in. Let me give the guys a heads up before you walk in and everything goes crazy. Then we'll have another situation." Lilly said, walking ahead of him.

"I already have another situation." Matt mumbled moving his leg trying to straighten out his pants as his eyes wandered over Lilly's rear end as she walked away.

Mate. Ryker demanded in his ear.

Duh Ryker, Duh. I'm working on it. Matt replied.

Matt waited outside the door until Lilly got back. She eyed him funny, giving him a questioning look as she did.

"Problems?" Lilly asked.

"Several but I'm working on them." He said, flashing her a charming smile.

"Ugh, come this way." She muttered to him as she started to lead him into the building.

They walked into the dark building. She heard Lilly mumble something about someone being dramatic and then the lights flicker on. Matt shields his eyes as they adjust. He raised an eyebrow well this certainly was dramatic.

"What no loud scary voice to welcome me? Who dares to enter? No? Nothing?" Matt laughed.

"Hush." Lilly said, grabbing his arm and pulling him along.

Lilly dragged Matt through a set of rooms that looked like a dinning room and living room. She stopped short in front of a wooden door. The same name Societatea Vânătorului was written on it. She pushed it open and pulled Matt into another room. Matt looked about the room confused why she basically had him sprint here. The room was an office lined with bookshelves and books covered them.

"Ok…? You know if you wanted me to be alone with you, you didn't have to drag me. I would have came willingly." Matt said, looking around.

"Sit." Lilly said, pointing to the chair.

Matt looked at her and shrugged, walking to the chair and sitting down.

"Good dog." Lilly smirked.

"Clever." Matt responded with a half smile.

"Lilly what is it, I don't have time for much. There's something going on and I don't know what-"

"Matt!" Logan smiled seeing him.

"Logan. Nice to see you." Matt smiled, getting up and shaking his hand.

Logan at first was pissed to find out that Lilly was his mate but over time Matt wore him down and now they are actually friends. Matt was working on wearing Lilly down. She still wouldn't even give him a dinner date. Logan rounded the desk and sat down. He gave Matt a puzzled look.

"I can't force her to go out on a date with you for the millionth time." Logan laughed.

"Yeah, yeah yeah. I'm actually here on behalf of Jace." Matt glanced at Lilly before looking back to Logan.

"What does Jace want? How's Nora? We haven't heard much from her since Kip." Logan said he sounded annoyed and disappointed.

"Nora is trying to balance many hats right now, Luna, Alpha, hunter, and wolf. You should check in on her. She could use a friend outside of us wolves." Matt smiled at him.

"I will have to do that." Logan said quietly.

"As for Jace we have a situation. So long story short Kip was working with the Alpha council which is like umm like congress…kind of for wolves. They make laws, we need to follow them, and they enforce them. Originally they were founded so not one pack would rule over the others. They are powerful and are High Alpha's which is above an Alpha. Ok. Background check; now juicy stuff." Matt said, leaning forward.

"You were always bad at the short part of the long story." Logan laughed, interrupting him.

"Bruce is power hungry and wants to finish where Kip left off. So far he hasn't made any moves yet but he is hanging out at our pack waiting. Another thorn in our side is Lance. He is an entitled brat basically and will do anything to get what he wants. -

"What does he want?" Logan asked, cutting him off.

"Right now it's Nora." Matt said, anger in his voice.

"How? I thought wolf law didn't mess with marked mates. It would interfere with the moon goddess." Logan said, shifting in his chair.

"Hey look at you reading up on us. Yeah Lance, don't care about that." Matt said with a smile and then frowning when he mentioned Lance.

"Ok, so Jace is going to kill him. There is one of your problems gone." Logan said with a shrug.

"Not exactly. Let me finish. Then there's Douglas. We don't know exactly what he wants but he wants to help us take down Bruce and Lance. We don't know if he is doing it for the good of all wolf kind or because he has an ulterior motive." Matt said suspensefully.

"Ok Jace kills Lance and takes down Bruce, problem solved. Don't see the point of your long drawn out story." Logan said, looking at Lilly.

"Bruce and Lance are High Alpha's ... .Alpha's have packs...packs have armies ... .tada." Matt smiled.

"So you're asking for backup." Logan said, rubbing his forehead.

"Ding ding ding! We have a winner, the handsome man behind the desk." Matt grinned.

"Let me get back to you. Right now they are not a threat to the human world. I have a lot going on here trying to build and train new recruits. I want to help but I need to think about it." Logan said, glancing at Lilly really quickly.

"Take your time and let us know." Matt said getting up.

"Lilly as always it's amazing seeing you." Matt said, bowing his head to her.

Lilly didn't say anything part of her wanted him to ask her out again. Deep down in her heart she wanted to say yes so badly but she couldn't bring herself to. She watched Matt walk to the door, her eyes tracing the outline of his broad shoulders. He paused, turning around.

"Bruce and Lance might just be a wolf problem but if Bruce was Kip's backer. The mastermind of the whole thing, after he gets done with the wolf world, where do you think he's taking his army next?" Matt paused before he walked out the office door.

Chapter Eighteen
Schemes

*L*ance barreled through Bruce's bedroom door. His shirt torn in half down the center. He was breathing heavily and pacing. Bruce looked up from the book he was reading, eyeballing Lance waiting for him to explain his intrusion.

"That girl." Lance said, rubbing his nose as he walked.

"Girl?" Bruce said, taking off his glasses and setting them on the side table next to his brown chair.

"Nora. Jace's mate." Lance grumbled, turning to walk across the room again.

"Ok…" Bruce sighed wishing Lance would get on with it.

"She ripped my shirt." Lance stumbled out, grabbing the side of his ripped shirt and flapping it at Bruce.

"Ok, really Lance, if you're mad about a woman ripping your clothes off then you have a different problem. Nora is beautiful, I wouldn't mind if she ripped my shirt off." Bruce chuckled.

"No, it wasn't like that, she was angry. She found out what happened to Jace and she wanted to rip me apart. The power. It wasn't anything I felt before. She is powerful. She is incredible." Lance said quietly.

"Well she is an Alpha right now. Jace is pretty powerful and she is his Luna so she shares his power. With that combo I bet she is powerful." Bruce rationalized picking up his book.

"No..I think it's more than that." Lance said softly, stopping in his tracks and looking at Bruce.

"Lance, I think you're elevating it all because you want her." Bruce said, looking down into his book.

"You're right, I do want her. Even more now. Jace doesn't deserve her. You're going to help me get her." Lance said locking eyes with him.

"Oh really." Bruce said looking up from his book his eyes glowing purple.

"Yes." Lance said, matching his stare.

"Why do you think I will meddle in this?" Bruce said his tone was threatening.

"If you don't…me and mine won't back your newest hobby any longer. You'll be on your own army wise and power." Lance sneered.

"What will you have me do Lance? She is already mated. She isn't going to just come to you. She is bound to him and loves him." Bruce sighed.

"It's simple. The only reason why she can't be mine. Is because of him. So we get rid of him." Lance smirked.

"Jace, you want us to kill Jace?" Bruce groaned.

"Yes." Lance smiled.

"You know he has backing, all other packs respect him. If we just go kill someone because you want their mate, we are going to lose respect. His beta will step up and we will have a war. The others will join him because of it." Bruce explained why it wouldn't work.

"No, what we do is make it seem like he did something….something unforgivable. Then we kill him. The other packs will be happy we took care of something so horrible and the girl will be mine." Lance smiled.

"It will have to be something good we frame him for. Bring Douglas and let him know our plans. Get his insight. Leave the girl alone till after all this is settled. We don't need anyone linking you to this and putting two and two together, about the girl." Bruce said, slightly annoyed but intrigued.

"Lance…you personally know what happens when your mate is killed. You sure you want to deal with that brokenness just because of your want for her?" Bruce asked, raising an eyebrow.

"She's strong. She's not going to break." Lance said to him so sure of it.

"If she's as strong as you said then you might be signing your death wish." Bruce smirked.

"I can handle her." Lance said to him.

"Clearly." Bruce said motioning to his shirt.

"As long as you help me with this I will do it like you say. Don't worry about the details that follow after.." Lance grumbled.

"Go on. You're interrupting me. Go talk to Douglas and come up with a plan." Bruce said, waving him off.

Lance rolled his eyes at the hand movement but he had got what he wanted. Soon Nora would be his. He stormed out of Bruce's bed room still mad. He was going to find Douglas and let him know that they needed to come up with a plan to take down Jace. He left Bruce's room in search of Douglas; ripped shirt and all.

"We need to stop this female Alpha. We need someone else in charge." Roger grumbled to the three other men sitting at the table.

"And exactly who do you think that should be?" Chad said.

Chad was a tall slender build of a man but his arms were riddled with muscles, he had deep brown eyes and sandy brown hair. He looked around at the others, Clay was built like a bear and had dark almost black hair that matched his eyes. Lastly Kendrick was the quiet one in the group, he had auburn hair and light green eyes.

"Obviously me, stupid." Roger growled.

"And what if we don't want it to be you?" Chad challenged.

"Which one of you three think you can run this pack better than I?' Roger growled, closing his fist around the steel cup in his hand, the metal bending beneath it.

"Clay! Clay should do it." Chad said, stirring the pot some more.

"Clay! Clay, you want to do this?" Roger growled.

"I didn't think about it. Having some power would be nice." Clay nodded.

"What, you don't want it? That's fine. Kendrick should, he seems the most sensible out of you two." Chad said his eyes flickering between them, he grinned watching the mayhem he was causing.

"No..No. I'm good." Kendrick said shaking his head, he didn't want part of this argument.

"Fine if Clay and Kendrick dont want to do it...I guess I will." Chad said locking eyes with Roger.

Roger growled standing up from the other side of the table. Chad chuckled seeing the rise he was getting out of him. He stood up to match his gaze and stance. Locking eyes with him, Roger began to growl more. They were still in the hall celebrating the new titles. They quickly drew Asher's attention.

"Problems?" Asher's voice chimed in their heads.

Roger locked eyes with Asher from across the way, the red glow coming through as his wolf pushed forward. He wanted to fight, and wanted to challenge him. He was not meant to be Beta; he and his female Alpha were weak and worthless. Chad glanced over his shoulder and smiled politely to Asher while clapping Roger on the shoulder.

"Chill out or we won't be able to make this happen." Chad mind linked Roger.

"No problems at all, just some friendly banter that got a little heated. We apologize." Chad mind linked Asher back.

"If you can't keep it under control, leave." Asher ordered.

"Yes Beta." Chad smiled at him.

The men looked at each other like school boys who just got in trouble. They all had silly grins. Chad settled himself back into his seat and glanced at Roger.

"If you want to be Alpha and leader. What do you propose the next move is?" Chad asked to take a drink of wine.

"We need to make an example. Kip had it right; fear is power." Roger said quietly.

"What kind of example did you have in mind?" Chad asked, letting out a long sigh.

"The ultimate one." Roger grinned.

"We scare one of those girls she placed in power." Roger mind linked the three men.

"Scare?" Kendrick mind linked back.

"Yes, scare them. Rough them around a little bit, make them fear for their lives." Roger mind linked them with a grin forming on his face as he did.

"A Little bit?" Clay said, his eyes flickering to Lyla.

"Yeah just a little bit, enough to scare them."
Roger said.

"How will they know it's not us?" Kendrick
asked.

"Disguise and we will do it when it's dark."
Roger replied.

"How far are you willing to take this?" Chad
asked, skeptical.

"As far as it needs to go. We instill fear, recruit
more of us and then overthrow. It's simple." Roger
said with a shrug.

"When are you planning?" Chad asked him
curiously.

"Why not tonight everyone is so happy and
carefree. It would be the perfect time. We will leave
pretending we're bored or angry with one another.
Then wait for one of those girls to head out. Then we
jump her." Roger explained his plan.

"Fine. We will see how this plays out for you. If
it doesn't then it's my turn." Chad said, agreeing.

"Fine… Ready?" Roger smirked.

"Ready for-

Roger stood up and threw the whole glass of
wine in Chad's face. Chad instantly reached for
Roger, he was going to murder him. Kendrick grabbed
a hold of Chad, while Clay grabbed Roger.

"Enough! Leave" Asher's voice bellowed
throughout the hall.

The men dropped their heads hearing the
command. Chad locked eyes with Roger like he
wanted to rip him apart. Roger blew him a kiss as he
started to leave.

"Step one in place." Roger mind linked him,
and he left the hall.

Chad let out a low growl as he grabbed napkins off the table and cleaned off his face. He threw them down grumbling as he and Kendrick left the hall.

Chapter Nineteen
Shiver

"Asher, how is everything going?" Nora mind linked him, sitting on the edge of her and Jace's bed.

"Everything is going good Alpha, What happened is everything ok?" Asher responded relieved to hear from her.

"Jace was injured by the Alpha council, it's what I was feeling. Everything is ok now, for the most part." Nora responded.

"Injured?" Asher asked curiously.

"Apparently if you insult them, there is some medieval tradition of whipping people." Nora said growling through mind link. Zara stirred in her becoming angry thinking about her mate being injured.

Jace heard her growling, He came over to the bed and sat behind her straddled her sides with his legs and pulled her back against his chest. She immediately felt better and nuzzled into his chest.

"Mmm, they can be a bit extreme. Jace ok?" Asher asked.

"Extreme is right. My wolf wanted to destroy them, it was hard to hold her back. Jace is fine now. You wouldn't even know it happened. He was back trying to piss them off seconds after he was healed." Nora smirked, mind linking him back.

"It's hard to control emotions when you're newly finding your wolf. It's understandable. I am glad he is ok. We will reconnect tomorrow Alpha. All is well here." Asher sent back.

"Thank you for everything. I couldn't be doing this without you." Nora responds to him.

"We couldn't be making the pack better without you. Night Alpha." Asher sent back.

Nora smiled softly, she really enjoyed working with him. He was going to be the perfect Alpha once she handed it over to him.

'What's the smile for?" Jace asked curiously, pressing his nose into her neck.

"Asher." Nora said, shivering against him as his warm breath teased her skin.

"Asher!" Jace growled, playfully nipping her shoulder.

"Not like that, silly. He is just going to be a great Alpha. I am happy for the pack. That's all... Jealous much." Nora chuckled.

"You should talk. I can't wait to see what you do when a female ogles me. The way Zara is, I'm sure I am going to have to restrain you." Jace smirked.

"First of all no one has ogled me besides Lance and secondly I will be fine." Nora sighed.

"Asher, if he wasn't so respectful Cole may have ripped out his throat." Jace said quietly.

"You leave Asher alone." Nora said, patting him.

Jace quickly spun her in his lap, his eyes glowing as Cole pushed forward. A growl lingering in his throat as she defended Asher. Nora laughed seeing his response. She gave him a look saying she was serious.

"Do you like Asher?" Jace said, the growl coming forward possessively.

"Yes, Why wouldn't I? He is a good guy." Nora chuckled knowing that's not what he was meaning.

Nora pulled away from him quickly and stood up with her hands on her hips. Jace inched forward, eyes glowing more.

"You like him?" Jace grumbled.

"Yes! I also like Dante and Matt and-

She was cut off by her own screech as Jace lunged at her. She jumped back giggling as he landed on the ground. She covered her mouth laughing at him until she saw he was getting up. He growled playfully at her before attempting to grab her ankle. She scooted away from him, still giggling. She hopped over him and rushed to the other side of the room. He was up on his feet in no time. He went to grab her again and she hopped up onto the bed. A smirk on her lips as he kept missing her. She backed away from him, standing near the pillows.

He stood up tall, a dangerous look in his eyes that said what he wanted. Nora always seemed to forget how he looked, like he could snap a grown man in two. Her eyes wandered over his broad shoulders and sculpted chest. His arms were muscles on steroids. Her heart raced in her chest as he looked at her with that look. Like he had cornered his prey. A smirk rolled across his lips as he watched her bite her lip, he could see her eyes studying him. She was debating on running. The predator in him wanted her to run. She found herself wanting to be chased but she was cornered. She looked behind him, seeing the door. She wanted to win, wanted to beat him to the door, but just to beat him a little bit. She in the end wanted to be caught. She tried summoning her powers but her body didn't recognize him as a threat so her powers were no use.

"We're fast. We can take him." Zara said excitedly in her mind.

Nora couldn't help but grin. Jace watched her waiting and the grin intrigued him. He wanted her to try to make a move. If she didn't soon he couldn't wait anymore. Nora was searching for a weak spot.

"He's impatient look at him. Wait till he moves and then we will get past him." Zara said intensely.

Nora locked eyes with him waiting. It was a stand off and it was killing her.

"Do something sexy, make him want to come here." Zara snickered.

Nora's eyes lit up at Zara's thought. She looked at Jace. She couldn't hide that she wanted him and it reflected in her eyes. She bit her lip and carefully pulled her shirt down off her shoulder. She watched his expression grow darker as lust and want flashed across his face. He moved closer to the bed as if ready to pounce. His hand gripped around the bed post as he stared at her. Nora pulled her arm slowly out of her shirt and up over her head. Her hair fell flawless down around her as she stood there in her bra. A coy smile on her lips as she chucked her shirt towards him. The shirt hit his chest and bounced back onto the bed.

That was all he could take. He crawled up on the bed after her. His plan was to pin her to the bed and her hands to the head board but as he got closer and reached for her, she moved. He landed flat on the bed. The thought of her running out the door in her bra drove him crazy. He heard her laugh as she dashed off the bed heading to the door. Cole panicked inside of him. Nora raced to the door with a huge smile on her face as she reached out for the door handle. She wanted to pull back and claim her winnings. The door wouldn't budge. That's when she felt him. Her heart spazzed in her chest as she watched his huge forearm stopping the door from opening. She felt his warm breath on the back of her neck and her whole body tingled.

He stepped into her pinning her to the door, his hand tangled into her hair pulling her head back gently but firm. His mouth went to her neck as he began to kiss on it. His mouth moved over her mark and the surge of intense feeling caused her to lean back into him. His mouth moved to her ear lobe as he playfully grazed it with his teeth.

"You shouldn't run from me, little hunter. I will always catch you." He whispered into her ear.

Her whole body vibrated and shudder begging to be touched by him. He let go of her hair and spun her toward him. Her hand caught herself on his chest. She ran her fingers down it. She watched him lean into her touch. Her hand traveled down over his abs slowly and teasingly. Then they began to trace his waistline. She wanted to play the game too. She placed small kisses along his chest and up to his collarbone. She watched him fight back shivers, As her fingers ever so slightly teased his pants line. She kissed his shoulder and then leaned up to his ear.

"You, catch me because I let you." She whispered a smirk on her lips.

Jace growled, it gave her chills he stepped into her more pinning her up against the door. His forehead rested against hers as his breathing increased.

"Run." Jace said daring her.

He stepped back just enough where she could sneak past him but close enough where he was still giving her chills. She nervously played with her bottom lip. It drove him insane, he wanted her mouth. If she didn't stop he was going to make up her mind for her. Her body screamed for her to run but to stay. She glanced to the bed and ducked out from under him racing for it. She could feel him behind her and as she reached the bed she turned to face him. She needed him.

His arms reached around her, grabbing ahold of her bottom and picking her up. She landed on the bed with Jace on top of her. He pinned her arms over her head with one of his hands; while the other hand he let one of his claws extend and he looped it in the middle divider of her bra. He pulled quickly up on the fabric, cutting the fabric into two freeing her breasts. His mouth immediately captured her breast. He sucked her nipple into his mouth. His teeth pulled on it as he bit down, sending a rush of chills through her. His tongue rubbed against her nipple as his teeth held it in place. Nora let out a small moan as she arched into him. Every flick of his tongue or pull of his teeth was sending her over the edge. She was already so ready for him. He began moving south and her body twitched at every touch of his mouth.

He grabbed a hold of either side of her pants and pulled. The bottom popped off and with one swift motion he had her pants off and on the ground. He kissed her skin right above her panties, her body quivering with anticipation. He grabbed her panties with his mouth, his canines descending. With a small movement of his mouth and the help of his hands, her panties were torn in half exposing her. He ran a finger down her center and watched her twitch with need. He entered her slit with his finger, her legs falling to the side to allow him access, as a wanting moan escaped her mouth. He found her bundle and began to tease it. Her hips arched into his hand craving more. He buried his face in her and began to tease her with his mouth. She arched against him, her legs shaking slightly, and her fingers entwined into his hair. Her head pushed back into the pillow as her body began to lose control and her mind gave into it.

She ached for him and wanted him. The throbbing at her center was begging to be eased. She didn't even realize he had gotten his pants off until she felt him press against her entrance. Her body immediately screamed yes as her ache was being answered. She arched into him craving and wanting more as he began to move faster. She matched his pace, her body throbbing and begging for release. He felt her tighten around him as he moved and it sent him over the edge. Nora clung to him as her release came. She tightened around him inside of her as he moved, causing him to release right after. Their bodies exploding with intensity.

Chapter Twenty One
Goodnight

Asher cleared his throat as the evening was getting late. After Roger and his friends left it was actually a celebration. The tension left and people relaxed but now it was late. He could fall asleep up there on the stage. He let out a loud yawn by accident. Jordan had already headed home; he had little ones and needed to get them to bed. Chance had checked out after a few drinks with his mate. Jaime had been waiting on Lyla but she gave up realizing Lyla was staying till the end.

Asher locked eyes with Lyla. He felt bad for her, for all the pain that she had to endure under Kip but was excited for her to start leading. It was like she was a phoenix rising from the ashes. He wanted to help her in any way. She felt his eyes on her, her forest green eyes locked with his. She raised a brow at him subconsciously pulling her curly blond hair over her shoulder. He shook his head letting her know it was nothing.

"I'm tired." Asher mind linked her.

He watched a soft smile across her lips as she nodded to him agreeing.

"I want everyone to go home." Asher chuckled as he sent the mind link to her.

"So you're beta and in charge tell them it's closing time." Lyla grinned answering him.

"Hmm you're right." Asher said as if it was something he hadn't thought about.

She chuckled hearing his tone. She shook her head slightly and then tapped her finger to her head as if telling him to use it. She stood by waiting for him to make the announcement to tell everyone or go home.

Asher cleared his throat loudly and the remaining pack members in the hall became quiet. All their eyes went to the stage as they waited for Asher to speak.

"Thank you all so much for celebrating today with us. Our pack is going to keep moving and growing in the right direction. You may continue the celebration elsewhere or in your homes but we are going to close the hall down for this evening. Thank you all again." Asher said, finishing the speech as he stood.

Lyla gave him a thumbs up from the crowd which made him chuckle.

"Walk you home?" He asked Lyla through a mind link.

He watched her debate with herself. She then decided that with everything going on it might be good to have someone walk her home. Her thoughts wandered to Roger and his friends. She nodded to him.

"Ok wait for me." Asher sent to her with a smile, a small feeling tugged at his heart that he hadn't realized before.

She smiled softly and began helping clean up as Asher finished up what he needed to do. Asher quickly thanked people for coming as he made his way about. His eyes flickered every so often to Lyla who looked flawless moving around picking up random things while keeping busy. He watched a woman come up to her and bowed her head. Lyla was taken back by it, not used to being in a position of power. The woman reached out and touched her hand. Asher tuned into the conversation the woman was grateful a female was in power and knew Lyla would help continue to guide the pack in the right direction. Lyla smiled and squeezed her hand back. The woman's husband came up behind her nodding his head to Lyla, agreeing with what his wife had said.

Asher smiled, it could work. They really could fix this pack. Hope stirred in him, as he watched a few more pack members thank Lyla. She was uncomfortable by it but her smile said that she was happy to be accepted. Asher made his way to her, she felt his presence and her smile grew.

"Beta." Lyla smiled, addressing him.

"Ready?" Asher asked, motioning to the door.

"Yes." Layla smiled, heading to the door with him to leave.

They walked in silence down the street. It was dark. There was no moon to light the way. The dull glow of the street lights only lit up small sections. Lyla didn't mind, they already had sharper vision from being wolves. Asher glanced at her wanting to talk but had nothing to say.

"Alpha ok?" Lyla finally asked, breaking the silence.

"Yes, her mate actually was in pain. She had to go take care of him." Asher explained roughly.

"Ahh, I hope everything is alright." Lyla said, looking at the sky as she walked.

"It should be, the Cross River pack has their own nuances going on but it's nothing Jace can't handle." Asher said, reassuring her.

"I guess that's the benefit of not having a mate. You don't need to worry about anything but yourself." Lyla said.

"I guess but it comes with other benefits." Asher chuckled.

"I'm good if mine never shows up." Lyla said quietly.

"That's funny, most wolves can't wait to find their mate, the other half of their soul." Asher said softly.

"I dont have the best of luck at things so he can stay away. With my luck, my mate will be someone like Kip." Lyla laughed.

"I don't see that happening for you." Asher smiled and shook his head.

"What about you? Have you found your mate?" Lyla asked him curiously.

"No. I didn't look for her, if she didn't cross my path by chance, I wasn't going to sort her out." Asher said.

"How come?" Lyla asked curiously, she then tapped him motioning for the alley.

"Because I wasn't going to bring her into this pack. Alley? Really?" Asher laughed.

"I understand…It's a short cut and this isn't some crime show. I am also not some damsel. I'm a wolf." Lyla laughed, stepping into the alley.

"Fine but if something happens you have to save us both." Asher smirked.

They started down the alley, hearing their footsteps Roger shifted in the shadows. Why were there two sets of footsteps? He glanced across the way to Clay who also heard it. Clay peered out and was shocked to see Asher walking with Lyla. Their plans instantly got canceled.

"Asher's with her!" Clay mind linked Roger panicking.

"Fuck." Roger responded.

"We can't go through with it." Clay said, involving Chad and Kendrick.

"The Beta is walking with her. We need to not do this." Kendrick agreed.

"Damn it. Fine, we will do this on a different day. Stay in the shadows." Roger linked them angrily.

"Do you really think we can fix all this damage?" Lyla said walking past where Roger and his buddies were hiding.

"I do, every place has people who don't like change but once they see it for the better they will fall in line ... .or I'll make them." Asher smirked.

Roger's anger flared even more at the comment, he was holding back a vicious growl as they passed. Kendrick sank further back into the shadows praying he wouldn't be seen. He bumped the dumpster he was near. Asher eyes flickered to it. His eyes searched for the cause of the noise. Lyla paused as she scanned the alley not seeing anything. She placed her hand up Asher's upper arm.

"It was probably an animal, cat, or rat; something trying to get food. Come on, we are almost out." Lyla laughed.

Something was telling Asher it was something more than that but he followed Lyla anyways. She smiled at him like he was being silly. His wolf inside of him was on alert though. He had felt it too. Asher walked Lyla the rest of the way out of the alley.

"Hey for the time being don't go that way anymore." Asher said, warning her.

"Really?" Lyla said about laughing but saw the look of concern.

"Yeah, I know you think it's silly but something had me on alert. Just be careful." Asher told her firmly.

"Oh ok. Thank you." Lyla said as they reached the girls' pack house.

Some of the females had grown comfortable living together so the ones that wanted to stay, stayed and turned it into their home. The others happily rejoined their family. She paused at the door feeling like she was supposed to say something else to Asher.

"Ok well get your butt inside so I can end this bad cop investigator show." Asher laughed.

Lyla smiled and bowed her head to him. "Good night Beta." She almost whispered.

She turned to start going up the stairs but Asher's hand caught her hand. She paused looking back at him a little confused. A look past over Asher's face, Lyla wasn't sure what he intended. She watched him double think what he was doing, whatever it was he decided against.

"Seriously, be careful. Just until everything is more settled." Asher said letting go of her hand slowly.

"I will." Lyla smiled with a nod and started up the stairs into the pack house.

Asher let out a sigh did he really think about kissing her. What was he thinking? He rubbed the back of his neck as he paused at the bottom of the stairs. Lyla reached for the door handle and she got a small feeling of sadness. Why was she upset he didn't kiss her, why did she think he was going to.

"Asher?" Lyla called to him, turning around her curls falling down around her face as she stopped at the door.

Screw it, he thought as he turned around walking back to her. He walked up the stairs quickly. If he stopped to think about it, he wasn't going to do it. His hand captured her face as he pulled her in for a kiss. Her heart pounding in her chest with nerves and excitement. She shut her eyes as her lips met his. Asher's other hand went to her lower back pulling her against him as he kissed her deeply. Asher pulled back slowly, ending the kiss. He wasn't sure what to expect from Lyla; she did kiss him back. He studied her face with a small smile on it.

"Good night."Asher said, stepping back from her.

"Mhmmm Good night." Lyla said with a small smile.

Chapter Twenty
Injured

*N*ora's phone vibrated, she rolled over tired trying to find the source of the noise, her hand searching under her pillow. Nothing was there, she then realized that it was coming from the night stand. It had been a long time since she had gotten a phone call. Now that she could mind link both packs there was almost no need for her phone. She grabbed a hold of it, trying to see. All her moving woke Jace and he grumbled next to her. His arm wrapped around her pulling her into him. She sighed happily feeling his warmth wrap around her. She saw Logan's name on the phone and almost sat up. She slid the phone to answer.

"Hello?" Nora said, almost worried she hadn't heard from him since they ended Kip.

"Hey Doll! Long time no chat." Logan's voice came through the phone.

"Yeah, I am so sorry, I've been so busy lately. I'm a bad friend! How are you?' Nora said her voice showing that she was actually sorry.

"It's ok and understandable being a Luna of one pack and Alpha of another must be overwhelming." Logan said, happy to hear her voice.

"Yeah but it doesn't excuse not checking on you." Nora said sadly.

"Shut up, anyway I need to come by and talk to your ass of a mate." Logan said in a playful voice.

Jace growled hearing the conversation in response. Nora chuckled lightly as it tickled her neck.

"Oh well tell him I said good morning beautiful." Logan laughed hearing the growl.

"Logan said good morning." Nora laughed.

"Doesn't he have wolves to hunt or some push ups to do." Jace grumbled.

"He said he needs to meet with you." Nora said, playing the middle person.

"We shouldn't meet here because of them. Why don't we meet at your pack?" Jace said, pressing his face into Nora's neck.

"Logan can you come to Red Woods pack today? Jace will be there and I'll also get to see you. You should drag Lilly with you and I'll bring Matt." Nora chuckled.

"Still trying to hook them up?" Logan laughed.

"Yup, once she realizes that Matt will be the best thing for her, she will thank me." Nora said as she tried to wiggle out of Jace's grasp.

"Ok see you around noon?" Logan asked.

"Noon sounds great." Nora said, swatting Jace's hand as it began to travel up her thigh.

"See you soon." Logan said, hanging up.

Nora pushed his hand away again and this time he pulled her into him and moved on top of her pinning her to the bed. Nora giggled as she tried to wiggle out from under him. Jace's grin grew at her struggle. He leaned forward kissing her forehead, then the tip of her nose, her cheek, the bottom of her jaw.

"Jace, we just made plans. I need to get back to Red Woods." She said, trying to ignore him.

He ignored her, as he began to kiss down her neck. Nora tucked her arms under his and wrapped them around his back. She then locked her legs around him, pinning him in the position he was in. His wicked smile spread across his lips, as he took this as a challenge. He went to move but Nora tensed up. Jace quickly realized that he was stuck. Nora chuckled as the realization spread across his face.

"So shower and go to Red Woods?" Nora smiled.

"Shower." Jace grinned and wrapped his arms around her, getting to his knees.

She laughed, hugging herself to him. He stood up at the end of the bed and carried her to the bathroom. Reaching the bathroom he set her gently down. Nora unwove herself from him and stepped back. She looked at him funny as mischief was written all over his face. She was just about to ask him what his expression was about, when he leaned forward and grabbed her shirt. He tugged and ripped in half down the middle.

"Hey!" She yelled, swatting him.

Jace laughed and scooped her over his shoulder heading towards the shower. She kicked lightly as he stepped into the shower.

"You're crazy! You still have boxers on, I still have my under-

Before she could finish her sentence she heard her underwear ripped and felt them fall down around her. She hit him lightly in his back. He laughed letting her feet hit the floor of the shower. He went to turn on the water. She looked at him a little annoyed but smirked. She eyed his boxers. As he turned to the shower, she quickly grabbed hold of the boxers with both hands and pulled hard. The boxers separated in her hands and she let out a loud laugh. She watched the boxers fall to the fall.

Jace choked back the laugh and turned around to face her, his eyes sparkling. Nora knew there was nothing but dirty thoughts going on in his mind.

"It's not sexy when you do it." He lied, smirking.

"It's fair! I have ripped underwear now you do too." She smirked, folding her arms across her chest.

Jace's smile grew as he watched her play tough. With one quick step to her, his arms captured her, wrapping around her. He hit the water knob on the shower and it turned on. He spun her into the water. She let out a yell as it hit her.

"Can you just behave for one minute? We have places to go." She growled at him.

"I can't help it. You're irresistible." He said, beginning to kiss her shoulder.

Nora smirked, she snuck her hand up carefully and grabbed a hold of the cold water knob. She quickly turned the knob on and turned in his arms. She then pulled him into the cold water.

"Oh shit!" He yelled as the ice water hit him.

Nora grinned as he quickly turned it back to warm water. He glared down at her and she shrugged.

"Problem solved….he doesn't seem to be interested anymore." She laughed, teasing him

"Oh give him a second." Jace said coming towards her.

"Jace I swear to god if you don't control yourself, I'm going to make you get out of this shower." Nora said firmly.

"Fine…Fine best behavior." Jace chuckled, reaching for the soap behind her.

Lyla yawned stretching in her bed, she slept great for the first time ever. The screen of Asher kissing her played over and over in her dream. She found a smile on her lips when she woke up.

"Breakfast?" Asher's voice whispered softly through Lyla's mind.

A silly smile spread across her face. Her stomach doing somersaults excitedly. It was like he felt her thinking about him.

"That sounds lovely, where?" Lyla responded.

"Men's old pack house, I'm cooking. Pancakes or Waffles?" Asher was sent back.

"Waffles." Lyla smiled.

"Waffles, coming up." Asher sent back.

"Waffles…with whipped cream and strawberries?" Lyla replied, a silly grin on her face.

"That sounds amazing….I love whipped cream." He sent back but the way he said whipped cream, made Lyla blush.

A dirty image of Asher spraying whipped cream across her personal parts and then submerging his face between her legs, mouth covered in white whipped cream, flashed in her mind. She blushed harder. She shook the thoughts away with a small smile. Lyla got dressed feeling overly happy. She couldn't wait to see Asher. She hurried down the stairs of the pack house and out the door as quickly as possible. She did one last whipped cream and face in the window of the door before walking out of it. She walked down the steps debating the quickest way. Alley, she thought even though Asher had warned her not to travel alone down it. The sun was just peeking out, sure it was dark but it was morning time and everything would be fine. She began walking towards the alley.

"On my way." Lyla sent him through mind link trying not to make her voice sound too excited.

"See you soon." Asher sent back, Lyla could hear the smile in his voice.

Lyla happily ducked into the alley, she wanted to be there as quickly as possible. Her stomach was fluttering around inside of her, a mixture of excitement and nervousness. She thought about him kissing her, her fingertips mindlessly touching her lips. She let out a small sigh, she wondered what he was thinking? Could he be her happy ending?

"Head in the clouds?" A voice came from the shadows to her right.

"What?" Lyla asked, confused . She went to turn to see where the voice came from but an intense sharp pain came to the back of her head.

She stumbled forward not understanding what was happening. The world rocked as she tried to get her balance. Something struck her across her face. She felt her eyes instantly swell. Someone hit her hard in the stomach. It all happened so fast she didn't even have a chance to fight back. The world around her went dark as the wind was knocked out of her.

"Asher..alley." She hoped the mind link went through before she passed out.

The mind link came through, Asher dropped the frying pan out of his hand. It hit the floor as he turned and ran for the door. He was panicking. He had such a bad feeling. His mind begging for her to be ok.

"Lyla…Lyla answer me back." Asher sent to her though mind link, running full speed.

When no answer came back, he ran harder and faster. Lyla, not responding to him. He knew she had to be hurt. His chest tightened as he pushed himself to get there.

---

*L*yla laid unconscious in the alley. The offender decided he wasn't done. Another swift kick to the ribs gave him satisfaction, although she was out cold he wanted to continue hitting her. He got grabbed by the arm.

"Let's go already before someone comes and finds her. More importantly, finds us." Chad said, grabbing Roger's arm.

"Delta my ass." Roger growled, kicking her again.

"Alright we've sent the message, let's go." Chad said, deciding to start leaving with or without Roger.

Roger watched Chad start leaving. He wished he could continue hitting Lyla. She was a poor excuse for a pack member never mind Delta; but Chad was right he needed to leave, He raced after Chad ducking out of the alley. No one was around, he smiled as he vanished.

---

*A*sher slammed into the side of the alley as he turned down it. In the middle of the alleyway he saw her. She was unconscious, her blond hair sprawled out around her. A wound from the top of her head was slowly dying, her golden hair red. He raced to her side. He had told her not to come down this way anymore. Kneeling in front of her, he panicked a little. Please be alive, he thought. He rolled her towards him. As he did he saw her chest rise and fall. Thank god, he thought as he looked her over. Her eyes were swollen and almost shut. He scooped her in his arms.

"Jordan. I need you. Bring supplies, men's pack house. I have a head wound and I'm not sure what else. Lyla was beaten and left in the alley." He mind linked Jordan as he began carrying her back to the pack house.

"I'm coming now, I have a medical bag ready to go. Is she conscious?" Jordan responded, Asher could hear the urgence in his voice.
"No." Asher replied back.
"I will be there soon." Was all Jordan said back.

Chapter Twenty One
Hurt

Asher kicked the pack house door open and rushed into the house. Lyla was groaning in his arms as she started to come to. He rushed into the kitchen. Spread across the kitchen island there was the breakfast he had prepared for them and just like she asked. Waffles with strawberries and whipped cream. Holding her against him he pushed the waffles off the island, and onto the floor. The plates shattered as they toppled to the ground. He sat her down on the large island in the middle of it. Asher rushed to see where the blood was coming from. It spilled onto the counter like the juices from the smashed strawberries on the kitchen floor. He had to roll her on her side. Holding her up with one hand he tried to piece through her hair to see. A large gash split her skull on the back of her head. She was hit over the back of the head with something. He set her back down. He needed water and something to apply pressure.

Fumbling around he found a tupperware large enough to fill with some warm water. He rushed about trying to gather what he could. He found two kitchen towels from the drawer as well. He hurried back to her. He dipped one of the towels lightly into the water and then rolled Lyla back on to her side. He began slowly and carefully cleaning the wound. The wounded continued to ooze and bleed. He took the other towel and held pressure to the back of her head. The white kitchen towel slowly turned red. He let out a breath trying to calm himself because he really didn't know what else to do.

"Asher!" Jordan's voice pierced the silence as he rushed through the front door.

"Kitchen!" Asher yelled back.

Jordan came rushing into the kitchen, pieces of the broken plates scattered further into the room as he hurried to the counter. A black duffle bag in hand. His feet kicking the broken plates across the floor. He ignored it and set his duffle back down next to Lyla as he began searching through it.

"I don't know what to do. She has a large gash on the back of her head. I tried cleaning it up the best I can and I'm holding pressure on it. It won't stop bleeding." Asher said to him.

"Head wounds bleed the most, don't panic." Jordan told him quietly.

He began laying stuff out on the counter. He kept pulling things out of his bag like he had a mini hospital in there. He had bandage supplies, items to suture and things Asher wasn't even sure what they did. He put gloves on quickly and then looked to Asher coming over to his side.

"Here let me see. Is she hurt anywhere else?" Jordan asked him.

"Her eyes look like they are swollen shut and I haven't checked the rest of her." Asher said, removing his hand from the back of her head and holding her steady on her side.

Jordan moved her hair out of the way and studied the wound. She looked like she had been hit with something metal. He wanted to say a pipe of some sort. The way the skin flayed outwards and looked like it had exploded. He wasn't sure how deep the wound went. He reached over grabbing a pair of hemostats and placed them gently inside the wound. Feeling around inside the wound he was relieved it didn't go into her skull. That her skull was still intact. Asher gave him a strange look.

"I'm trying to see how deep it goes." Jordan explained

Asher nodded and continued to hold Lyla on her side. Jordan nodded to a stack of gauze on the table. Asher reached over with one hand and passed them to him. Jordan took them and dabbed the wound lightly.

"So the bleeding isn't bad. She got a few little vessels that are going nuts, which is causing all the blood. I can suture them and the wound up pretty easily. She will be good from there." Jordan explained.

A feeling of relief washed over Asher as Jordan motioned for him to place a hand on the wound and hold the gauze to it. Jordan then began moving all the supplies he would need closer to him. Asher watched him begin placing sutures. Jordan sutured the inner part of the wound before moving on to the skin. The longer Asher looked the more and more angry he became. He was going to find who did this and hurt them. How did anyone think this was acceptable?

Lyla winced as the last two sutures were placed in. Jordan wiped the wound making sure the wound had stopped bleeding. He nodded to Asher letting him know he was finished. Asher laid her gently back down on her back on the countertop. Jordan looked at her eyes touching her around them. He felt a small break in her orbit. He frowned slightly, it would heal and luckily for her she was a wolf so it would heal quickly. He moved on to her ribs. He touched them lighty feeling the bones. There were no breaks. He lifted her shirt looking at them. They were riddled in bruises.

"She has a broken eye socket and her ribs are badly bruised." Jordan said to Asher as he looked for something in his bag.

"Everything should heal pretty quickly." Jordan said, grabbing some bandage material.

Jordan then stopped what he was doing and went to the fridge. He grabbed a frozen bag of peas from the freezer. As he made his way back towards the island, he grabbed the towel hanging off the stove. He wrapped the bag of peas lightly in the towel before walking back to Asher. He handed Asher the peas. Asher looked at him confused, he wasn't sure what Jordan wanted him to ice.

"Her eyes, lightly." Jordan said going back to his bandage material.

Asher lightly held the frozen bag of peas across Lyla's eyes. He did his best not to apply pressure but just hold it there.

"Wrapping her ribs will help with the pain. It would be easier if she was awake." Jordan frowned as he walked back over.

"Why would it be easier?" Asher looked up from focusing on holding the pea's in place.

"Cause then she could sit up." Jordan said with a small smile on his face as if Asher asked a silly question.

"It's ok I can hold her up." Asher said ignoring the look and going to pick her up.

"I'll need her shirt off." Jordan said quietly as he came over to the island.

Asher nodded he slowly rolled up her shirt just exposing the area Jordan would need. Jordan raised an eyebrow at him, but ignored Jordan's look. Jordan shrugged and Asher held her up in a sitting position. He began wrapping her ribs. Several passes later and two different materials, her ribs were wrapped up. Jordan went to his bag putting things away. Asher unrolled her shirt. He laid her carefully back down on the counter top. As she touched the counter top of the island, her eyes began to flutter open. She could barely open them from how swollen they were. She let out a long groan as she tried to sit up.

"Lyla it's ok I got you, lay down." Asher said to her, placing a hand on her shoulder to keep her laying down.

"Asher?" Lyla said his name hearing his voice.

She was so confused she wasn't sure what happened. She slowly raised her hand to her head and felt a wet substance. She suddenly remembered something hitting her. Everything hurt she curled into herself trying to find comfort. She whimpered softly.

"Hey, you're going to be ok. You got banged up pretty bad. Jordan's fixed you up." Asher said, trying to figure out how to comfort her.

"Have her take these for pain." Jordan said, handing him two little oblong pills.

"Water." He said to Jordan nodding towards the fridge.

Jordan opened it, looking into the fridge. He saw the small water bottle and he grabbed it. He cracked the top open and handed it to Asher.

"Lyla taking these will help." He said handing her the pills.

"What is it?" Lyla asked, confused.

"It's for pain." Jordan said from behind Asher.

Lyla took the pills and placed them into her mouth. With shaking hands, Lyla took the bottle of water from Asher and drank some. She sat up looking at him, the best she could through her swollen eyes.

"What happened?" Lyla asked him quietly.

"I'm not sure. Do you   remember anything? Saw who attacked you?" Asher asked her, trying not to sound too alarmed.

"No, I was walking and they hit me from behind. Whatever they hit me with knocked me out." Lyla said quietly.

"It's ok, we will find out who did it." Asher said a growl in the back of his throat.

"We already have suspects." Jordan said his tone also turned angry.

He had been calm the whole time he needed to treat Lyla but now that she was ok. He could feel his blood boiling. He would be livid if this was his wife or daughter. Asher glanced over to Jordan, his emotions reflecting his as well. He was starting to shake thinking about what happened.

Chapter Twenty Two
Responsible

*N*ora and Jace walked into the pack house. Something was happening and she could smell the blood. Jace tensed up on the side of her not sure what was happening. He was getting himself prepared for a fight if needed. Nora began to follow the smell of blood. Jace caught her hand, telling her to wait. She let him go first as they walked towards the kitchen. Nora could feel everything in her body ready to fight. She felt the energy growing in the pit of her stomach. She could recognize the feeling now and was becoming more and more capable of using her power. She followed behind Jace ready to use it if necessary.

Walking into the kitchen, her heart dropped. Lyla was sitting on the counter with a bag of frozen peas to her face. Her golden blond hair was stained red with blood. Jordan was packing up and Asher looked up, his eyes filled with anger, saying he could murder someone. Nora moved out from behind Jace and rushed over to Lyla.

"Oh my god! What happened? Are you ok?" Nora asked, getting to Lyla's side.

"I was -

"She was attacked but you would know that if you were here, like an Alpha should be." Asher growled, the amount of anger coming off of him was intense.

Jace growled and bowed up, stepping in front of Nora. Jace's eyes glowed fiercely, feeling like his mate was being attacked. Asher growled and stepped towards him. Jordan backed away not wanting to be in the middle of his Alpha and Beta's fight. Lyla lowered her head and started to feel sick. She reached out to tell Asher to stop but he pulled his hand away from her giving her a look saying that this needed to be said.

"How dare you talk to her like that!" Jace yelled in Asher's face.

"Because it's true she should have been here!" Asher yelled back, spit flying out of his mouth and hitting Jace on the cheek.

As the spit droplet hit Jace's cheek. Jace wiped his cheek off, his eyes narrowing as Nora saw every muscle in his chest and arms tense. Asher bowed up again. Nora winced, this was about to go to blows. She took a deep breath and shoved herself in the middle of them. As she did her body yelled danger and zapped both Asher and Jace. The jolt sent them both backwards two steps, leaving them rubbing the spots on their chest and arms that touched Nora. Nora's eyes were glowing as she looked at both them.

"That is enough." Nora growled.

Jace growled, his eyes still locked in on Asher. Nora sent her aura out as she growled again. It gained Jace's attention, Asher flinched trying to fight against her aura due to how upset and mad he was.

"If you were here the pack wouldn't think it is acceptable to attempt anything like this!" Asher growled.

Jace let out a low growl and hit the counter top. A large crack went down the center of it. Asher reacted and went at Jace. Nora shut her eyes and placed her hands outward. They both crashed into her and she let out a strong enough burst of energy. Jace and Asher landed on their butts on the floor. They both looked shocked as they looked up at her.

"I said that is enough!" Nora yelled

She looked down at both of them, daring them to challenge her. Her eyes glowing the brightest shade of amber. She could feel her skin vibrating with energy as she waited to see if she needed to jolt them again.

"Asher, you need to stand down now." Nora yelled locking eyes with him, she sent her aura out over him until he bowed his head.

Nora looked to Jace who seemed to have a smirk on his face thinking Nora was siding with him and he had won. Nora narrowed her eyes at him as she locked her jaw annoyed.

"You need to stop! Asher is right, I should have been here! If it was your pack and your members you would be beating yourself up and not forgive yourself." Nora said, still standing between them with her arms stretched outwards.

Jace made a small face knowing that what she said was right. He still wanted to rip him limb from limb for disrespecting and talking to her like that.

"Woah looks like we showed up to the party late." Matt said walking into the kitchen with Lilly and Logan.

Logan watched Nora standing between Jace and Asher. He immediately rushed around the island and stood next to her. He didn't know if she was fighting both of them but all he knew was whatever side Nora was on he was backing her up. Jace growled seeing Logan standing between him and Nora. He got to his feet angry. The growl made Asher angry again and he stood up.

"What are you doing!?" Jace growled at Logan.

"I don't know what you're thinking or doing Jace but I am not letting you hurt Nora." Logan said.

Lilly went to back her brother up and Matt's hand captured her waist. He pulled her back against him. She hit his chest, her stomach doing a summersault that she tried to ignore.

"Listen gorgeous, it's fine. From what I gather Nora got in between something. Jace wouldn't dare touch her." Matt explained to her.

"Let go of me." Lilly said not to put up a fight.

"Only if you ask nicely" Matt chuckled.

Lilly sighed, not wanting to add more drama to what was already going on. Her body just reacted and leaned into his. She couldn't deny how good it felt.

"Logan get out from between me and my mate." Jace growled.

"For fuck sake!" Nora yelled.

"Logan, I appreciate you coming to my rescue, I missed you! But Jace isn't being an ass to me. He's being an ass to Asher. Now all this nonsense is going to stop now or I am going to lose it." Nora yelled.

Logan laughed turning to face Nora he wrapped his arms around her and squeezed Nora lightly. Jace grumbled seeing him touch her but Logan stepped away. Which made Cole back down.

"Missed you too." Logan said, leaning back against the counter.

Logan glanced over to Lyla who seemed to now be hiding her face. She scooted off the counter. Asher helped steady her.

"What happened?" Logan asked concerned.

Lyla backed away from him. She was feeling funny. Her wolf inside was acting drunk. She liked the way the man called Logan smelt and kept wanting Lyla to go to him. She felt her heart racing in her chest but between the pain medicine and being out of it she didn't know what to think about the sudden rush of emotions.

"Lyla what's going on?" Nora asked her, looking at her worried.

"I don't know." Lyla said feeling overwhelmed.

"Lyla, why don't you go get some rest…Asher, can she stay in your room while we get everything figured out?' Nora asked him.

"I think that would be good." Asher said to Lyla.

"Are you sure?" Lyla asked him again, trying her best to shove down the urge to reach out and touch Logan.

Logan was studying her. She was acting so funny. Maybe the head injury has got her confused, he thought.

"Yes. We need to make sure you're safe. It would make me feel a whole lot better if you were here anyways.' Asher said, reassuring her.

"If you say so." Lyla said but wobbled.

Asher didn't even ask and scooped her up into his arms. He looked over his shoulder at Nora before leaving the room.

"I'm going to get her settled and then I will be back down to talk." Asher said, trying his hardest not to sound aggressive.

"That sounds good." Nora said calmly.

Asher exited the room carrying Lyla close to him. She sighed happily in his arms. She could get used to being in his arms, she thought. Her wolf however whimpered.Why was she sad? Lyla thought as Asher carried her upstairs.

"What the hell is his problem?" Logan asked, his face scrunched like he tasted something gross.

"He's an as-

"He's upset. The pack here before was very against women's rights basically. They were not allowed to do anything and were looked down upon. When I became Alpha I made changes quickly. Now there is a group of men trying to send a message. I named Lyla Delta last night." Nora started to explain cutting Jace off.

"So why is he angry with you when you're doing all the good things?"Logan asked with a shrug.

"Because I haven't been staying with the pack. We've had some issues at Cross River as well and I left last night because Jace was injured. The attack happened last night. Asher feels like if I was present more here at Red Woods and not bouncing back and forth between the two packs, there wouldn't have been an attack. ...He's probably right." Nora sighed, guilt overwhelmed her.

"Nora, that attack would have happened with you or without you. That was a send a message attack. Those people don't care who is here. They are on a mission." Logan said firmly.

"Hunter boy's right." Jace said.

"Asher is also right. I need to be here." Nora sighed.

"So what's the move Luna?" Matt asked as he rested his chin on the top of Lilly's head, his eyes flashed as his wolf pushed forward.

"We find out who did it but right now we wait for Asher." Nora sighed, she already knew who did it.

Chapter Twenty Three
Planning

"What are you going to do?" Jace asked, annoyed.

"Might make people think twice before doing anything like this." Nora said, trying not to argue with Jace.

He gritted his teeth, he was trying to be understanding but he had a lot going on. The idea of Nora being away from him more than she already was made Cole upset. Nora felt his emotions and frowned slightly.

"Jace it's just until we get this mess sorted out and have people that need to fall in line…fall in line." Nora said, trying to explain to him.

Jace clenched his jaw, he couldn't argue. He understood the pressure and responsibility of being Alpha. He had been doing it for so long now. He forgot what it was like starting up. He glanced at Matt who shot him a sympathetic look. He got it, Matt was away from Lilly often because she wasn't a wolf and didn't understand the mate bond. She was slowly starting to feel it. She would never feel it like another wolf would but their bond could be strong, if she would stop fighting it.

"What do you need us to do boss lady?' Matt asked, as he leaned down and rested his head on Lilly's shoulder.

Jace looked at him, looking upset because he called Nora boss lady and not Luna. He growled slightly. Nora tapped him, knowing exactly what he was being testy over.

"Luna…bossy lady, same thing." Nora groaned.

"What do you need from us Nora?" Logan asked, ready to assist however he could.

"I need to find out who did this. Part of me wants to alert every woman in the pack to not go anywhere alone but at the same time I don't want to give the assholes doing this anymore power." Nora grumbled.

"Warn the woman but not the pack." Asher's voice said coming into the kitchen.

"How's Lyla?" She asked with a frown.

"Resting." Asher answered shortly.

"I will alert the women only and then we need to brainstorm." Nora said quietly.

Her eyes glossed over in the next breath as she put a message out to all women in the pack.

"Hello all this message is for only the woman in the pack. There's been an attack, it was meant to send a message to the women . Do not go out alone and travel in numbers. We are strong, we are powerful, and we will not let low life cowards threaten, place fear in, or hurt us. The woman attacked is doing well and will heal. Do not let any men know that this message has been sent. These cowards will not have an ounce of our concern. I promise you I will find these attackers and bring them to justice swiftly. We are the glue that keeps this pack together and strength. We will show them that. If you have any threats sent to you or concern, come to the men's pack house and see Beta Asher or myself. We will get through this and come out stronger than ever."

Her eyes resumed and brought focus back into the room. She sighed deeply, rubbing her head. She needed to fix this quickly.

"So the first obvious suspect. Roger and his friends. Just because they hate women in power doesn't mean we can go out and arrest them. We can certainly bring them in for questioning. The only problem I have is if they somehow managed to lie during their oath to me. How am I supposed to know if they are lying or not?" Nora frowned.

"You'll know." Jace said from her side.

"He's right. There will be something that will tell you." Logan followed up behind Jace's comment.

"Ok so I guess let's go round them up. Logan, are you ok waiting to discuss the second part of problems until after this?" Nora asked him.

"Yeah and I will gladly come to help you." Logan said with a reassuring nod.

"Second set of problems?" Asher asked her

"It's Cross River business but may concern Red Woods soon. I will fill you in at the same time I do Logan. That way I can tell everyone the same story once." Nora said a little bitterness coming out in her voice, as she was still hurt that he blamed her for Lyla.

"And the hunter needs to know?" Asher asked with a weird look.

"He's my friend." Nora said shortly to him.

She then without any more words turned on her heels and began walking to the doors. All those that were coming better follow her because she was not waiting.

"Nora?" Lilly's voice chimed up as Nora got close to her.

"Yeah Lilly?" Nora asked with a small smile.

"I have an idea for your problem." Lilly smiled at her, a hint of mischief in them.

"What is it?" Nora asked, she couldn't help but smile as she did because of the look Lilly had on her face.

"I actually have two ideas. One is pretty simple: you just go out at night alone, when they go to attack you, we are there to catch them, and kick some ass. Or you appoint me whatever title Lyla has until she gets better." Lilly smirked.

"Make you a Delta? " Asher said, confused.

"That's what I said, pretty boy." Lilly said to him, annoyed.

"You're not a wolf or in this pack. Could you even hold your own if a wolf attacked you?" Asher asked, making a face.

A low deadly growl came from behind Lilly. Lilly's back vibrated as Matt was becoming angry with Asher. Asher locked eyes with Matt, a small amount of surprise in Asher's eyes as he didn't think goofy Matt to sound so lethal .

Asher was taken back at the intensity of Matt's growl. The way he could switch from being fun and goofy, to calm and deadly was unnerving.

"Calm down guard dog." Lilly chuckled tapping Matt's forearm that was wrapped around her.

Jace tensed up in response to Matt. He would not tolerate anyone trying to intimidate a member of his pack. Nora chuckled and then began laughing. She couldn't take all the emotion going on. All the men in the room looked at her like she was crazy.

"Nora?" Jace asked, coming up to her, touching her shoulder lightly.

"You guys broke her finally." Logan said, shaking his head.

"You guys are absolutely ridiculous." Lilly sighed.

"Hush Lilly." Logan said to her.

"No she's right. It's like being stuck in the boys locker room and you are all bowed up about which one should be the quarterback or some shit. I can't take it. Next person who argues or tries to piss off the other I'm going to zap you. Zap you like one of those bug lights." Nora said, wiping her eyes.

"Bug lights?" Matt smirked from behind Lilly.

"Yes firefly! One those light bugs fly into and it shocks them." Nora said, laughing still.

"Ok, ok. Maybe you need some rest." Jace said going to pull her into a hug.

"No, I need you all to listen. Stop trying to decide who is the bigger, badder wolf in the room and shut up before I show you all what big and bad is." Nora said, her eyes glowing as she threatened them.

"Ok, love. We're listening." Jace said, pulling her into him, a smile on his face as he watched her threaten them all.

She inhaled his scent, he was like some instant calming drug. She looked around the room and everyone was looking down like a bunch of little kids that got scolded. Except for Lilly who found this all hilarious. She gave her a look that said you go girl and it made Nora smile.

"Ok so back to what Lilly said. She's right. And Asher you're right she is not part of the pack about her not being in the pack but it's the perfect reason for her to have an even bigger target on her back. She's not a wolf, worse she's a hunter, and now the new delta until Lyla is up and walking around." Nora smiled.

"Lilly, you sure you want to play bait." Logan asked concerned

"Thank you, I was about to say something. I don't know if this is a good idea. Yeah you're a badass but we don't know how many men have done this. You could get ambushed." Matt said, his eyes glowing icy blue.

"Pssh I don't have to worry about anything. You will be there in a heartbeat if I am in trouble. Don't underestimate yourself." Lilly chuckled, throwing her head back into his chest, looking up at him.

He grumbled wanting to fight and protest more but he buried his face against her shoulder and her scent made him relax. He let out a long sigh.

"Fine." He grumbled, pouting a little bit.

Lilly laughed and turned in his arms. "It's going to be fine, you should remember I'm a badass and can kick your ass, never mind some pathetic wolf preying on women."

He made a face again. Lilly didn't know why but she wanted him to stop being worried. Before she could process what she was doing she leaned in and kissed him lightly on his lips. Matt completely froze, he didn't believe it just happened. His wolf was freaking out inside of him. The most Lilly has let him do is hold her. Lilly was surprised but covered it up quickly by going to step back away from him. Nora had a giant grin on her face.

"So now what's the next step?" Lilly said as she ignored everyone's surprised look.

Chapter Twenty Four
Hunter girl

"The next step is to head to the hall, where I summon everyone and tell them you're the new Delta." Nora said to Lilly.

"So we seriously think this is a good idea?" Asher asked, finally settling down.

"It's what we got." Jace said something finally after everyone had quieted down.

"It will work. It will make whoever is trying to terrorize the women; even more mad that Lilly isn't in the pack and she's a hunter. Nora's right." Jordan followed up Jace's comment with this.

Nora nodded and then wiggled out of Jace's grip and began walking towards the door to the kitchen. Jace gave her a weird look but followed her, wondering what she was up to. Logan followed behind her.

"Where are we going?" Logan asked following them.

"To the hall. I swear you guys are the sharpest tools in the shed." Nora laughed.

"I'm going to go check on Lyla and head over." Asher said to Nora before she headed out from the kitchen.

"Ok." Nora nodded with a small smile, she could tell Asher was starting to grow feelings for Lyla.

It could also be the reason why he was so angry with her. Part of her said he was right. A pack isn't made to be without their Alpha and she had been gone more than she had been here. She frowned, she needed to fix things. She walked through the pack house heading to the outside door, everyone starting to follow her like little ducks. Jace caught up and grabbed ahold of her hand walking by her side.

Matt watched everyone slowly start leaving the kitchen, he was hanging back. Once everyone had left Lilly went to follow and Matt caught her hand. She turned around looking at him confused and then she saw his face. Panic raced through her. His face was full of want.

"No, now listen wolf boy I.. I was confused for a second but-

She couldn't finish her sentence, Matt's arm wrapped around her waist pulling her towards him. She went to protest but her body crashed into his. She was fighting with herself again. The butterflies in her stomach wanting every part of this but her brain screamed he's a wolf. He's supposed to be your enemy.

"What hunter girl, do you think that was a kiss?" Matt smirked.

"Matt-

Matt's lips pressed into hers hard and demanding. Lilly tried to fight it. Matt wasn't letting her fight him anymore, his lips pulled against hers demanding she cave. The spark and chill it sent through her body she couldn't deny him any longer. She kissed him back fiercely, giving in. Matt's hand moved down from her hips and slid down over her ass cupping it as he slipped his tongue into her mouth.

Their tongues began to battle as if trying to show who was more in charge. The heat rose in Lilly's cheeks as she felt warmth spread through her. Matt lifted her against him, she wrapped her strong fit legs around him as he carried her to the island. Matt let her bottom hit the island, not breaking the kiss. Lilly's fingers entwined into his red hair as if she was trying to hold him in place.

Matt's hands began to wander down her body. Each touch of his fingers against her made her skin on fire with want. She moved into him more, she needed to be closer to him. Matt pulled back from the kiss. Lilly instantly got angry, she didn't want the kiss to end. She went to pull him back into the kiss but Matt buried his face in her neck kissing it. Lilly sharply inhaled as he pulled some of her skin into his mouth, sucking on it gently. Lilly arched into it, another small moan escaping her mouth as her hands traveled along his chest. A tingling sensation ran down her legs. She pulled his shirt into her hands; as if it was the only thing keeping her upright. Matt tugged her shirt down off her shoulder as his mouth began to move down her shoulder biting it softly.

"Where the hell is Matt?" Jace asked, sitting in the car.

"Give him a second." Nora giggled.

"Why are you giggling?" Jace asked, a playful smile on his lips.

Her giggle instantly made him want to pin her down and get her to giggle more.

"Just give him a minute." Nora said, laughing at his look and tapping Jace.

Logan got in the car sighing loudly as he all but slammed the door. Jace shot him a look as if it said don't you dare slam the car door.

"What's your problem?" Jace asked him.

"Damn sister of mine. Everything is always on her own clock." Logan grumbled.

Nora let out a few more giggles, waiting for the boys to catch on. Jace shot a look over to Nora and she started laughing more. Jace let out a growl at her which did nothing but make her laugh more.

"Keep it up, chuckles and I'll give you something to laugh about." Jace said his eyes flashing mischief in them.

"What's so funny…I'm lost." Logan asked.

Nora began laughing more as Jace reached across the car to get her. He made a face reaching for her as everything clicked.

"Oh for the love of god I don't have time for this." Jace grumbled, pulling back.

Jace's eyes glossed over.

"No Jace!" Nora said, seeing his eyes gloss over as she wacked him softly in the arm.

"Matt! Get your ass out here!" Jace's mind linked him with an order.

Matt growled. Lilly let out a small noise as the growl vibrated against her breast. The sensation caused goosebumps and chills to run through her instantly. Matt lifted his face out between her breasts as he grumbled some more. Lilly looked confused at him seeing his eyes come back to normal.

"What?" She asked.

"They're waiting for us gorgeous." Matt said, kissing her neck once more.

"I completely forgot about them." Lilly said breathless as she leaned into his love bites more.

"Me too." Matt groaned, pulling back.

As he did he pulled Lilly's shirt back into place. Adjusting it appropriately before stepping back away from the island. He held his hand out to her, she sighed, taking it. She scooted down off the counter and stepped into him. He couldn't take her being close, his eyes glowed slightly he pulled her against him. She looked confused for a second.

"What?" Matt asked her.

"Your eyes, why are they glowing ice blue?" She asked.

Matt couldn't tell if she was worried or intrigued. He smiled a little bit worried how to answer her. He had finally got her and he didn't want to scare her off. He knew the wolf thing was a struggle for her.

"It's… Ryker..my wolf." Matt said quietly.

"Oh. you're going to have to explain all that to me at some point." Lilly said softly.

"I definitely will. Come on before I get yelled at again." Matt laughed, grabbing a hold of her hand.

"What?" Lilly asked, confused following him out to the living room.

"It's also a walky-talky." Matt laughed at his own joke tapping his head.

"Wolf thing?" Lilly laughed walking with him to the door.

"Yup." Matt said, holding the front door open and letting her out.

"Great, he's grumpy." Matt chuckled, looking at Jace's car.

"That's fine. I'll tell him to shove it. Come on." Lilly laughed, grabbing Matt's hand once more and walking to the car.

"Please don't." Matt laughed getting to the car.

"No promises." Lilly chuckled as Matt opened the door.

"Move over losers." Lilly said, poking Logan in the arm.

"About damn time you got out here." Logan grumbled scooting over behind Jace.

"Oh hush, you're lucky I'm here to help you." Lilly grinned, getting in and scooting over to the middle seat.

Matt got in the car and shut the door. He looked over to Jace who was looking at him through the rearview mirror. He had a frown on his face for Matt keeping him waiting.

"Glad you could make it." Jace said to him before starting the car up.

"See Logan, you be more like Jace. He is happy and grateful to have Matt." Lilly smirked, turning the sarcastic comment of Jace's around.

Matt smirked at Lilly. Lilly scooted over to him and Matt lifted his arm so she could lean against him. Matt wrapped her arm around her holding her close. Logan shot Lilly a look asking what's up. Lilly stuck her tongue out at him.

"Your mate seems to have finally given in. I'm happy for you…don't hold me up again." Jace sent it to Matt via mindlink.

"Thanks Alpha." Matt smiled back.

"Yay!!." Nora sent to Matt via mind link.

Matt laughed out loud as his eyes returned to normal. Lilly shot him a look and then shook her head.

"Wolf thing." She mumbled adjusting his arm against her.

Chapter Twenty Five
Announcement Two

Nora stood in the hall pacing on the stage. She had sent a mind link summoning all pack members to the hall. She had ordered food and drinks to be prepared as part of another celebration. Jace was watching her pace wanting to make her relax but knew she had to get it out of her system. In her head she kept telling herself that she was strong and had this. The door opened and the first member walked in. Nora straightened up and put on a smile. Her nerves in her stomach bubbling and flipping about.

"Welcome please have a seat at whichever table you like." Nora greeted.

A few more members started piling in. Her stomach tightened with each new person. Jace came over to her and took her hand. She felt a wave of calmness rush over her. She smiled saying thank you to him. He winked at her and the bubbles in her stomach turned into butterflies. She leaned up and kissed his cheek.

"Remember you killed a whole mess of Lobo's and Kip with just one touch. You have this. You are amazing." Jace whispered in her ear.

"I love you." The words fell out of Nora's mouth and panic swept over her.

They hadn't said it. Yes they were mated but what does that mean…what if he didn't love her back. She started to feel like was going to throw up. She suddenly felt his arm around her waist. He pulled her fiercely against her and crashed his lips into hers. He kissed her deeply and passionately. Nora's legs went weak from the kiss. The hall around them went silent. He let Nora go, pulling back he looked at her brushing her raven colored hair from her face.

"Nora, I've loved you from the moment I saw you. I love you too." He said, kissing her forehead.

Nora pulled him into another kiss not caring that the hall was slowly becoming full. Jace kissed her back wrapping his arms around her as he did. He heard someone clear their throat behind them. Jace growled, pulling back from the kiss. He saw Asher waiting on the stage with a small smirk on his lips knowing that he had pissed Jace off. Jace narrowed his eyes at Asher before Nora tapped him lightly. Roger and his men entered the pack hall a prideful smile on their face like they knew something no one else knew. She felt Jace stiffen beside her and she squeezed his arm trying to calm him.

Another growl was heard as Nora tried to figure out where it was coming from. Jace stepped away from her catching Asher who was the one growling, his eyes locked on Roger and his friends. Jace pulled him back to the back of the stage, Asher then turned his anger on Jace.

"Stay out of my way." Asher growled.

"Get yourself in check! You'll fuck this whole thing up." Jace growled at him letting go of his arm and shoving it away

"Don't tell me what to do." Asher growled more.

"I will." Jace said, starting to bow up at him.

"Hello everyone and thank you for coming on such short notice. We have more news to celebrate and I'm hoping to give these announcements quickly. You're welcome to eat and drink here again but if there was something I took you from, feel free to go back to it after the announcement is made." Nora's voice echoed out over the room, the room going silent.

Jace looked to Asher and sighed, shaking his head before walking back towards the front. He hung out in the back area of the stage not wanting to shadow over Nora, as she did her thing. He watched the crowd studying each person trying to figure out which person was the one they suspected. Asher came out from the back and stood next to Jace, his face angry as he looked out over the pack.

"I am going to make the new announcement quickly so as to not keep you all too long. Lilly, can you come out here please.' Nora called behind her.

Lilly walked out on stage and the room's feeling changed. They all looked a Lilly with uncertainty. Nora smiled as Lilly came to stand next to her. Matt was just beyond the stage staring down the crowd. If anyone made a move towards them he would make sure no one got to that stage.

"As you know Lilly is a hunter. She is one of the hunter's who came and assisted us take down Kip and help change this pack for the better. That being said, Lyla is currently not feeling well and will be resting until further notice. That leaves a temporary position for Delta open in our pack. I need all the help I can get." Nora paused letting the crowd take in what she had just said.

Logan was scanning each and every wolf as well. The men standing behind Nora and off to the sides were ready for anything. Logan saw looks of confusion on most of their faces but there were a set of four men in the very back who looked proud. Logan's eyes flickered over to Asher and he was locked in on them. These must be the ones he assumes did it.

"So what does Lilly have to do with all this? We need to make our alliances stronger. As you know Cross River is our strongest ally just for the fact that Jace is my mate. Right now we do not have any other allies. So in order to expand our pack's strength's we are going to grant Lilly the title of Delta until Lyla is back up on her feet." Nora announced and waited for the backlash.

An overwhelming amount of feelings rushed forward. Confusion, anger, uncertainty. No one in the room was happy about this. Then the tinge of rage came forward. She waited for some to speak up.

"Alpha I mean no disrespect but she is a hunter. Yes she helped save us but for as long as wolf history accounts hunters have hunted wolves. Do you think that is…this a little umm..

"Wrong!' Roger stood up from the back, he couldn't control his anger.

Nora smiled seeing him triggered. Lilly nudged her briefly as if to say haha it's working as she waited for Roger to continue to move forward through the crowd.

"Yes, for as long as history can account hunters have hated wolves and vice versa. This is about moving forward. These hunters are here to help support us, not attack." Nora said, ignoring Roger's face.

"Do you all see what she is doing to this pack?" Roger growled standing in front of the stage.

"She's changing and ruining everything!" Roger yelled.

Jace growled, not able to fight it back; the growl was echoed by Asher and Matt stepping forward. Roger's eyes flickered up to the stage. Nora was standing silent letting him have his say. She wasn't bothered in the slightest by his ranting. The only thing that reflected anything was her eyes. Her eyes were glowing. A soft reminder to the room that her wolf was just under the surface if she needed her.

Let's just kill him. If we rip his throat out in front of everyone then no one will question us. Zara muttered in her head, Roger was annoying her.

Sometimes I question how you are my wolf. Nora told her back but a smile appeared on her lips.

Why because actions are better than words? Zara grumbled.

Not every action is appropriate, hush you're distracting me. Nora said to her

This action is appropriate. He's challenging us, so we shut him down. Zara said back like her statement was a no brainer.

Hush. Nora said.

Nora wasn't sure what just happened. Jace was by her side in two steps as if protecting her and Lilly looked like she was ready to fight. She focused back on what was going on, Zara distracted her.

"She's not fit to be Alpha." Roger yelled out over the crowd.

"How dare you!" Asher growled, stepping forward.

Jace watched Asher with a little surprise. The anger and power rolling off of him was strong and almost impressive to Jace. Jace and Cole were two seconds away from killing Roger but he paused hearing Asher. He was almost tempted to see where this would go.

"How dare I? I-

"Nora has freed us. Do you not remember the fear, the panic of doing anything that could be remotely considered wrong and being punished. I know several of you didn't even come out of your homes anymore. The women here have never even known a normal life. You weren't even allowed to live with your wives and daughters. Do you not remember a time where Kip was attempting to take them as his own to create his own offspring. Then trying to create those monsters. Do you really think life was better?" Asher bellowed out over the crowd.

"How many of you lost someone because they said the wrong thing, or were in the wrong place?" Asher said, reminding them the conditions they used to live under.

"Those are all minor things, What she is trying to do is wrong." Roger growled.

"Minor? Was it your wife or daughter, brother or son that was killed in front of you because they didn't bow their heads quick enough. Did someone try to take your mate away from you just because? Did your mate die fighting because your bond was too strong and she couldn't bear having another?" Asher growled at him, stepping down off the stage.

"Maybe nothing happened to you but you are one of the few and lucky ones. So shut up and sit down." Asher growled, squaring off with him.

"I..

"Roger, go sit down." Another pack member said from the crowd.

"Yeah, Beta Asher is right. Alpha is changing things for the better. Sit down." Another member yelled.

"You are all so foolish. This pack is going to crash and burn." Roger said, looking Asher dead in his eyes.

Chapter Twenty Six
Confrontation

*A*sher stepped into him accepting his challenge. Roger growled, bowing up at Asher. As they tried intimidating each other. Clay, Chad, and Kendrick were up at the front trying to back up Roger. Jace jumped down off the stage landing neatly next to Asher. He growled fiercely, the power rolling off of him was intense even if you were not in his pack it made you want to buckle. Clay locked eyes with Jace deciding he would take him on. Logan hopped off the stage on the other side of Asher, Chad squaring off to him.

"I've always wanted to take on a hunter." Chad smirked.

Logan didn't say anything but grinned at him, it almost threw Chad off a little but he was waiting for Roger to make a move. Kendrick looked around, seeming like he was torn. Matt was next to Logan in a heartbeat watching Kendrick. It was going to be an even fight if there was one. Lilly was watching Nora, everyone's eyes were flickering from the men to Nora. Nora's eyes glowed brighter as she stepped down off the stage with such grace you would have thought she floated down. Each step she took the power coming off of her got stronger. She was drawing on the energy around her as she was walking. She wanted Roger to feel it. Wanted Roger to know that these men would back her up but the real threat was her.

She walked down the center of the men squaring off with each other. Asher and Roger were the only ones close enough to actually being able to throw blows if they wanted to. As she walked between each man, they seemed to step back from her. Roger saw her coming and wasn't going to let her get in the way. He brought his fist back as Asher was distracted by Nora and brought it forward.

Nora moved with speed she didn't realize she had. Her hand captured Roger's fist as it went to land a punch on Asher's jaw. She stepped in front of Asher, holding Roger's fist. Roger's eyes were huge with disbelief.

"No one will hurt any of my pack members any more." Nora growled, as she squeezed his fist.

Roger tried to fight against it but he couldn't. Where did she get this strength from? She was just a woman he thought, trying to push his fist forward. Nora sent a surge of energy into his fist. The painful jolt buckled Roger to his knees. Chad, Clay, and Kendrick all backed away seeing Roger brought to his knees.

"If you don't like how the pack is being run you can leave." Nora growled down at Roger.

"You are not fit to be Alpha." Roger said through gritted teeth.

"Then you can leave." Nora said, letting another jolt go into his hand.

She watched him buckle more, the only thing at this point holding him up was Nora holding on to his hand. Roger went further into the floor as Nora let more energy slip from her into him. She looked over at the other three standing there wide eyes, as a woman took down their friend.

"The offer is extended to all of you as well." Nora growled looking at them.

Chad, Clay, and Kendrick backed away. Nora looked down at Roger who had buckled onto the floor and she let him go.

"Get out of my hall." Nora growled.

"You three, come pick up your friend." Nora said, throwing Roger's hand back at him.

Nora stepped back into Asher. He caught her by her arms steadying her. Nora's body was still on defense. As Asher touched her body shocked him. He quickly dropped his hands from her arms, shaking his hand trying to get the tingles out of it. She tried to calm herself down but her body was still recognizing threats. She smiled her sorry to Asher as she stepped away from him. She walked carefully back to the stage. She cleared her throat as everyone was watching. Chad and Clay helped Roger up. They began helping him out of the hall. Kendrick hanging back.

"Kendrick." Clay called over his shoulder.

Kendirck shook his head, he didn't want to go with them. Chad looked at Kendrick confused. Clay groaned his annoyance as they all but carried Roger out. Kendrick looked at Nora and bowed his head, going to find a seat quietly. Logan, Asher, Jace, and Matt are still guarding the front of the stage.

"Ok so any other objections to my new announcement?" Nora smiled out over the pack, her eyes still glowing intensely.

The pack members were silent, she was worried maybe she had scared them. She didn't know, she sighed a pain forming in the back of her head.

"Thank you Alpha." A small voice came from the crowd.

Nora looked up and a young woman was standing up, she bowed her head respectfully. Soon several more women stood up and bowed their heads in thanks. Then followed the rest of the pack. She felt grateful that she had not scared them and that they were thankful she was their Alpha. She didn't want to fail them.

"You're welcome. I promise to keep trying to improve things for the better here." Nora said with a smile.

"You are all welcome to stay and eat." Nora smiled.

The pack members smiled, some got up to leave cautiously. Uncertain if it was ok or if they were doing the right thing.

"You may go if you need to. If I took you from something please don't feel obligated to stay any longer." Nora said so pack members did not feel awkward.

Asher came back on stage with Jace. Logan and Matt were still at the front of the stage guarding it. Jace went to touch Nora's arm and he got zapped.

"Sorry I'm not doing it. I'm not sure how to turn it off." Nora whispered to Jace.

"It's ok, I'm sure once your adrenaline goes down, your electric shock shield will too." Jace chuckled.

Roger got to his feet outside. Shoving Chad and Clay off of him. He growled fiercely becoming filled with rage over what just happened. He looked angrily at Chad and Clay.

"There's something not right with her." Roger yelled.

"What?" Chad asked.

"I don't know, there is something not right and we're going to find out what. Right after we kill that hunter girl." Roger said quietly.

"We kill the hunter girl and we could be put to death. We are lucky we havent been caught for what we did to Lyla." Chad said quietly

"We won't get caught." Roger said like it was nothing.

"Kendrick, he clearly is out." Clay said quietly.

"We need to keep him silent, he could get us caught." Chad said quietly.

"Well we kill him too." Roger shrugged.

"Kill Kendrick?" Clay asked.

"Yeah we are in the kill or be killed part." Chad said, rolling his eyes.

" I just." Clay said quietly but then looked at Roger and nodded in agreement.

"How are we going to do this?" Clay sighed.

"We wait till they leave. Kill Kendrick tonight and hopefully the hunter girl. If not the next night." Roger shrugged, putting no real thought into any of it.

"Sounds promising." Clay muttered.

"Do you want to die too?" Roger growled at him.

"No not really, which is why we need to be careful." Clay growled back.

"Let's go somewhere else and talk about this." Chad said quietly.

"Kendrick will be easy. He will come to us apologizing and will just take him out then." Roger said, still talking.

"The hunter girl should be trickier. She might be brave though and she seems like a risk taker." Roger said thinking out loud.

"And she most likely knows about Lyla being hurt in the alley." Roger continued talking.

Clay and Chad continued listening to him as they walked. They were not sure where he was going with this. They both glanced at each other as they were walking, sharing the same thought.

"And she will want to prove herself." Roger chuckled, slowing down.

"Roger what the hell are you talking about?" Chad grumbled.

Roger stopped in front of the alleyway pausing to look back at Chad and Clay, a sly grin on his face. He pointed to the alleyway and smirked evilly.

"She is going to come into the alleyway. She's an arrogant hunter. She is going to want to, one prove herself, two she's going to investigate the area where the first attack happened and three she will find her way to the alley and we will attack her there." Roger smiled.

"Ok." Clay said, confused.

"So get in the fucking alley and hide." Roger growled.

"What about Kendrick?" Chad asked.

"We will mindlink him to meet us here." Roger sighed.

"Who says he's going to come?" Clay asked.

"He will." Roger sighed.

"Ok then." Chad shrugged.

"Just get in the alleyway and freaking hide. I never met people who question someone so much." Roger grumbled walking into the alleyway.

"This is gonna be a long freaking night." Clay groaned going into the alley.

"Yeah and we didn't even get any food." Chad mimicked Clay's tone.

"Shut the fuck up." Roger's voice echoed in the alley getting annoyed with the two of them.

Chapter Twenty Seven
Waiting

Nora settled into the chair on the front of the stage. The pack mood lightened and those that stayed were laughing and eating in no time. Nora was starting to relax. Asher and Jace approached the chair next to her. She smirked seeing the power struggle going on. Asher moved for the chair and so did Jace. Nora's smirk was becoming more and more of a grin as she watched them shuffle over the chair.

"I'm her Beta." Asher finally said.

"Well she's my mate." Jace growled.

"This isn't your pack." Asher said, matching his growl.

Nora started laughing which broke their tension. Jace loved her laugh and it made him smile.

"Something funny?" Jace smirked at her, daring her to continue laughing.

She couldn't help it, she felt a tear sting her eye as she grabbed her belly and chuckled more. Jace walked over to her and Asher took the opportunity to sit in the chair. Nora saw his quick childish sit down in the chair and lost it. She was laughing so hard she couldn't breathe. Jace went to her with a low growl in his chest as he approached her. The pack members went quiet not sure if the growl from Jace was threatening but their alpha isn't showing any signs of being afraid. He leaned into his hands on the back of the chair blocking her from moving. Her laughter turned into a giggle as he leaned down towards her.

"What's so funny?" He asked her inches away from her face.

"You." She chuckled.

As Jace growled in her face, a few members of the pack stood up. Nora laughed at his growl, her hands captured his face and leaned up into his lips. Her mouth tugged on his lower lips. She growled back at him for the first time. He instantly wanted her even more, his knee went between her legs as he slid her forward, his arm wrapping around her waist pulling her against him. His mouth kissed her deeply. Nora's arms wrapped around his neck, her fingers finding their way into his hair, kissing him fiercely back.

"Seriously?" Asher sighed, rolling his eyes.

"All the time." Matt said, walking towards him as he threw a grape into his mouth; Reaching Asher he leaned against Asher's chair.

Asher gave him a funny look. Matt offered the cup of grapes to him and Asher frowned his eyebrows at him waving his hand no. Just then Lilly walked by with her own plate of food. Matt followed her with his eyes. She blushed a little at him and he couldn't help himself.

"You're on your own man." Matt said, clapping Asher on the shoulder, he shoved the cup of grapes towards Asher before he took off after Lilly.

Asher watched Matt stalk Lilly and then sit down next to her. Without even asking he pulled her into his lap, wrapping his arms around her. Asher glanced over to Jace and Nora who were still kissing. He sighed but then found himself thinking of Lyla. He hadn't been interested in anyone for a long time.

"Hey." He sent Lyla through mind link

He looked around the room, part of him wanting this to be over. He wanted to get back to the pack house and check on her in person.

"Hey." She responded back and her voice sounded unsure.

"How are you feeling?" Asher asked his voice, trying not to show concern because of the way her voice sounded.

"Foggy still. My head hurts real bad. How's it going?" Lyla asked.

"Make sure you're resting. It's going. Part one of pissing off the bad guys is complete." Asher sent back to her laughter in his voice.

"I am. Part two is?" Lyla asked Asher back.

"I'm assuming catch the bad guys but we haven't discussed it. I know Lilly is going to be bait." Asher sent back.

"Lilly?" Lyla asked concerned.

"Nora's friend." Asher answered.

"Is she prepared for what she could be going against?"" Lyla asked concerned.

"Yes, she's a hunter." Asher responded.

"Oh well then she will be good to go." Lyla said feeling better.

"Are you still in my room?" Asher asked, the question he hoped wasn't weird.

"Yeah. Is that ok?" Lyla asked.

Asher could tell she was trying to hide the concern in her voice and he knew it was to do with her still being there.

"Yeah, actually I would feel alot better if you stayed there till I got back. If you're ok with that?" Asher sent back quickly wanting her to know she was not putting him out

"Ok, I would like that very much." Lyla sent back a smile in her voice.

"Ok I will see you soon." Asher sent back his own smile coming through the mind link.

"Kendrick, meet us in the alley." Roger's voice came through in a mindlink for Kendrick.

"What? Why the alley?" Kendrick sent back, he felt nervous all of sudden hearing from Roger.

"Just come." Roger said annoyed back.

"Fine." Kendrick sighed.

Kendrick looked around the hall, sweat beading across his forehead instantly. He struggled with what to do. He had been friends with Roger for as long as he could remember, they even grew up together. He was like an older brother to him. Kendrick sighed and got up from his table slowly. He quickly and hopefully without notice made it to the door. He walked out of the pack hall quietly, trying not to draw attention.

Asher was watching the room wanting people to hurry up and leave, when he spotted Kendrick sneaking out. He didn't know if he was excited to see him going or concerned because it felt like they were that much closer now to part two.

"Nora!" Asher mind link her trying to get her attention away from Jace.

She stirred hearing the mind link. Jace pulled back. Just as Asher mind linked Nora, Logan came over and nudged them. He had been watching the room the whole time and once he saw Kendrick leaving he came over to let Nora know.

"Look, member number four is leaving." Logan said motioning to the door as Kendrick ducked out.

Jace and Nora's eyes went to the door and saw Kendrick quickly duck out. Nora frowned. She was hoping maybe he would change his mind about following Roger.

"Did you want me to follow?" Logan asked.

"No, it's fine." Nora said, making a face.

"So since you guys are interrupted now what is the plan?" Asher said coming over.

"Well it's simple. We wait until it's dark and everyone has gone home. Lilly will head out by herself to the alley, We will split in two. Half of the group goes to the back of the alley, the others blocking the front of the alley where Lilly will enter. That way they won't be able to escape. We will leave shortly after her, giving the illusion that she's alone." Nora said quietly.

"Does Lilly know?" Logan asked, he was now showing concern for his sister.

"Yeah she came up with most of it." Nora nodded.

Lilly looked over at the four of them talking and by the look each one of them were giving her, she knew they were talking about the plan. She winked and gave a thumbs up. Matt raised an eyebrow at Lilly's motion and then looked behind him. He looked even more confused as he saw Logan, Jace, Asher and Nora looking their way.

"What's up with them?" Matt asked.

"I'm assuming they are talking about the next step in the plan. By my brother's face he's worried. I was letting them know I was cool with being the victim still." Lilly chuckled at the word victim.

"Don't say that word. I swear you let something happen to you, I will not forgive you." Matt said to her his face became serious.

"Kind of a silly statement, if something happens to me, you most likely won't be able to be mad at me. I'll either be badly hurt or dead." Lilly shrugged, eating a piece of cheese off her plate.

"Don't say that shit." Matt growled.

"Well it's true." Lilly smirked seeing Matt get upset.

"It's not funny." Matt said again, giving her a look telling her much it bothers him.

"No but it's true. Do you give this lecture to your soldiers that go to war…nope so hush and enjoy our time before I have to go play damsel in distress and then kick some wolf ass." Lilly chuckled, throwing a piece of cheese at him.

"You better not let anyone of them touch you or I promise I will kill them." Matt said sternly as he pulled her into him.

"Yes dear." Lilly chuckled, leaning into him.

Chapter Twenty Eight
Practice

Kendrink walked down the road for some reason he was feeling sick about this. The sky was dark now but the stars and moon were covered by clouds. There was barely any light except for the street lights. It added more to his feeling of dread. He shouldn't be feeling this way but he was. He dragged his feet across the black concrete as he started walking closer to the alley. Maybe he should tell them he was tired. He didn't want to do anything like they did the last time in the alley. Roger was too much of an extremist, maybe it was time for a change around here. Maybe he could talk Roger into it before he got them kicked out of the pack. Rogue life wasn't a good life. He spotted the alley. He would talk to Roger to try to get him to see the light and if not he would just go home.

Getting to the alley he tried looking down it. He didn't see any of them down there. His stomach dropped a little but as he walked slowly in. Where were they? The alley felt darker than normal. He reached the middle of it and wondered if they had left already. He turned to start walking out when he heard a noise behind him. He jumped a little bit at the sound of the noise.

"Jumpy Kendrick?" Roger chuckled, coming out of the shadows.

"Yeah it's a little creepy." Kendrick said, shaking his head at him.

"What did you need Roger?" Kendrick asked him, as he looked around the alley.

"How was the little party?" Roger asked bitterly.

"Same as the last time." Kendrick said with a shrug, wondering why it sounded like Roger had his feelings hurt.

"Really." Roger said almost like he didn't believe him.

"Yes. Are you ok?" Kendrick asked him confused.

"Make any new friends?" Roger asked, his tone starting to get mean.

"No, I sat at the table we normally sat at. Ate and was about to head home when you mindlinked me." Kendrick said to him, his face getting more confused, the more Roger talked to him.

"So you didn't tell anyone about what happened to Lyla?" Roger asked, stepping closer to him.

"No Roger. Is that what you're worried about?" Kendrick asked almost hurt the way Roger was acting like he would betray him.

"Should I be worried?" Roger said, stepping even closer to him.

"Roger, I wouldn't betray you. You've always been like a brother to me." Kendrick said back but he didn't like the look flashing in Roger's eyes; so he took a step back.

"A brother?" Roger asked, continuing forward.

"Yes Roger we grew up together, I've always looked up to you. Besides, even if I wasn't loyal to you, I was still here. It would make me guilty too. Why would I do that?" Kendrick said his voice was getting shaky as he was starting to feel cornered.

Kendrick could see the end of the alley again, if he was quick enough maybe he could run? Maybe he would make it out? He didn't know why but right now everything was telling him he was in danger. Roger was starting to look more and more dangerous as the minutes went by. He was regretting even coming. He glanced behind him judging the exit as he took another small step back. Movement in front of him brought his attention back. Clay stepped out from the shadows behind Roger.

"See I told you we could trust him." Clay said to Roger.

"Yeah, he's good." Chad said from behind Kendrick.

Kendrick glanced back to where the exit was and now saw Chad in his way. Even though they were saying they could trust him and he was good, Kendrick didn't feel safe.

"Roger. This is all a mistake. We need to just back away from this whole plan. It could be good for us here. Who cares if the girls have some freedom." Kendrick said, trying to get Roger to see.

Roger put his head down for a second. It looked like he was debating everything Kendrick had said. Chad and Clay even got confused about what was going on. They were waiting to see what would happen too. Clay secretly hoped Roger would change his mind. Clay didn't want to see Kendrick hurt. He didn't really think Roger would hurt him but part of him said that Roger would and could hurt him. Roger took several minutes and then looked up to Kendrick. He gave him somewhat of a smile.

"You know you're right. I..I just struggle with changes. If I accept all this then I don't know where my place is in this pack anymore. I think that's what my problem is." Roger said sadly to Kendrick walking towards him again.

Kendrick was listening to him and felt bad for him. He was worried about change. Roger had always been an enforcer and if change happened he didn't know what that meant for him.

"Roger, we can find something for you to do. I get change is scary but sometimes scary is good." Kendrick said to him with a smile.

"Kendrick, I'm glad you said that. It makes me feel so much better. I'm glad I changed my mind." Roger said, reaching him and putting his hand on Kendrick's shoulder.

"Good. You just need to talk sometimes. I know that's tough for you." Kendrick said to him with a smile.

"I'm sorry brother." Roger said softly, stepping into him for a hug.

Kendrick went to hug him back but at the last minute Roger grabbed Kendrick's neck and with one swift motion jerked his head to the side. A loud bone snapping crack radiated around them. In that one quick minute Roger snapped his neck. Kendrick didn't even have a chance to fight back. Roger let go of Kendrick and Kendrick's body hit the cold hard ground, the sound bouncing off the walls of the alley.

"Oh fuck!" Clay yelled, as he looked at Kendrick's lifeless body.

"Shit." Chad whispered in just as much shock as Clay's voice had.

"He's..dead." Clay whispered.

"Yes he's fucking dead." Roger said, rolling his eyes.

"Holy shit you killed him." Chad stuttered out.

"Yes you dumb fucks. Do one of you want to come over here and I'll show the other a reenactment of what happened so we can make sure?" Roger growled.

"Stupid ass wanting us to accept change." Roger mumbled kicking Kendrick's body.

Clay felt like he was going puke. He knew Roger said he was going to do it but he didn't think he would actually do it. He thought maybe he was bluffing. Worst-case maybe scare Kendrick into being quiet, break an arm or leg something not kill the poor kid. Clay could feel the bile rising in his throat. He looked at Chad who was just completely blank staring down at Kendrick's body as if he was waiting for him to jump up.

"Ok if you two don't stop acting like babies and get your shit together I am going to kill you both too. I can do this alone but I can't leave people around to tell about it." Roger smiled a smile that would make even the toughest person's skin crawl.

Chad looked to Clay who didn't know what to say. It sounded like a joke but the way things just went down and his smile, Clay didn't want to risk it. Clay reached down and grabbed Kendrick's shoulders and motioned for Chad to grab his feet.

"Great choice boys! Great choice. Now hurry the fuck up." Roger laughed looking at the entrance of the alley.

"Hide him behind the dumpster." Roger said motioning to the dumpster in the back.

Chad and Clay began carrying Kendrick's body quickly to the back. They were used to being tough but they were tough guys together. They never thought something like this would happen. This was all getting too crazy and fast.

"I can't believe he fucking just did that." Clay mind linked Chad.

"Shut up, shut up." Chad sent back panicked.

"He can't hear us, I'm mind linking you." Clay said quickly, glancing at Roger who was pacing and talking to himself.

"I know I just can't deal with it anymore, just be quiet till this is all over." Chad sent back wanting to get out of this situation as soon as possible.

"Ok so the pregame run through was perfect. We need it to go down exactly like that. So get back to where you guys were. When hunter girl walks in I'll distract her talking trash. You two block her exits and then bam she'll be dead before she knows it." Roger laughed.

Chad and Clay stayed quiet as they went to their hiding spots. Both sick to their stomachs as they waited for Lilly to come through.

"Are you still sure you want to do this?" Matt asked Lilly for the fourteenth time.

"Yes and if you don't stop, I'll beat your ass and then go kick theirs." Lilly said, tugging on his shirt as she threatened him.

"I mean we could go find some place just me and you. I will gladly let you beat my ass." Matt smirked, stepping into her.

"Lilly in all seriousness Matt's right you don't have to do this." Nora's voice interrupted Matt's playing.

"Nora I got this." Lilly said, tapping her hip.

Nora didn't realize this before but as she looked down at Lilly's hip she saw knives on either side of her hip. Lilly saw Nora's face and smirked. She took a step away from Matt who grumbled about it. She gave him a look saying wait. She kicked the heels of her boots together and knives popped out the toes. She then bent down and pulled two more blades out of the sides of her boots.

"I'm packing, and I'm skilled. Not to mention my pretty hair clip in my ponytail is also a weapon." Lilly winked.

"Ok then…Sooo note to Matt don't ever piss her off." Nora chuckled.

Matt smirked, pulling Lilly back to him. " I kinda like her when she's spicy."

"Matt, keep it in your pants for two seconds." Jace grumbled behind Nora.

"Pssh Alpha, you should talk, if Luna so much as looks at you a certain way or laughs a certain way and lord knows….ok ok shutting up." Matt started to say but the glare he was getting from Jace made him stop.

"All right Lilly you walk in there, we will give you a ten minute head start. Matt and I will go through the front. Jace and Asher you will take the back. Logan, you're going to the rooftop." Nora nodded to each person as she gave direction.

"Everyone good?" She asked after pausing a second, she could hear her own heart pounding in her ear.

"As good as can be." Matt muttered.

"Ok let's do this." Lilly grinned.

She squeezed Matt and pecked him quickly, going to leave. Matt growled and pulled her back into him. His hand went to her face as he pulled her in for a deep kiss. It was the type of kiss that made Lilly's knees go weak and she leaned into him. When she pulled away from him, she was breathless. Matt pressed his forehead against hers.

"I mean it, be safe." Matt said as if he was saying a threat but his eyes looked like he was pleading with her.

"Don't be late, lover." She smiled, kissing his nose before slipping out of his grasp.

Matt watched her blond ponytail swish as she walked away from him. He knew she was powerful. He knew she was capable. He finally got her and he was watching her walk away from him. She was his heart walking away and he would do anything and everything to protect it. Matt let out a long breath out putting his hands behind his head as he watched her until he couldn't see her anymore.

Chapter Twenty Nine
Red Riding Hood

"Let's go Matt." Nora nudged him.

Nora smiled as she began walking down the road slowly after Lilly. Matt had been trying so hard to resist the urge of running after Lilly. Jace and Asher had left several minutes ago to ensure they had the back blocked off. Logan had headed to the rooftop. He somewhere had gotten a rifle.

"Matt. She said not to be late." Nora laughed, calling to him as she walked down the road.

Matt shook his head and hurried after her. He was scared. Afraid something would happen to Lilly. He would lose it, Ryker would lose it. He had been begging Matt to shift for the last twenty minutes. He kept going on about how he was faster in wolf form and stronger. Matt kept reminding him that they didn't need to beat Lilly there. If he needed to shift he would. He looked up at the night sky and begged the goddess to make sure Lilly was protected.

Lilly reached the alley and she smiled to herself. She wanted to strut in there pretending to be some helpless, harmless red riding hood. She wanted the basket and everything. Oh grandma ma what big eyes you have. She laughed to herself. Looking into the alley, She felt her heart speed up in her chest. Go time she told herself as she stepped into the alley.

The cold brick walls seemed to close in on her as she walked down the alley. Her boots echoing off the walls. This was the perfect place to be attacked, she thought. She took a breath and put her guard on high alert. The whole time she tried her best to act like she was carefree. She heard what sounded like someone sliding their foot on the ground behind her.

"Hello, hello Blonde." Roger snickered from behind her.

"I believe it's Delta to you…Mohawk." Lilly smiled brightly.

"You are not my Delta." Roger growled.

"Hmm funny I think I am. You really need a better hobby, hanging out in alleys is pretty lame and sad. Are you sad?" Lilly smirked.

"How dare you." Roger growled.

"I think that's what I am supposed to say…remember Delta. I have a boss title and you don't." Lilly said just poking the bear making him angrier.

Roger growled and it echoed off the walls. Lilly shrugged like it didn't matter. She wanted him to get himself so worked up he went into a blinding rage. She heard movement behind her and she sighed.

"Of course the bad guy would have back up. Really can't settle your own problems alone. Need your friends. Pathetic." Lilly chuckled.

She glanced over studying Chad and Clay. They seemed uncomfortable with everything like they didn't want to be involved. Roger looked at them and smiled.

"Grab her." Roger ordered them.

"Roger, I don't know about this." Clay said, stepping back slowly.

"Yeah, let's just let it go." Chad whispered.

"Cowards! Really fine, I'll do this myself." Roger growled lunging at Lilly.

Lilly squared off waiting for him to get near her. Roger growled, the growl became louder and fiercer as he got closer to her. Lilly stepped to the side as Roger came running at her. Stepping to the side she threw her elbow into his face. Her elbow smashing into his nose. An instant crack was heard. Blood poured down the front of Roger's face as he stumbled forward smashing into the ground. Lilly twirled around a small smile on her face as she waited for Roger to get up from the ground.

Roger slammed his fist into the ground. The front of him was covered in blood and dirt from one simple blow from Lilly. He looked up at her from the ground in anger. Rage and hate filling him. He stood up growling. He looked at her. He wanted to rip her apart piece by piece. He let his claws extend down and he ran at her. Getting close to her he began slashing at the air. Lilly reached into her side pockets pulling out her daggers.

She dodged his slash as he kept trying to slice into her. He backed her up against the wall but she was quicker than him. She used the wall as leverage and flipped over the top of Roger. As she did she stuck her dagger out. It pierced into his shoulder running downwards into his back as she flipped over the top of him. Landing neatly on her feet she yanked the blade out of his back.

Roger let out a loud yell as she yanked the blade out. He swung around his claws slicing across her midsection. Lilly reacted to the searing pain by slamming the hilt of her dagger into his face. Chad and Clay looked at each other and decided they were out. They were done with Roger's madness.

Roger head butted Lilly in the face. She stumbled backwards in a daze.

"Cowards." Roger yelled to Chad's and Clay's back as they hurried out of the alley.

Chad and Clay ran to the back exit of the alley, it curved right before exit. They were relieved when the exit appeared. They bolted to it, pushing themself harder to reach it. As they reached the exit Jace and Asher stepped in front of them. Chad and Clay rammed right into Asher and Jace.

"Going somewhere?" Jace growled.

Chad and Clay froze looking at each other; they didn't know what to say. Chad hung his head lower. Asher growled at them and they looked sick.

"Kendrick is dead." Chad whispered.

"Roger murdered him before we could even understand what he had done." Clay said, adding to Chad's whisper.

Jace growled looking at Chad and Clay. He nodded to Asher before walking into the alley. Asher grabbed them both by the neck holding them in place.

Roger swung as Lilly was still foggy, she barely dodged the blow. Roger fist grazed her chin. He slashed at her with his open handed claws. It shredded her shirt, leaving more wounds. Her white shirt is now turning red. She laughed looking at it.

"What are you laughing about?" Roger growled backing Lilly into the wall.

Lilly laughed louder at him. Roger snatched Lilly by the throat and applied pressure. She locked eyes with him, a smile still on her face. She dragged her fingers across his cheek scratching him. He acted like it didn't phase him. She laughed harder at his tough guy response.

"Stop laughing. Why are you laughing?" Roger yelled.

"Because you touched me." Lilly stopped laughing and smiled.

"I'm about to kill you doll." Roger said, squeezing her neck tighter.

"You touched me and I'm dating one of the big bad wolves. You're dead." Lilly managed to get out as Roger began choking her.

"What.. big bad what? What wolf do you think is big and bad? No one is here to save you, blonde." Roger asked, confused and snickering.

---

*L*ogan took aim on the rooftop, he could see Roger pinning Lilly up against the wall. He didn't have a shot, he risked killing Lillly if he took it.

"Fucking move." Logan whispered.

He couldn't, there was no shot. His mind screamed to do something or Lilly was going to die. He took his shot aiming for Roger's leg. The bullet flew towards Roger, hitting him in the back of the leg.

---

*R*oger felt his leg buckle and he was confused. He didn't let go of Lilly though. Before he could process what just happened, a red wolf was racing towards Roger. It ran up the brick wall next to them. Kicking off it, the red wolf sailed through the air towards Roger. It's mouth hung wide open. As it got to Roger, the wolf grabbed ahold of Roger's neck. It's teeth sinking in, blood instantly began to pour out from the wound. The wolf jerked it's head quickly to the side. The wolf's teeth sinking further into Roger and ripping into his flesh. He pulled Roger off Lilly and with one more jerk, Roger's head came smooth off. Roger's headless body sunk to the floor.

The wolf dropped Roger's head out ofit's mouth. Roger's head bounced across the alley floor. The wolf didn't even look back but rushed over to Lilly.

In an instant Matt was standing in front of Lilly, his hand cradling her face, as he studied her. Her eyes connected with him and she smiled. She let out a small sigh of relief seeing him.

"You were almost late." She chuckled.

Matt began looking at all her wounds, becoming angry that he didn't bolt down the alley sooner. He pulled her into his arms, cradling her into his chest and began quickly walking out.

"I told you not to let him touch you." Matt said to her, his voice worried.

"I'm fine, just a bunch of scratches." Lilly said to him.

Matt grumbled walking out of the alley holding Lilly to him. Nora was pacing waiting for a sign she was needed. Seeing Matt holding Lilly she rushed to them. Nora looked over quickly.

"Get her to the pack house, I will have Jordan meet us." Nora told Matt.

Chapter Thirty
Wolf Talk

*M*att felt his lungs burning as he held Lilly to his chest, racing to the pack house. Seeing it he felt relief. He didn't know how badly she was hurt. She was tough and she could put on a good show. She was still human, she couldn't heal herself. She could break and be broken. She could die. Matt's stomach twisted in on itself as the thought crept into his mind. Matt was panicking on the inside but he was like stone on the outside. Lilly shifted in his arms, wincing in pain as she did. He gritted his teeth, her pain felt like his own. Worse, he couldn't fix hers. If he could he would kill Roger all over again but slower.

Jordan met him at the door shaking his head, already assessing the scene in front of him. He was angry seeing another woman attacked.

"Get her inside and to the kitchen." Jordan said as Matt reached him.

Matt brushed past him hurrying into the kitchen. The counter top of the island was still cleared off from Lyla laying on the island. Matt gently set her down on it, trying to be careful so he didn't hurt her more.

"I'm not glass." Lilly teased him but no response came from Matt.

She wanted to see his smile, something that showed her he was ok. She didn't know why but it was making her upset to see him so upset.

"What the hell happened?" Jordan growled, setting his medicine bag down on the table.

"Roger attacked her." Matt growled.

"Roger, that bastard. I hope we caught him." Jordan said, beginning to put out his supplies.

"He's dead." Matt said coldly.

"Dead?" Jordan asked quietly.

"I killed him." Matt said, his voice emotionless.

Lilly looked at Matt. She had always seen his goofy side, the playful, flirty, and silly person he was. Seeing him now and the way he spoke gave her chills. Jace had said Matt was lethal and she had seen him fight but this, this was deadly.

"Good." Jordan said shortly.

"Matt, I promise I'm ok." Lilly said, sitting up and wincing.

"I'll need her shirt off to see the wounds." Jordan said shortly.

Matt growled at Jordan not meaning too. Ryker was on edge and was confused he was seeing everyone as a threat. Ryker didn't want Lilly exposed in front of him. Lilly chuckled a little bit and it grabbed Matt's attention.

"Are you ok?" Matt asked her, concerned by her laugh.

"How long have you been naked?" Lilly smirked.

"What I?" Matt then realized he had shifted back from wolf form and didn't bother putting on his spare clothing he had stashed outside the alley.

"I had other things I was worried about." Matt said with a smile finally cracking his face.

Lilly shifted and began trying to pull her shirt up, she winced a little bit and then looked at Matt annoyed.

"Do you want to help me or should I ask Jordan?" Lilly smirked.

Matt moved quickly to help her with her shirt. Lilly was now sitting on the counter top with her shirt off. Matt stiffened seeing the claw marks across her stomach and rib cage. He knew it was bad from the amount of blood on Lilly's shirt but this looked brutal. He realized he had never seen a human hurt before. Most of the time it was other wolves and no matter how bad it was, it was never really that bad because they healed so quickly. Matt looked to Jordan concerned.

"Matt, you're going to have to move and control your wolf. I am going to have to touch her to clean the wounds. I am not a threat and have my own mate." Jordan told Matt calmly as he began moving towards Lilly.

"Why does any of that matter? You should be asking me if I am ok with it." Lilly asked, confused by Jordan's statement.

"Well, I can clearly tell he is your mate, by the over protectiveness. Secondly, I don't feel like fighting with his wolf who might try to kill me for touching you. And yes of course I should ask you." Jordan said, sighing.

"Can you lay back on the counter?" Jordan asked her as Matt moved out of the way.

Lilly watched Matt and she could tell he was fighting with himself. She laid back on the counter and then held her hand out to him. Matt smiled a little bit. The fact that she wanted him made him happy. He went over towards her head and entwined his fingers into her hand.

"So are you ever going to stop trying to fight every guy that comes near me?" Lilly smirked, wincing as Jordan began cleaning her wounds

"It's a wolf thing." Matt shrugged, squeezing her hand a little trying to get her thoughts off of what Jordan was doing.

"Explain to me so I don't have to think about the pain." Lilly said to him with a small smile.

"The short answer is No. Ryker, which is my wolf's name. He is very protective over you and what's his is his. Think of how a…

"Dog?' Lilly chuckled, teasing him.

"I was going to say think of how wolves are in the wild. It's like that. However when a wolf marks their mate the intensity tends to go away little. It's not an overwhelming uncontrollable urge." Matt explained to her.

"So most of these can stay open and should heal up nicely. I will put a bandage around your torso. There is one on the abdomen I want to suture close. It's just too risky to leave open. I don't have anything to sedate you here. We can head to the hospital-

"No do it here." Lilly said shortly.

"Lilly, that's going to hurt." Jordan said, almost confused.

"I'm not going to a hospital. So suture me up or call Logan, he'll do it." Lilly said quietly.

"Logan?" Jordan repeated the name confused looking at Matt.

"My brother. Your choice Doc." Lilly said, shrugging on the table.

"Are you sure, this is going to hurt." Jordan said quietly.

"This isn't my first time." Lilly smirked.

"Matt-" Jordan started to protest.

Matt studied her face for a minute. He had noticed that her eyes showed a little bit of fear when Jordan mentioned the hospital. There was something there, he wanted to ask her what was wrong and why she was afraid but he wasn't going to push her. He looked at her face. He wanted to know what she had been through. Why had she been sewed up by her brother in the past? So many questions.

"Either your wolf doctor does or you can bandage me up and Logan will fix me up later. I am not , I repeat not going to a hospital." Lilly said going to sit up.

Lilly looked to Matt for help and he felt his chest tighten. He inhaled and let out a breath.

"If she says she got this, then she's got it. Do it." Matt said to Jordan.

"Alright then." Jordan grumbled going to get his suture kit.

Matt took a seat next to the counter, his arms wrapped around Lilly's shoulder area in a form of a hug. His mouth next to her ear.

"Are you sure about this?" He whispered to her, his stomach felt nauseous for her, the thought of her going through more pain.

"Matt, I have been a hunter since I was a child. This…this is nothing." Lilly said back her voice went a little dark for a second.

"Lilly-

"Tell me more about the wolf stuff, if you're going to be my lover then I need to know more." Lilly smiled playful as she said the word lover.

"Lover?" Matt smirked.

"Mhmm one of them. I mean you look like a fine specimen." Lilly chuckled, eyeing his very fit and muscular naked body.

"One of them." Matt growled, the thought of Lilly being with anyone else made Ryker jealous.

"Mhmm." Lilly chuckled.

Jordan sat down beside her mentally preparing himself for what he needed to do. He didn't like hurting people and she was human so he expected this to be horrible.

"Ready?" Jordan asked her.

"Ready." Lilly said in a sing-song voice.

Matt grabbed her shoulders lighty to keep her in place. Lilly rolled her eyes at him but if it was going to make him feel better and got her sutured up without going to the hospital then she would ignore it. Jordan pierced the suture needle through her flesh and out the other side of the wound beginning his first stitch. He glanced up expecting Lilly to move but she remained perfectly still. She shut her eyes as he pushed the needle through the other side.

"What's marking?" Lilly asked, her voice calm and steady.

"It's a ritual kind of. A male wolf will bite his mate on the crook of their neck. The mark that's left there lets others know she has a mate." Matt explained.

"That's kind of over the top." Lilly chuckled.

"No laughing." Jordan said and smirked he didn't expect to say that to her.

"The whole walky-talky thing, how does that work?" Lilly asked as Jordan continued sewing her up.

She closed her eyes tighter as the pain began to get worse. She knew he was having to do a layer inside where the meatier part of her flesh was and then a layer to close the skin. She winced giving into the pain a little bit. Each tug of the suture pulling through her skin, each poke of the needle burned and stung. Matt squeezed her shoulders seeing her in pain for a brief second.

"We can communicate through our minds. If a wolf is part of a pack he has an open radio to anyone in the pack." Matt said, trying to take her mind off of the pain.

"That sounds like it could get really annoying." Lilly smiled.

"It can be sometimes, I never really thought about it. It's been that way my whole life. Just like Ryker we share one body and one mind." Matt said with a shrug.

"Wait so your wolf can talk to you?" Lilly asked, opening her eyes and looking at him intrigued.

"Yeah, he can definitely be annoying but he's also a part of me so it would be a little weird without him." Matt smiled.

"So he can tell you what he wants for dinner or if he's mad?" Lilly said, trying to understand.

"I mean I guess, most of the time Ryker wants out to run. He wants you and then he's there when I have heightened emotions…he's not always saying the right thing. Most of the time egging me on to fight." Matt laughed.

"He wants me?" Lilly asked quietly.

"You are also his Mate. He wants you to meet him and wants to..wants us to mark you and make it official. That's our latest argument." Matt said awkwardly not knowing if this was the right time.

"Do you want to mark me?" Lilly asked, she was worried but something made her excited about it.

Matt struggled with his answer. God yes he wanted to mark her. Wanted to tell the world that she was his and no one else's. But no he didn't, she was a human part of him was afraid of what that could do to her. Wolves also mate for life…humans didn't.

"No and yes." Matt answered honestly.

"Why no?" Lilly asked quietly.

"All done." Jordan announced triumphantly.

Matt let go of Lilly's shoulder and sat up straight; he was happy for the interruption. He didn't want to let Lilly see him vulnerable like that yet. He was this cocky strong goofy person. He didn't want Lilly to know that he was terrified that she might decide this wasn't for her.

"You are an amazing young lady. I have never seen someone tolerate something so well. Especially a human. That was remarkable." Jordan said motioning for her to sit up.

"Gee thanks Doc." Lilly laughed.

"Let me bandage you up and then you'll be good to go." Jordan smiled brightly, happy to have that all done and over with.

"Jordan I am going to go get some clothes, will you stay with Lilly till I get back." Matt asked but more so told Jordan.

He quickly kissed Lilly on the forehead before Jordan or Lilly could say anything and walked out of the kitchen.

Chapter Thirty One
Interrogation

"Jace, come home now! I swear I am going to start a war. You need to get here now!" Dante yelled through the mind link at Jace.

Jace was walking back down the alley towards Asher, when the mindlink hit him. There was so much emotion and power behind it that Jace stumbled. Jace looked to Asher concerned. He walked to him quickly, his eyes searching for Nora.

"Dante what's going on?" Jace asked calmly back.

"The council has Sarah in the old dungeon and is questioning her. They won't let me see or speak to her. I don't know what's going on but in a minute I am going to smash open the door and kill them all I swear it." Dante said.

"Dante breath, you're her mate. Do you feel pain?" Jace asked as he reached Asher.

"I need to leave now somethings going on at my pack. Tell Nora I will get with her in a little bit but I need to go now.' Jace said quickly to Asher.

"Everything good?" Logan asked, coming up behind him.

"If I don't get there quickly it won't be. You and Asher look after Nora or else." Jace said and then shifted in front of them.

"We got your girl." Logan told Cole, Cole growled slightly at Logan but nodded before rushing off.

Jace decided to shift, Cole would get there quicker. From the pain and panic in Dante's voice he needed to be there soon. If Dante started a war over this, he wouldn't blame him. If anyone attempted to do the same to Nora he would destroy everything and everyone that stood in his way.

---

*I*t was dark but she was used to things like this. She sat in a chair in the center of the room. The council members hanging out in the shadows. Trying to intimidate her. They had not lived in Kip's pack. They didn't know what she had been through. What she could take, this was nothing.

Sarah could feel Dante's anger and panic. She could almost hear him pacing the floor upstairs. He must know. She frowned thinking of him being panicked or upset. She wanted to let him know she was ok. She could still mindlink him as of right now.

"Hey, I'm all right. I'll let you know if I'm not." *Sarah sent it to him.*

"If they touch you Sarah they are dead, all of them dead ." Dante sent back to her, the rage and anger radiating through the mind link gave her a chill.

She knew he was serious. She smiled softly thinking about how he would break down the door and come save her if needed. Lance came forward with a stupid grin on his face. He stopped in front of her looking her over as if he was sizing her up. He titled his head to the side as Sarah's eyes came back to focus.

"Talking to your mate or Alpha?" Lance asked with a small smirk on his lips.

"My mate." Sarah said shortly.

"Hmmm we should fix that." Lance announced walking over to the over side of the room.

"Can I ask why I am here? And what do you want?" Sarah said politely.

She knew right now she had to tread lightly. They were the council they were all knowing, all right and could do whatever they pleased. If they said you had red hair and your hair was brown your hair was now red. She hated the system but right now she couldn't do anything about it. Lance smirked, he was the sadist of the bunch. Sarah knew it when she locked eyes with him for the first time. There was always one, in the group. One who got off on pain and hurting others. She glanced at Bruce, the one who was the leader. He planned everything and came up with what needed to be done but didn't want to get his hands dirty. Her eyes then settled on Douglas, then there was one who was in it for the ride. He didn't agree with anything but kept quiet waiting for his opportunity. He would do whatever worked best for him.

She knew these men, lived with them, grew up with them. They may have different names, different faces and different titles; but they were not any different. She knew the game and she could play. Lance came forward holding chains. She wanted to roll her eyes. She knew the chains would be soaked in wolfsbane. wolfsbane limited a wolf's ability. They would say it would be so she couldn't communicate with the others. So she couldn't lie. Lance stepped forward, he was wearing black gloves to protect himself.

"Sorry sweetheart this is going to burn." Lance smirked as he presented the chains to her.

"What? Why? What did I do wrong?" Sarah said meekly, she rolled her eyes in head.

She knew what she was supposed to say. She knew how they wanted her to act. So she would play. She knew that if she acted tough it would be worse. That their interrogation would go further then just that. She had seen it happen. If they were anything like Kip it would escalate and quickly. She didn't want that to happen. She liked her skin where it was.

Images of Kip skinning a girl in front of her flashed before her eyes. The poor girl he thought was talking to another pack. Seeking help, letting them know what he was planning. The girl was just trying to leave. She remembers everything, the smell of her blood in the air. Watching her skin peel from her meaty fleshy muscles. He tortured her for hours and had all the women he thought were strong watch. To scare them into submission. The poor girl died hours later in severe pain. These councilmen knew none of that. So she would play the game. She didn't want Dante getting hurt because of her.

"Darling you didn't do anything wrong. It's part of the routine questioning. So we can make sure you are truthful and not seeking answers elsewhere." Bruce said from the shadows.

"But it will hurt." Sarah said, making sure she sounded afraid.

Lance's smile grew seeing her shiver and then the fear in her voice. He grinned, he lived for this stuff. He felt himself grow hard in his jeans as he moved closer to her with the chains. She pushed back into the chair.

"Dante, they're going to put wolfsbane soaked chains on me. I wont be able to communicate with you. Do not freak out, it is normal. I promise I am ok. If I am not, you will know. Do not do anything that could get you hurt." Sarah sent it to him as quickly as she could.

"I..I love you." Sarah added and then chains
were dropped down on her.*

Lance grinned as he laid them across her
chest. He placed them around her wrists and down
across her lap. The chains burned into her. Hissing as
they touched her skin. She winced and then
remembered she was supposed to act like she was in
more pain. She began moving and shifting like she
was on fire.

"Please no. It hurts." She cried letting them
have what they wanted.

"Darling it's just until we are done questioning,
that's all." Bruce said, coming out of the shadows.

She bowed her head waiting for the rest of it.
This couldn't be the end of everything. She was trying
to focus on Dante's pacing footsteps upstairs.
Knowing he was close by brought her comfort to her.

"Ok first question, what is your name and
whose pack do you belong to." Bruce said coming
forward and standing in the little bit of light that was in
the room.

"Sarah and I swore loyalty to The Cross River
pack and their Alpha Jace Knight" Sarah answered,
purposely leaving out her last name.

She knew she had to give some error so that
they could have something to not pick at. That way
they can correct her and make her answer fully that
way when they started with the real question they
would believe what she said.

Lance came over and pressed on the chains
so they sizzled into her thighs. She winced and shut
her eyes against the pain.

"Your whole name." Bruce said firmly.

"Sarah Alexander." Sarah said her eyes stayed
down as she spoke.

Lance pulled on the chains and brought them up to her neck. She wasn't quite sure why he was attempting to hurt her some more. Her body was starting to respond to the wolfsbane. She slowly started to ache and shake.

"You need to look at us when you speak, answer the question in its entirety." Bruce instructed.

"Do you understand?" Lance snickered as he pushed on the chain some more.

The chain burned into her neck, asSarah struggled to find her voice.

"Yes, Alpha council." Sarah said, lifting her eyes as she spoke and locking onto Lance's.

Chapter Thirty Two
Loophole

Dante could feel her pain but it was dull, like it didn't really hurt her. He was staring at the door debating on breaking it down. Noah was howling and crawling on the inside of him. Everything in him was telling him to go get his mate. His body was shaking from holding himself back. He pressed his hand to the door. He knew it would take one small hit and the door would crumble.

He felt more stinging pain but no emotion from Sarah. He tried to reach out to her through a mind link but it was like he was hitting a wall. He shut his eyes connecting the dots. Sting burning pain and no ability to mind link. Wolfsbane, they were poisoning her. He knew it was for questioning.

How dare they. Noah growled inside of him.

Dante brought his fist back and slammed it into the door. Wooden pieces shattered about the stairs leading down to the interrogation room. A piece of splintered wood landed on the concrete floor and skidded towards Lance. A malicious grin spread across his face. He glanced up the stairwell waiting for Dante to come down. He knew Dante wouldn't be able to hold it together. Now he would have the war he was hoping for.

"No!" Sarah yelled seeing the wood, it felt like her heart stopped as she looked at it.

Her stomach knotted and twisted inside of herself. She knew that if Dante came down here seeing her like this his wolf would lose it. He had already gone against the council orders by disturbing them, if he did anything else they could kill him. Sarah was terrified. Her eyes watching them as they looked to the stairs waiting. Bruce and Lance stared up the stairs waiting for their prey to come down.

Dante couldn't take it anymore staring at the gaping hole he had just made. Seeing the door gone. Noah pushed him forward. He prayed he would be strong enough, if he could kill just one of them and set Sarah free that would be enough. He would die for that. He went to step onto the first stair accepting his fate.

Something strong grabbed a hold of his shoulder stopping him from moving forward. He was thrown backwards, hitting the kitchen island. As he hit the island he fell to the floor staring up. Jace stood their breathing heavy. Dante knew he ran all the way here. Jace looked him over before turning to the empty space where the door was.

"Stay." Jace orderedDante, his Alpha aura rushing into Dante in case he had second thoughts about not listening.

"Jace you can't." Dante whispered.

"Stay." Jace growled and began walking down the stairs.

Dante flinched trying to stop Jace but the command he gave him was too strong. He watched his Alpha walk down the stairs not knowing what would happen next.

*J*ace walked down the stairs slowly as if he wasn't walking to his possible doom. He was thankful he got there before Dante could venture down into the stairs. Dante would have killed one of them and then there would be a war. Jace wouldn't have let them kill Dante.

"Well it looks like Jace will be down a Beta." Lance's voice said happily.

"No, Dante, go back. I am fine! I promise. Go!" Sarah pleaded seeing someone starting to come down the stairs.

"Oh it's too late now darling. You will be mateless too. Sad day." Lance snickered.

"Why exactly will I be out of a Beta?" Jace's voice echoed in the dark cell.

"What?" Lance asked, confused hearing his voice.

"I said why would I be out of a Beta?" Jace said, stepping down onto the concrete floor, his eyes locking with Lance's.

Anger and confusion flashed in front of Lance's eyes. He wasn't supposed to be there. Lance tensed up.

"Jace." Bruce announced, like it was a pleasant surprise.

"How?" Lance muttered with a frown.

"Why was I not alerted that you were questioning one of my pack members?" Jace said firmly, glancing at Sarah.

He studied her quickly making sure she was ok. She gave a quick nod seeing him assessing her to let him know she was fine.

"You were not on premises." Bruce said, taken back by his question.

"Per wolf law you are to alert the Alpha of the pack whenever interrogating a member of his pack. Furthermore it states that if you are questioning a female member of the pack you are to allow the Alpha present or another high ranking pack member." Jace said his tone was strong but not insulting.

Bruce was taken back, he was not sure what to say. Jace was right and he was testing them. If Bruce didn't acknowledge the law and went against it; Jace would have the right to challenge him and he was not ready for that. He didn't have his pack here, He didn't have the strength and power right now to fight him. This was supposed to happen at a later date. Lance was looking at Bruce dumb founded. He was waiting for Bruce to give him a say so.

"Well you are here now, we were just setting up. So shall we begin?" Bruce asked, trying to back pedal.

"No, the protocol has already been broken. You haven't even informed me why you are questioning her." Jace said standing his ground.

"Because we can." Lance growled.

That was the answer Jace was hoping for. He needed them to say that they were doing things to abuse their power. Bruce tensed up at Lance's answer grilling him from across the way. He knew that Lance had just fallen into Jace's trap. Jace was holding back a smile.

"Are you saying that you are abusing your power and rights as the Alpha council?" Jace asked politely.

Douglas smiled from the darkness. He caught Jace's eye and as Jace glanced at him he nodded letting him know that was a smart move. Bruce sighed frustrated.

"Let her go." Bruce muttered.

"What?" Lance said his voice barely a whisper as he was not sure if he heard Bruce right.

"I said fucking release her!" Bruce screamed.

Jace didn't even look at Bruce as he became upset. Jace kept his expression blank. He didn't want to give Bruce any chance to go back on his command. Lance growled at Sarah. He was angry and didn't bother putting the gloves on. He pulled the chains off her. The chains burned into his skin as he did. He didn't care, he was so angry. This was disrupting his plan. The longer it took to come up with some false information to accuse Jace with, the longer Nora was not his. The burning from the chain was a reminder to him of his own pain of not having what he wanted.

As he raked the chains off of Sarah, burning and pulling some of the skin off of her wrist Jace flinched trying not to react, his wolf angry for how Lance was doing it. Sarah remained still. She was a statue waiting to be released. Once the chains were off of her Lance slammed them on the ground. Lanced stomped his feet on the ground glaring at Jace and went to the back corner of the room, pouting like a child.

Jace went to Sarah and helped her slowly up. Jace could hear Lance grinding his teeth in annoyance. Sarah stood up slowly, blood dripping from her wrist. The place where the chain had been pulled off too hard. Jace helped her walk slowly to the stairs.

"Bruce, we can't let this happen." Lance sent through mind link.

"You should have kept your mouth shut." Bruce growled back through mind link.

"There's no way this is a loophole for them." Lance sent back angry.

Bruce was searching his brain trying to find something, a code, a law, a loophole where they could hold Sarah and question her but nothing was coming up. Jace was right they needed to inform him first and then invite him to the session before even attempting to question her. There was no way around it. Bruce bit his lip watching Jace walk Sarah slowly up the stairs. As the light shined down from the kitchen. Dante stepped into the doorway relieved to see Sarah. Jace moved behind Sarah helping her up the stairs and guiding her to Dante. Dante looked to Jace wondering how the hell he pulled this off.

Seeing Sarah, Dante was overwhelmed with relief. She was safe. Sarah had burns from where the chains were resting on her. There was blood but she was overall fine. Dante felt relaxed as he pulled Sarah into his arms. His hand cradled the back of her head as he kissed the top of her head.

"Thank you." Dante whispered to Jace, grateful.

Jace nodded his head to Dante and went to go finish walking up the stairs, leaving the council in the black hole they belonged in.

"Jace." Bruce's voice called up the stairs to him.

Jace paused, waiting for Bruce to continue talking. He knew by the way he said his name that it was not a question. It was something spiteful coming. He expected backlash but not this quickly.

"Jace Knight Alpha of the Cross River Pack. The Alpha Council summons you for a questioning session. We are here to find out information regarding the downfall of Alpha Kip of the Red Woods pack. We must inform you there is possible evidence of your involvement." Bruce's voice echoed up the stairs.

Dante stiffened his eyes going to Jace. Dante's eyes began to glow ready to fight for his Alpha if needed. He had formally requested his presence and informed him of why and since he was Alpha he did not need to tell anyone. Jace's beta was present.

"Alpha." Dante whispered looking at him, all he had to do was say the word and he would fight by his side.

Jace reached forward and squeezed his shoulder tightly.

"I Jace Knight Alpha of Cross River command that you, Dante Ortiz, Beta. Are now acting Alpha in my place. Until further notice, you will guide and manage the pack. If anything happens you are to take over my duties until I can or permanently." Jace said formally to Dante.

Dante swallowed hard not liking any of this. He knew it was what needed to be done when an Alpha was sent to questioning. Questioning could sometimes take days or go for however long the council saw fit. Sometimes the Alpha did not come back. Dante studied Jace, he would not allow Jace to be taken from them.

"I, Dante Ortiz, accept responsibility for the Cross River pack until you do return." Dante said to Jace letting him know that he was not leaving them.

Jace squeezed his shoulder and walked down into the darkness where the council was waiting for him.

Chapter Thirty Three
Pain

"*H*ave a seat." Lance snickered as Jace's feet hit the concrete floor of the basement.

Jace went to react. He wanted to grab Lance by the throat and squeeze the life out of him. He hated his smug attitude and he acted like a spoiled brat, ninety nine percent of the time. Jace walked over to the chair and sat down. He pushed the chains away from the chair, not reacting to the wolfsbane. Bruce raised an eyebrow at him. Lance smirked.

"No, not there." Lance chuckled.

"In that old tub." Lance finished after he laughed.

Jace looked back at the old metal claw foot tub in the room. He had never used it but he knew what it was for. You would submerge your victim in a bath of wolfsbane. It was worse than the chains drenched in it. Jace sighed standing. He shook his head slightly and walked over to the tub going to climb in.

"No strip first." Lance smirked.

Jace let out another sigh and kicked off his shoes. He pulled his shirt up over his head and then dropped his pants. He left his boxers on, he wasn't taking them off and they would just have to deal with that. He climbed into the old metal tub and waited. Lance sent out an order for the wolfsbane bath to be made and they were at a stand still for the moment. Lance kept eagerly looking over at Jace,

"What do you like what you see?" Jace cracked a smile as he leaned his head on the back of the tub.

He knew he was poking the bear but he didn't care. Lance growled at the comment. He hated Jace with a passion.

"You won't be so smart mouthed once the water comes in. Go ahead, have your moment." Lance said to him.

"Speaking of the water, I am more of a lukewarm type of person. If you could make sure they get the temperature right. You know, not too hot, not too cold." Jace said, his smile growing.

"What are you fucking Goldilocks?" Lance growled, gritting his teeth.

"Exactly see you get it. I knew you would! You're the smart one. Do I get bubbles or rose petals?" Jace continued making light of the situation.

"You're not going to have a tongue in a minute." Lance said growling, stepping forward.

"Lance, if we take out his tongue, how is he going to answer questions?" Bruce said, stopping Lace.

Lance growled angrily. He began fidgeting. He grabbed a knife off the interrogation table and was squeezing it in his hand. Bruce was watching Lance shake as Jace got the better of him.

"Lance he needs his tongue but he could use some wounds so that the wolfsbane settles into his blood better. Nothing too extravagant but go ahead." Bruce smiled.

"Douglas go help hold Jace still while Lance runs the knife over him." Bruce ordered.

Douglas grumbled like he was put out. He got up and walked over to Jace holding his shoulders . Lance walked slowly over to Jace as if he was enjoying every step he took. He twirled the knife in his hand as if he was trying to scare Jace.

"Lance hurry the fuck up. I have no time for the dramatics." Douglas growled.

Jace smirked at Douglas' comment which enraged Lance. Lance crossed to the tub quickly. He pushed the blade into his Jace's chest skiing downwards. Jace's skin peeling away from itself as the blade slid effortlessly down his center. Jace winced but didn't respond to it. Lance became angry, adding another long slice across his stomach. Jace shut his eyes and began to zone. Lance was becoming angry that Jace wasn't responding. He had a third slice from his collarbone down to his belly button. The sharp stinging burning sensation Jace tried blocking out.

"Lean forward." Lance order.

Jace waited for Douglas to let go and shifted forward trying to ignore the pain from the wounds. Lance began tracing the newly formed scars on Jace's back from him being whipped with the knife. Several long seconds Later he stepped away Jace's back covered in long slices. He tried hard to block out the pain, he knew Nora might feel it. He didn't need her feeling this.

Lance finished just as the water was being brought in. Several large pots were being carried in by Jace's pack members. Dante had grabbed a pot of water just so he could go down and check on Jace.

Nora knew Jace was gone the minute he left she could feel his panic but she couldn't reach him. She was confused by why he blocked her out. Asher walked with her back to the pack house. They had waited until the pack police showed up to take Chad and Clay away. They also waited for the cleaners to show up and take care of Roger's body.

"I'm sure he will let you know soon. He seemed rushed when he said he had to go. Some small problem, that's all. If it was something serious he would tell you." Asher said looking over at trying to reassure her.

"The last time he blocked me out the council ended up whipping him." Nora said growling slightly.

They walked into the pack house. Jacob had just finished up fixing Lilly and Matt was cradling her to his chest. Nora smiled seeing them. Jacob looked up at Nora and nodded to let her know everything was ok.

"Matt, feel free to use any rooms upstairs. I am sure Lilly wants to rest." Nora smiled at them.

"Thank you. I think that would be best." Matt said, kissing the top of Lilly's head.

"I think we should-

Nora started to say but a sharp sting burning pain running down her chest caught her off guard. She winced leaning forward on to the counter. Asher and Matt stopped looking at her. She shook her head saying she didn't know what that was. Then it happened again. She let out a small yelp leaning into the island. Her back began being attacked and she gripped the counter fighting through the pain.

"Nora?" Matt said concerned, he sat Lilly on a chair and quickly went by her side.

Asher was there grabbing a hold of her shoulder trying to steady her. She began to shake through the pain. Sweat beading across her forehead. The pain was quick, sharp. It stung.

"What's going on?" Matt asked, panicked.

"I don't know, it feels like my skin is being torn." Nora said, gripping the counter.

"Cole." Zara whimpered, feeling the pain as well.

Nora heard Zara's cry and knew that it wasn't her pain. She tried to talk but she couldnt it hurt too much. Matt lifted her shirt searching for wounds or marks. Maybe she had hurt herself in the process of everything at the alley. Asher was studying her face trying to figure out what was going on. Then it stopped. Nora let out a long breath and went to stand up. A rush of burning hot pain covered her body. It hit her hard and fast. It instantly blinded her and she collapsed onto the counter. The world went black for a moment as the pain was overwhelming. She sank downwards towards the floor. Matt and Asher went to her side catching her.

"What the fuck is going on!" Matt yelled.

Jacob rushed over and began assessing her while she was unconscious. He was confused nothing physically was wrong with her but her body was reacting like she was in severe pain. Suddenly a jolt went through the men. Matt, Asher and Jacob all jumped back as electricity zapped them. Nora's eyes flew open and she sat up gasping. Asher went to help her up.

"Don't touch me." Nora ordered.

Asher looked hurt but followed the order. Nora could feel the energy running wild under her skin. Her eyes glowing bright as she tried to get a hold of it.

"If you touch me I will hurt you. Not meaning to but my body is unsure of the threat right now." Nora explained quickly.

"What do you mean?" Asher asked, confused.

"I will explain another time." Nora said, getting to her feet.

The pain subsided but was still there. Nora knew the pain wasn't hers. It was Jace's. Her body, not understanding why she was in pain, was seeing everyone as a threat. She needed to get to Cross River. She needed to stop what was happening to Jace.

"What's going on?" Matt whispered looking at Nora.

"It's Jace. Someone's hurting him. It's his pain not mine." Nora explained quickly.

Matt growled hearing his Alpha was being hurt. He looked to Lilly torn between his mate and his duty. Nora saw him and his emotional dilemma. She smiled.

"Matt you stay. I will take care of whatever or whoever is daring to touch him." Nora said the wave of power coming from her made everyone in the room wince.

Matt, Asher and Jacob all bowed their heads in an automatic response to the power wave, trying to show submissiveness so it might not affect them. It could be painful fighting against an Alpha's aura but this was more than that.

"Someone needs to come with you." Asher said his head still bowed.

"You need to stay and take care of the pack. Matt, you need to take care of Lilly. The pack needs Jacob just in case. I am fine solo." Nora said, each word out of her mouth felt like a command.

"Luna, I can't let you go alone. You know Alpha would kill me." Matt said quietly.

"What's going on? Woah what's the deal with the energy in here?" Logan announced walking in the room.

"Dude Nora you look like a christmas tree. What's up with you?" Logan asked, concerned going to her.

"Logan dont touch me right now, the whole power thing is going haywire. " Nora told him quickly knowing Logan would understand.

"Gotcha so why are you on overdrive?" Logan asked quickly.

"Someone is torturing Jace. I need to get back to Cross River now." Nora said, beginning to walk to the door.

Logan looked at Lilly, she mouthed the word go to Logan and nodded that she was fine. Logan looked to Matt who looked like he was struggling and torn between Lilly and Nora.

"I'll go with you. If he's got my sister. Then I got your back." Logan said the following after Nora.

"Asher, I am sorry but I have to go. I know I promised to stay but Jace-

"Nora I'm sorry about earlier. You don't need to be. Go. Go save your mate." Asher said to her with a noded.

"I will be back soon. I have no clue what I am walking into or what I'm about to do, be on stand by just in case." Nora said to Asher but looked over at the men in the kitchen.

"I will put a call into our hunters. We will back you if needed." Lilly said her tone was strong and firm.

"I will reach out and let Dante know you're coming." Matt said quietly.

"No, don't. If he knows something they might hurt him too. I wanna surprise them." Nora said.

"Them?" Logan asked, confused.

"The council. I will explain on the way. Your car here?" Nora asked.

"Of course.' Logan said following Nora out of the kitchen.

"Good you'll need something fast to meet me there." Nora said as she got to the pack house door.

"Meet you?" Logan said, confused.

"Yup see you at Cross River…hunter boy." Nora smirked as she stepped out the door, her feet hit the gravel walkway.

She shut her eyes and shifted quickly. Logan took a step back as a light blinded him. Where Nora was standing was a white wolf with gold highlights through her fur. It wasn't gold per se but like sunlight had kissed the tops of her fur. The wolf's eyes were the color of embers from a fire. This wolf was different and had its own glow about her.

"Nora?" Logan said, taken back by the way this wolf looked.

The wolf nodded to him before taking off. Logan watched the wolf sprint to the forest. Logan snapped out of his awe and bolted for his car.

Chapter Thirty Four
Surprise

The water hit Jace's wounds as it began being poured into the tub. The water hitting his open wounds caused him to grab the sides of the tub and grit his teeth. The water was like pure fire as it slowly began to encompass his body. He shut his eyes trying to push the pain away. He had to focus on anything else. He was terrified that Nora might feel what he was feeling.

Nora. His mind began to flood with images of her. Looking across the night club his eyes landing on her immediately knew what she was and what he had to do. The way she was dancing and moving like she was lost in the song playing. The first night they were ever intimate, him chasing after her as she laughed trying to hide from him. The pain disappeared. He leaned his back on the back of the tub zoning out on memories.

The tub was filled up to his chest. He felt chains being locked around his wrist. The chain was then looped under the tub. They then attached it to his opposite wrist. He was now locked in the tub. Jace didn't even flinch or move when the chains clasped around his wrists.

"First question. What is your name?" Bruce said moving forward out of the darkness.

Jace smirked, he hated questioning. They always start with basic questions to ensure you're following directions and can set up a baseline..

"My name is Jace Knight, Alpha of the Cross River Pack." Jace answered,

"Good." Bruce said shifting as if he was trying to decide the next step.

"I like long walks on the beach, star gazing, and home cooked meals." Jace added a cocky smile on his face.

Douglas cracked a smile trying not to laugh. Lance growled, grabbing a hold of the knife he used to slice his skin. He walked to the tub, anger and excitement oozing from him. He took the knife and ran down Jace's exposed arm. Jace didn't move, did not respond. Lance moved back triumphant like he had shown Jace.

"I don't know what's wrong with your hearing. I said long walks on the beach, not knife slices on my arm. I don't know what shit you're into but I'm good thanks." Jace said not moving a muscle.

Douglas coughed to cover up his laughter. He had never been in a questioning before where someone was bold like this. They normally try to please the council so the torture would be over quickly.

"I will cut out your tongue!" Lance yelled, stepping towards him.

"Lance! We need his tongue where it is." Bruce yelled at Lance.

"Well he needs-

"What he doesn't need is fingers." Bruce grinned.

Zara raced through the woods, hunks of dirt kicking up as they were tossed behind her. Her eyes focused as they raced home. She felt an overwhelming burning feeling and had to push it from her mind so it didn't affect her. She had to get to Jace.

Zara I know you are strong but I think I need to handle this in human form first. Then shift to you if needed. Nora told her as they weaved in and out of passing trees.

What. No, I'm ripping their throats out. Zara growled, spotting the wall that blocked Cross River from the rest of the world.

Zara with the way I'm feeling right now, my powers will do us good. Let me go first. I swear to you if you can't handle it, I will let you take over. Nora said back to her.

Zara was quiet for several seconds. They reached the wall. Zara stepped back and pushed off the ground. Her paws ran across the cement wall as she scaled it. They landed neatly on the other side. An alarm was tripped as they touched the top of the wall, a siren going off warning the pack that a breach in the perimeter was made. Zara didn't even respond to the noise. She could see the pack house and was bolting to it.

Fine, you go first. Zara said as she hit the driveway pavement of the pack house.

Thank you. Nora said to her, she wanted them to be a team not a power struggle.

Zara stopped at the door and pulled away allowing Nora the energy to push forward for the shift. Zara bowed her head and then transformation began. Nora's bones popped in and out of place. They both urged the shift to happen quicker than normal. A few seconds later a very naked and glowing Nora stood where the white wolf was. Nora walked up the stairs of the pack house as Logan's black car pulled into the driveway.

"Do you feel that?" Bruce asked suddenly.

Lance was looking over all the tools he could possibly use to cut off Jace's fingers. He was dabbling with a guillotine looking tool when it hit him in a wave. The power. Someone with immense power had come.

"I feel it." Douglas whispered, unsure of what it meant.

"Who has power like that?" Lance whispered.

Jace tried sitting up but he was strapped down. He knew somewhere deep in his gut it was Nora. He was worried. He had felt her power before and it was crippling strong. It had drained her the last time she was using it this strongly. He was afraid of what it would do to her and lastly the council was about to find out how strong his mate was.

A blinding light came from the top of the stairs and it began to light up the darkness in the room. Lance, Bruce, and Douglas shielded their eyes as the room filled with light. When the light settled. Nora was standing in the basement. The power radiating off of her made them want to buckle to their knees. They fought hard against it. Nora's eyes were glowing the brightest they had ever seen. They were the color of embers from a fire. Jace shifted in the tub trying to see her.

Anger rushed over her as she saw her mate, bloody and submerged in water. She knew from the pain she felt the tub was laced with wolfsbane. Denying Jace the ability to heal or have access to his wolf.

"Release him." Nora commanded.

The command sent out into the room made each man shift forward involuntarily to go do what she had ordered. They fought against it. They all shifted away from her trying to get away from the overwhelming feeling she was giving off. They fought hard against the urge to fall to their knees, bow their head, and submit.

Nora growled that no one listened and moved to the tub. She grabbed a hold of the chains, the wolfsbane stung but didn't seem to affect her. With one quick motion she pulled gently and the chains came off.

"How dare you go against the order of the council." Lance yelled and stepped towards her.

His hand reached for her to pull her away from the tub. Her body sensed the threat coming. As soon as Lance's hand grazed her skin, a jolt of energy was sent out. It poured into Lance sending him flying across the room like he had been struck by lightning. He hit the wall and slid down to the floor. He whimpered curling into himself the pain coursing through him like electricity. Bruce's mouth dropped open as he couldn't believe his eyes. Nora didn't even move. She glanced at the stairs hearing footsteps and knew it was Logan. Logan rushed down the stairs, blade in hand ready to fight.

"Woah! Nora, you're glowing." Logan announced when he realized everyone was back away into corners and there was no fighting going on.

"A hunter! You dare bring a hunter. Wolf laws say all hunters are to be exterminated like the pest they are." Bruce yelled, sending out his aura trying to overpower Nora.

"He's my friend. And no one will touch him." Nora announced.

She felt Bruce's aura. It was annoying like a mosquito buzzing around trying to get attention before it bit you. She waved her hand and pushed it away. She didn't know that was possible but it felt like she could do it, so she did. Amazingly it worked.

"Logan, can you help me get Jace out of the tub?" Nora said, walking the rest of the way to the tub.

Logan nodded and got to the other side of the tub. Nora grasped Jace's bloody forearm and Logan grabbed the other. They nodded to each other and pulled him out. The wolfsbane didn't even affect Nora.

The council had been waiting to see how she would react touching it. The fact that she didn't even whimper amazed them.

"You never thought I would be your knight in shining armor uh?" Logan said to Jace as he draped Jace's arm across his shoulder helping him steady.

Jace just smiled for once he was thankful for Logan and Nora's relationship. Nora stepped away from Jace and locked her eyes on Bruce. She stepped forward standing tall.

"You and your council are leaving my lands tonight. I say lands just in case you think about going to Red Woods. Get out of this basement and leave now." Nora gave orders. The force of the power she sent out with the command, made Bruce's head buckle into submission for a second.

"You have no right to tell-

"I do not care. Get out or I will let my wolf out and she will rip your throats out." Nora threatens him.

"Are you threatening the Council? Do you not understand? Little girl you are about to start a war." Bruce said, standing up tall and threatening her.

"I'm not threatening. I am making promises. Stay and find out if they are real." Nora growled.

Douglas was the first to move. He moved past Bruce, Bruce looking betrayed as he did. He didn't want any part of this. The power Nora was sending out was starting to make him feel sick.

"Douglas!" Bruce yelled, as he watched Douglas go up the stairs.

Bruce locked eyes with Nora fire burning in them but then it died out. He sighed exhausted from trying to match her. He glanced at Lance who was still on the ground. He walked over to him, grabbing him by the arm and yanking him up. Lance let out a small noise as he did.

"This isn't over. What you have just done here you will regret full force." Bruce announced as he got to the stairs.

"No I won't." Nora growled.

Bruce tried staring her down one last time. Nora shut her eyes channeling everything she had and sent it out into the room. The wave made Lance fall into the stairs and caused Bruce to grip the railing trying to not fall over.

"You have fifteen minutes to get off my territory." Nora growled.

Bruce shoved Lance up the stairs as they both hurried out. Nora felt them shift into their wolfs forms as if they needed to escape quicker. She listened to them. Everything about her was more intense. She could hear them run through the house, out the door and head towards the woods.

Chapter Thirty Five
Saved

Nora was on high alert as she waited to see if they were coming back. She felt stronger and more intense. Her body vibrated with her power. After several seconds she looked over to Jace. He was struggling trying to get out of the tub. The large chains weighed him down. Nora rushed to Jace's side. She reached to grab the chains and Jace tried moving away from her. She looked confused and then decided She was going to pull him out of the water. She watched him flinch as she came near, again. What was going on?

"Jace?" Nora asked quietly.

"Cut the chains, don't touch the water and do your best not to touch the chain. It's all drenched in wolfsbane." Jace said slowly trying to talk through the pain.

"What can I do to help?" Logan asked, waiting to be some type of help.

Jace shook his head to Logan as he struggled to keep himself calm. Logan came behind Jace and wrapped his arms around him. Pulling him slightly up out of the water. Trying to keep as much of Jace's body out of the poison.

"I don't need help." Jace grumbled feeling a little relief from having some part of himself out of the water.

"I'm not helping you." Logan smirked.

Jace didn't have the strength or energy to fight him. Nora frowned, looking around the dark room there was nothing she could use to cut the chains. She searched the small rolling table still finding nothing big enough. She needed bolt cutters. Dante, she thought.

"Dante, I need bolt cutters." She mindlinked him.

"Ok what's going on? Where are you?" Dante asked back quickly.

"In the basement I need them to free Jace in a hurry." Nora sent it to him quickly.

She looked over at the tub, she could just drain the water. She could deal with the pain for a second. She walked over to the tub straining to see where the drain was. Jace had his eyes shut and his head tilted back as he was trying to not focus on the burning pain running through his body. He had sweat beads across his forehead.

"Dante's going to bring bolt cutters." Nora told him, as she got closer to the tub.

Jace managed a nod but still had his eyes shut. Nora peered into the tub, she could see the plug at the foot end of the tub. The stoppers chain was removed making it harder to pull. She gritted her teeth taking a deep breath in. She glanced at Jace to make sure he still wasn't looking. He would be angry if he knew what she was about to do.

Do it. Zara said in her mind.

Nora felt strength from her wolf pour into herself. It wasn't like the strength already resonating inside of her. She at that moment didn't realize that she had more than one energy in her. She thought it all came from the same place but until that moment she realized she had never pulled on her wolf before. It was all from her hunter side. She gritted her teeth and plunged her hand into the water. Acid, acid was the only thing she could think of to describe it. It felt like her flesh was going to peel from her bones. She braced herself on the side of the tub as her fingers painfully grazed the stopper.

"Nora." Jace attempted a growl.

He felt the pain from her and opened his eyes slowly. He gritted his teeth seeing her reaching into the water. He tried to sit up but the longer he was in the wolfsbane the weaker he had got. He pulled on the chains trying to get free to stop Nora from hurting herself.

"Woah Nora! Let me help." Logan said his arms still wrapped around Jace trying to hold him up out of the water the best he could.

"Just hold him." Nora said through gritted teeth.

Nora finally managed to pull the stopper out of the tub pulling her hand out of the water as quickly as she could. She grabbed her hand with her other hand. The water stung as her hand touched her injured one. The water quickly drained out of the tub and into a drain in the floor.

"Nora, what the hell were you thinking?' Jace growled as the water disappeared he could feel his strength slowly coming back.

Nora didn't say anything she was looking at the chains still keeping Jace in the tub. She had an idea. She needed to be careful not to hurt Jace. She closed her eyes pulling on her hunter side, she felt the normal tingle and energy begin to surge.

Zara, do you think you can help? Nora asked her as she stepped towards the chains.

"Nora, what the hell are you thinking? The chains are lace in wolfsbane as well stop hurting yourself." Jace growled.

"Shh." Nora said, shutting her eyes trying to reach Zara.

Zara was weak from earlier the wolfsbane had poisoned her and she could feel her exhaustion. Suddenly the same strength came to her. Zara didn't respond but she felt there with her. Nora opened her eyes and grabbed ahold of the chain. It burned, her eyes glowed intensely as she pulled and twisted the chain. A loud crack was heard as the chain snapped. Nora dropped the chain from her hands and stepped back feeling weak as Zara slipped away from the forefront. The chains were broken from the tub, put still wrapped around Jace and attached to his wrist.

Jace looked surprised as he chain fell away. He was amazed that Nora was able to do that. She stumbled back a little bit. Jace waited a few seconds letting some more of his strength come back before he could lift the chains off himself. Logan helped lift the last bit of chain off of Jace, before Jace shrugged his grip off of him. Logan dropped his hands away from him and held them up defensively. He gripped the sides of the tub trying to pull himself out. Nora was there at his side in seconds. She looped her arms under his arms.

"Nora the water is still on me, it's going to hurt you." Jace said anger still in his voice.

Nora ignored him and helped lift him out of the tub. His flesh touching hers felt like acid. She pulled him out of the tub and they collapsed backwards onto the cement ground. Jace landed on top of her. He quickly rolled off of her, breathing hard. Nora winced, waiting for the pain to stop. She stood as soon as she could. She grabbed a metal bucket that was on the ground and went over to the sink. She filled the bucket up with water. She walked slowly over Jace. He was laying with his back on the ground, his eyes shut, his breathing starting to resume back to normal. Nora dumped the water over him.

"Hell Nora." He yelled as the cold water hit him.

"We have to rinse the wolfsbane off you." Nora said quietly her skin still hurting as she walked back over to the sink and started filling the bucket again.

"Could you not make it freeze?" Jace smirked, starting to feel better.

Nora smiled carrying another bucket filled with water over to Jace. He shut his eyes as she dumped the water over him once more. His skin finally felt better and like it was not on fire. The sounds of footsteps rushing down the stairs echoed in the darkness. Nora turned ready to fight.

"Dante." Jace whispered knowing right away it was him.

"Nora!" Dante yelled coming down the stairs holding the bolt cutters.

Spotting her he raced over almost slipping on the water. He held the bolt cutters out to her. A confused look on his face.

"Why did you need bolt cutters? The council left?" Dante asked one question after another.

"Jace was in a wolfsbane bath and chained to it. I broke the chains and scared off the council." Nora said quickly, her eyes looking over Jace.

She frowned seeing the long thin cuts across his body. He wasn't healing that part of him would be the last to restore after something like that. Nora kneeled next to him, she put her hand out wondering if she could do what she did last time. Give him some energy to speed up the healing process.

"Nora! Don't you dare touch me," Jace ordered while sitting up.

"But-" Nora started to protest but Jace held up his hand.

"You already drained yourself of doing everything that you just did. I can feel how exhausted you are. We need to get out of this basement. You might not feel it but you need to get the wolfsbane off of you as well." Jace said quietly.

"How did she run off the council?" Dante asked in a whisper.

"Tell me you didn't feel the power surge going on?" Jace sighed.

"That power was Nora? I thought it was all three of the council mixed with your aura." Dante said in disbelief.

"Nope." Jace said with a half smile on his face.

"Shit Nora." Dante whispered.

"Logan?" Dante said, looking at him.

"Howdy." Logan smirked, nodding his head at Dante.

"Come let's get out of here." Nora said quietly as she ignored the sting for the wolfsbane still on her skin.

She started on the stairs, Jace, Logan, and Dante walking behind her. She wanted a shower and a nap. She got to the landing waiting for Dante and Jace. She could hear them whispering in the shadows.

"We need to prepare for a war. The council isnt going to take being threatened and chased out lightly. They will come back with numbers to make an example out of us." Jace said to Dante.

"I can't believe she has that much power. I thought I was just confused by the power surge. She is stronger than the council." Dante whispered back.

"I know and now the council knows. It worries me. All I know is they will want her. To keep or kill her I don't know." Jace said quietly.

"They can try." Nora said from the top of the stairs, she was leaning against the door jam.

Jace smirked hearing her response.

"You don't hurt people I love." She added with a smile.

Chapter Thirty Six
War

    Nora stepped away from the doorway and a rush of fear went through her. She was worried about the consequences of what just happened. She needed to let Asher know. Logan stood just off the way from the kitchen looking at her strangely.

    "Asher something happened, I need the pack to be put on lock down." Nora sent to him

    "What happened?" Asher sent back.

    "I chased off and threatened the council when I found them torturing Jace. They had originally tried torturing Sarah. They called it questioning." Nora explained.

    "That power surge….was that you?" Asher asked, he had felt it miles away.

    "I think so. I kind of went a little extra glowy this time." Nora said quietly.

    "Damn. So war is coming. Don't worry, I'll keep this pack safe." Asher sent back.

    "Have Lilly and Matt stay there, it's not safe for them to be moving right now." Nora sent back.

    "Will do Alpha….be safe." Asher sent back.

    "You too." Nora replied.

    She glanced at Logan who was still staring at her. She gave him a look wanting him to explain. He let out the breath he was holding and then opened his mouth to talk. Nothing came out at first and she watched him try again.

    "What the hell was that? I went to follow you down and I was literally thrown back by some invisible force. I don't know how anyone could have stood near you for long. Whatever you were radiating was insane." Logan said, trying to process.

"I found a way to tap into something and now I feel like a bomb from the way everyone keeps looking and saying things about the force or power I was giving off." Nora sighed, feeling awkward.

"It's fine we will figure this out. Logan, you need to stay here tonight. We just declared war." Jace said shortly after coming out of the basement, his body was still shaking from recovering from the wolfsbane poison.

"Ok…regroup in the morning? You look like hell." Logan said, looking Jace and his wounds over.

"Yes, let's regroup in the morning. Thanks." Jace smirked at Logan's comment.

Logan nodded and began to make his way through the pack house heading to the stairs. He had no clue what he had just felt but all he knew was he had never felt anything like that. He was worried. Worried for Nora and then worried for hunters. Nora was an ally but what if things ever went south. Shut up, he told himself as he began to climb the stairs. Nora is your friend. He reiterated to himself.

They ran hard and fast through the woods. Bruce's wolf in the lead trying to put enough distance between him and her. The power flowing off of her instantly made him sick. The others didn't feel that way but maybe she could control how people felt around her. Bruce had instantly felt his stomach twist and turn when she walked in. Lance was too caught up in being excited seeing her and then had felt pain. Douglas needed away from her the overwhelming need to submit coursed through him. Three wolves raced off into the woods not speaking to one another. They got to the safe cabin within the hour. Bruce shifted in front of the cabin into his human form. He punched open the door and it swung open as he stepped inside. He let out a loud growl as he walked into the center of the cabin. Douglas was the next to shift and he walked to the far corner. His mind raced as he was trying to process everything.

"What the fuck was that? How did she do that?" Lance asked loudly as he stumbled into the cabin.

"How the fuck do I know! Do you think I would have ran if I knew the answer to either of those questions!" Bruce screamed.

"Do you think it's because she's an Alpha and a Luna? There's a double strength there." Douglas said, trying to process.

"I don't know…could be. But she shouldn't be that powerful. I know Luna's draw on their mates authority and Jace is powerful. He comes from a long line of powerful Alphas. Even dating back to the originals but he still doesn't have power like that. He would if he had joined us when we asked but it wouldn't have been to that extent." Bruce was rambling on at this point trying to think things through as he talked out loud.

'She is still mine." Lance announced, as if that was somehow possible.

Bruce narrowed his eyes at Lance. He crossed to him grabbing him quickly by the neck. He squeezed Lance up against the wall. Lance narrowed his eyes on him. He was tired of Bruce thinking he was better than anyone. He was not above him. Douglas and Lance had let him run the show because they didn't care for it. But he was not the leader. They were all equal. Lance captured Bruce's neck with his own hand squeezing back. A look of shock went across Bruce's face. He was stunned that Lance would challenge him.

"You forget Bruce we are all equals. You are not above me. If you touch me you better be ready for me to fight back." Lance growled.

Bruce didn't respond but locked eyes with him, his eyes glowing. In return Lance's eyes began to glow and he let his canines fall down. He smirked looking at Bruce deadly.

"Just say when Brucey." Lance dared him.

"That's enough. I am going home. I am getting my troops ready. Securing my pack and will be in touch. You two can stay here and tear each other apart over a girl who most likely could kill you both in an instant. If her powers are that strong. But I am going home to prepare for war. If you didn't realize that's what's coming." Douglas said, walking to the door.

He watched the realization hit Bruce and Lance before he stepped out into the cool night air. He glanced up at the stars looking for the moon. He needed guidance for the longest time he had been sitting idly by while those two clowns ran the show. It was time all of that stopped. He needed to connect with Jace and not get himself killed.

"*I* don't know Jace, I'm torn." Nora said loudly pacing around his office.

She thought about letting Asher just become Alpha now. If she could step back from Red Wood maybe the council would not attack them. She also thought they would just because and she also needed the numbers if this really meant war.

"Tell me what you're thinking." Jace said trying to get comfortable on the red couch in his office.

Nora had kept him up all night. The sudden realization that they were in danger set in and now she was trying to solve the world's problems overnight. Dante was already passed out in a chair across the way.

"You said they each have an army." Nora said again for the tenth time.

"Yes, love." Jace said quietly, closing his eyes.

"Technically we have two if we lump Red Woods and I am sure the hunters would help if needed to but I don't know." Nora said, slumping down on to the desk.

She was torn, she didn't know how to help. They were in this mess right now because of her. The council would be coming for her and she just wanted to make sure no one else got hurt. She needed to solve them. She laid her head down groaning. Jace got up and sighed. He walked over her, a small smirk on his lip. He scooped her up into his arms and pulled her against him. She sighed happily against him.

"I will contact Zeke and Chadwick. You don't realize how much of an impact you have made. You saved the Black Sands pack, freed the Red Woods. The hunters are growing because you built a bond between the wolf packs in the area with them. You are mated to one of the fiercest Alphas in the land. And you are incredible. You have some type of insane strength and gifts in you. We will be ok." Jace whispered to her.

She bit her lip. She wasn't worried about her. She was worried about them, the wolves, the hunters, the packs. Everyone but her. Jace sat there saying she was a gift but she felt like the only gift she brought anyone was chaos and death. She would find a way to save them without anyone getting hurt. Even if that meant she went to the council alone.

"Hey, what are you thinking in there?" Jace asked, feeling all sorts of emotions rushing off of her.

“Nothing and everything.” Nora sighed.

“Come on, after everything you're exhausted. The packs are on high alert, we will be ok for tonight. Bruce is going to need to regroup and then gather his armies before they can actually attack. We will know when they start making moves.” Jace said, rubbing her arm softly.

“All right.” Nora said softly, she enclosed her fingers around his hand and he led her out of the office.

Nora paused in the doorway and looked at Dante. She reached down and poked him gently. He jumped up looking around his eyes glowing slightly. He was on high alert since everything went down.

“Go check on Sarah and spend time with her.” Nora said quietly.

“Did we decide anything?” Dante yawned.

“No, not yet..” Nora sighed, tapping his shoulder before heading out.

“It will be ok.” Jace said to them both walking out the door.

It will be ok. We will make sure of it. Cole said to him, his voice holding promises that Jace already knew. They would take on armies for her. Walk through hell to make it ok.

Chapter Thirty Seven
Crumble

*D*ouglas crossed the border into his land. He took a deep breath, the smell of pine wrapping around him. The temperature was slightly colder than the surrounding areas. He let out the breath he took in. He was happy to be home. He walked down the pebble path towards the lodge looking pack house. He made it through the gate and passed their border. No alert, no siren nothing. They were not used to being worried about any threat. Their Alpha was a council member. No one dared to come on their land uninvited. Walking into the hall of the pack house there was silence. The pack house felt almost like a resort in the mountains. Very rustic and woodsy, He knew it was late but was surprised no one was up and about. He went to his office and sat down in his chair in front of the fireplace.

"Samuel."He mind linked his beta.

There was no response, Douglas realized he had to be sleeping. He leaned back, shutting his eyes, sleep creeping up on him. He shook his head trying to shake it away as a yawn escaped his lips. It was now setting in how easily they could be attacked.

"Samuel!" He summoned him again through mind link, this time louder and with more force.

"Alpha, are you ok?" Samuel replied sleepily but with concern.

"Yes, office now." Douglas replied.

Moments later a tall sandy-haired man walked into the office. He was in boxers and t-shirt when he walked in rubbing his dark forest colored eyes. He let out a yawn before sinking into a chair opposite of Douglas.

"We are going to war." Douglas announced as Samuel sat.

"War?" Samuel yawned again.

"Yes." Douglas replied shortly.

"Who is the council wanting to destroy this time?" Samuel said not one ounce of concern in his voice.

"The Cross River Pack." Douglas frowned.

"Jace Knight's pack, the Cross River? Why would they want to make him an enemy? He is one of the stronger Alphas, if not the strongest. This will not be their normal go in attack and pack up by lunch time." Samuel groaned.

"This will be an actual war." Samuel added becoming more awake as he took in the information.

"We are not backing the Council." Douglas said almost cautiously, announcing his secret finally.

"We're not?" Samuel said, surprised.

"No Bruce and Lance need to be taken down. For years I sat by as those play boys did what they wanted to better themselves and not wolf kind. I'm done with it. Seeing Jace and how strong his pack is. He and his Luna will be the one to end them. I will be backing him." Douglas said grimly.

He watched different emotions pass over Samuel's face. Shock, worry, fear, and then excitement. Samuel sat up a little straighter and smiled.

"It's about damn time." Samuel said with a grin.

"I need you to go to Jace's pack as quickly as possible. I need to send you so they know I am truthful. If I send my beta it means that I am committed. We need to start preparing. Have Dalton start prepping for war. Do not say anything to anyone yet about this conversation. I also need you to leave tonight to go. Bruce and Lance are still too wrapped up in themselves right now to be paying attention to us." Douglas explained.

"Gotcha, I will be back by nightfall." Samuel said, standing with a nod and walking out of the office quickly.

Samuel paused in the doorway looking over his shoulder to Douglas. " This is going to be the most important fight The Silver Mountain pack has ever been in. We are finally standing for something."

"It will be. Maybe things will finally start being the way they were intended to be." Douglas said with a nod.

Douglas smiled; he hadn't even told Samuel to go yet and he was already to leave. He had hated the council for years. For years Douglas had been promising him that they would recede from the council. Samuel was excited to finally be doing it. Their pack, the Silver Mountain had always prided themselves on doing what was right. They had gotten away from that over the years and it was time to get it back. Samuel nodded to Douglas as he ducked out the door.

Bruce squared off with Lance as they both released each other and backed away. Tension was high as they glared at each other. Bruce was shaking slightly as Lance's chest rose and fell rapidly matching the beating of his heart in his chest. He was fighting the urge to shift and rip Bruce apart.

"So What you think because you're Bruce McHenry Alpha of the City Lights pack with all your fancy shit you deserve the girl." Lance growled tensing up as he spoke.

All the muscles in Bruce flexed immediately as Lance dared to speak to him in such a manner. He let a low growl rumble through his chest, letting him know he was unhappy. Lance smirked in response, still not backing down.

"Oh and what the Dark Water pack deserves her? Lance, you deserve her? You're an entitled brat whose daddy paved the way for him. You have never done anything by yourself or for anyone else. You do not deserve anything." Bruce growled.

"I do deserve her!" Lance growled, all of the muscles in his arms and chest flexing.

Lance felt his fangs come down as he began to almost twitch from not attacking Bruce. Bruce stood quietly calming himself, he wanted Lance to explode. Bruce grinned at him.

"You deserve nothing. You are worthless." Bruce whispered.

At that moment Lance lunged at him going for his throat. Bruce saw him coming and wanted him to. Bruce dodged the attack and countered it. He forced his wolf claws to come out. As Lance lunged at him he shoved them into Lance's chest as he attacked. Lance winced at the pain but the pain didn't stop him. He continued moving closer to Bruce. Bruce's eyes widened in surprise. He had expected Lance to back down, to be in pain. Lance drew his claws as he continued forward. Bruce's knuckles now pressed against his chest. Bruce's claws sticking out the back of Lance. Bruce felt the cabin wall hit his back. He didn't realize he had been backing away from Lance. Bruce tried pulling his own claws out of Lance but Lance was too close, he had no way of retreating. He struggled pulling on his hand trying to release his claws so he could get space between them.

Lance grinned watching Bruce panic. He winked at Bruce and then slowly pressed his claws into Bruce's stomach. Bruce let out a small yell of pain as he felt them puncture his abdomen. Bruce's free hand went to try to stop Lance from pushing them further into his stomach. Lance smirked watching Bruce make a poor decision. Lance acted quickly and plunged his free hand's claws into Bruce's throat. Bruce's eyes widened as he quickly realized his error. Bruce gripped Lance by the arm as his eyes started to roll back into his head. Blood seeping out around Lance's claws.

"You're right, I only do what's good for me. You should have stayed good for me." Lance said as he pushed his claws sideways and out of Bruce's neck.

Blood poured down over Lance's hand and Bruce's body. Bruce's body slumped downwards pulling Lance with him, as his claws were still inside of Lance's chest. Lance grabbed ahold of Bruce's hand and yanked it away from him. He then stepped backwards letting Bruce's body slump to the floor. Blood puddles surrounded Bruce's body as it emptied itself. Lance smirked, holding his chest. As Bruce died a rush of power went into Lance. He shut his eyes, enjoying the feeling. He had just become the Alpha of City Lights and Dark Water. He dared someone to keep her from him now.

He opened his eyes. The bright glowing of fluorescent purple radiated out of his eyes. He kicked Bruce's body away. He began walking to the cabin door. He smiled and sent a message to his beta.

"Dalton, we are upgrading. Get the pack ready for war. I will be home soon." Lance snickered through the mind link.

"Alpha, your aura feels strange? Are you ok?" Dalton was sent back concerned.

"That's because I am an Alpha of two packs and soon to be Alpha of all Alphas. We will dominate them all shortly. I am more than ok." Lance chuckled.

"Of Two packs?" Dalton asked, confused.

"I killed Bruce. Prepare the pack we are going to war!" Lance sent back excited.

"With who, Alpha? Douglas?" Dalton asked, a little worried.

"Cross River and if Douglas dares stand in our way and not join us. We will destroy him as well." Lance said fiercely.

"Jace's pack? That Cross River?" Dalton said letting the worry slip through.

"Stop asking questions and get to doing what I said." Lance ordered.

"Yes Alpha, Sorry Alpha." Dalton said quickly back.

"Also we will need to prepare the pack for my Luna. She will be coming back with me. She needs the best of everything. Make sure her room is done up. Have the girls get it ready." Lance smiled.

Dalton wanted to ask him who his Luna was and what he meant but he didn't want to push his luck. He bowed his head even though they were mind linking.

"Yes Alpha." Dalton said quietly.

Chapter Thirty Eight
Guarded

Dante walked sleepy and sluggish down the hall. The thoughts of war in his mind. He had been there before. He wouldn't have second guessed it and he didn't this time. He just wanted to know when they were going to be able to not be constantly defending themselves. He paused at his door. Sarah. She was hurt from being in wolfsbane cuffs but she didn't act like anything happened. He felt a spark of anger. Some horrible things had happened to her. He took a deep breath trying to push those thoughts away as he walked into their room. Sarah was curled up in his bed sleeping. The blanket wrapped around her midsection, her leg draped over it showing her bottom off just slightly. He smiled softly and walked over to the bed. He pulled his shirt up over his head and then unbuttoned his jeans, letting them slide off of him. Stepping out of them he went to get into the bed, that's when he noticed. Sarah's breathing had increased, she was flinching and whimpering in her sleep.

"No! Stop! leave her alone. I did it." Sarah mumbled and then winced like something had hit her.

She let out a small yell and then whimpered. Her body began twitching. Dante scooted into bed and pulled her into his arms. She began fighting, swinging, scratching and clawing. Her fingernails dug into his arms as she opened her eyes. Her canines descended as she went to sink her teeth into her attacker.

"Sarah." Dante said, trying to get her attention before she sank her teeth into him.

His voice hit her and she froze. Her vision came to focus and she realized it was Dante who had her and she was no longer in the basement locked away at Red Woods. Dante released his hold on her and kissed her forehead. A rush of relief rushed over Sarah followed by guilt, as she looked at the claw marks he had on his shoulders and forearms. She frowned deeply looking at his expression. He didn't look hurt or worried, he looked at her with concern and it filled his eyes. He was hurt but hurt for her. What had she gone through all these years?

"Dante, I am so, so sorry. I ..I thought I -

"Sarah, it's ok. What was all that?" Dante asked, pressing his lips once again to her forehead.

"Nightmares." Sarah said shortly.

"Nightmares? " Dante asked quietly, he knew them all too well. He wanted to know what hers were.

"Red Woods was terrible for women. I have nightmares from it all. It's fine. I am strong and will be fine." Sarah said dismissing it.

"Sarah it is not fine and it's not a matter of being strong." Dante said softly.

"It's ok." Sarah said, pulling back from him.

"It's not. Sarah that was trauma. That wasn't just, oh I got in trouble alot like you've said to me in the past, when I've brought up the little whimpers you make in your sleep." Dante said, trying not to sound angry.

"It doesn't matter. Things happened. I don't need you looking at me like..like that." Sarah said, waving her arm at him.

"It does matter and looking at you like what? Concerned?" Dante said, trying to keep his voice from being upset.

"Like I'm broken." Sarah yelled as she got up.

Warm tears pressed against her eyes, wanting to escape. She felt her chest tighten, she didn't want him to know. She didn't want him to think less of her. She didn't want to think about those things. She started towards the door.

"Sarah!" Dante yelled to her and started to go after her.

"Dante, I need some air. Please." Sarah said not looking back at him as tears slipped out of her eyes, her voice shook a little.

Dante's gut tightened and he resisted the urge to pull her into a hug. To hold her, kiss her and tell her how perfect she was. He gritted his teeth, and didn't say anything. If he opened his mouth he was afraid the wrong words would fall out and he might push her away. She waited by the door for a few seconds and then she walked out of it. Dante watched her disappear as the door closed. He sunk down on the bed trying to figure out how he could help her.

He waited several minutes before going to look for her. He wandered through the pack house and down the stairs. Walking out towards the kitchen he found her sitting just by the back door. The door wide open, her knees curled up to her chest with her hands wrapped around them. She was shaking off and on. Dante walked quietly over to her sitting down next to her. He reached out and touched her arm gently, not saying anything. She didn't move for what felt like forever but when she finally did, she moved into him. His heart stopped aching for a moment as he moved his arm around her pulling her closer.

"I'm sorry. I didn't mean to push you." Dante said into her hair.

"I'm sorry. I have a hard time being vulnerable and talking about things that have happened. As long as you were good and followed the rules. Were seen but didn't make a sound. Did as you were told . You were safe…but all bets were off if Kip was in a bad mood." Sarah said quietly.

Dante didn't say anything, just held her tightly and listened. He didn't want to make her feel worse and he didn't want to say the wrong thing. Dante almost wished Kip wasn't dead so he could kill him, himself for causing so much pain to Sarah.

"I was so worried when that door flew open. I thought it was you coming down the stairs." Sarah said quietly.

"It was. Jace got there in time to stop me." Dante said quietly.

"Thank god. I was praying you wouldn't come down. I couldn't handle it if you were hurt." Sarah said quietly leaning against his chest.

"I would have killed them all for touching you." Dante growled.

"Dante, they could have killed you and then what. I couldn't have dealt with that." Sarah said sadness in her voice.

"Maybe, but I would have killed at least one of them." Dante grumbled.

Sarah was quiet; she didn't want to start an argument over things that didn't happen. She leaned further into him, inhaling his scent which instantly made her feel peaceful. Dante's hand traveled down her arm looking them over as he did. She was healing pretty quickly.

"Wolfsbane doesn't bother me a whole lot." Sarah said quietly.

"I see that….that's almost incredible. It's one of the most toxic things of our kind." Dante said, running his finger over the small burn the chains left on her skin.

"I guess with years of it being used on you, you build up a tolerance." Sarah said with a shrug.

"I'm sorry you had to live like that all those years." Dante said, trying to keep his wolf and anger at bay.

"It's ok, I helped a lot of girls. I don't know what would have happened to them if I hadn't been there. There is a silver lining in all of my scars." Sarah smirked.

Dante kissed the top of her head wrapping his arms tighter around her. He was never going to let anything happen to her again. Even if he had to risk his own life for hers. Not one thing was touching her, ever.

"You are amazing." Dante whispered to her.

Sarah smiled brightly at him. She chuckled and shook her head lightly. Dante tapped her nose, shaking his head back at her. She laughed and bopped him back on the nose. She then took a breath and looked up at the night sky. She suddenly became serious again.

"Dante I may be able to tell you someday but right now, I want to forget that part of my life. The only good thing was that it led me to you." Sarah said, looking at the bright moon.

"I won't push. You can tell me one day when you're ready." Dante said following her gaze to the moon.

"Thank you…bed?" Sarah asked, starting to get up.

"If you want to. I know from my own nightmares that sometimes I just want to stay up after." Dante said and a yawn escaped.

Sarah smiled at his yawn and then tapped his hand lightly as she stood. She shook her head and motioned for him to follow her.

"No, you look exhausted and I sleep much better in your arms. It's like they keep that part of my mind at bay and only good dreams happen." Sarah smiled at him.

"I sleep better with you as well.' Dante smiled at her.

"Nightmares?" Sarah asked curiously.

"Nightmares…I'll tell you about them one day. We can share battle stories." Dante winked at her.

She chuckled her response as she began walking towards the exit of the kitchen. Dante yawned again standing up. He shut and locked the pack house back door. He checked it over once more before going to Sarah. She held out her hand waiting for him. His hand caught hers and he wrapped his fingers around hers. As they began making their way back to their room.

Chapter Thirty Nine
Intruder

Nora woke up just before the sun was coming up. She glanced over to Jace watching him sleep peacefully. She watched the slow moonlight dance across the floor and touch upon his face. Nora smiled wondering how he could sleep so well with everything going on. She turned over on her side to look at him better. She brushed the dark almost raven color lock of hair out of his face. He didn't even move, his breathing didn't change. He was still so peacefully asleep. She stood walking over to the window. She was afraid for the future, scared of what it meant now that her secrets were out. Now that she had declared war. She didn't want anyone else getting hurt. She was staring out the window when a strong feeling hit her. It was like something broke. She felt a shift in power. Something big had just happened.

Jace sat up seconds later, he was breathing heavily like some had thrown cold water on him. Nora turned from the window looking at him confused.

Did you feel that?" Jace asked her to kick the blankets off of him.

"That weird snapping breaking feeling and then it was almost like a power shift?" Nora said calmly.

"Yes, exactly. Why ...never mind you're different. I need to contact Zeke and Grayson now. Something just happened." Jace said standing up quickly.

"Jace, it's barely dawn and what do you think happened?" Nora asked, confused by why he was so upset.

"Every Alpha is awake right now, I can assure you. A council member died and by the way it felt, another council member killed them and gained their power." Jace said, looking for clothes.

"You know all that from that feeling?" Nora asked, watching him rush about the room.

"Yes, the dynamics are set up so when we pledge loyalty to an alpha or the council you form a bond. When that bond is broken you feel like. Like how you knew I was in pain. I just don't understand why this didn't affect you like it did everyone else." Jace said, looking at her.

"Hunter thing?" Nora asked, giving an answer.

"Maybe?" Jace said, then pulled his shirt over his head.

"The consequences of killing a council member is death. Most are not strong enough to fight the bond anyways. What just happened was another council member killed the other to gain power. I am almost positive they did so to become stronger to take on us. To take you. I am worried about Douglas, he was always the one out of the three that wanted to do the right thing. At the same time I can see Bruce and Lance fighting over who gets to lay claim to you. So I am not exactly sure right now who's alive and who's dead." Jace said, pulling his pants up.

As Jace finished his statement his phone on his nightstand started to ring. Crossing the room he knew right away it would be Zeke. He picked up the phone but before answering he took a deep breath and then slid his phone to answer.

"Zeke." Jace said quietly.

"Yeah I felt it too, we have a situation…The council is after Nora." Jace said quietly.

"They were here investigating after Kip, they know about what Nora can do and I am assuming this surge in power is because one of them wants her for themselves." Jace explained.

"Yes damn it! They know she's my mate. They don't care if you know how they operate." Jace sighed sitting down on the bed.

Nora turned to look back out the window, slowly but surely she watched lights in the houses of pack members turn on. The world around them is waking up to uncertainty. Nora's chest tightens. Flashes of her past and death come to her mind. She felt like she was an omen for death. She looked out the window at the houses and wondered if they would die because of her. She wouldn't allow it.

"Alpha." Asher came through mind link.

"I'm awake." Nora responded.

"Did you feel that?" Asher asked her quietly.

"Yes it's the first step for them in declaring war, one has taken out the other to gain power." Nora said quietly.

"We will be ready, Alpha. Dont worry. We will protect you and this pack." Asher said and it made Nora's stomach turn.

She didn't reply, the urge to throw up started creeping up her throat. There was a knock at the door to their room and she knew it was Dante before even going to the door. She opened it putting a finger to her mouth letting Dante know to be quiet. She nodded to Jace who was still on the phone with Zeke. Jace spotted Dante and waved him in. Dante nodded his head respectfully to Nora and then walked by her.

"Call Grayson. We need to start making moves now. Zeke is willing to back us." Jace said quickly pointing to the phone on his computer desk.

Dante nodded and went to the phone quickly. He scrolled through the contacts and found his number before hitting send. Nora could hear the phone ringing. She needed air. She walked across the room and opened the balcony door, stepping out onto it. She went to the rail grabbing a hold of it. The urge to throw up is even stronger now. Her knuckles turned white as she held onto it for dear life. She looked up at the sky looking at the bright moon, her gut asking for help.

Nora, why do you plead with me? She heard her voice, as if it trickled down from the moon itself.

I don't want anyone else to die or get hurt because of me. Nora said back tears swelling up in her eyes.

Then don't let it happen. She answered simply.

How? How do I do that? I am just me. Nora said, trying not to be angry at such a simplistic answer.

Nora you are just you. But if you don't know what you're capable of then I can't help you. She said sternly.

I-

Nora I warned that war would come if you let others know of your power. Now you must find it within yourself to do what's right and protect those around you. I have given you everything you need. She said her tone was flat.

But how will I know what to do? Nora said, fighting back tears

It is in you. You need to listen. You need to trust yourself, your hunter self, and Zara. You are capable. She said then as if the moon knew she was done it dimmed.

Nora gritted her teeth, some freaking answer she thought squeezing onto the railing. She was trying to block out the noises of Dante and Jace on the phone. Trying to block out the overwhelming feeling slowly choking her. She tore her eyes from the sky and looked out over the field. She saw something. She squinted, pulling on Zara to help sharpen her vision. It was a person.

"Jace!" She mind linked him.

Jace was outside in seconds and the look on his face worried as he pulled the phone from his ear. Nora put a finger to her mouth and pointed down towards the intruder. Jace narrowed his eyes seeing the man.

"Is he alone? Did you see anyone else?" Jace's mind linked her back.

Nora shook her head, her eyes locked on the man who was still approaching the pack house. Dante came outside seconds later hanging up the phone with Grayson. Dante looked over the rail, Nora knew Jace had mind linked him.

"Dante, you go around back, I'll head through the front. Nora stay here and keep an eye on him." Jace sent in a mind link to the three of them.

Dante nodded his response and ducked out of the balconey. Jace went to move to the door but stepped back. He pulled Nora into a fierce kiss which took her by surprise before he disappeared as well. Nora shook her head, a small smile on her face as she kept her eyes on the man creeping about. Nora spotted the boys. Dante coming around from the back and Jace from the right side. The man was still walking straight for the pack house.

"He's going for the front door." Nora mind linked Dante and Jace, her voice confused.

"I got eyes on him." Dante said back.

"Same. Keep closing in on him." Jace was sent back.

The man started climbing up the stairs to the pack house front door. She watched him notice Jace and Dante. He began to back away. She wasn't going to let him get away. Her eyes glowed brightly as she debated her next move.

Do it! We got it! Zara said, anxious and excited, in their mind.

She grabbed a hold of the railing stepping up into it. She felt panic but it wasn't hers. Then Jace's voice chimed in her head.

"Nora don't we have him." Jace yelled at her through mind link.

Nora smirked and then jumped off the balcony. She felt the air blowing through her hair as the ground was coming at her fast. She hit the ground fast, landing neatly behind the man, in a crouch position. The man froze, seeing that he was now blocked in from all sides. Dante and Jace appear on his left and right. Nora slowly stood up from the ground. Her eyes glowed fiercely. The sun rising behind her gave her even more of an amber glow.

Jace was glaring at Nora, anger rolling off of him as he channeled it toward the intruder. Dante was bowed up and ready to fight. The man locked eyes with Nora and took a step back. The power she had scared him.

"Can we help you?" Nora asked with a calm, chilling smile.

The man was tall, his eyes were a deep green and he had sandy brown hair that was ruffled into a mess, like he had just rolled out of bed. He backed up putting distance between himself and Jace. He then raised his hands up defensively. Jace stepped closer closing him in, his eyes glowing a fierce ice blue as Cole was just below the surface ready to rip this intruder apart. The man backed up into the pack house door. His back pressed up against it, as Jace cornered him in. The man held his hand up to Jace as if telling him to wait. He gritted his teeth and Jace was wondering who exactly he was. He could feel that he was powerful and his gut was telling him he was from the council.

"What are you doing creeping around my land?" Jace growled.

"Douglas sent me. I need to speak to you urgently." The man said quickly.

"Douglas?" Jace said surprised, he had been expecting something from Lance.

Nora growled fiercely behind him and Dante's eyes glowed ready to shift. The door behind the man opened and Sarah was standing behind the opened door, eyes glowing. She had heard the commotion and felt Dante's anger. The man almost fell into Sarah, her growl made him step forward into Jace.

"Yes, Douglas is my Alpha. My name is Samuel, I am his Beta. I am here not as a threat. I would have brought an army instead of just myself if I meant to do harm." Samuel said, trying to make them see.

Being Doulas's Beta he was stronger than most Alpha's just by being connected to the council. However Jace had always made him question if he could actually take him. He glanced over his shoulder at Nora whose eyes were glowing as bright as the sun and knew that she had power stronger then his. He could feel it radiating off of her and she hasn't even called fully upon her wolf. This was the girl that was starting the wars.

"Eyes off my mate." Jace growled, stepping closer to him.

"I am no threat to her or your pack." Samuel said his eyes glowing purple to remind Jace just who he was.

"Douglas did say he wanted to go against Bruce and Lance at some point." Dante grumbled but not letting his guard down.

"He could have an army waiting for him just outside the border." Sarah said, grilling him.

"I don't. We can either fight or talk. I am ordered to give you a message so do you want to talk, hear the message or fight." Samuel said his wolf pushed underneath his skin letting him know he could shift in a second if he needed to.

Sarah and Dante's stance buckled a little bit, feeling Samuel's power. It annoyed Jace, he growled slightly seeing Samuel affecting Dante and Sarah. He went to step into Samuel, when he felt Nora's hand on his shoulder. She moved to his side, Jace fought with the urge to block her from Samuel. Nora studied Samuel; she wasn't getting any threatening vibes from him. Her danger alerts were not going off.

"Nora, Alpha of Red Woods and Luna to Cross River." Nora said, introducing herself and holding out her hand to Samuel.

Jace smirked a little knowing instantly what she was doing. If Samuel was a threat Nora's hunter senses would take over and he would get a jolt of energy that would send him flying. He watched Samuel slowly take her hand in his. He got small little zaps of electricity but nothing major.

"A female Alpha? And a Luna?...Impressive. Samuel Beta of Silver Mountain." Samuel said, shaking her hand firmly.

"He's telling the truth. Let's go inside." Nora said letting go of his hand and nodded to Sarah to let them pass.

"Luna, are you sure?" Sarah said quietly.

"Yes he means us no harm..today." Nora smiled, slipping her hand into Jace's before walking past Samuel.

Dante blocked the stairs leading away from the pack house and nodded to Samuel to follow. Samuel gave him a strange look before walking passed Sarah into the pack house. Sarah glared at him before she walked by. Samuel glared back at her a small amount of his power rolling off him just to let her know, he may be acting nice but he was powerful. Sarah bowed her head as he walked past in response to it not out of respect. Dante came to her side putting his hand around her shoulder.

"You ok?" Dante asked her while watching Samuel's back follow Jace and Nora.

"Fine, he just wanted to show off." Sarah mutters, making a face.

Dante growled wanting to fight Samuel because he dared to threaten his mate. Sarah smiled and looped her arm through his, rubbing his arm calming him. She motioned for him to follow Samuel.

"Have a seat." Jace told Samuel as they walked into his office motioning to the chair in front of his desk.

Jace rounded the desk still holding Nora's hand. He pulled his chair out motioning for Nora to sit. Nora pecked him on the cheek as she sat down across from Samuel. Jace leaned on the tall chair protectively over Nora. Jace's eyes locked on Samuel watching him intensely. Cole is still pacing inside of him, still on edge.

"I'm assuming you all felt the surge in power?" Samuel began.

Jace nodded looking like he was interested but looked like he was more on edge. Nora smiled lightly and reached up and grabbed Jace's hand trying to calm him.

"Lance killed Bruce and is now in the process of taking over Bruce's pack. Lance will now have two armies." Samuel started.

"Fuck." Jace whispered and Nora looked up at him.

"I never thought Bruce would be the one to be taken out. He was always so political. He had a loophole and back door way to everything. Lance was always just a hot head with too much of daddy's money." Jace said, shaking his head.

"Well I guess it's a good thing it's Lance and not Bruce then." Nora said, Jace and Samuel looked at her like she was a little crazy.

"Lance is a hot head and he's blinded by what he wants. He doesn't see the bigger picture of things. Bruce was secretive and coordinated. At least we know what Lance wants and know how he will act." Nora said, looking from Samuel to Jace.

Jace smiled and leaned down kissing her on the top of her head. " You are always so smart my love."

"I try." She smirked at him and she saw the small reaction Jace tried to hide, she knew exactly what her smart comment and smirk would do to him.

She chuckled knowing that this was not the time or place. That he couldn't act on it. She grinned seeing him look at her and she knew that he knew she had done it on purpose. The look he gave her told that she was in trouble when they were finally alone.

"My Alpha sent me to you, to let you know we will back you. We know Lance is bringing war to your front door and we will stand with you." Samuel said proudly.

"Tell your Alpha to be ready. Lance is not going to wait. He is never one to wait very long when he wants something." Jace said, almost growling.

"We have been wanting to take the council down for years. The corruption has worn heavily on my Alpha but to keep our pack safe he had to stay. Now with this opportunity to do things right. We will not fail." Samuel said his voice was firm and strong as he spoke.

"We are having a meeting today with three other packs, they all are backing us as well. Can your Alpha attend?" Jace asked, his eyes still on Nora.

"Unfortunately no. He doesn't want to show his backing just yet. He doesn't want to risk Lance knowing. If Lance thinks my Alpha is on his side, we can use this to an advantage. He needs to remain at Silver Mountain keeping our pack safe until the moment is right." Samuel explained.

"Figures." Jace grumbled now, trusting them less.

"Jace it makes sense and if they are true to what they say. Then it would be greatly beneficial to know what Lance is planning. Douglas could be our inside man." Nora said, looking at Samuel.

"Fine. Let your Alpha know that if he is not true to the words you said here today, that I personally will rip his throat out." Jace growled his eyes glowing ice blue as he spoke.

"He won't go against us." Nora smiled looking at Samuel; she sent her aura out towards him heightening Jace's threat.

Samuel's eyes widened a little bit as he felt her power. It was just a small ounce of power but it felt equal to his own Alpha's. He looked at her confused.

"What are you?" Samuel asked, looking at her.

"Complicated." Nora chuckled.

"Now that the meet and greet is over. You have a few hours before the meeting. You're welcome to take a nap in one of our rooms, shower and get something to eat. I assume you've been traveling all night." Nora said to Samuel as she stood.

Jace smirked a little at the way Nora threw her power out over Samuel. He took her hand in his and began walking out of the office. Dante and Sarah had been guarding the door.

"Dante have Samuel here set up in one of the rooms. Sarah, we need a perimeter check. Alert the guard Zeke, Grayson, Asher, and Logan will all be coming in just a few short hours. Inform Wyatt as well, I know the hospital has him busy lately but I need him by our side right now." Jace said, giving orders.

"Yes Alpha." Sarah and Dante said in unison with a nod before heading out.

Chapter Forty

History

Nora wandered into the kitchen. It would be minutes now for the other packs to start arriving. Lori had whipped up something to make it more casual. Even though they would be talking of war, food always seemed to make everything better. Nora reached over and plucked a red grape off its vine and bit into it. She zoned out everything rushing into her mind.

"It's not good to hold things in constantly." Lori said softly.

"I'm just worried." Nora said, grabbing another grape.

"War is scary, that's normal to be worried." Lori said with a small smile.

"It's not the war part that scares me. I'm worried I can't keep them all safe." Nora said, hearing it outloud made her stomach clench inwards on itself.

The rush to vomit again hit her. She turned, grabbing a hold of the sink and preparing to empty her stomach. She turned on the sink, cupped her hands and let them fill with water. She splashed the water over her face. Trying to let the cold water chase away the feeling.

"Luna, you will do your best and that is all that is expected of you." Lori said coming over with a cool rag and placed it on the back of her neck.

"Thank you." Nora said quietly.

Jace walked into the kitchen raising an eyebrow at Nora, a concerned look on his face as he walked over to her. He rubbed her back trying to sooth her.

"You alright love?" He asked her as he leaned over and kissed her shoulder.

"I'm ok." Nora smiled at him, putting on a brave face and trying somehow to block her emotions from him.

He frowned a little but his attention was taken back by Asher walking into the kitchen. He nodded to Jace and then bared his neck to Nora. She shook her head at him. She had told him several times that he needed not to do that.

"How's the pack?" Nora asked Asher as he walked in.

"Lyla and Chance are running the show right now. Getting rid of Roger has settled everything. The pack instantly felt lighter. We have locked up Clay and Chad until we can discuss consequences for them. Lyla is doing much better. Logan, Matt, and Lilly are just behind me. " Asher said, summing everything up.

"That's good. I'm glad things are moving along. I'm glad Lyla is healed and back to herself again." Nora smiled at him.

"Jace!" Zeke said his aura wafting into the room as he stepped into the kitchen.

"Zeke." Jace smiled walking over to him, He reached Zeke and slapped him on the shoulder.

Zeke mimics the same action they both laughed seeing each other.

"It's good to see you." Zeke smiled at Jace.

"Unfortunately it is the same thing as the last time we met." Zeke added with a chuckle shaking his head.

"Hopefully this will be the last time we meet for anything like this." Jace said, stepping back from Zeke.

"Nora. You look radiant as always." Zeke walked over to her as he moved to hug her. Jace stepped in between them, blocking the hug.

"And look very hand- " Nora went to give him a compliment back but Jace growled.

Nora chuckled, shaking her head. She stood on her tippy toes and kissed Jace's cheek which instantly melted Cole.

"I forgot how poss- I mean protective your mate is." Zeke laughed.

Before Jace could even respond Chadwick and Grayson walked into the kitchen. The oversize kitchen was quickly becoming crowded. Chadwick locked eyes with Nora and was overcome with emotions. He had never got the chance to meet the woman responsible for saving him and his pack.

Chadwick walked over to Nora slowly looking at her in wonder. Nora looked at him confused. He came over to her and took her hand softly in his. He then kneeled and pressed his forehead into her hand. Nora looked at Jace a little panicked.

"I am forever in your debt." He whispered against her hand.

Grayson came over following suit kneeling behind his Alpha, bowing his head. Nora looked to Jace for help but he just gave her a small smile.

"We will fight for you and with you." Grayson said from behind Chawick.

"Thank you." Nora said and then kneeled down on the ground so her and Chadwick were level.

"I know you feel indebted to me but I want you to not make decisions based on that. If your pack cannot handle war right now then do not do it. I do not want to risk any more lives or lose anyone." Nora said, placing her hand on his shoulder.

"Jace, why don't we go to the dining room? There's more …air." Nora said feeling like the room was closing in on her.

"This way." Jace announced before walking toward the kitchen exit.

"Your Luna is remarkable." Zeke said to Jace as he walked through the door.

"She doesn't call you Alpha though." Zeke said, pausing, getting a read on Jace.

"She is the only one allowed to call me by my name. She is my equal. You'll understand if your Luna ever comes out of hiding." Jace winked at him.

Zeke smirked, shaking his head as he went out. Asher was like a bodyguard over Nora; he was watching each Alpha carefully. He almost fell over when Nora got on the ground and kneeled with Chadwick. He walked over to Nora and offered her his hand up. Chadwick raised an eyebrow as another man helped Nora up and not her mate. He looked at Grayson with a questionable look.

"That's her Beta Asher of Red Woods."
Grayson sent him back.

"I forgot she is both Luna and Alpha. She is incredible." *Chadwick sent back to Grayson.*

He then found Nora's hand dangling in front of his face. She smiled down at him offering her hand to help him up. He smiled, taking it and allowing Nora to help him up. The strength he felt as he touched her hand, amazed him. She looked at him confused and Asher narrowed his eyes at him seeing the look on Chadwick's face. Nora shook her head to Asher and patted his shoulder as she walked by him heading out of the kitchen.

Walking into the dinning room Zeke and Jace were already discussing plans and attack methods. Nora made a face as those two were always the first to jump into anything. Just then a small wave of power was felt. The Alphas in the room stiffened knowing that kind of power comes from the council. Zeke looked to Jace worried as if to say is it happening already. Jace sighed and shook his head.

"I wanted to wait till you all were here. Samuel beta of Silver Mountain, Douglas's Beta will be joining us." Jace announced as Samuel walked into the room.

Asher stiffened up defensively and moved closer to Nora. Chadwick and Grayson were on high alert. While Zeke seemed to just study Samuel as he walked in.

"Good afternoon." Samuel said with a nod to them all.

"I want to start by saying My Alpha and our pack is on your side. I can see the wheels turning from some of you about if I am a threat or not. I came alone, no army. I am here as proof of Alpha Douglas's support." Samuel said, his voice full of authority.

The room was silent as they all took in what they said. The council had made themselves a reputation for being misleading and dishonest over the last few years so everyone was skeptical.

"Let's have a seat and we will begin discussions." Jace announced taking a seat at the head of the table.

Grayson and Chadwick sat side by side off to the right. Nora made her way to Jace's right side sitting down. Zeke sat across the table from Nora and Asher made sure he was right by her side. Samuel wanted to display that he was there as an equal so he sat next to Asher. Leaving the other head of the table open. Jace took note of it, raising an eyebrow at Nora. She smiled saying she saw it too.

"Ok, is this everyone?" Zeke asked quietly looking over the table, there were four packs in total.

"No." Nora said with a smile as she felt the hunters walk in.

Samuel stiffened as the scent of hunter made its way into the room. Samuel looked to Jace who seemed unbothered. Chadwick tensed up but Zeke and Grayson who already knew about Jace's alliance were not surprised. Logan walked into the room.

"Sorry we're late, you know love birds and all." Logan smirked as he nodded behind him to Lilly and Matt.

"Hunters." Samuel growled standing up aggressively.

"Ok Wolfie? Did someone not give you the memo?" Logan smirked as his eyes flashed danger.

"Wolfie! How dare you." Samuel growled.

"We have an alliance with the hunters. They have assisted us in the past with critical issues. They are safe here on my grounds." Jace said locking eyes with Samuel.

"Do you know what the law says!" Samuel shouted.

"Here we go." Logan said, rolling his eyes.

"It's an old law we chose to see past it." Jace said a growl under his voice.

"Hunters are…are

Samuel was cut off as Nora slammed her hand on the table standing up, letting a little bit of power roll out into the room. Her eyes glowed slightly as she turned to face Samuel.

"Hunters are welcome. If you can't understand that. Then you will need to contact your Alpha and let him know he will be fighting alone. Hunters here fight by our side and vice versa." Nora growled.

Samuel felt her power and tried to fight it by sending his own power out. The room felt the power war and Nora didn't seem phased by it. She pushed out hers more calling on Zara to help her. Samuel's forehead began to sweat.

"Nora just say when." Logan said, stepping up.

"That is enough." Jace growled hitting the table.

"Samuel back down or get off my land." Jace growled fiercely.

Samuel was on the verge of buckling from facing Nora. So he gritted his teeth and withdrew his aura. He sat angrily.

"Does she not know our history with them?" Samuel asked Jace.

"You do not know your own history." Nora said quietly.

"Hunters were once wolves." Nora said quietly.

Chapter Forty One
Preparing

"*H*unter's were once wolves?" Samuel laughed, shaking his head.

Jace looked at Nora nervous, he didn't want her to explain. He was begging her with his eyes to stop. They didn't need to know. He was worried that if she told them the other packs may turn on them. He didn't know if he would be strong enough to protect her. He glanced at Dante who shifted his stance nervously.

"Yes. Hunters date back to the original bloodlines of wolves. The two powerful families. However one was cursed to become something strong enough to hunt wolves. Hunters. The wolf blood line faded out amongst them as time went on but in the very beginning they were wolves." Nora said ignoring the glances Jace was giving her.

"Well that is some fairy tale. Who exactly told you this?" Samuel laughed while the room was silent.

"The goddess." Nora said quietly.

"The moon goddess, the mother of all. Spoke to you." Samuel said in disbelief.

"Mhmm. Now if you have any other issues I suggest you leave." Nora said sweetly.

"There is no such thing. You are either a hunter or a wolf. There is no inbetween. I'm sorry Jace but your Luna spins some stories." Samuel laughed.

Asher stood up, his chair being thrown out behind him, as he turned to Samuel. Anger coursing through him.

"Do not speak about my Alpha in such a manner." Asher growled.

"Sit down mut." Samuel said sending out his power

Asher tried hard to fight against it but couldn't. Nora stood up, her chair being thrown back against the wall as she did. Her eyes glowing and her body radiating energy like nothing no one had felt before. She locked eyes with Samuel and slowly began walking to him. Each step she took felt like she was sending electricity in the air. She grabbed a hold of Samuel's arm. He began wincing in pain.

"I am both Hunter and Wolf. This is just my hunter's side. You do not want to meet my wolf." She whispered into his ear.

Samuel whimpered, fighting in the chair to get his arm free from Nora. Jace stood slowly and fought against the waves of energy Nora was sending out. He made it to her side and placed his hand on top of hers. Ignoring the pain. Nora blinked her glow fading as she felt Jace. She let go of Samuel's hand and stepped back into Jace. He wrapped his arms around her tightly. She looked out across the room. A mix of emotions. Logan, Asher, Dante, and Zeke impressed and were proud. Chadwick and Samuel were scared when Grayson seemed to just take it all in.

"Let's move on shall we." Jace said his voice was powerful booming out over the room.

Nora leaned back into Jace, letting his presence calm her as she dropped Samuel's arm. Matt was standing behind Lilly smirking as he wrapped his arm around her waist. Samuel glanced another small look of surprise as he saw another wolf with a hunter. He looked like he had just entered another world. Nora smirked, sitting back down in the chair. She nodded for Logan to join them.

"Logan, is I guess you could call the Alpha of the hunters. He is also my close friend. If it wasn't for his group of hunters we would not have freed The Red Woods Pack and Black Sand pack. They are willing to help us free ourselves from the rule of corruptness the council has been pushing." Nora said powerfully looking out over the room.

"Your hunters helped us?' Chadwick said, looking at Logan as he took a seat.

"Honestly until Nora, I would have let you all kill each other off. I thought wolves were bloodthirsty, murdering fiends. Then I bumped into Nora and realized we could co-exist and just because there were some bad apples doesn't mean you all are." Logan explained quietly.

"We want what you want. A world where we can both live without worrying the other is out to get us. That there are rules and boundaries that you don't cross. Useless blood shed doesn't solve anything." Logan continued.

"We are with the hunter." Chadwick said firmly.

"We've been fine with the hunters since we fought side by side. We were hesitant at first but these are not the hunters from our ancestors' past." Zeke said, adding to Chadwick's comment.

"Ok well that sums that up. Sorry Wolfie looks like we got voted in the club." Logan smirked winking at Samuel.

"Moving on." Jace announced to let his tone show his Alpha status as he requested in his chair.

"Ok so we are all here because war is coming. What we just found out a few hours ago is that Lance has murder Bruce and taken over his pack as well. His destination is here." Jace said quietly.

"I am going to be honest with you all and up front. Lance wants my mate. He is starting a war with me over her. Now I know this doesn't concern most of you. She is not your mate but what I want you to think about is this. If he is willing to go to war with me over wanting my mate. Then what will stop him if he wants something from your pack. Land, resources, or just because. He is willing to break laws just because he wants something. He is a spoiled child and needs to be stopped." Jace said, watching each one of their faces.

"Jace is right, if he is going to war with Jace over his mate he will do as he wants with each of our packs. There will be no stopping him." Zeke said, scratching his forehead as he spoke.

"Why does he want your mate?" Chadwick asked.

Jaced looked at him debating he was trying to come up with something that won't lead to more questions. He was still trying to keep as much as he could about Nora and her gifts a secret.

"Because he's Lance. He's a pig. You can't deny…Jace don't hurt me but your Luna is stunning. Plus she has dual roles which causes her to have power. The first female Alpha is a big deal. Lance has always taken things he wanted without consequence." Zeke chimed in.

Jace was grateful and let the comment about Nora's beauty pass. Nora smiled at Zeke thanking him for the comment. Jace gave her a look and she made a kissy face at him. He grumbled slightly and she smirked. He narrowed his eyes at her letting her know she would get it later. She then chuckled.

"God, I'm surrounded by Love birds." Logan said, making a gagging noise.

"You'll find yours soon enough." Nora whispered to him.

"Nope, never. Can we get back to talking about war." Logan said, making a face.

"My Alpha is going to act like he is with Lance, that way we will have all the inside details. He will move with him and then when he goes to attack we will be with you. He will be using both armies. From experience a single army of the council can wipe out a pack." Samuel said, his voice very matter of fact as he spoke.

"Well it's a good thing we have allies." Nora said with a smile, looking around the table.

"My pack is still recovering in numbers but we will offer up what we can." Chadwick said his tone had a hint of sadness to it.

"Chadwick we completely understand. Help us how you can, we do not want anyone to be vulnerable. I think everyone should leave men behind to defend their packs just in case Lance suddenly becomes a war general and decides to split his armies. We do not need our homes not protected." Jace said quietly.

"What will come of it all once Lance is gone. All of that?" Zeke asked quietly, you could see his wheels spinning.

"Does Dogulas think he is going to be King and we will go back to the dark ages?" Grayson said, speaking up for the first time.

"Yeah we do not need anyone else power tripping." Dante said from Jace's left.

"No the council was a good foundation. It was left unchecked but in the beginning it was, what it was meant to be. I say we evaluate, appoint new people. Maybe even more people so not one person is more powerful than the other." Jace said, thinking out loud.

"Power comes from bloodlines, we all know that. Someone will be more powerful just by default." Chadwick stated.

"Yes but look at us now. This is what's supposed to happen when a threat comes along. We are supposed to unite, come together and solve it. It has nothing to do with bloodlines." Jace said, shaking his head.

Nora watch Jace and how he handled everything. She smiled proudly at him. He was meant to do this. He fit perfectly in the role. He was leader, a true alpha. He did it in a way of respect and trust. He had power but he never used it unless he absolutely had to. She glanced at Asher and saw the same traits and qualities. When this was all over with, he was going to be an amazing Alpha.

"Love?" Jace sent Nora in a mind link seeing the look he gave him and then the look she gave Asher.

"Nothing. You're doing great." Nora said, smiling at him.

"What's the next step?" Logan asked he glanced to Lilly as he spoke, trying to gauged where she stood.

"You go home and prepare your armies. The advancement will be coming any day. We shouldn't draw the attention of humans. If this could somehow go down not on pack lands but not near humans it would be best." Nora glanced at Logan, who nodded in an agreement.

"That's easier said than done. There is very little land not occupied. How will we know when Lance is making his moves." Zeke asked.

"There's a valley north of here, no humans and no wolves. If we can trap his armies in the valley, the battle should be over quickly." Logan said solving the battlefield problem.

"My Alpha will let me know as soon as plans start being made. Once he is, I will inform you all. Your contact with my Alpha will be limited due to him trying to stay under cover." Samuel said locking eyes with Jace.

Jace stood. Now there was a plan. Nora stood as he did. He walked over, slipping his arm around her waist and pulling her towards him. He looked out over the table. He knew in his heart this would be the new council. He glanced at Logan, they might freak out a little bit when he brings up the idea of a hunter sitting at their table, but it will be for the best.

"Our lands are always open for any of you. Whenever you need help, just ask. Go home, prepare your troops, spend time with your loved ones. It will be here before we know it. If any of you wish to stay, my pack house is open to you." Jace said with a nod of respect to them.

Chapter Forty Two
Wrong

A few moments later maps were sprawled out across the dining room table. All territories joined at the valley. Lance and Bruce's territories were north west of the valley. Nora's eyes traced the valley. Zeke was to the east, Chadwick to the south, and Jace with Noras's pack were south east. Silver mountain with Douglas was northwest. The council would have to travel downwards to get to them. She watched Jace go over this with Asher and Logan. He was trying to see what pack would be willing to travel north to loop around them, just in case Douglas backed out on them. They needed to cover all bases.

Their voices blurred together and Nora started to feel sick. The constant nagging of this was her fault and strangled her heart. It wrapped around her lungs, choking her. She began to feel her light headed and vision blurred. She didn't want to pull Jace away from the meeting. She quietly excused herself into the kitchen.

Water. Zara yelled at her.

Nora nodded as she fumbled towards the sink. She blindly turned on the water and cupping her hands she brought it to her mouth drinking it quickly. She then caught more water in her hands and splashed her face with it. The shakiness was starting to subside.

Air. Zara said this time not so firmly.

Nora looked to the kitchen door and saw the outside. Just seeing outside made her feel better. She turned off the water and walked slowly to the door. She didn't want to rush in case she fell out. She pushed open the screen door and stepped outside. The warm sunlight hitting her skin and the cool breeze danced across her hair, flipping it behind her. She inhaled shutting her eyes, instantly feeling better. She smiled, enjoying the moment of silence.

Silence. The word echoed in her brain. There was no noise, no sounds. No birds chipping, the wind didn't rustle the leaves. She felt her breathing catch in her throat. She was scared to open her eyes. Something was telling her not to.

Nora, somethings wrong. Zara whispered to her.

A strong smell drifted into her nostrils. She tensed up afraid of what it could be. Her body shaking and vibrating telling herself there was danger.

It smells, like fire…blood. Zara said registering the smell for Nora, who was choosing not to.

Damn it Nora, open your eyes! Something is wrong. Let me have control. Zara growled at her.

Nora tried to ignore Zara, she didn't want to see. She didn't want to know.

What if we can help? What if someones hurt? Nora, we are strong. Open your eyes, move. Zara commanded her.

Nora bit her lip nervously, opening her eyes. The world was gray, smoke filled the air. She looked down at the wooden railing in her hand that she was gripping on to like it was the only thing holding her in place. It was charcoal. She let go of it quickly and it crumbled. Nora stepped down the stairs, looking around. Blood, it made her sick to her stomach. She followed it to the driveway of the pack house. It was painted red. Pack members that she didn't remember their bodies were scattered about. Throats ripped open, eyes looking in horror. She turned quickly to the pack house. Red and orange Flames danced across the roof with black smoke pouring out. It was getting thicker and thicker. The air she couldn't breathe in. The smoke blinded her as she tried to travel through it. She couldn't see her hand in front of her face. She crashed down to her knees, trying to force air back into her lungs. Her hands held her hands, holding her chest as she gasped.

Jace! Her mind shouted as she made her way to the door, stepping over bodies.

She pushed open the door and it crumbled away underneath her touch. Turning to a pile of black ash in front of her. She watched the dust float out of her hand before stepping into the house. Entering she saw Asher on the ground mouth open like he had been screaming. His abdomen was sliced open and had several wounds covering him. Nora knew he was gone, she began moving faster, her heart pounding in her chest. She moved through the room that was burning looking to see who she could help.

Lilly was on the floor, next to Matt clinging to him. Her throat sliced open, blood had poured down from her gapping neck down onto Matt's dead body. She was holding him before she was killed. Nora felt sick, getting to the kitchen she saw Sarah impaled by a spear, her body slumped over not breathing. The room is on fire around them. Nora needed to find Jace. She saw Dante collapsed in the doorway to the basement. Nora shut her eyes as she felt her chest collapse inwards just as he was in the doorway. She moved towards Dante, she knew before she even touched him he was dead.

"Down here." A voice called from the darkness of the basement.

Nora froze, she didn't recognize the voice. It wasn't Jace's and she was confused. Maybe it could be Lance but from what she remembered it didn't sound like his.

"Nora move yourself, time is running out." The voice commanded.

Nora gritted her teeth, she let out a slow breath and she stepped over Dante's dead body. She started down the dark stairs. The room was filled with smoke and the fire danced along the walls. She could feel the heat but it didn't look real. She wanted to reach out and touch the flames to see if they would actually burn her.

"Nora." Jace's voice hit her like a ton of bricks.

Nora turned on her heels looking for him frantically. Her eyes were trying to see through the smoke and darkness. She walked towards the middle of the room. Her foot hitting something. The smoke rushed out as if someone had opened a door, pulling all the air out. The hair on her arms and the back of neck stood up as she looked down at the blood stained table. Her stomach twisted inside of her, as she felt the air in her lungs rush out. She couldn't breathe. She grabbed a hold of her chest stepping back away from the table. Tears streamed down her face as she felt her legs buckle.

"Jace." She whispered seeing his mutilated body.

He had wounds covering his entire body. Long lacerations where his skin was flayed opened. She then realized his head was separated from his body. She slammed into the wall, realizing that everyone she loved was gone. Sinking to her knees, shaking as her world was ripped away from her again. She fought the urge to vomit as she tried to breathe. She couldn't breathe. How did this happen?

"Nora." She heard the voice again, but this time it was female.

She looked around the room not seeing anyone. She tried to get up but her legs felt like jello. She looked at the fire around her and decided that she wasn't moving. That if this place burned down then she was going to burn with it.

"Nora, get up now." A voice said loudly and filled with anger.

Nora's head popped up and the woman from before walked towards her. Light radiating out around her as she stood in front of Nora. The fire in the room disappeared and the darkness brightened.

"Goddess." Nora whispered, unsure if she was really seeing her again.

"We did not make it through the last time so you can sit here and give up." The Goddess said to her with anger radiating off of her.

"There's nothing left for me if this is what has happened." Nora said defeated.

"This is what's to come. Something bad is coming and you are the only one who can change this outcome. You need to be smart and careful to save your loved ones." She said with a long sigh looking at Nora.

"I haven't even shown you what will become of you." The Goddess said, waving her hands.

It was cold, the chill hit her first. She felt metal around her hands. Her mouth tasted of blood, she was weak and tired. She moved her foot and she heard the sound of chains dragging across the floor. She focused her eyes trying to see in the darkness.

"I've tried to be nice, Nora." A bitter voice said from the corner.

"You're so beautiful and to have to chain you down here like a wild animal is…so..sad." Lance's voice said from the corner.

Nora felt sick, she tried to turn her head away from him but she felt something heavy around it. It was a metal collar. Nora was completely shackled to the wall, she was propped up against. She hated him, rage burned in her stomach. She wanted to rip his head off of his body. She tried to call on her powers, she felt them stir but something suppressed them. She moved her arm and tried to tug on the metal shackles to break free. She then saw an iv port strapped to her inner arm. She looked at it confused.

"We figured you out." Lance said quietly stepping into the dim light.

Nora looked at him confused about what he had done.

Zara? Nora tried calling on her wolf. She could feel her but it was like she was locked away. What was happening.

"What did you do?" Nora growled at Lance.

"You should have just came to me. This would have gone so much better. I had a beautiful bedroom suit for you. Servants to wait on you. I might have even spared Jace's life…well maybe not your mate. He would have kept coming for you but all your friends didn't have to die. Maybe I could have kept Jace down here and let you visit him like he was a pet or something but no. You wanted a war." Lance said, shaking his head.

"The war happened?" Nora whispered.

"I guess that's what you could have called it. We dominated. Now I am Alpha of all Alphas. King. You could still be my queen. There could still be a happy ever after for you Nora." Lance said quietly.

"How did you win? We had armies." Nora asked, trying to move some more.

"We had more than just armies. We had an unstoppable army. Bruce was right about Kip. Those bird brains just weren't seeing the big picture. Be my Queen Nora, there's nothing left for you. Do you really want to rot down here?" Lance asked in his voice, almost pleading with her.

"What do you want from me?" Nora asked, letting her head slump back against the wall.

"Your power. Your body and a son. A son with your power and my blood line would be unstoppable." Lance said quietly.

"Maybe friendship but we won't push it." Lance smirked.

Nora felt her stomach turn in on her. She was going to vomit, she turned her head trying to stop the waves of nausea. A son…the words bounced around in her head. Then her mind screamed Jace! As she thought her world was collapsing. Tears began to flow down her cheeks. She had thought about a family but it was with Jace. A little boy or girl with his ice blue eyes and jet black hair. Jace chasing after them in one of the gardens. She couldn't breathe. Jace was gone. They were all gone.

"Nora I know this is a lot but this is where you are at right now. It's going to go my way regardless. You just need to choose how you want it to be. I can have my way with you, you can be pregnant down here, birth our son down here, and then never have anything to do with him. Or you can have a beautiful bedroom suit, be a queen, maybe enjoy you know and raise your baby. Think about it." Lance said as he began to leave.

His footsteps echoing as he left felt like nails in Nora's coffin. This can't be happening, this can't be real. This is all wrong. Her mind screamed.

Chapter Forty Three
Can't

  *J*ace's stomach dropped to his knees. His heart sank. He was overcome with an unnerving feeling. He looked around the room confused at who was giving off these feelings. Fear hit him like a wave. His eyes darted around the room. Where was she? He could feel her pain coursing through him. He stood up from the table knocking his chair over as he began to look for her.

  "Nora!" He yelled not caring how he looked in front of the other members.

  "Nora?" Dante asked, confused.

  "Nora!" Jace yelled again.

  "Alpha! Jace what's going on?"' Dante asked, trying to get him to focus.

  "Somethings wrong, where did she go?" Jace said his voice coming out as angry as he headed towards the kitchen.

  "What do you mean something is wrong?" Dante asked him his voice trying to calm him.

  "Dante I fucking feel her, she hurt or something. Somethings fucking wrong! I need her now." Jace yelled, his eyes flowing.

  "I'll go towards the living room and out front." Asher said

  "I'll go check upstairs." Dante said getting up and racing towards the stairs.

They all scattered as Jace walked into the kitchen trying to feel for her. He shut his eyes focusing on her scent, her fear overwhelming him. He needed to find her. Why was she so scared? She felt like she was drifting from him. He felt like his bond was slipping from her. He rushed into the kitchen slamming into the countertop island. Where was she? He saw the back door wide open.

"Nora!" He yelled rushing towards the door.

He nearly fell down the stairs. He was going so fast. He looked out over the grass, his eyes searching. He shut his eyes trying to calm himself long enough to try to zone in on her. He inhaled deeply trying to slow his heart rate and breathing down. Taking a minute he heard her. She was sobbing softly. Where was she? He caught her scent, the smell of warm vanilla invaded his nostrils, as his head snapped in the direction. He rushed around to the front of the house, his eyes searching for her. He saw her and his heart dropped. He rushed to her but slowed down as he got there. She was curled into herself on the driveway, sobbing uncontrollably. He dropped to his knees going to touch her. A jolt went through him, sending him backwards. Her body was in protection mode.

He gritted his teeth, he needed to wake her up. She was in some weird state. He wasn't sure how to reach her. He walked over to her cautiously, kneeling down in front of her. He wanted to reach out and pull her into him. Wrap his arms around her and tell her everything was ok.

*S*he stayed curled up in the darkness. This couldn't be her life, they couldn't all be gone. She wasn't going to give this monster a child. Her poor child, Lance, would use her child for evil things. She couldn't let that happen. Why was her body not working? She looked down at the IV port. It had to be this, whatever they were putting into her. She tried to curl her wrist inwards, the shackles going between the two handcuffs were preventing her from getting to the port. She moved her head down towards her arm. Maybe she could reach it with her mouth. As she leaned forward the chain attached to her collar snapped her head back.

"Ahhhh!!!!" She yelled, slamming her feet down.

This was not happening, she wasn't going to stay down here and rot. Rot and serve him. Jace fought to the end. They all fought to the end. She was going to. She gritted her teeth looking at the IV port. It was coming out. She wiggled the chain up towards the forearm of her arm, trying to loop it into the IV port. If she could just get it so she could yank it out with the chain maybe her powers would come back. Maybe Zara will come back. The sounds of footsteps coming back may freeze her and stop her attempt. She scooted back into the stone wall. Praying Lance wasn't coming to touch her.

"Nora." A voice said as it was coming closer.

"Leave me alone." She shouted back.

"Nora." It came again, as the person walked into the room. Light following them.

"Goddess?" Nora asked hopefully.

"Nora this is what will come! Fix it. I've done all I can for you." She said fading out.

"No wait, how do I fix it! Please tell me how I can stop this. Wait! Please! Don't leave me." Nora begged as the light disappeared out of the room.

Just before it completely faded, she felt a tug on her arm. The IV port was torn out. Blood started to seep down Nora's arm. She felt her body shift and change. She began to hear footsteps again. No not yet she thought, she felt Zara stir within her. She wasn't ready. She couldn't fight yet. She was panicking. She needed to hide the blood. She tried tucking her arm behind her but with the shackles. She had no way. She acted like she was cowering, trying to curl into herself. The footsteps entered the dark room and stopped. Hurry, she thought to herself, commending her body to work faster.

"Nora." The person in the doorway whispered.

"Go away." She growled.

"Nora please, wake up." The voice said again.

"Wake up?" Nora said, shifting trying to peer through the darkness to see who was talking to her.

"Nora!" The voice yelled and began walking to her.

Nora tried backing up, she wasn't sure who this person was or why they were yelling her name There was fear and panic around them.

Zara, are you back yet? I need you! Nora yelled in her mind.

Nora I'm trying. Zara said back to her, *her voice faded and distant, like she was miles away.*

"Nora! Come back to me! Wake up!" The person yelled, dropping to their knees in front of Nora.

The voice hit her with pure emotion. He was afraid…He. He smelled so good. Nora reached out slowly, her hand shaking as she touched the person kneeling in front of her. She tucked her hand under their chin and lifted it. The piercing ice blue eyes stared into her soul as they looked at her.

"Wake up please." Jace said to her, his voice breaking her heart.

Nora felt something pull her back into the wall but the wall was gone. She was sucked out of the dark room and pulled by some unseen force. She fought against it trying to get back to Jace. She was thrown backwards into nothing. She began swinging her arms trying to fight it.

"Jace! Jace!" Nora screamed .

"Open your eyes. Shh, I got you. I got you." Jace said ignoring the painful jolts, Nora was sending into him.

Nora's eyes flew open. They were filled with fear and panic. She stared at him as it finally registered he was really there. She reached up and touched his face. Electricity flew from her fingertips to his cheek. He winced trying his hardest to ignore it. Nora quickly realized she was zapping him this whole time he was touching her. She shut her eyes, forcing the energy down. She pretended in her mind she was packing it up and putting it away. The shocks became less and then finally stopped.

Jace grabbed a hold of her better wrapping his arms around her. He kissed the top of her head, Nora's head rested against his chest. She could hear how fast his heart was beating. How frightened he was.

"Nora, where did you go?" Jace whispered.

"I..I don't know. I..it can't happen. It won't happen." Nora said, her voice shaking, as her eyes flooded with tears.

"What happened? What did you see?" Jace asked her, as she pulled away from him.

"You're here?" She asked, touching his face.

She ran her hand down the side of his cheek, her thumb brushing his strong jaw line. She pressed her forehead into his. Her breathing was still rapid like she had just run a mile. Her body was shaking from the trauma.

"You..you were gone. They were all gone." Nora said, her voice cracking as she buried herself into his chest.

"Nora, I'm right here. No one is taking me from you." Jace vowed to squeeze her tightly.

Jace looked her over, trying to see if there had been any injuries. He glanced down at a weird mark on her arm. The mark was just about where her arm would fold. What was that from? The front door of the pack house slamming open drew his attention.

"She's not inside!" Dante yelled as he came flying through the front door, panic written across his face.

Asher followed quickly behind him rushing to get to her. He froze seeing her wrapped up in Jace's arms. His eyes began searching the surroundings for the person who hurt her.

"I've got her. She's ok. I'm gonna get her inside." Jace said scooping Nora into his arms and cradling her against his chest.

Jace began walking quickly to the house, holding onto Nora like his life depended on it. Nora looked up at his face, watching the emotions run across it.

"I am not going to let it happen. It's going to be ok. I'm going to fix it." Nora whispered.

Chapter Forty Four
Leaving

*J*ace walked out of the room shutting the door quietly. He wasn't sure what just happened but he was shaken to his core. When he couldn't find her, he panicked. The only other time he felt fear like that was when he thought he had lost her. He paused outside the door listening for her. He could hear her steady heart beat and her breathing. He let out a breath and ran his hands over his face, trying to calm himself some more. He straightened up and put on a strong face and headed down stairs.

"What the heck was that?" Dante asked in a whisper coming over to Jace.

"I don't know exactly." Jace answered.

Asher came over along with Logan both their faces filled with concern. Jace studied them, debating on what he wanted to say.

"I'm not sure what just happened. It was like she was stuck in a nightmare. She was saying things about how she saw everyone gone. I don't know what that means. She is upstairs resting. Everyone is to leave her be." Jace said, looking at them as he made his way around them.

"You know how Luna can …well you know she's different. Do you think she saw something that could be true?" Dante asked cautiously.

Jace stopped in the doorway to the dining room. His shoulder tensed. He gritted his teeth. He was worried too. Nora was different. He was trying not to let his concern leak out of him. He hadn't had a chance to talk to her. To see what actually went on. He turned slightly. He swallowed trying to think of something to say.

"Since this the inner circle and you all care for Nora. I honestly don't know. I don't know what she saw. I don't know if it can or will come true. Nora has had a lot of trauma. She had lost her entire family before she came here. All of them, murdered. Now you all are her family. She doesn't want to lose any of you. It could be fear and worry making her see things." Jace said softly.

"All I know right now is that we need to prepare. Prepare for everything and anything. A war is coming and I will not lose her….or any of you. So let's gather ourselves and go stare at that map some more." Jace said with a small smile on his face.

"I'm going to make some coffee first." Asher announced heading to the kitchen.

"I'm getting a beer." Dante said quietly.

Asher shook his head walking back to the dining room, Logan following after him. Logan was quiet. He seemed deep in thought and he was keeping his emotions in check. Jace, getting to the dining room, remembered that he needed to ensure the walls were secured.

"Matt up patrol and I want you to make the first round. Check everything thoroughly. You may bring Lilly with you." Jace sent it to Matt through a mind link.

"Yes, Alpha." Matt responded shortly.

____

*J*ace had set her down on their bed quietly. She had pretended to fall asleep in his arms. It wasn't hard to fake, she was exhausted from what she had just gone through. She knew he didn't understand and didn't know what to do. He had mumbled to himself about needing to send scouts out to re-enforce his walls. She could feel his eyes watching her as he looked down at Nora. She held still pretending she was peacefully sleeping. She almost shivered when he brushed a strand of her dark ebony hair out of the way. Anymore of a touch and she would have blown her whole cover. She heard him take a deep breath and headed out of their room. She knew He would come check on her shortly.

Nora waited until he shut the door, she listened to his footsteps growing distant. She needed to make sure he was out of reach. She laid frozen on the bed for several seconds. She stayed there until she could no longer hear Jace. She sat up frantically. She needed to keep her emotions in check. Being bonded to Jace made him feel what she felt. She began pacing. She had to prevent what she saw from happening but how? She wished she saw how the battle had gone. Was it a surprise attack that went wrong? She ran her hands over her face. She needed to prevent it. She needed to stop it from happening. She needed to break it down.

She walked to the bathroom, she needed to calm down. She flipped on the switch to the light. The bathroom glowed a soft golden color. She walked over the sink and turned the handle. She cupped the water in her hands while still thinking. She splashed it over her face. As the water droplets fell off her face, she let out a long breath.

What did she know? She knew the war happened, everyone died and she ended up locked in a basement. Not going to happen, she reminded herself. Ok the war needed to be avoided. How could they win against Lance with no war. What did Lance want? Lance was after her. The words bounced around off the walls inside her head. Lance was after her. If she went to Lance there would be no war. No war, nobody dies. That was it. She thought, staring at herself in the mirror. She needed to find out how to get herself to Lance.

Jace would never let her go, He would say it would be too dangerous. She would have lots of trouble sneaking away. She needed to go now. She knew Lance was from the north west.

Zara, do you think you could find him? Nora asked her.

We get close enough, we know what he smells like, I could track his scent. You really want us to do this? Zara asked.

Do you want all of our loved ones to die? Do you want Cole and Jace to die? Nora asked her tone letting her know that it wasn't a real question.

No. Zara growled.

Well then this is what we need to do. Nora said back to her walking over to the desk.

What are you doing? Zara asked her, annoyed.

Shouldn't we trust our mate though? Zara added.

I am leaving a note. Did you not see the vision? Do you want to end up like that? Nora asked, clenching her fist.

No. It was dark and cold where I was…like before. Zara whimpered.

Fine, then we go to Lance. We save everyone. Nora confirmed and began writing on the paper.

Dear Jace,

I am so sorry to do this. I can't let anyone else die because of me. I can't let you die because of me. I will find a way back to you. I promise. I will. Do not come after me. I will work this all out. Trust me. I love you with all of me. I'm sorry.

Nora.

Now what? Zara sighed.

Nora walked to the window, looking out of the window. She felt Zara sigh again more loudly as she opened the window.

When we do come back, he is never going to let us in a room with windows. Zara groaned.

Nora laughed as she opened the window and swung her body outwards. Her foot dangled in the air as she looked down at the ground. Three stories up was a long way to fall. She had done it once before and she knew she could do it again. As long as her powers kicked in it would be no problem. It didn't make her stomach feel any better. The fire burning in it from nerves. Nerves because she was leaving, nerves because in seconds she may be falling to her death, and last she was afraid she might never see Jace again.

She knew if she stayed he would die. She had to leave and risk it. She took a deep breath and leaned. She let her body go limp and then she leaned, tumbling into the air. She felt her body go numb as if it was some type of defense mechanism. She squeezed her eyes shut holding her breath, repeating over and over again in her mind "please work." Praying so hard her powers were kicked in and kept her from slamming into the ground. She opened her eyes, seeing the ground coming at her at light speed. No! She screamed inside her mind.

Then as if she had bungee cord wrapped around her toros, she was pulled back. The movement prevented her from moving forward. The world slowed down, she began to float down towards the ground. She felt the relief wash through her. The ground was there in no time and she was just dangling above it. The earth floated up to her and she placed her big toe on it. Touching it making sure it was real, like she was going swimming. Testing out the waters to make sure it was just right. She then sat her whole foot down the other following suit.

"Thank god." She whispered when both feet were on the ground.

"Now to start moving." She announced as she started walking north west, it shouldn't be long. She thought.

Chapter Forty Five
Lighted Path

Nora ducked into the tree lines and took off running. Her lungs burning inside her chest as she dodge branches getting to the fence line. She was avoiding the security cameras she knew Jace had laced through out the pack lands. She got to the outer wall and felt her stomach twist.

"Your doing the right thing." She whispered to herself before she started climbing the stone wall.

Getting to the top of the wall she stood on the ledger looking down. She gritted her teeth wondering if she was doing the right thing. She looked up at the moon, feeling her heart beat fast in her chest.

"I don't know if this is the answer but I am going to need you with me along the way.. I won't let them all die." Nora whispered to the moon.

The moon seemed to glow brighter, lighting up the forest around them. She took a deep breath before jumping down. Landing neatly on her feet she quickly started through the woods. She was not sure which way to go but started traveling in the direction she thought Lance's pack would be. The moon light shimmered down from the dark night sky and danced upon the woods floor. It began to make her a path. She took a breath with a smile coming to her face.

"Thank you." Nora whispered.

She felt Zara press against her skin, wanting to come out. She was restless. She didn't want to leave. She was struggling. Nora tried to calm her as she began following the lighted path. She needed to get as much distance between her and Jace before he knew she was gone.

Shift. Zara said quietly in their mind.

Can you handle that right now? Your emotions are all over the place? We need to keep going forward. We go back, they all die. Nora said back to her, making sure she got the point across.

No, I know this. It just sucks… I am faster than you. Shift and I will get us there. Zara said with a grumble.

All right, I am trusting you. I know you can. Nora said back to her.

I got this. We will get to that bastard's place in no time. Zara growled.

Nora nodded, and closed her eyes letting Zara push forward and take control. A few painful seconds later Zara was out and Nora was along for the ride. Nora was nervous. Zara was loyal and she understood wanting to be next to Jace. She knew her wolf side was the more emotional one. She felt her nerves growing as Zara stared at the lighted path. Zara lifted her head, smelling the air. She looked down the lighted path and then back the way she came from. Nora felt the conflict pulling inside of them. Nora didn't say anything, she let Zara decide. She had to trust her. Zara whimpered and then took off down the lighted path.

Lance paced the hall of the City Lights pack. He decided to come here first to make sure everyone fell in line. He could feel the anger and hatred from some of the pack members. He knew it would be there but as long as everyone fell in line, he didn't care if he was liked or not. He had called a meeting and people were shuffling in. That would be the first thing to be addressed. He liked his pack members to do exactly what he said, when he said. He wasn't one to wait. If he said jump then they all better jump the instant his sentence was finished. They all needed to pledge their allegiance to him and they needed to do it quickly. He knew Jace. He wasn't sitting idle by waiting for Lance to make a move, he was preparing an army.

Jace was likable and a leader. People just followed him. Lance knew he would have others. He already knew the Red Woods pack would be with him because Jace's Luna is the Alpha of it. She would be his Luna soon enough he thought, jealousy and anger rushing through him as he thought about Nora. The pack members began lining up and Lance stood over them. He wanted them to know he was above them.

His eyes began scanning the crowd. He was searching for Bruce's Beta. He spotted him walking through the door, the man's body was completely tense. He looked like his skin was going to tear away from his muscles due to how tight he had all his muscles flexed. He saw Lance lockeyes with him. Rage flashed in them but he quickly tried to stop it. Lance smirked, this poor beta was so loyal to the decreased Alpha. Lance marked it as a good thing and decided to give him a second before condemning him. Looking out over the pack, he was met with blanket stares.

"Hello all and welcome. I am your new Alpha Lance. You all know of me from the council and being Alpha of the Dark Water Pack. Well today I will be combining our pack. Things will go on the same for the most part." He began saying, greeting the pack.

Several gasps were heard and they began to mumble. How did Bruce have such a dramatic pack? Lance groaned.

"Where is Alpha Bruce?" Someone called out from the pack.

"Ok so I guess we will start with the dumb questions. This is the last question I am answering today. I am a very impatient person, I don't like to be questioned. On top of all that we got things to do." Lance said, adding a growl to his voice.

"Bruce is dead. I am your Alpha now. We need to make all of it legal right now but everyone standing up in a group and pledging loyalty to me and then we can get on with it." Lance said in a rush.

"How did he die?" A tall man asked, ignoring everything Lance had just said.

"How?" Lance growled becoming annoyed, his pack wouldn't dare question him, never mind question him after he said no more questions.

"Yeah, how did he die? Why are you in Alpha mode here?" The man said, his voice changing.

"What is your name? Come forward." Lance asked motioning him to come up to the front.

"Brian." The man said to him as he reached the front of the pack, standing inches from Lance.

"Brian he died…like this." Lance said, stepping into Brian his claws drawn.

He grabbed the back of Brian's head and shoved his claws through Brian's throat, his other hand punching him in the rids. On impact his claws went into Brian's stomach. A loud shriek rippled through the pack as Lance took a step back pulling his claws out of Brian. Blood spraying all over him as Brian's body dropped dead.

"Any more fucking questions?" Lance yelled out over the crowd.

Lance stood staring out over the crowd, Brain's blood running down his hand, staining his skin bright red. Blood splatter across his face. His wolf inside begging for more. One more person just wince, look the wrong way at anything. Hamiliton wanted more blood.

The crowd went instantly quiet. Lance snapped at a woman standing by a table. She was freaking out. The look on her face said that she didn't want to die next.

"Towel…go get me a towel." Lance said, rolling his eyes.

"Now the rest of you pledge." Lance growled.

The crowd shifted not sure how to start or what to say. He looked out over them and spotted Bruce's beta. He snapped at him and motioned for him to come up the front. Fear poured out of the pack as Bruce's beta began making his way up to the front. The pack was afraid for him. They obviously cared for him, Lance noted.

"Beta, I would like you to lead your pack in the declaration of loyalty to me … .now" Lance growled.

The woman bowed her head and rushed over holding the towel out to him. Lance took the towel and began cleaning the blood off his face. He saw the woman was still waiting and motioned her to go back to the crowd. Lance cleared his throat, becoming annoyed now.

"I Emanuel." Emanuel, Bruce's beta started waiting for the pack to chim in.

The room filled with I and peoples names. Lance smiled happily, finding himself a chair in front of everyone and having a seat.

"Of the City Lights pack pledge my loyalty and service to Alpha Lance." Emanuel said slowly so the pack could follow.

Power began to flow into Lance; he could feel a bond building and grow with the City Lights pack as each member finished their pledge. By the end of it all Lance felt all powerful. Being the Alpha of two packs felt like he was on some type of drug. He felt unstoppable. His eyes glowing the brightest purple as he looked over the crowd. The pack is waiting for instructions.

"Excellent. Perfect. Now that's out of the way. I need you all to cancel all your duties and plans. You all need to start combat training and make yourself ready. A war is coming and we will be bring it." Lance smiled brightly, the rush of worry collapsed into him.

That was one thing he hated about being Alpha, you feel what your pack feels. Right now they are pathetic. He growled fiercely over them and their thoughts stopped as they froze in place.

"I will not be an Alpha to a bunch of cowards." Lance growled.

"Get out of my sight and get yourself ready. Emanuel see that they are training." Lance announced.

"It will be up to you all if you live or die. Train like your life depends on it because it does." Lance snared.

"Someone show me to my quarters." Lance announced standing up, stepping over Brian's dead body.

Zara put her nose to the air tracking the scent of the three council members. She raced off into the distance. The moonlight light is still lighting the way to go. She knew she was far outside their pack's territory now. The air felt different, the ground was harder,and everything shifted. She just couldn't tell if they were in Bruce's territory or Lance's. Everything smelt like both Bruce and Lance. She kept to the path the moon set for her.

If we were headed to Lance's shouldn't we start smelling the ocean? Nora said inside their mind.

That's what I was thinking. I'm starting to smell …like city air. The world opens up near the ocean but this doesn't look like that. It looks like we will be hitting a…. City. Zara said as she stopped short at the edge of the forest.

As if she summoned it with her thoughts a black tar road appeared leading the way to a city. The city seems to sparkle and shimmer in the distance.

City Lights, we are at Bruce's pack. Lance must have come here first to ensure he was asserting himself into full power. Nora said in their mind.

Zara just growled her response, she was shifting in place debating on stepping onto the road. Nora could feel how nervous her wolf was. She tried to calm them both. Zara's mind kept going to the thought of being locked away again.

Zara, I will not let that happen. We are trying to avoid all that remembering. Nora said to Zara.

So what's the plan? Zara asked her.

I don't really have one. Nora said back to her, honestly.

So we're just going to stroll up there? Zara said back.

Ummm. Yeah pretty much. Nora laughed, a little nervous.

I hope you're ready for this. Zara said, stepping out onto the black tar and began walking down the road to the city.

What are you doing? Nora said, kind of panicked.

Walking up to the gate. Zara said, confused.

Wait, wait, wait. Let me regroup for a second. Nora said her voice shaking a little bit, images of her dream coming into her head and the dark room.

Zara stepped off the road and ducked into the woods. Zara was now trying to calm Nora. Zara began to pace because it felt like that was what Nora was doing inside of them. Zara could hear her mumbling.

Nora, talk to me. Let's walk through this together. Zara said to her.

Ok so if we sneak in we will look like an enemy. Walking in is the best choice, it shows that we are not hiding anything. Nora began to explain.

Ok. Zara said not understanding why they were discussing this because that was exactly what she was doing a minute ago.

I think I got it. You're not going to like it and I need you to find a way to play along. Nora said to Zara.

What do you mean? Zara asked now on edge.

We need Lance to believe we came here to be with him. If he thinks we don't want Jace and want him. He won't lock us away. Nora said quietly knowing what Zara's response was going tobe.

Are you insane? No. We should go in there and kill him. I can't do that. Jace is your mate, Cole is my mate. We are not doing that. I won't stand for him to touch us. Zara growled fiercely in their mind.

Do you want our mates dead? Nora said her voice was cold and short.

No. Zara answered begrudgingly.

Then we play pretend and we will kill him. Nora said, her voice deadly.

Fine, let's do this. Zara growled.

Let me have control. I am going to make an entrance. Nora said with a smile in her voice.

I'm trusting you. Zara said softly before letting Nora push forward.

Nora's body cracked and shifted back into human form. She stood up in the grass, sharp little pieces of twigs digging into her feet. She slipped back on her clothing that she snuck out with. She took a deep breath and shook her arms, trying to shake away the nervousness coursing through her. She took a step out onto the tar and her stomach sank. She reminded herself what she needed to do and what she was trying to prevent as she made her way towards the city.

The road led to gold gates, they were as tall and sparkled in the setting sun. There were no guards that she saw. Where was everyone? She thought. Well it was time to make herself known. She shut her eyes, pulling her energy out. She knew if she drew enough energy to herself Lance would feel her. She opened her eyes, her body vibrating. She pulled on Zara for strength and her eyes began to glow. She then reached out and tapped the lock gate. The gate busted open by the smallest tap of her finger. The gate swung back and slammed into the cement wall.

Knock, Knock. Assholes. Zara chuckled in their mind as Nora stepped through the gate.

Nora laughed hearing Zara's comment but quickly regained composure. She needed to be strong and focused. Her eyes narrow in on a tall building. It was white and etched in gold. She knew that this was their pack hall. She shut her eyes and she could feel the energy in the room, inside the pack hall. She knew the whole pack was in there. She let another wave of power and energy flow out from her. She was sending a message giving them the smallest taste of what she was. She knew Lance already knew what she was capable of.

Lance stiffened up in the hall. A wave of something powerful coming rushed into him. He pressed back into his chair, trying to recover from it. He looked around the room. The pack coward, they thought it was him. He was more powerful now but this was not him. He was concerned, a little voice in his mind asking what if it was Jace. How would he not sense him until right now. Lance stood up looking about the room. The whole pack was here. He realized his mistake. He was focused on everyone pledging their loyalty to him and gaining power that he left the pack lands completely opened. He gritted his teeth, trying to calm himself.

"All members that are on patrol duty need to go back to their stations now. We may have a situation on our hands." Lance demanded.

He watched the pack members shuffle about and start making their way to the door. He felt like he knew someone was going to report Jace's pack was surrounding his land. That the war was here. Jace was quick but he didn't think he would be this quick. Lance hadn't even had a chance to summon His own Dark Water pack here yet. A pack member reached out to open the door and was thrown back.

Lance watched the man hit the ground and skid across it landing right in front of him. Everyone else quickly backed away. As the door opened swung open wide. The power radiating through the door was blinding, people were fighting, going to their knees to submit. He felt this once before and he knew who it was.

She stepped through the door, her long raven hair falling down her like it was blowing in the wind. The energy coming off her was making her skin glow. Her honey eyes beamed, like she was some goddess. The pack members looked at her like she was one. Some of them shield their eyes as if it was too much to look at her.

"Nora?" Lance said fighting his hardest to stand.

"Lance." She smiled, walking down the walkway to him.

"Are you alone? " Lance asked, confused.

"Of course. Why wouldn't I be?" Nora asked, adding a cute chuckle to her voice.

"Where is your mate and his army?" Lance demanded.

"Oh my …hmm mate." She said it was annoying, as she stepped up one of the stairs.

"Jace. You are aware, we will be going to war. With your mate and his alliances." Lance said, narrowing his eyes at him.

"War. If that's what you want to call it." Nora laughed again, closing the gap between them.

She let her eyes wander over him, turning the energy off just a little so he could see her looking at him studying him. Lance felt his chest tighten a little bit and became confused. Nora leaned against his chair, she reached out and ran her hand down his arm. Small little twinges of electricity brushed against his skin. She controlled the energy to let him feel just the tiniest bit. She was hoping it would fool him into thinking he was getting a butterfly sensation from her.

"I know about the war. I knew the minute you killed Bruce. Once I felt that I knew what I had to do." She smiled, Lance staring at her like a deer in headlights.

"What do you mean?" Lance asked quietly.

"Well you see Lance, I need a man who can match me. I know you feel my strength. I know you can feel my power. I also know that you're not afraid of it. I know your ambitions match mine. You want to be Alpha of all Alpha's. King of all kings. I can help you with that." Nora said, getting dangerously close to his ear.

Her breath tickled his ear and he felt shivers rush through him. His wolf pressed forward, wanting her. The power and energy she gave off made his wolf crazy and he wanted her as his own.

"What is it that you want? If I allow you to help me?" Lance said, trying to take back authority.

"Well every King needs a Queen. Every Alpha needs a Luna." Nora said, licking her lips as if they were dry.

"You have a destined mate. The moon goddess blessed you with Jace and you're telling me that you want to walk away from that." Lance said with a growl, not believing her.

"The moon goddess got it wrong. Jace should not have been my mate. He is weak, timid and can not handle me. He is nothing but a burden and would have me hide my powers away. Which is a blessing from the moon goddess." Nora growled, the anger more coming from Zara and then insulting their mate but she used it like she was angry with Jace.

"How do-

"Lance, I need someone like you. You have vision, power, strength and do I frighten you?" Nora asked, her voice low and seductive.

"No. You do not frighten me." Lance said, it was a little bit of a lie but he was making himself believe it.

"Be my King and we can rule everything together." Nora said, whispering into his ear.

Chapter Forty Six
Pretend

Lance tingles all over hearing her whisper such words into his ear. He pulled back looking at her, studying her trying to see if she really meant it. He wanted it to be true. His wolf wanted it to be true. If she meant it they could really conquer the world together. He looked at her neck, jealousy coursing through him.

"His mark." Lance whispered to her, nodding at her neck.

Nora's heart sank, she knew right away what he was implying. It was sacred. It meant she and Jace were forever connected. It was more special than a wedding ring. She sat down on his lap to confuse him and hoped to hide her immediate sadness. She wiggled slightly just to add more destruction into her motive.

"What about it?" Nora asked, turning to face him.

"It means you belong to him." Lance growled.

"I belong to no one." Nora growled, running her finger tips down the side of his face.

"You need to belong to me." Lance growled back.

"And my word is not enough?" Nora said her voice was coy.

"Sorry Doll, actions talk." Lance said, eyeing her suspiciously.

Nora decided she was done with this bullshit. She jumped off his lap, she allowed her anger to flow out of her. Everyone in the room became instantly timid as they felt her anger.

"Is this not enough action for you?" Nora stood up stomping her foot, a tidal wave of energy flowing out of her.

She watched Lance fight with himself to find some type of bravery. He stood slowly trying to match her. A part of her wanted to know if she could just kill him. She frowned not knowing if she had it in her.

"The mark links you to Jace. Regardless of your actions. If you wear his mark. Your loyalty is to him." Lance said, folding his arms across his chest.

"So you won't take me up on my offer until the mark is gone?" Nora asked him, rolling her eyes.

Lance stood there quietly, crossing his arms. Nora was chewing on the inside of her cheek trying to contain herself. She could taste the blood from the hole she was making in it.

Let's just kill him now. I don't think anyone here would stop us. Zara growled inside of her.

I'm not sure. Nora said nervously to her.

She rolled her eyes and began walking down the platform. The pack members shifted away from her as she started making her way to the door.

"Where are you going?" Lance growled, coming down the platform and following after her.

"Well I really wished you would have taken my offer. I am attracted to you and think that we would do great things but if you are saying me coming all the way here without Jace knowing. Betraying him and presenting myself to you is not enough then I am leaving. Maybe another Alpha somewhere will see my potential." Nora said with a shrug and turned to leave again.

Lance was off the platform and to her faster than she could take steps. He caught her by the arm pulling her back. Nora tried to control her body from attacking him. She knew he was getting small little jolts of electricity by the way he was trying not to flinch. Nora's body right now wanted to send him flying across the room.

"I didn't say any of that." Lance said his tone was a mixture of want and anger.

"Well that is exactly what it sounded like." Nora said back to him annoyed.

"Why don't we go talk in private." Lance smiled at her.

"I'd like that." Nora said, forcing it out, she wanted to puke.

She did not want to be alone with him whatsoever but she had to play this part. She had to do this to save everyone, to save Jace.

"Excellent. I will take you to the room that is adjacent to mine. There is actually a conjoining door." Lance smiled at her, offering his arm.

"That sounds lovely." Nora smiled sweetly, looping her arm through his.

"You must be hungry, tired, and wanting to take a bath." Lance said, trying to be a gracious host.

"Yes, actually I traveled very far and very fast." Nora said quietly.

"I will bring some food." Lance said as he began guiding her out of the hall.

They arrived in the room in no time. Everything in the pack was connected by sky bridges or tunnels. The city was stunning. It was night and every single building was covered in twinkling lights. The city shimmered and glistened like it was christmas. They stopped in front of a large white door, the trim of the door had golden etchings on it and then the handle looked like a crystal. Lance took a key out of his pocket and unlocked it. He let the door swing open slowly and then motioned for Nora to walk in.

If he touches us you shift and I will rip his throat out. Zara growled inside of her.

The room was huge. You entered into a sitting area where there was a small white leather loveseat with large buttons and a matching lounge. Lance grabbed a hold of her hand seeing her look around and he led her into the room more. Through the sitting area was a step up and opened into the bedroom area. A large four post king size bed was in the middle of a platform and shimmering gold curtains were draped down around the bed. Through the bedroom was a master bathroom. There was a giant claw foot tub that was begging for someone to soak in it up to their chin and an all glass shower. There was a gorgeous old style vanity all set up and ready to be used. As she took everything in words from her vision popped into her head.

"You would live like a queen, I have everything ready." Lace said quietly

This was her room. He had already begun to plan this. He walked over to a wall and tapped the wall. The wall opened up, revailing a walk-in closet. He stepped into it motioning for her to come in. Nora followed him. She looked around at the walls full of clothing, shoes, and jewelry. They were all her size.

"Like?" Lance said quietly as if he was searching for approval.

"It is stunning." Nora said quietly, seeing clothing in her side meant the vision would have played out exactly how she saw it.

It made the situation so much more real. She took a breath in moving to look at the clothes. Running her hand along the outfits trying to clear her head.

"The clothes all look to be about my size." Nora said quietly.

"Pretty amazing uh." Lance smiled.

"Why is the clothing all my size?" Nora asked curiously, she knew the answer but she wasn't sure if he would be honest.

"Well lets just say I had a feeling at some point you would be here." Lance smiled at him.

Nora chuckled to the response not knowing what to say and not trying to think about the images she had seen. She ran her hand down a satin nightgown and wanted to cringe. She couldn't see herself wearing that for him.

"I personally like red." Lance smirked, nodding to the red night gown next to it.

Play along, play along. She reminded herself in her head as she let go of the satin blue nightgown she had touched.

"You should get comfortable.' Lance smiled still staring at the red night gown.

"Well that would be nice. I would really love to eat something and then take a bath." Nora said, walking over to the bathtub.

Lance raced her to it, turning on the water. He walked over the cabinet next to the tub. He opened it and Nora saw tons of items for the bath. Nora watched Lance take out some bath oils and bath salts. He came over and began making up the tub for her. Nora smiled, watching him carefully. Lance looked at her and wanted to tell her to undress and get in the tub. He wasn't going to push her this time around but in the future she will quickly learn what Lance liked and disliked.

"Ok, I will let you relax." Lance said standing up and moving away from the tub.

"Thank you." Nora said back politely.

"I will have a meal left on your table out there." Lance said to her with a nod.

"Before I go we need to talk about that mark." Lance said with a frown.

"Fine…what do you want to say about it?" Nora asked him, settling into the chair next to the tub.

"I say it needs to come off." Lance said quietly."

"Well how do we do that?" Nora growled asking.

"You reject your mate." Lance said like this was the final test of loyalty.

Chapter Forty Seven
Gone

"I just reject him and it goes away?" Nora asked, sounding like she was curious.

"Yup it will hurt but the mark will burn off. Few seconds poof gone." Lance said, looking her up and down.

Nora gritted her teeth, Zara began howling inside of her as she felt Nora debating it. Lance leaned against the wall folding his arms across his chest looking at her skeptically. Nora fidgeted slightly.

"If you don't reject him, how is this going to work? I doubt you would want to be bonded to him. If everything you have told me has been the truth." Lance said anger bubbling inside of him, as he looked at Nora with narrowed eyes.

"How do you reject someone?" Nora asked, delaying it more.

Nora, we can't reject our mate. I do not know if I can let you. It hurts..it hurts just thinking about. Zara whined inside of her.

Nora felt her chest tense up and she felt like she was getting out of breath. Zara's panic and pain rushed into her. The back of her neck started to feel warm and it started to spread over her body.

"It's easy. You just say I Nora of well I guess your of both Red Woods and Cross River reject Jace Knight. And then you're all done. Easy peasy." Lance said his forearms flexed, she could see veins extending on his arms.

An image of Jace beheaded popped into her head, the darkness.The cell that was her home. She knew it had to be somewhere below them. Flashes of everyones death popped into her head and her eyes began to glow.

Let's just kill him right now. Zara growled inside of her.

The idea made her want to consider it. She even stepped forward towards Lance, her eyes glowing bright, her body vibrating. She just needed to touch him and she could drain him of energy. His body would not be able to work and everything would shut down. She smiled at him trying to throw him off but he could feel the power rolling off of her. He tried not to act afraid. She then paused, she remembered something from her vision. Lance had some secret weapon or at least that's what she thought and felt. She paused.

Nora I can't. Zara whimpered.
We won't. Nora said back to her.

She then slammed her hand to her neck and shut her eyes. She felt her neck burning as she focused on the energy she was pulling from around the room. Focusing on what she wanted. She imagined her energy pouring into the mark and fixing her skin. It weaving itself back together and then the mark disappears.

"Aahhhh!!' She let out a small yell as she held her hand in place while the energy burned into her.

"What. What are you doing!" Lance yelled asking.

"Stop. stop." Lance said, panicking and not understanding.

Nora pulled her hand away and let out a long breath. Her body shaking, she felt like she had just pressed an electric rod to her skin. Taking another deep one and letting out as she tried to focus on anything but the pain.

"You…" Lance said quietly walking towards her, his eyes focused on her neck.

"You..you reserved your mark?" Lance said, moving her hair and looking at her perfect skin.

"It's like it was never there." Lance said, taking his pointer finger and running it over her skin.

Nora flinched slightly because her skin felt sun burned. She almost expected blisters to be there but her skin looked and felt flawless.

"Even when you reject verbally your mark burns away but there is still something, some tiny scar or mark." Lance whispered, pulling his shirt collar to the side.

Nora's eyes landed on his neck. He had been marked at one point. She could see the small outline that was faded if you looked close enough. The only thing that was throwing her off was that it looked smudged and black.

"See. But you, your skin looks like it's never been touched." Lance said, amazed still staring at her neck.

"Believe my intentions now." Nora said with a small smile

"It will be like I am the first person to mark you." Lance said his eyes flashing lust as he stepped into her.

"Hold on cowboy, we need to become friends first." Nora said, putting her hand to his chest.

"Excuse me." Lance growled.

"No sir. I am not like other girls. We have mutual power, mutual authority. I am not some hopeless pup dying to be your mate. We will do this right. Business friendship and then lovers." Nora said, stepping into him and running her finger down the side of his neck.

Lance felt chills rush over him, he caught her chin with his hand. He ran his thumb over her lip. Nora smirked and then bit his thumb lightly, letting one of her canines nick his thumb. Lance pulled back a small smile on his face as he studied her.

"You are not like other women. Fine, I will court you. But I am not a man who likes to wait. Do not play games with me." Lance said, his eyes trailing over her body.

"No games promise… well there will be but you'll like them." Nora chuckled, her laughter sexy.

Lance felt himself stiffed at her response. He was trying his hardest to control himself. He stepped back from her trying to get some air in between them.

"Dinner tonight. I will be back shortly. Get yourself settled. I will send someone up to help you get ready. My Queen." Lance said, stepping forward, grabbing her hand and kissing the top of it.

Nora pretended to blush and giggle. Lance looked proud of himself as he nodded to her and hurried out the door. As the door shut Nora collapsed her hand over her mouth. Tears flowed from her eyes as she silently began to cry. Her hand went to her neck. Her mark is gone. She sank to her knees as she leaned back into the wall shaking. Her connection to Jace is gone. She couldn't feel him like she once could. Zara howled like cries in her mind.

"Zeke and his pack will be here tomorrow, we need to start moving. I need to get intouch with Douglas and find out exactly where Lance -

Fire. His neck was burning. He let out a loud groan of pain as he grabbed his neck with his hand. The pain flowing through him sent him forward like someone punched him in the gut. His mark. His mark was burning. Terror spread through him as he braced himself.

"Alpha!" Dante yelled and panicked.

"Nora! Go! Nora! Something's wrong. My room!" Jace said, grabbing Dante by the shirt and pushing him as he collapsed in pain to his knees.

Dante saw his mark and knew what he was saying and bolted towards the stairs. Matt heard Jace and began coming down the stairs. He almost crashed into Dante.

"Nora!" Dante yelled, pushing Matt out of the side as he rushed past him.

"Nora?" Matt asked worriedly running up the stairs after Dante.

Dante crashed into Jace's bedroom door. He could still hear Jace groaning in pain downstairs. The door was open, it flung open as he crashed into it, giving away to his weight. Dante came crashing down onto the floor.

"Nora!" Dante called, fear was washing over him, as he tried to get up.

When someone's mark burned it was from their mate. They were either in pain or worse. Or you were being rejected.

"Nora!" Matt said, rushing into the room behind Dante, he jumped over Dante who was getting himself off the ground.

Matt looked at Dante like he was crazy just standing there. Matt began looking around the room. He didn't see her. He moved into the bathroom quickly. She wasn't there either. The window was open and the cool night breeze blew in from it. Dante saw the piece of paper first and walked over to it. A groan from the door caught Dante's ear and he turned, seeing Jace bracing himself against the door. Sweat beaded across his forehead and he was pale.

"She's not here, Alpha." Matt whispered.

Dante glanced over the paper and he felt his stomach twist. He heard Jace growl at Matt's response.

"What do you mean not here?" Jace growled anger coursing through him as he started walking towards Matt, his eyes glowing.

"Alpha." Dante whispered.

Jace couldn't hear him; he was locked in on Matt as if Matt was the cause of all this. Matt bowed his head trying to show submission to Jace.

"Jace!" Dante yelled, Jace's head snapped towards him.

"She left." Dante said quietly, holding the paper out to Jace.

Jace took the paper in his hand, his hands shaking as he tried to read over it.

Dear Jace,

I am so sorry to do this. I can't let anyone else die because of me. I can't let you die because of me. I will find a way back to you. I promise I will. Do not come after me. I will work this all out. Trust me. I love you with all of me. I'm sorry.

Nora.

Jace crumpled the note in his hand and marched to the bathroom. He hit the light switch so hard it broke as he turned the light on. He walked over the mirror, turning his head and growling, his eyes landing on where his mark should be. It was gone. Like it had never been there. His stomach collapsed on itself. He felt like he was going to vomit. He didn't know what this meant. He tried to search for her with his mind, trying to lock in on her. He couldn't feel her. The porcelain sink in his hands cracked. He was holding on to it so tight. Dante slowly walked into the bathroom. Seeing Jace's blood dripping down his hands from the sink cutting into his hands.

"Jace." Dante said softly.

"My marks it's gone..it's gone. I .. I can't feel her." Jace whispered, his voice sounding broken.

Dante hung his head, he didn't want to think about it but that usually meant the person was dead.

"What the hell was she thinking?" Jace said, shaking.

"Jace." Dante said, walking over to him and trying to move his hands from the sink.

He grabbed Dante and slammed him against the wall. He was shaking so violently that he was shaking Dante as he held him to the wall.

"Jace."

"Dante my mark is gone...I can't feel her..she's..she's-

"Alpha, your mark is gone, it's not black." Matt said, walking into the bathroom.

"What?" Jace said quietly.

"When your mate dies it turns black." Matt said calmly trying to get Jace to calm down.

Jace's eyes seemed to clear up, he looked like he realized he had pinned Dante to the wall and he took a step back.

"Alpha, she is still alive." Matt said, reassuring him.

"So she rejected me?" Jace asked, confused.

"I don't know what she did. Rejection there would be some mark, a scar, something fade but Alpha your neck looks like it's never been touched." Matt said to him, sounding confused.

"What did she do?" Jace asked out loud as he walked back to the mirror.

"I don't know Alpha…the Luna… She's different." Matt smiled saying it.

"We need to move. We need to find her. She's going to Lance." Jace said, stepping back away from the mirror.

"How do you know?" Dante asked, confused.

"Because she's trying to save us all." Jace said shortly walking out of the bathroom, blood droplets from his hands being torn left a trail behind him.

Chapter Forty Eight
We Wait

"*I* don't give a fuck what he's doing I need to talk to him now." Jace yelled into the phone, the phone receiver almost buckling in his hand.

"Would it be more discreet if I just showed up there?" Jace growled.

Dante was across the way talking to Zeke and Matt was on the phone with Chadwick. They were telling them that they were moving now. That they were not waiting for Lance to make his move. Nora was gone and Jace was seeing red.

Logan walked into the room and locked eyes with Jace. Jace almost looked happy to see him. In Jace's mind if anyone cared for Nora close to how he did it was Logan. He nodded to him and let him go back and then went back to his phone call.

"I need to know where he is. It would be quicker. I don't have time. Let Douglas know if I don't have an answer in a half hour, I am moving. Remind him that he may council but he does not want to make an enemy with me by keeping me waiting." Jace threatened.

Asher walked in his face showing his concern. He didn't mask it. He looked around the room. He knew his Alpha was gone, he couldn't feel her. He had been trying to mind link Nora since this morning.

"Nora." Asher said sharply looking at the men in the room, Logan shook his head saying he didn't know anything yet.

Matt held his finger up to Asher as he quickly wrapped up his phone call. Matt hung up the phone and looked to Asher and Logan going to catch them up.

"Nora left." Matt started and as soon as those words came out of his mouth Asher cut him off.

"What do you mean left?" Asher asked, his voice holding anger.

Logan shook his head and frowned he knew before Matt even said the words. He knew his friend, he knew Nora. She was selfless.

"She went to Lance." Matt said and heard a loud growl coming from Jace as he slammed the phone down.

The phone shattered into pieces on the desk, the receiver in pieces in his hand. Dante kept on with his phone call acting like Jace had not done anything.

"What the hell do you mean she went to Lance? What the hell did he do?" Asher growled looking at Jace.

Jace looked at Asher and hearing the comment his body shook. He was going to rip Asher apart. Jace came charging towards Asher. Asher bowed up ready to finger. Logan shook his head stepping between them. They both didn't see it coming. Logan hit Asher hard in the stomach, sending him backwards into the wall. He caught Jace by the shoulders locking eyes with him.

"Stop. We need him and his help if we want to get her back." Logan said firmly.

Jace froze hearing Logan's words. He looked at Asher gritting his teeth as he stepped away.

"He says one more dumbass comment like that, Red Woods will have a new beta." Jace growled.

"So if he didn't do anything why did she leave?" Asher winced, getting off the wall.

"Because she's Nora. Because she loves us idiots too much. She's afraid of her loved ones dying. I should have seen this coming." Logan said, shaking his head.

"She went because she doesn't want us to get hurt." Matt said, shaking his head.

"She should have said something." Dante grumbled as he ended his phone call.

"We wouldn't have listened anyways. This war was happening regardless." Matt said.

Jace was stressed running his hands over his face and through his hair. They didn't know where Nora was. Didn't know where Lance was. Each second that passed he felt more and more like he couldn't breathe.

"Zeke is with us." Dante said, trying to make Jace feel better.

"Chadwick too." Matt said with a nod.

"Obviously Red Woods." A feminine voice said entering the room.

"Lyla?" Asher said he thought he came alone.

"I knew something was wrong with Alpha so I came to check." Lyla told him.

"Jace we need to think this through, I am with you and my hunters too but we can't go blindly rushing into wherever Lance is. The valley was a safe plan." Logan said, watching Jace carefully.

His voice hit her like a hot wave. The world around them slowed down and she locked in on Logan. His scent invaded her nostrils. He was intoxicating. Her wolf cried inside her begging to be near him. Lyla felt like she was in a haze.

Jace gritted his teeth and stepped towards Logan. It didn't phase Logan. He locked eyes with Jace. He knew Jace wasn't in the right frame of mind and he was ready for whatever emotional outburst he might have.

"You think I don't know that" Jace growled.

The growl at Logan was all it took and Lyla was in between them shoving Jace. Her eyes glowed amber as they locked into Jace's, her fangs descending. The amber color of her eyes made him think of Nora and he stopped moving.

"Back the fuck up." Lyla yelled in Jace's face.

"What the hell? Woah..Hi..miss?" Logan said confusedly, touching her arm slightly.

"Hey, hey I got this. I appreciate it but I got this." Logan said to her softly.

Lyla felt an instant chill run through her as Logan's hand touched her skin. Goosebumps spread up her arms, as she inhaled sharply. Logan looked completely confused at her reaction.

"For the love of god." Jace mumbled getting a hold of himself and going back to his desk, he wasn't about to fight over Logan never mind fighting a woman.

"Are you ok?" Lyla asked him, her breath shaking.

"Um, are you?" Logan asked, confused.

"Yeah I'm fine." Lyla smiled sweetly to him.

"Ok then umm anyways back to what I was saying. Jace, I am with you but let's be smart." Logan continued stepping around Lyla.

Lyla's eyes ran over him as he stepped around her. Her wolf inside began howling. The word mate bouncing around inside her head. She looked at Logan and everything in her told her she belonged with him. She stepped up with him, ready to defend him against anyone.

"Oh hello again." Logan said, confused, looking at Lyla.

Matt began laughing hysterically in the corner. Jace sighed, frustrated looking at Lyla.

"Look, I will not hurt him. No one here will. He is a friend and ally. Calm down. Or leave." Jace said to Lyla.

"What?" Logan said confused and looked back at Matt who was still laughing.

"Ok.. Miss. I am a hunter, I may not be a wolf like you all but i can't certainly fight and hold my own. I am very well trained." Logan said, looking at her baffled.

"What am I missing?" Lilly asked, walking into the room and looping her arm through Matt's who was still chuckling.

"Logan is Lyla's mate." Matt laughed again.

"What..shut up no way." Lilly laughed.

"Mate?" Logan asked, focused on looking at Lyla.

She was gorgeous and he felt a pull towards her. The minute he actually looked at her. His stomach flipped nervously inside of him.

She bit her lip and nodded like it was a secret that wasn't supposed to be told yet. He looked around the room like he was unsure what he was supposed to do. He then saw Asher. He looked hurt. He remembered how closely Asher had cared for Lyla when she was hurt. He felt instantly bad.

"Asher-"

Asher shook his head, cutting him off. " We need to plan now. All this will have to wait. Welcome to the wolf family I guess. We need to figure out how we are getting Nora back."

The broken phone began to ring. Jace looked at it confused before picking it up.

"Douglas?" Jace's voice said as he put his hand up telling everyone in the room to be quiet.

"Ok we will be ready to move at dawn. The other packs are on their way. We will surround the city and make moves from there." Jace said, looking about the room.

"Ok we will meet there beforehand." Jace said before hanging up.

"What is it?" Asher asked.

"Lance is at City Lights. They have spotted Nora. She was talking about being his queen." Jace said, flexing his jaw.

"You know that's not true even if she said it." Dante said to Jace reassuring him.

"She's using it to get close to him." Matt said, nodding.

"He must have made her get rid of the mark. To prove she was no longer connected to you." Dante continued.

"She's clever. I just hope she knows what she is doing. He better not fucking touch her." Jace growled.

"We are meeting with someone from Douglas who plans to formalize everything just outside the City Lights border. We will game plan there and then attack. Zeke and Chadwick are on their way with their packs." Jace said quietly.

"I will have my hunters get ready. We need to be prepared for Lance's pack to show up. We may be able to move on him at City Light but he will call for reinforcement the minute he knows we are there for him." Logan said quietly.

"Douglas is going to cover that part." Jace said quietly.

"We better come up with a just in case Douglas doesn't hold his part of the bargain piece." Logan said quietly.

"I agree. We will see how many numbers we have. Asher maybe Lyla could take a portion of Red Woods and Cross River and go where Douglas would be. Dark water packs can only come at us one way. If we ensure to block them then the main attack should go well." Jace said thinking out loud.

"That sounds reasonable." Asher nodded.

"I will go get my pack." Asher said quietly.

"I will go contact my hunters." Logan said looking to Lyla like he wanted to say something but didn't know what. He smiled at her before leaving.

"Ok what now?" Lilly asked out loud.

"We wait.." Jace said, his voice angry and filled with dread.

Chapter Forty Nine
Acting

She stretched outwards, her fingers running over soft smooth surfaces. She rolled over hitting pillows. She must have fallen asleep. She was exhausted, running away and using so much of her powers. She didn't know how she got onto the bed though.

"Oh you're awake?" A small voice said that sounded almost excited.

Nora moved her head in the direction of the voice. A small girl stood just beyond the closest doorway. She was moving clothing into the closet. She had light brown hair and light brown eyes. She smiled brightly at Nora.

"Hello?" Nora said, sitting up.

"I'm sorry to have woken you. I would have had to go soon anyways but you were sleeping so soundly. I took your measurements while you were sleeping. All this clothing here in the closet should fit you perfectly." The girl smiled again.

"Ok…what's your name?" Nora said, pinching the bridge of her nose as she was getting a small headache.

"Polly." The girl smiled.

"How did I get on the bed?" Nora asked her looking around the room, it was just herself and Polly.

"I came in after knocking several times.You were asleep against the wall with your head on your knees. I helped you into the bed. That was not a comfortable way to sleep." Polly smiled.

"Thank you." Nora smiled back to her, the girl was overly happy.

"Alpha would like you to attend dinner with him. In about twenty minutes. You have all the clothing you will need. There is makeup and hair supplies in the bathroom. Anything else you need just ask me and I will get it for you." Polly said with a nod walking to the door.

"Ok Thank you." Nora said going to stand up.

She still felt so drained. She watched Polly smile at her once more before leaving. Nora walked over to the closet. She was amazed looking at the amount of clothing that was in there. She must have slept really hard. She tilted her neck to the side as she tried to stretch out the muscle in it. A small ache forming at the base of her skull. She shook it off looking in. Dinner she thought. She needed to look the part. She stepped into the closet running her hand over the as she walked into the closet.

"Ok sexy…demanding…in charge." She said to herself.

Her eyes landed on a black dress that shimmered in the light. The shimmer had a blue tone to it. It had a heart shape neckline that plunged and would show off her breast.

"Sexy, demanding, in charge." She said, pulling the dress off the hanger.

She found a pair of dark heels and walked to the bathroom. She felt empty. She felt lonely. She took a deep breath as she flipped the light on in the bathroom. As the light flipped on she found herself staring into the bathroom mirror.

Her eyes immediately went to her neck. Her eyes teared up seeing her skin not marked. She shut her eyes letting out a small breath calming herself. She looked at the dress, sexy, demanding, in charge. She repeated to herself as she slipped off her clothing. The black dress had a long slit up the side of it. She walked over to the vanity that was in the bathroom. She sat down in front of the vanity.

"Twenty minutes." She repeated what Polly told her.

She pulled open the drawer looking into a variety of make rolled forwarded. She frowned deeply seeing the makeup. Thoughts of Joel running through her head. His voice said "Do curls! Excitedly as she looked at herself. She never really did make up but when she needed to he was always right there. Thoughts of everyone she loved who had passed entered her mind. Joel, her parents, her brother. She felt shaky, closing her eyes and she felt Zara trying to comfort her. She was there because of them. She was not letting that happen to her pack and her mate. No one else was going to die.

She grabbed a bright red lipstick and popped it on to her pouty mouth. Her lips instantly looked more desirable. She fumbled around the drawer looking for mascara. Finding it she applied it to her eyes. She sighed looking at herself. She pulled her wavy hair up into a bun and then pulled strands of curly pieces of hair down around her face. There was a rose hair clip rolling around in the drawer. She grabbed it and placed it in the bun, which turned it instantly into an elegant updo. She stood and walked over to a floor length mirror in the corner of the bathroom and turned it. She fit the part she was playing perfectly.

She slipped the dark black heels on. Took a deep breath reminding herself why she was doing this and walked out the bathroom.

As if they knew a knock came to the door. She was ready. She walked to the door and opened it. Lance was standing there. She didn't expect to see him. She had thought someone would escort her to him. His mouth dropped seeing her. His eyes wandered over her body. The dress hugged every inch of her in all the right spots. His eyes lingering on her breast, her hips, and then moving over the slit in the dress that when she moved showed quick flashes of her thigh. He pulled his bottom lip into his mouth as he looked her over.

"Hungry?" Nora flashed him a smile, her voice playful as her eyes teased him.

"Starving." He answered back his voice full of unspoken promises.

"Well I guess we should get to dinner." Nora smiled, stepping out of the doorway of her room.

"Yes..Dinner." Lance said, offering her his arm.

They walked down a long hall and to a stairwell. It was a different way then they came before. Lance watched her the whole time as she tried to remember where she was. She knew he was trying to confuse her. He smiled watching her figure it out.

"Just taking precautionary measures, doll." Lance said to her nodding for her to go through a doorway.

"From me?" She laughed innocently.

"Oh I think you know it's you, I need to protect myself from." Lance said his voice was dangerous.

"Well I think you should consider yourself lucky then." Nora smiled, his voice matching his.

"And why is that?" He asked her to pull on her arm gently, making her stop.

"Because I'm here. Choosing you. " Nora said, spinning herself towards him and stepping close to him.

Lance felt his breath catch in his throat. His stomach twisted with excitement. His eyes locked with her perfectly pouty lips.

"I wouldn't play with fire." Lance whispered to her.

"I am fire." Nora whispered back to him, running her hand gently down the side of his cheek.

Lance felt a shiver go through him at the slight touch. His hand catching hers as he stopped her from moving it away. His eyes glanced at the door behind her. Something crossed across his face, she couldn't figure out what emotion it was but it was like he was debating something with himself.

"Come with me." Lance said, leading her away from the door.

Shit. Nora thought as she tried to hide the dread that pitted in her stomach.

No, we are not sleeping with him. Zara growled at her.

No. No. we aren't. Nora agreed, she started coming up with a plan to shock him if he tried. Maybe she could shock him enough to make him unconscious and somehow make him think that they did.

"Hey relax, it's nothing scary. I want to show you something. It's business." Lance smirked.

Lance started leading her down the stairs and at the very bottom they approached a door with a keypad. Nora began to get vibes remembering Kip and his experiments. Nora locked down her emotions. She needed to see this. She needed Lance to think she was with him one hundred percent. He got over to the keypad and looked at it with a smile on his face. He motioned for her to come to him. She gave him a sexy smile trying to keep her disguise up. She stepped into his arms and Lance pulled her back against him. He went to cover her eyes with his hands and she moved her head away.

"I will give you the code once…you give yourself to me. Until then this is just a friendly precaution." He whispered into her ear.

"Hmm, ok I'll play." Nora smirked, letting Lance place his hands over her eyes, she purposely wiggled into him.

Her ass brushing against his pelvis made him catch breath in his throat. He tried to ignore it as he punched in the code of the key pad. Nora pressed back into him again.

"You're playing dirty." Lance whispered to her, as the door made a clicking noise as it unlocked.

"I think you rather enjoy it." Nora laughed playfully.

Chapter Fifty
Deja Vu

Lance chuckled at her moving closer, it was a daring chuckle almost as if he wanted to push her to see what she would do or say more. The door popping opening caught her attention and she stepped forward. She walked across the threshold and she froze. Deja Vu came rushing back to her. Everything was white, the halls, the ceiling, and the floors. An eerie hospital vibe crashed down around her. She looked back at Lance who closed the door and offered his arm to her once more. She tried to control her anxiety that was flooding into her. She took his arm and he began leading her down a hallway. The hall opened up to glass walls looking into hospital rooms. She clenched her jaw, as they stopped at the first room. She could feel herself shaking as she tried to control herself. Alarms going off in her head as her body screamed danger.

"You ok." Lance stopped suddenly looking at her with suspicion.

"Honestly…no." Nora laughed lightly.

"Explain." Lance ordered for some reason becoming upset, he was wondering if she was having second thoughts.

"You are not the first man to lead me down into an underground hospital." Nora said being completely honest.

"What do you mean?" Lance said softing his voice, he was suddenly upset that he may have upset her with his tone.

What the hell's wrong with you? Hamilton said sharply in his mind.

Nothing, I just like her. We should like her if she is to be ours. Be quiet. Lance snapped back.

"Kip. The last time I was in a set up like this someone was trying to experiment on me." Nora said guard.

"How fucking dare he. If he was still alive I would kill him myself. Did he touch you?" Lance asked part of his statement sounding like he was some knight in shining armor, then it seemed to turn dark.

"No, he met his end quite quickly." Nora said, flashing him a smile.

"Good. Kip had it wrong. You can't use humans." Lance said, letting go of her hand and walking over to the thick glass wall.

"Bruce became obsessed with the idea of super beings. He began trying the formula Kip had discovered on everything." Lance began saying.

Lance nodded glancing back at Nora as the nurse in the room motioned for someone to be brought in. Two large men dragged a younger man into the room. Nora stepped up to the glass to her stomach twisting and turning inside of her.

"You see, they need to be wolves already. Kip's plan didn't work because the human bodies were not strong enough to withstand the change. This is a rogue. No pack, no power, no authority. The bottom of the wolf kind." Lance said snarling a little as he explained to Nora what a rogue was.

"But." Lance said as he motioned for the nurse to go to the next step.

"If we injected them with Alpha blood with few tweaks we have made in the lab then we get-

"A Lobo." Nora whispered.

"A what?" Lance asked, looking at her confused.

"It's what we were calling the things Kip made. Do these ones die?" Nora asked, hoping the answer was yes.

"Uh?" Lance asked, confused.

"I mean do they actually last. Kip would have these creations and they would give out. It was like their bodies couldn't handle what was happening. They would die because of it." Nora explained.

"See now that's the interesting part. They are wolves on steroids. Just watch in a few seconds his muscles will have muscles. He will look hideous. His body will be that of wolf and human but he will be fast and super strong. Imagine a whole army. We would never have to worry about our pack suffering from war. We would just unleash them." Lance smiled proudly.

Within a few minutes it was just as Lance said. The poor young man mutated into this half wolf half human monster. His fangs were descended, drool pouring out of his mouth. Claws were his fingernails should be. He stood up right and tall. His eyes were hollow, they constantly glowed purple as if he was stuck in a shifting mode. The poor young man had turned into something out of a nightmare.

"How do you control them?" Nora asked, looking at the creature.

"Well they are wolves. So before we turn them I have them pledge themself to me. They accept me as Alpha and once they are turned I still have that bond over them." Lance said excitedly.

"That's amazing. So they follow your command because you became their Alpha." Nora repeated trying to make sure she understood.

"Yeah it's that easy." Lance said with a shrug.

"Do they have the same weakness as we do? Mistletoe, Mountain ash, wolfsbane?" Nora asked as she studied the creature.

"Silver." Lance said quietly.

"The others, yes. It aggravates them but what kills them is silver." Lance said with a shrug.

"How many do we have?" Nora said trying to match his excitement and using the word We so Lance would think she was with him.

"Ten so far. The rogue has to be just right. It's a strange process." Lance said as if he himself did not understand it.

"Ten's not a lot." Nora said with a frown.

"No, Doll, but ten with you by my side is enough." Lance said, putting his arm around her waist and pulling her into him.

"You give me a lot of credit." Nora smiled, shyly at him.

"You have no clue what you send off or how it feels. Jace is a fool to let you go and not encourage your gifts. But his loss is my gain." Lance smiled brightly.

Nora smiled and moved closer into his arms acting like his words were something special. He squeezed her a little and then looked down at his watch.

"Hungry?" Lance asked, nodding for her to follow him.

"Yes." She said shortly, she wanted to say no.

Lance went to walk away but stopped. He stepped toward Nora. Her body told her to back away but she knew she couldn't react like that so she wanted Lance to trust her and accept her. It was the only way her plan was going to work. Lance looped his fingers around her necklace. She looked at him confused. She was almost afraid he would know it was the necklace Jace gave her. The one that blocks her hunterside from other wolves.

"This is stunning." Lance whispered as if he was captivated by it but there was a tinge of something else, maybe jealousy.

"My mothers. That's all that I have left of her. I don't ever take it off." Nora whispered, the vulnerability in her voice was true.

"Your mother?" Lance asked, letting the onyx drop gently back down on her skin.

"Killed by rogues last year." Nora said her sadness was real and sold the story.

"I am so sorry." Lance whispered, touching her cheek lightly.

"It's gorgeous like you. It's intense and has a mystery to it. You shouldn't take it off. It suits you perfectly." Lance said, taking her hand in his and leading her. She wanted to puke from his affection.

Seeing Lobo's back again and this time stronger was making her nervous. If they kept making them Lance could succeed. She needed to stop them from making more. She knew this is why Jace had failed in her dreams. They would have never known that Lance was making an army of Lobo's. They would have never thought Bruce was the one following through with Kip's botched work.

Lance approached the door and the same type of keypad was on the inside. She needed to get the code. Lance motioned for her to stand in front of him. She stepped into his arms. He put his hand over his eyes, His breath tickling the back of her neck. She cringed trying not to let the idea of him touching her float through her mind. He then reached forward with his other hand going to the keypad.

Slow it down. Nora thought as her body began to tingle.

The world slowed down instantly around her. All of the danger warnings and pent up nerves had her energy and power ready to go. She moved her head out of his hand. She then watched him punch the four digit key code in. 1....5.....9...7. She then quickly slid her head back into his hand. His hand neatly covered her eyes. She took a deep breath in and let it out. She was trying to calm herself. There was one person that could instantly calm her. She thought of Jace, his warm touch. His scent, and his powerful deep voice. The world snapped back into place and the door creaked open.

"This is way Doll." Lance smiled at her as he led her down another long hallway.

This was again a different way but what he didn't realize was Nora was memorizing everything. She knew the hallway before the wall was off white and plain. While this hallway had stainless steel baseboards. She would find her way back to the lab one way or another. She would find her way back and destroy everything. After the lab and the Lobo's were gone. She would deal with Lance. She wished she could talk to Jace. She wished she could tell him everything.

They ended back at the wooden doors and she knew these led to the dining hall. She wondered if it would be the rest of the pack or if it would be just her and him. The doors flung open and all of City Light's packs were sitting cafeteria style at long wooden tables. She didn't know why she felt nervous but she felt like something was about to happen.

Chapter Fifty One
Dinner

*L*ance tugged on her hand guiding her into the hall. Upon entering it everyone bowed their heads and did not dare look up. Lance smiled widely as he continued to the front. Nora studied the pack as she went through. She wanted to know if they were loyal to him or not. If they were not and were by force, she might be able to start a rebellion here and that would give her more to work with. Lance led her to the front table. There were five chairs. He pulled out a chair to the left of the middle one and motioned for Nora to sit. She smiled brightly at him as if it was so sweet of him. Like she enjoyed all of this. Once she was sitting he pushed her in. Only then did she realize she was seated at the Alpha's table. She looked at the empty seats next to her. She counted five and her mind automatically started Alpha Beta, Gamma, Delta and Luna. She was sitting in the Luna seat. She felt her jaw flex as Zara growled inside her mind.

We will not be his Luna. Zara growled.

I know, we need to play along and play the part. I'm coming up with something. I need you to relax. We might not even need to have a war if we can pull this off. Nora reminded her.

Drinks came out. A young man who wouldn't even raise his eyes began pouring red wine into her glass. He went to pour some into Lance and he waved it away. He snapped his fingers and another young man came out with a different bottle.

"Bourbon? I assumed you would enjoy the wine but you have surprised me so far." Lance asked Nora.

Nora nodded her answer. He motioned for the man to pour some into a glass for Nora. She didn't want to drink either but she kept reminding herself she needed to act like she was enjoying herself. Lance picked up his glass and raised it to her. She smiled happily and clinked her glass against his. Lance took a large sip, the bourbon burning his mouth as it warmed his throat and stomach. Nora took a small sip, the smell of it bothering her. She set the glass down, finding it odd. She had a fair amount of alcohol in her life. Especially after her family was murder. It never bothered her before. Lance snapped his fingers and carts of food came out. The same young man that brought her drink out brought her plate of food. Uncovering the dish it was an orange pale looking soup. The smell hit her nose and she felt instantly nausea.

"Its butternut squash soup ma'am. I can take it away if you don't like it. It is just the starter. The main course will be out shortly." The young man said kindly.

"That would be great, thank you." Nora smiled at him, covering her nose to keep from smelling it anymore.

"You ok?" Lance asked curiously watching the interaction.

"I got sick once off of butternut squash and haven't been able to eat it since. Instantly turns my stomach." Nora chuckled, reaching over and touching his forearm as she talked.

Her touch sent shivers through him and he loved it. He nodded and smiled at her. Leaning over towards.

"I will outlaw butternut squash then." He smirked playfully.

Nora laughed like it was the sweetest and funniest thing she had heard. She squeezed his forearm as she did. She felt gross like she was some love sick teenager but her acting was working. Lance placed his hand on top of hers and patted it. He then stood and looked over the pack. They instantly went silent seeing him stand.

"City Light pack, I would like to introduce to you my guest of honor. Nora Alpha of Red Woods pack-

Mumbled went through the crowd as he stated Nora was an Alpha. Nora smiled hearing the words and questions of how a female was Alpha. Lance sent out his aura silencing them as he glared.

"Yes you all heard right. Alpha and Red Woods pack. She is the first female Alpha known to our times. She is incredible and earned the title. " Lance said, glancing back at her.

"She is also your soon to be Luna. In two days time, we will hold a ceremony. Dark water will arrive here by that time and we will unite our packs. We will be the most powerful. Three packs will become united. Red Woods, City Lights, and Dark Water. Once we have united, I will mark Nora and you will all pledge your loyalty to her as my Luna. I will need your ceremony planner to see me after dinner. Enjoy your food." Lance said a huge smile on his face as he sat down and the main course began to be severed.

"I will have the dressmaker come by your room in the morning. I think we incorporate all colors of the three packs. Red, black, and gold. It will be beautiful. Not as beautiful as you." Lance smiled at her.

She forced a bright smile and squeezed his hand before she began to feel shaky

Luna. Two days. Mark her? The words bounced around in her head violently as if they would scrambling her brain. There was no way she was letting Lance mark her. Her blood boiled as she thought of another man besides Jace marking her. She knew it was Zara fueling her anger as will, she was beyond upset. The plate sat down in front of her and she stared at it, trying to wheel her emotions back in. She needed to stay in character. She needed to like the idea. The food smell hit her and she needed to vomit. Her legs felt like they were jello.

"Ma'am are you alright?" The young man asked her as he sat down her food.

She knew without even seeing a mirror that she was pale. She could feel the color drain out of her face. She could feel her mouth beginning to make extra saliva like you do right before you vomit. She felt a cold sweat running down the back of her neck. The smell of the food made her feel worse.

"Nora?" Lance asked her now, looking at her concern.

"Lance, would it be ok if I retire for the evening. I'm afraid I've used a lot of energy traveling here and then with the rest of the excitement." Nora smiled at him.

"Of course, it was silly of me to think that it wouldn't have drained you. Polly." Lance called out to the crowd.

Polly stood up and came over to the front, bowing her head to them.

"Polly please see Mistress Nora here back to her room. You are to bring her anything she requests or needs." Lance ordered her.

"Yes Alpha." Polly said bowing

Nora smiled at Lance before trying to stand. The movement made a wave of nauseousness rush through.

Zara I need your help to power through this. Nora begged her.

I'm trying, I feel it too. Zara said, sounding just as sick.

Polly saw her looking sick and offered her hand. Nora smiled and took it and they made her way out of the room quickly. Polly knew something was wrong.

"Bathroom. Please." Nora said as her stomach lurched.

"This way, there's a private one right here." Polly said, grabbing her hand and leading her down a hall.

Nora hit the bathroom door quickly, seeing the toilet she rushed to it crashing on her knees in front of it. Before she could even lift the seat her stomach began to empty. She was shaking from how violently she was puking. She felt a cold wet rag on the back of her neck as Polly gathered her hair into her hand and helped hold it back. After what seemed forever she finally stopped. She instantly felt better. Polly held a cloth out to her and Nora wiped her mouth.

"Thank you so much. I am so sorry." Nora said, standing with her legs feeling weak.

"Don't worry about it. Let's get you to your room so you can clean up." Polly smiled brightly at her.

Polly kept a close eye on Nora as they walked to her room. Nora could feel her studying her but it wasn't a judgmental one. It almost felt like Polly may care for her. Polly opened the door for Nora. Nora smiled at her as she went in. Closing the door Polly didn't say anything but went to the closet grabbing her a night gown and then stopping by the small fridge in the room getting her water. She held both out to Nora as she sat on the bed.

"Do you like tea?" Polly asked her.

"Yeah, although right now everything seems to be making me sick. The bourbon smelt funny, the soup, and the food. I didn't even have a chance to see what that was." Nora said quietly, maybe it was nerves.

"It's not nerves, The way you traveled here and walked in here. I know you are not a nervous person." Polly said quietly, as if she was reading Nora's mind.

"Maybe, it's just all too much." Nora whispered, she felt at ease with Polly.

"Let me get you the tea. It is soothing and is designed to help with nausea." Polly smiled at her and then started to open the door.

Polly paused at the door making a small face before looking back at Nora.

"How far along are you?" Polly asked.

Chapter Fifty Two
Surprise

"*H*ow far am I..what?" Nora asked, repeating what Polly had just said but her hand instinctively going to her stomach.

"How far are you along…with child?" Polly asked, her voice low just above a whisper.

"With child." Nora repeated again, she could feel the acid crawling up her throat as her chest felt like it was going to collapse on her.

"You are pregnant right? The smells? The vomiting." Polly asked, pointing to Nora's stomach.

"I..I..I don't know." Nora whispered as fear spread through her.

"How long ago was your heat?" Polly asked her, still talking quietly.

Nora sunk down onto the bed. If she was pregnant she had now put her unborn child in danger. It was fine when it was just her life. She could feel the color drain from her face. She wasn't far along, maybe six weeks she thought to herself doing the math.

"Don't worry, I won't say anything….but you're going to have to think of something. You won't be able to hide it forever." Polly said quietly.

Zara can you tell? Nora asked her as she realized what Polly meant.

"I think you understand but I'm going to say just to make sure. He will kill your baby before it is born. He is an evil man and jealous. If you are carrying another man's child he will make sure that child is not born." Polly said, frowning.

"Polly, are you loyal to Lance?" Nora asked her as Nora's eyes studied her.

"As loyal as can be." Polly winked.

"The rest of your pack?" Nora asked, trying to figure out her odds.

"Same..there is a select few who are more loyal than others " Polly said leaning towards the door.

"What about with Bruce?" Nora inquired.

She was unsure; If the pack was still loyal to Bruce then the odds were with her but she needed to know what kind of pack this was.

"In the beginning Bruce was a good man. He wanted nothing but the best for his pack. Then everything changed. He went to the extreme. He thought he should be king of everyone with an unstoppable army. Kip was promised to be his equal when they rose to power. Kip was just his work horse. Towards the end Bruce was no longer the Alpha we knew and needed." Polly said, her voice becoming sad.

Nora felt relief. If this pack was ok with what Bruce had been doing. There was no hope for them.

"I will go get that tea I was talking about." Polly said walking out of the door.

"Polly you're coming back right?" Nora asked her quickly, her voice showing fear.

"Yes ma'am." Polly smiled sweetly at her.

We are. Zara's voice came through.

How do you know? Why didn't you tell me if you thought we were? Nora said back to her frustrated and scared.

I knew something was different but I didn't know what. You've been tapping into some of your hunter powers so I just assumed it was that. I can feel the baby now. Zara sent back.

Nora's heart sank thinking about how she was away from Jace. How this should be something exciting to tell him but she was there now, scared. Polly said she had to do something fast before Lance found out. She would not let him hurt her baby.

"Alpha." Asher's voice came through mind link.

"Asher!" Nora sent back completely shocked.

She had forgotten that she could mind link them still. She had severed her ties with Cross River when she removed Jace's mark, disconnecting from him meant disconnecting from the pack. Asher was her pack.

"Thank god. Alpha are you ok? Are you hurt?" Asher said through mind link to her.

"I am fine. I have a plan, don't worry. How is Jace?" Nora asked, saying his name, her heart sank further into her stomach.

"He's coming for you. He almost lost it when his mark disappeared. He thought the worst." Asher said his voice was a little emotional, she could tell he had thought the worst as well.

"You need to delay him somehow. I have a plan. Tell him the Lobo's are back. Bruce was the mastermind behind Kip. That's why the council didn't do anything when he tried to tell them about Kip. I need to get rid of the Lobo's before we have the packs go to war. If I don't we will all die." Nora said firmly.

"We have fought the Lobo's before. We can fight them again. You need to be back with us." Asher was sent back.

"Asher these Lobo's are different, they are not using humans. They are taking rogues and making them strong. They are different. I need to take them out before we can arrange an attack." Nora ordered.

Asher was quiet as if trying to find away to convince her that they needed to come get her and not wait. He couldn't disobey her orders.

"Inform Jace this information at once and tell him he needs to wait." Nora ordered him.

There was silence. She had expected more of an argument or a fight over it but there was nothing but silence. Nora took a deep breath and started thinking about what she needed to do.

"Jace says he's coming for you whether you like it or not. He also said to tell you not to put yourself in danger and he is…angry with you for doing whatever you did to your mark." Asher said, sounding like he was trying to summarize what Jace must have been telling him.

Nora smiled, feeling like she was actually able to hear from Jace. She was frustrated he wasn't listening but at least she was kind of hearing from him.

"Tell him he needs to wait. I have a plan to take out the new Lobos and then I will let you know to tell him to attack." Nora said firmly.

"He wants to know the plan. He's not agreeing to anything till then." Asher said back his voice firm as if it was Jace himself talking to her.

"In two days' time, there is going to be a ceremony. Red wood is invited. It's a merging of packs. I will have Red Wood come here. Lance doesn't know how big Red woods is. We can hide some of Cross River there. Then just before the ceremony I will take out the Lobos. I feel the City Light's pack wants to be rescued. Bruce went off the deep end and now Lance is in charge. I feel if we can take out the Lobos and then surround the city. City Light's pack will turn against Lance. " Nora explained her plan.

"Jace agrees with the plan, he's asking what type of ceremony?" Asher sent it back to her.

Nora bit her lip, she didn't want to tell Jace. She didn't need him changing his mind but yet she was having trouble lying to him. She sighed.

"Making me his Luna." Nora said quietly, almost wincing as if she knew the pain it would cause Jace.

"Umm..he's angry, lots of angry words." Asher said quietly.

"Tell him it won't happen. The plan is to have him overthrown before that takes place." Nora said, making sure her voice was firm.

"He said he will lose his shit if you get hurt." Asher said back and she knew that putting whatever Jace had said lightly.

"Tell him I love him too." Nora laughed.

A soft knock came from her bedroom door. Nora quickly ended the mind link as he door creaked open. Polly came back carrying a silver tray. On the tray there was a silver teapot and matching cups. She smiled walking over and setting the tea tray down. She then poured the tea into the silver teacup and held it out to Nora.

"This will ease your stomach." Polly said.

"Thank you." Nora said, taking the cup from her.

Nora took a long sip, she felt the warm liquid move down her throat and into her stomach once the liquid spread out through her stomach it instantly made her feel better.

"Polly, I am going to take down Lance." Nora whispered to her

"I know." Polly smiled at her.

"Will you help me?" Nora asked her to take another sip.

"Yes and I know others that will help too." Polly smiled brightly at Nora.

Chapter Fifty Three
Pregnant

"Sleep for now Miss. I will bring you some more tea in the morning to get ahead of your nausea. Take this." Polly said, pulling something out of her hair.

Polly was holding a beautiful silver and blue hair pin in her hand. She looked confused at Polly but the blue in the hair pin kept her attention. It was the color of Jace's eyes and her emotions were getting the best of her. She realized how much she missed him. Polly smiled at her, placing it in her hand.

"It's going to have multiple uses." Polly said nodding to it.

"What do you mean?" Nora said looking over the hair pin and then she noticed a small break in the metal.

Nora pulled on the bottom of the hair pin and it exposed a thin sharp blade. Nora smiled surprised at Polly.

"I can tell you're strong but every girl needs added protection. Speaking of protection; wedge something in the door tonight to ensure no one can get in." Polly said walking towards the door.

"Thank you again." Nora said, grateful.

"Don't worry about it. I feel like you are going to be the person to end this all so it's the least I can do." Polly smiled, stepping out into the hall and shutting the door.

Nora walked to the door. She made sure it was close and then locked it. She looked around. Sitting in the corner was an oversized chair. She went over to it and pushed it in front of the door. No one was coming in. She felt safer but she was still worried. She walked over to the bed sitting down. She placed her hand on her stomach. She swore her stomach was already growing, her breast already starting to ache. She felt nervous. She knew nothing about being pregnant. She knew the basic stuff but had no idea what to expect. She then felt even more worried. Not only was she pregnant but her baby would be a wolf and hunter. Besides her, the baby was going to be the first of his or her kind. She didn't know anything about werewolf pregnancies. She needed to talk to someone. She couldn't ask polly, she didn't need Polly knowing she was only part wolf. Lyla or Jaime she thought to herself.

"Lyla?" Nora sent through mind link waiting quietly for her to respond back.

"Alpha are you ok? I heard you went to City Lights. Please tell me your fine." Lyla's voice rushed through the mind link.

"I am ok. So far everything is going as planned. How are things there?" Nora asked, trying to find a way to bring up pregnant werewolves without being suspicious.

"We are mobilizing to move. Jace and Asher are in a meeting regarding what to do next. Jace is..umm very worried about you." Lyla said, choosing her words carefully.

"He's just upset I left. If he listens to me everything will be ok." Nora chuckled.

"Who is staying behind to ensure the remainder of the pack is ok?" Nora asked.

"Jaime or I, we are not sure yet." Lyla said her voice sounded tired but trying to stay strong.

"Lyla there is a woman here pregnant. I'm worried about her. How long are wolves pregnant for?" Nora asked, finally coming up with a sly way to ask.

"Three months if she's having one can be a little longer if she has multiple babies." Lyla said her voice was a little confused.

"Only three months! Why do they grow super quick? How long till they start to show?" Nora blurted through mind link her panic mode in overdrive.

"Wolfs grow faster and stronger than humans. They do not need the nine months to become full term. Alpha, are you ok?" Lyla asked worried and suspicious.

"Yes I am fine. Sorry I still don't know alot about things I guess. When do you think the other woman would start showing?" Nora asked, trying to hide her nervousness.

"So a pregnant wolf can start showing anywhere from six weeks to eight weeks at the earliest. It happens pretty quickly. It's like they are normal one day and then wake up with a belly." Lyla said her voice was still confused.

"Ok." Nora sent back her hand pressing on her belly, afraid at any minute now she would look pregnant.

"Alpha, are you sure you are ok?" Lyla asked quietly again.

"Yes Lyla. Have Asher mind link me once they are on their way. We have only tomorrow to prepare for everything. I still have a lot more work on my end. Send my love to Jace for me. Let him know I miss him and I will see him soon." Nora said going to end the mind link.

"**W**e are moving now. I am not waiting. I want her back now." Jace growled, his eyes glowed fiercely as he grabbed a hold of the table.

"I know but Alpha has a solid plan. We should trust her." Asher said, trying to calm Jace.

"I am starting to move out Red Woods to be there in time for the ceremony. You can give us as many Cross River packs members you want. Lance has no idea how big Red Woods is. Dark water is also heading that way. So there will be two armies to fight if we act rash." Asher added, trying to stop Jace from seeing red.

"It's the only option we have." Jace growled seeing his hands were tied.

"Dante, I think Sarah should go. She's strong and was once part of Red Woods." Jace said, waiting for Dante's response.

He could see Dante debating himself part of him wanting to ask him not to send her but he understood where he was coming from. Not only was Sarah strong but she was skilled. He bit his lips looking at Jace. He nodded as if he couldn't say the words.

"We should send someone from the inner circle as well." Lyla said walking into the room.

"Like who Dante can't go Lance has seen him enough and knows he's my Beta. Matt and his charm has made himself known. Asher is already gone and we can't send Logan; he would be found out instantly." Jace answered her back.

"I would like to go." Lyla said, looking at Asher.

"You're already part of Red Woods, that's not a problem." Jace said dismissing her thought.

"Wyatt should come. He's a doctor and Lance doesn't really know him." Lyla said, accidentally blurting the doctor's part out.

She wanted Wyatt to come because she was almost positive Nora was pregnant. She didn't buy anything Nora had told her about a girl there. She was too worried and too emotional for it to be someone else pregnant.

"Why would it matter if he was a doctor?" Jace asked his brows coming together as he spoke.

"Um because…in case someone gets hurt." Lyla answered, looking at the ground, her mind screaming shit.

"Lyla." Asher's voice came from behind her, his beta aura making her bow her head. She might be the Delta of the pack but Asher still held rank over her.

"It's nothing." Lyla growled.

"Lyla, if you're hiding something it will be worse when I order you to tell us." Asher growled back his eyes, glowing amber as he looked at her.

Jace clenched his jaw impatiently waiting for Lyla to say what she knew. The amber glow of Asher's eyes made him even more upset. It reminded him more of Nora and how she was not here.

"Lyla, if you know something, say it now!' Jace growled turning towards her, his eyes glowing like ice as Cole pushed forward.

"I…I think Nora is pregnant." Lyla blurted out and then covered her mouth quickly.

"What?" Jace said his voice shook a little bit from his emotion, he suddenly felt sick that she was there pregnant. He quickly became angry because he wasn't there to protect her.

"I am not sure but she was asking a lot of questions about wolves and pregnancies. She said that there were some there she was worried about but her reactions. I don't know. Wyatt should go just in case." Lyla said.

"Fuck Wyatt. I'm fucking going." Jace growled, the desk starting to break under his clenched hands.

"Jace-" Asher started to say but suddenly he was grabbed a hold by Jace, his shirt twisted in Jace's hand

"You, you can mindlink her. Mind link her now!" Jace yelled his fangs descending as he was becoming closer and closer to shifting.

"Alpha." Dante said, stepping closer to him and going to put his hand on his shoulder.

"Don't fucking touch me Dante. Asher mind link her now!" Jace yelled so loud the walls felt like they were shaking.

"I will if you calm the fuck down." Asher growled back.

Jace locked eyes with him, Cole wanted to hurt someone. He was pacing and howling inside of Jace, All Jace could think about was getting Nora. He let go of Asher and stepped back, his whole body shaking as he fought against the urge to shift. Asher nodded to him and his eyes glossed over.

"Alpha?" Asher mind link her.

"Asher is everything ok? You should be getting rest and preparing to head out tomorrow." Nora told him her voice was a little confused.

"Alpha, I need to ask you something…Jace wants to know if you are…if you're pregnant." Asher sent back quietly.

"He what?" Nora asked, trying to act surprised, damn Lyla she thought.

"He is about to explode so Alpha please just answer if you are or not. No disrespect intended." Asher sent back his words were rushed.

"Tell Jace I am..I am." She whispered.

"Alpha, I think you should tell him the truth. Lying might make it worse. I will tell him whatever you need me to. I am loyal to you." Asher sent back, cutting her off.

"Damn it Asher, I am so scared right now. I had a solid plan walking in here but now I don't know if it will hurt…hurt the baby." Nora sent back her will to be strong, starting to buckle to the fear.

"We will work through this. What were you planning on doing?" Asher sent it back to her.

"What's taking so long, Asher." Jace growled, stepping towards him.

"I was going to do what I did to Kip, to Lobo's here and then destroy everything, the lab, all of it." Nora sent back quietly.

"That killed you last time. Jace marking you somehow brought you back." Asher sent back panic in his voice.

"I know that but I have Zara now. I have her ability to heal." Nora said, trying to reassure him.

"Alpha, we need to think more about this but right now I need to know if you want me to be Jace." Asher said Nora could feel that he felt threatened.

"Tell him I love him. Tell him I will do everything to protect our baby and that I will see him in no time. Tell him he is an ass for finding out this way." Nora sent back.

"She says she loves you and that she is going to do everything in her power to protect your baby." Asher said and then stopped as the words baby hit Jace.

Asher watched Jace buckle forward and brace the chair in front of him. Jace hold body shaking like he couldn't control what was happening.

"She says she will see you again in no time and remember she says this. You're an ass for finding out this way." Asher said a small smile on his face at getting to call Jace an ass.

"I'm fucking going now." Jace said as the chair that was once holding him up went flying into the way.

The chair hit the wall shattering, Dante dodged a chair leg as it went by his head. Dante looked to Asher wishing they could mind link. Any second they might be fighting Jace to stop him from going after Nora.

"What the hell is going on here?" Logan said, walking through the door.

Jace's eyes were glowing and his chest was rising and falling. Dante and Asher looked like they were a mixture of scare but ready to fight.

"Nora's pregnant." Jace said his voice and body shaking more as he said it, he was fighting Cole for control more than he had ever in his life.

"Bloody hell." Logan whispered, realizing what was going on.

"I'm fucking going after her now. She's not spending one more second near that fucking monster." Jace growled, Cole's claws emerging from his hands.

"Alpha you can't." Dante said, stepping towards him.

"Are you going to stop me?" Jace said anger rolling off him in terrifying waves.

"Alpha, think of Luna." Dante said, trying to calm him down.

"I fucking am!!" Jace yelled, going to swing at Dante.

Logan snatched Jace up, yanking his arm up behind his back and slamming him down into the desk. No one ever realized how strong Logan is until moments like this. Jace began to attempt to shift. Logan ripped off a chain around his neck with his free hand and threw it down on Jace's back. The chain burned into his back stopping the shift.

"Fucking think Jace! You go in there like this he will kill her. He will kill her before you can even get to her. She will die and so will your child. Fucking stop! Get a hold of yourself. We need to be smart." Logan yelled at him.

Dante and Asher both looked at each other in shock as they watched. Logan's words hit Jace like a tidal wave. He sank further into the desk. He needed to calm himself but the fear was sickening. All the thoughts of what could happen to Nora and their child were overwhelming him. Jace took a long breath in holding it and then letting it slowly out. He did this again.

Cole the dumb hunters right. We do this and we kill her. Jace said to Cole.

Cole didn't say anything but accepted it. He gave back full control to Jace. Cole's emotions leaving Jace let him have more control. Logan held onto him to ensure he wasn't faking it.

"Get off of me Logan." Jace said quietly.

"You good?" Logan asked not to ease up.

"Yeah let me up." Jace said his voice was not as angry as it was.

Logan took the necklace off Jace's back and released him. Jace stood touching his back lightly feeling the burn the necklace made as he watched Logan put it back around his neck

"Silver infused with mountain ash, mistletoe, and wolfsbane." Logan winked at him.

"Covering your bases." Jace grumbled to him before turning and looking at Asher.

"Tell her I love her more than she knows and I will see her soon. To be safe no matter what." Jace said quietly, the weight of the world felt like it was on his shoulders.

Nora waited in the silence, she could feel stress from Asher. What was wrong? She felt nervous sitting in her dark room, staring at the door. She didn't want to go to sleep but she was so tired. She was waiting for something to come through the door. Her body was on high alert because it knew they were in enemy territory even though she was pretending. She wasn't to the point of tingling but she felt like she was in some weird stand by mode. She felt her eyes getting heavy as she began to sway on the bed. She kept trying to make sure she stayed awake. She wanted to see if she could sneak down into the lab and get more detail. She felt her body topple over as she hit the bed, collapsing in exhaustion.

"Nora." Her voice was enchanting as she sang Nora's name, calling to her.

Nora grunted slightly, she was so tired. She needed sleep. She turned slightly on to her side.

"Come now Nora, that's no way to act." The voice chuckled even the laughter was like music.

"Hmm?" Nora asked, trying to open her eyes.

"We don't have much time." The voice said, becoming impatient.

Nora sat up and forced her eyes open. She was surrounded by darkness, she was nowhere. There was nothing. A glowing light came from the far side of the room which outlined her. She knew her right away and smiled.

"Hello Goddess." Nora said sleepy.

"You really like throwing wrenches into the world." The Goddess said as she walked over to Nora, the light blinding her as she approached.

"What do you mean?" Nora said, trying to squint to see her.

"The baby is early." The Goddess said.

"Excuse me?" Nora said, confused.

"The baby was supposed to happen but after. Now we have to figure out how you're going to stop everything without harming yourself or child." The goddess said annoyed.

"The baby…you knew about my baby?" Nora asked even more confused.

"Yes, the baby will unite everyone and everything. Bring everything to a full circle to the original way it was. Hunter, wolf, and human. The baby will be of all worlds with the strongest blood lines." The Goddess said to her, the words seemed like they echoed around the darkness.

"The corruption will end with you. You and Jace and your child. The universe needs this to work. If it goes the other way, Lance will have his army. He will bring terror to wolf kind and it will spill over into the human world. With his army and you as his power cord nothing will be able to stop him. If he doesn't find out about the child, he will lay his claim to you and think it was his. Or if he finds out the child will be held and used as a weapon against you to do his bidding. Then the child" The Goddess explained.

"I didn't sign up for this! My baby didn't sign up for this! What gives you the right to decide!" Nora felt like she was going to vomit and a wave of anger rushed over her as she stood up.

The glow coming off of Nora almost matched the goddess light as she stepped towards her. She was angry, how dear she let this happen.

"Why don't you stop it!" Nora yelled her light getting brighter.

"Because I can't. I am bonded." The Goddess yelled back but her voice was not full of anger like Nora's but sadness.

"I would but I can't. I can only help." She said quietly to Nora.

"Come here." The Goddess said, holding out her hand to Nora.

Nora hesitated but reached for it. As the goddess touched her hand she felt a wave of power surge through her. It was more intense than anything she could create. She almost went backwards from the force. The Goddess waited for Nora to regain herself before asking for her other hand. Nora was nervous, her hand going to her stomach worried about the baby inside. What if this would hurt her growing child.

"It will not." The Goddess whispered.

Nora took a breath and placed her other hand inside the Goddess's hand. A small burst of the same power flowed through her. The Goddess then leaned forward and placed her lips to Nora's forehead. Nora felt warmth flow through her and something divine. She couldn't describe it but she instantly felt peace and power all at once.

"Nora, I place my blessing on you and your children." The Goddess whispered as she let go of one of her hands and placed it on Nora's stomach.

"I am Goddess of the moon and mother to the child of the moon, I bless you with all of my being." She said loudly.

As she finished her statement a wind rushed through Nora. Her hair flew back over her shoulders as her body began to vibrate. A light radiated off of her so bright that it matched the light the goddess had out shone her for a second. Once the blast of light faded, Nora continued to glow. She noted that the Goddess looked tired and her light had dimmed.

"This will help you. This will ensure your child can withstand what you need to do. Use my blessing wisely, I only get to give one out every few centuries." The Goddess smiled.

"Your light?" Nora whispered.

"It takes a part of me each time I do it." The Goddess said letting go of her hand and touching her cheek.

"You are so very special Nora. Go save the world." The Goddess whispered and tapped her on the forehead.

Nora's head fell back and she crashed onto her bed. Her head hitting the bed made her jolt up. She was out of breath as if she had been running.

"Alpha, Jace says to tell you he loves you more than you know and he will see you soon. To be safe no matter what." Asher's voice came through the mind link.

She ran her hands down her arms. She felt different, she felt like she had so much energy. She felt amazing. She felt stronger, more powerful. Did that really happen? She thought almost scared she made it up. She closed her eyes thinking of her powers and a glow began to come off of her skin. She blinked and it was gone. She was in more control. She could end this. She could do what needed to be done. She had everything she needed now. Well almost she thought sadly.

"Jace." Her mind wanted to reach out to him, she wanted to hear his voice

Her voice echoed into his mind. It didn't feel like a mind link but something deeper. Something more connected, something stronger. Jace shook his head, he had to be making this up. Too much stress.

He shut his eyes wanting it to be true. His mind says her name back Nora.

"Jace!" Nora sent back, how was it possible?

"Nora? How are you doing this?" Jace asked her.

"I'm not really sure but god it's good to hear your voice." Nora sent back her voice, almost tearful.

"I'm coming for you. I will be there in no time. I will be there." Jace vowed.

"I know you will be. I love you so much. I promise I am fine..actually I'm better. I'm stronger and different." Nora said, trying to explain.

"I love you. What do you mean? You're making me worried." Jace was sent back.

"The Goddess said she blessed me. I thought it was a dream but look I can mind link you. I am more in control of power and its different kinds of power. I can't explain it." Nora said quietly.

Jace was quite taking everything in. He had heard of the Goddess blessing their kind when needed but it was very rare and almost never happened. The Goddess wasn't allowed to interfere often.

"Jace, have everyone start moving out tomorrow. This all needs to end tomorrow night." Nora said quietly.

"Nora the baby." Jace said quickly.

"The baby is fine, the Goddess blessed the baby too. The baby will withstand anything that I need to do to stop all of this." Nora sent it to him.

"Nora, I can't lose you. I need you to be careful. Wait for me to get there, don't do anything rash. We will have the manpower. Everyone is behind us. Everyone is uniting." Jace said, his voice going back and forth between ordering her and almost pleading with her.

"It will be ok. I can feel it. I will see you at sunset tomorrow." Nora sent him back.

"Sunset?" Jace asked, confused.

"Yes, have everyone ready at sunset. Red Woods is moving out tomorrow morning, leaving shortly after them. Dark water will be here in the morning for the ceremony. It will all be over by sunset tomorrow." Nora said, forming her plan.

"I will be there but Nora you wait for me. Don't do anything. Remember you died the last time. I don't know if you can handle something like that again. Let us handle it. Three armies plus hunters against two is not bad odds." Jace said, trying to make her see.

"I love you. I will see you at sunset tomorrow." Nora said not promising anything to him.

"Nora!" His voice was angry as he shouted her name.

She wasn't going to argue with him. She knew he would be here. Their armies will be back up if there is anyone resisting after she destroys the Lobos. She laid back down and actually felt like she could sleep peacefully.

Chapter Fifty Four
Tea

A knock at the door woke her up. As soon as she opened her eyes a wave of nausea hit her. Her hand went to her stomach as she slowly sat up. She put her feet on the ground. The cold hard wood helps fight back the nausea. She stood up realizing she had forgotten that she blocked the door with the chair. The knock came again.

"One minute." Nora said loudly to the door as she began to move the chair away from the door.

She choked back a gag as she stood up right. She took a deep breath in before unlocking the door. She needed cold air. She opened the door and then looked for a window. She didn't even care at this point who was at the door. She crossed the room to the window. She grabbed a hold of the soft white curtains, tossing them aside. She was getting so warm so quickly. The floor length curtains swung back at her and she became frustrated. Yanking them hard to the side. The curtain rod fell down off the top of the window. She braced for it to hit her. A jolt flowed through her and as the rod went to land on her. The curtains were thrown across the room. The curtains landed neatly on the bed and the rod rolled to the bedroom door.

"Incredible." Lance said as he stopped the rolling curtain bar with his foot.

Nora wanted to vomit more hearing his voice. She unlocked the window and pushed it up. The cool breeze hit her quickly and she instantly felt better. She glanced over her shoulder looking at Lance and forced a smile.

"Thank you." She said with a wink, adding a more adorable smile.

"You..you are everything the moon Goddess has chosen for me." Lance grinned.

Nora wasn't aware of it but when her body went to protect herself, her body shimmered and glowed. A light seems to encase her. Lance was in aura and at the same time so excited that she was going to be his.

"Plans for today?" Nora asked, turning from the window to face him.

"I had come up here to talk about your outfit and ceremony plans." Lance said, holding his hand out to her.

Nora placed her hand in his ignoring the fact that his touch made her skin crawl and burn. He led her over to the small couch and motioned for her to sit. Nora sat as she did, she suddenly realized she was in her pajamas. She adjusted her shorts that were riding dangerously up. Lance watched her his eyes following every curve of her sun kissed thigh. He cleared his throat like something was stuck in it and sat closely next to her.

"So the ceremony?" Nora asked shifting a little trying not to make it known that she didn't want to be next to him.

"Yes..um..I..the..Ceremony.." Lance said, stumbling over his words as his eyes ran over Nora, her tank top dangling just a little too low, her shorts riding up just a little bit too much.

It was all making him crazy. Her perfect sun kissed glowing skin begging for him to touch it. He moved closer to her his fingers twitching and yearning to just touch her. He placed his hand on her thigh.

Be calm, don't react, don't react. Nora was telling herself slightly, she had to play the part, had to protect herself, and her baby. Pretend he's Jace, she felt a part of her heart break as she said those words to herself.

Nora flipped a switch, her eyes looking him over. She smiled seductively at him as she watched his eyes flash with lust in them. He ran his hand up her leg, his tongue playing with his teeth as he did it. Nora smirked, leaning towards him.

"Ceremony." Nora said the words in a whisper hoping it would put him back on track and not let this go any further.

"The ceremony will be held..held.." Lance said, his hand running into the soft light blue fabric of her shorts.

"Will be held?" Nora said her voice quietly as she tried forcing back the fear of what he might do.

It happened too quickly, her body didn't have time to react. Lance slipped his hand towards the center of her legs, his hand brushing against her. Nora let out a surprised noise and Lance growled. His other arm wrapped around her waist pulling her backwards. In one swift motion he had laid her back on the couch and was straddling her. His face buried into her neck as he began to kiss and nip her neck. Nora fought with herself trying to control her body from shocking him. It was right under the surface of her skin if she needed it. She could feel it building and building. She felt her teeth graze the spot where he would mark her and she panicked. A jolt of energy radiated out from her hitting Lance in the mouth as his fangs lowered. He scooted backwards holding his mouth. It felt as if he bit something metal, his teeth and mouth vibrating. The vibration made his teeth tingle.

"What the hell?" He whispered, rubbing his jaw, his eyes narrowed as he looked at Nora.

Nora opened her eyes and realized she had been squeezing them shut for fear of anything further happening. She couldn't help but smile seeing him massaging his face, looking at her so confused.

"You ok?" Nora said sitting up and putting a caring hand on his shoulder.

"Yeah I..I'm. Nothing." Lance chuckled.

A loud knock at the door drew his attention. A thought of wonder stretched across his face. He looked back at Nora as if to ask who would be coming to her room this early. She shrugged. Lance made a face and got up off the couch. Nora took advantage of it to head to the closet. She wasn't leaving herself open like that anymore. She ducked into the closet trying to find the quickest thing to throw on. She saw a dark blue bathrobe that went well past her knees. She grabbed ahold of it and wrapped herself in it. She didn't want to risk undressing and have Lance come wandering into her closet.

"Nora." Lance called from the door.

Nora tied the bathrobe around her tightly before walking out into the room. She looked at Lance wondering why he was calling her. Polly's head popped up over Lance's shoulder as she stood on her tippy-toes.

"Polly." Nora smiled brightly seeing her.

"Morning ma'am I brought your tea for you!" Polly smiled.

"You're wonderful!" Nora said with a bigger smile.

"I've brought you a few cookies and a biscuit as well." Polly said as Lance stepped beside and allowed Polly into the room.

"Alpha, did you want me to have something brought up for you?" Polly asked so innocently and politely.

"No, I have matters to attend to. I better get going." Lance sighed deeply like he had just missed out on something important.

"Nora, I will have your gown brought up at four. That will give you exactly two hours to be ready. The ceremony starts at six. The marking will be at seven." Lance said casually as he walked to the door.

"See you soon." Nora said with a bright smile.

"Not soon enough." Lance smiled back walking out the door.

As soon as the door shut, she felt all the tension rush out of her. She grabbed the small waste bin and her stomach began to wrench. Bile came rushing up her throat and emptied into the trash can. Her stomach emptying the only thing it had in it. She was shaking. She didn't know if it was the baby making her sick or the thought of Lance having his hands and mouth on her. She felt a damp cool cloth on the back of her neck. Polly then gathered Nora's hair into her hand and held it while Nora finished.

"I'm so sorry." Nora said to her as she grabbed a tissue from the end table wiping her mouth.

"It's all right, Miss." Polly said, stepping away from her.

"Please call me Nora." Nora said to her shaking her head, like it was silly for Polly to call her ma'am and miss.

"M.. Nora drink the tea slowly, it will settle your stomach." Polly said, catching herself from calling her Miss.

Nora nodded, sitting back on the couch. Polly took the tea and handed her the cup. Nora took it into her hands, the warmth from the white teacup rimmed with flowers; felt amazing against her cold hands. She took a small sip shutting her eyes as she did so. The minute the liquid hit her mouth her stomach felt instantly better.

"Polly I don't know what witch craft this tea is but thank you so much." Nora said, feeling her stomach instantly relax.

"I am so glad I could help." Polly smiled sitting down next to her.

"You have no idea how much you helped. Your timing was amazing. I think he would have..god I don't want to think about what he would have tried if you didn't come check on me." Nora said, taking another sip of the tea to ensure the nausea didn't come back.

"So what's the plan today?" Polly smiled big.

"I need to get into that lab." Nora said that was her only plan really.

"Well let's start planning on how we are going to do this." Polly said, holding out the tray of cookies and biscuit.

Chapter Fifty Five
Our Girl

Nora took a bite of the biscuit, the flaky butter bread melted in her mouth and her stomach instantly purred in happiness. Polly let out a chuckle as she heard it too. Nora smiled devouring the rest of the biscuit. She wiped her mouth taking a sip of her tea. She felt a hundred times better. She nodded her thanks to Polly as she cleared her throat before going to speak.

"We have nine hours until the ceremony starts." Nora said to Polly.

"I need to get in the lab just before the ceremony. That way it will be mostly empty and Lance will be preoccupied." Nora continued pausing to take another sip of her tea.

"I have connections down there. There are people who are being forced to do this. They don't want to be a part of it and they don't want to be creating those things. They will be able to guide us through the labs." Polly explained.

"Well we need to find some way to sneak away then. I will say there is something wrong with…it would need to be something with the ceremony. Lance would make anything else wait." Nora said thinking out loud.

"The dress." Polly smiled as the idea entered her head.

"He is very vain and conceited. If it has to do with how you would look then he would make an exception for it. He would want his soon to be mate to be absolutely perfect in every way." Polly smirked.

"Perfect. So at five as I am standing there waiting for everything to begin. We will have an accident with the dress. I will need assistance so I will have you come. Then we go to the lab." Nora smiled happily as everything was coming together.

---

*J*ace paced the dark gray concrete in front of the gate. He was waiting for the last army to show up. Jace's pack hasn't shifted yet but Chadwick was here with what they could spare in wolf form. The green eyes glowing out from mostly dark brown wolves letting them know whose pack they were with. Logan was on a motorcycle in front of a hummer filled with his hunters, as well as a large black truck. Matt was standing by it talking to Lilly. Jace could tell by the way he was moving that Matt was telling Lilly about being careful. His eyes went to Dante, his arm wrapped around Sarah rubbing her arm softly as if the same thoughts were running through his mind. Wyatt was alone; he had Abby stay behind. She was running the hospital in his absence. Jace locked eyes with Dante and if Dante could almost read his mind, he shook his head no.

"You're staying back. In all of this I am being reckless. You and Sarah stay behind." Jace order.

Dante flexed his jaw going tight and every muscle tensed. He stepped away from Sarah. Sarah looked at him confused wondering what he was doing. Dante slammed his fist into the wall next to the guard station. Letting out a loud growl. Matt's head snapped in the direction of the noise and immediately began to move, his eyes glowing ice blue looking for the threat. Jace shook his head.

"Who's going to have your back!" Dante yelled at him through mind link as his chest moved rapidly, blood dripping from his knuckles.

"I need someone to take over the pack if I don't make it back. It's you. That's what being beta means. Do your duty." Jace snapped and let his alpha aura roll off of him targeting Dante.

Matt felt it and realized there was something going on between Dante and Jace.

"Be right back, gorgeous." Matt said, kissing Lilly's hand quickly before walking over to the scene.

"Hey dude, chill. What's going on?" Matt said coming up to Dante carefully, he could feel Noah wanting to shift.

"'I'm being fucking benched." Dante growled out loud, the anger rolling off of him was dangerous.

"Shit." Matt whispered before glancing at Jace whose stare was deadly.

Dante was flexing his jaw off and on as he tried to disobey the command Jace had given him. Jace held on locking down the command.Sarah came over to Dante and entwined her fingers into his.

"Dante." Sarah whispered.

The way she said his voice, the feel of her skin.The rush of calm Sarah gave him every time she was near. He dropped his head bowing to Jace. Giving into his command.

"I got him Dante. Don't worry. I got him." Matt promised to Dante.

"I know you will. If I can't go, I'd rather have you there. I know you will. Keep your freaking self safe too. I can't lose your goofy ass too." Dante said, clapping him on the shoulder.

Dante looked at Jace hard one last time before walking off with Sarah. He was still angry as he walked away. Matt glanced at Jace giving him a small smile before heading back over to Lilly.

"Love ya too brother. Keep the pack safe while I'm gone." Jace sent to Dante, through a mind link as he went back to pacing.

"You come back. You hear me. I swear you freaking don't I will kill you." Dante said, threatening him.

"If I don't come back…I will be dead." Jace snickered through mind link.

"I'll bring your ass back to life and kill you all over again. Try me….love ya too." Dante sent back.

A smile actually made it across his face as he continued to wear a path into the cement. Logan looked over to him and nodded asking if everything was good. Jace nodded back letting him know things were fine.

"What the hell was that?' Lilly asked as Matt came back.

"Dante is beta…he has to stay behind in case Jace doesn't come back. Dante was pissed about it." Matt explained shortly.

"Oh." Lilly said her eyes were going to the woods, she shifted in her chair.

Lilly's hand went to her bow and dagger as if she was seeing a possible threat. Matt followed her gaze, something was moving through the forest up ahead. The forest glowed white. Matt nodded to himself knowing right away what it was.

"Zeke. Moonlight pack is finally here." Matt said to her and he watched her relax.

Jace felt a little lighter watching the large group of wolves with glowing eyes emerge out of the forest. They walked down the concrete road towards Jace. Zeke was in wolf form and stopped just in front of him. He shifted, bones snapping and popping into place as he shifted into human form.

"It's about damn time." Jace smirked seeing him.

"You know Moonlight is always fashionable late." Zeke said knowing damn well they were not late, this was all happening a lot earlier then they had planned.

Zeke wouldn't have said no to Jace. If they had told him the second they came up with the plan to attack Lance that they were going right there and then, he would have gone. Nora was amazing, she made Jace a better person. He was already an astonishing leader but he was…the only word for it was better with Nora. Nora had saved them all before. Zeke and his pack would lay their lives down for her if needed.

"This everyone?" Zeke said his eyes scanning, he could tell which pack was what by the glow their eyes gave.

Black sands had almost their whole entire pack here. The green glow of their eyes was almost eerie against the dark backdrop of the evening. Jace's pack hadn't shifted yet but he knew all the humans were Jace's and then were hunters. His eyes locked eyes with Logan he was fidgeting on his motorcycle waiting for the cue to be told to go. Logan nodded his head to him, acknowledging his presence.

Red Wood had their entire pack there. The amber color reminded him of Nora. He knew that the pain Jace must be feeling not having her there was excruciating. Asher's wolf Xander was enormous in the front, he was on the verge of pacing as well. Suddenly Xander's hackles went up and a low growl began to rumble through him.

Jace's head moved in the direction that Xander was growling at. Jace tensed up seeing a set of purple glowing eyes walking down his driveway. Moonlight pack quickly surrounded the unknown council wolf. Jace quickly made his way toward the unknown wolf. Moonlight pack stepped out of his way as he moved. Reaching the small dark chocolate brown wolf, Jace narrowed his eyes at him.

"Shift!" Jace bellowed at the wolf.

The wolf slowly began to shift. The longer it takes to shift shows inexperienced and it is very painful. The young man collapsed to the ground breathing heavily. Jace didn't care, he reached down and yanked the young man up by his arm.

"Who is your Alpha and why are you here?" Jace growled, seconds away from letting loose on him.

"Douglas. I am here to tell you they are already moving to City light's. I am your good faith person and communication to Alpha Douglas. He says to tell you he is still with you." The man said quietly.

"Good. I would hate to have to kill the entire council." Jace growled letting go of the man.

"You, you're with my pack. This way." Jace growled at the man who had landed on the ground.

He nodded, standing up slowly and began walking behind Jace. He looked out over his pack, his home, his family, and lastly his friends. He never thought he would see the day when they would all unite over one cause. It was all because of Nora.

Jace nodded to each leader of the group and began to move to leave. Matt hopped off the truck Lilly was in and jogged up next to Jace, taking Dante's spot to his right. He nudged his Alpha lightly.

"Let's go get our girl." Matt said to him.

Jace growled a little at him at mentioning Nora being anyone's girl besides his. Matt chuckled lightly. Logan revved his motorcycle, as the cars behind him turned on. Jace's eyes flickered over each pack as they moved towards the forest. Matt was right. His words echoed in his head. Let's go get our girl.

Chapter Fifty Six
Smoke and Mirror

*J*ace took off into the forest. Once inside he shifted into Cole. He shook the tension off as he shifted. The moon light hitting Cole's dark almost blue coat. It shimmered. He lowered his head and glanced back at his pack. A howl went up and Cole took off. The look was telling them to keep up. He was not waiting.

One by one they all shifted and followed the dark shimmer of Cole taking off in a flash. Nothing was keeping him from Nora any longer. He bolted dodging the trees as he passed them. A fallen tree limb in front of him. He felt the air as he jumped over it landing on the other side. Zeke, Chadwick, and Asher followed behind. Their pack followed one by one after Cross river. At a point they would branch out and surround City Lights but as of right now they ran in unisom. The hunters took what roads and paths they could to get there.

Jace looked up at the full moon and it seemed to sparkle back at him. The moonlight seemed to call to him and he felt something guiding him through the woods. As if the moon was lighting the way to Nora. Cole chased after the light hard and fast. The ground gave way to his enormous paws as he pushed himself to go harder and faster with each step he took.

Nora was standing in the walk in closet looking at the gown hanging there. Someone came by and dropped it off. Polly had been her saving grace, the urge to rip the gown into shreds came over her seeing it when the poor young wolf handed it to her. It represented everything she hated. Represented Lance's and she would never be his. She is now in the closet staring at the gown. The gown was thought out well. It was actually stunning. The gown was heart shape and around the neckline was the deepest shade of red, it faded down the toros to a dark blue black and then flared out down the skirt to a white. The gown sparkled all the way down it. The colors of the sparkles follow suit of the shades, red at the top, blue, and white at the bottom. She knew without asking the dress represented three packs becoming one. Red Woods, Dark water, and City Lights.

"Ma'am, they are asking you if they could come in for hair and make up." Polly said hanging in the doorway of the walk-in closet.

"Polly…if I have to tell you to call me Nora again, swear I'm going to-

"Nora." Polly laughed, saying her name and cutting her off.

"Send them away. I am wearing my hair up and makeup will be simple." Nora said curling her nose as she said it.

"I will try." Polly laughed.

Nora reached out and touched the dress. Electricity coursed through her as she did and the world went dark. She walked in the darkness trying to see where she was. A spotlight hit her. The light bouncing off of her, the action making her look down. She was wearing the dress. Each small movement caused a disco ball of light to bounce off of her.

Smoke invaded her nostrils. Fire, the word rang through her mind as she recognized the smell. Fire what could be on fire? A flash of light blinded her and then she was surrounded by smoke. She coughed, the smoke rushing in.

She saw the entrance of the hall, large doors covered in dark ash reached towards the ceiling. She went to step over one of the scorched bodies. The air from her passing over hit the body and it instantly disintegrated. The ash floating up around her. She felt sick to her stomach. Where was she?

The room shifted and the light faded out. She was standing in the middle of City Lights hall. Everything was back to normal, nothing was on fire. Her tri-color dress sparking in the candle light, candles spread out along the room. Lance pacing the front stage as he kept looking to the door. Suddenly a siren screamed, catching everyone off guard. The members stood looking around. The siren meaning danger. The door was kicked open and in the entryway was Jace. Her heart sped up seeing him, a smile coming to her lips excited to see him once more. But the more she looked at him the more she had this unsettling feeling. Something was wrong.

He was covered in blood. His chest rising as if he had been running for days. Behind him with the same absent dead eyed look was Logan, Asher, and Matt. Each of them covered in a fair amount of blood. Lance shifted back towards the wall of the stage confused. The members in the hall shrink away from the doorway frightened of them. Frightened of the anger and rage rolling off them. Why were they so angry? Nora walked towards Jace.

"Jace, What's going on? Are you ok?" Nora asked quickly, walking to him.

He acted as though he didn't see her or hear her. She went to reach out and touch his chest but she fell right through him. As she tumbled through her, she caught herself just on the other side. She was now standing outside the hall. Jace standing in the only entrance and exit. What was going on? Nora thought going to touch Jace again. Her hand didn't even touch him. He stepped into the hall, a small scream from the members as they moved further away from him. It didn't phase him. Logan stepped up next to him, looking at all the candles. Jace nodded to him. Logan reached over grabbing a candle. Matt passed a bow and arrow to Jace. Jace held the arrow over the flame of the candle Logan was holding. The arrow caught fire. Jace fired into the back of the room. The arrow landed in Lance's throne light chair. The chair caught fire quickly. Jace nodded to Logan and Matt who then began to move about the hall knocking candles to the floor.

The room quickly began to catch fire. The members began to scream and hold each other as the flames grew. Cross River began to leave Jace still standing in the entrance way.

"Jace!" Lance yelled, it was a mixture between a plea and order.

"You will all burn." Jace yelled, slamming the doors shut.

"Lock it up. No one comes out." Jace growled.

"Jace! Wait, you can't! There are innocents in there. Jace!" Nora said, running towards the door trying to pry it open from where Matt and Logan barricaded it shut.

"Jace!" Nora screamed as she turned to yell at him.

"Jace you can't! You are not a monster!" Nora continued to yell.

She found him with his head bowed, shoulders down in defeat as he towered over something.

"Jace?" Nora asked moving towards him, not sure why he all of a sudden looked so crushed, the members around them held the same presence.

What was going on? She then saw Wyatt holding someone. As she got closer she realized it was not just someone. It was her. Wyatt held her collapsed and limp body out to Jace. He wrapped his arms around her pulling, Nora into his chest. Wyatt didn't have to say it allowed, they all knew she was gone.

"I told you to wait." Jace whispered, his voice breaking.

The screams in the background from the burning city light members echoed the pain.

"We got here too late." Logan whispered, the pain the same as Jace.

"Why wasn't she by the hall." Asher said angrily.

Jace let out a heartbreaking growl like noise as he clutched Nora's body to him. The noises shattered her.

"Nora?" Polly's voice snapped her back to her reality.

"Polly?" Nora asked breathlessly.

"Nora are you ok? You're shaking." Polly asked her to touch her forehead.

Nora was also clinging to the tri-color gown as her hand trembled. She looked about the room carefully. It didn't happen. She thought relief was going through her chest.

"Polly, we need to go now. We need to get in the lab now. If we wait, we will still lose everything. I need to be in the hall and not leave." Nora said, connecting the dots.

“Ok..Ok. Let me make a few adjustments and get in touch with a few people. I will be right back for you.” Polly said with a nod.

“Ok.” Nora said quietly, still staring down the gown.

Thank you. She thought. She knew the Goddess had said no more help from the other day but the vision was her way of warning her.

Chapter Fifty Seven
Groundwork

Polly rushed out of the closet but Nora caught her wrist, her eyes still on the dress. The images of what would come if she didn't get this right tugged at her heart and tightened her chest.

"Polly, we need to get all the Lobo's in one room. I need to do this in one shot." Nora said, taking her eyes off the dress and looking at Polly.

Polly's eyes were filled with concern. Polly's eyes studied Nora's face, worry coming across hers.

"Nora, how are you doing this? Like I've heard what you can do and felt the power you have but …will you be safe?" Polly asked in her voice, wanting the reassurance that Nora would tell her yes.

"Yes." Nora answered, giving Polly the answer she wanted. The truth was she didn't know.

Polly stared at her hard for a long minute and then nodded to her before heading out of the closet. The door to Nora's room shutting behind Polly as she left echoed in the emptiness of the room.

Nora searched the closet for something simple to wear. She grabbed a pair of black jeans pulling them quickly on. She grabbed a plain black t-shirt dropping it over her head. She bent down grabbing a pair of boots and walking out of the walk-in closet. Getting to the doorway she glanced back, the shimmering sparkle of the tri-color dress catching her eye.

"It's not happening like that." She told the dress as stepped out of the walk-in closet.

She plopped down on the couch pulling on one of the boots. Her mind raced trying to figure out she was going to destroy all the Lobos. She needed to make sure she did it quietly. Her power was not exactly quiet. She needed to not die either. She ran her hands over her face as she let out a sigh.

We got this. Zara's voice came through.

I know but there's so much at stake right now. Even if I destroy the Lobo's if it does kill us…Jace…. Did you see? Nora said back to her.

I saw. We're not dying. Zara said back, determined.

I love your confidence in us but the last time I did this we did. Nora said quietly.

It's different now. We're stronger, connected. Both sides of you have been merging together. And the little one. The little one is giving us strength. Not to mention the Goddess blessed you. We're not dying. Zara said firmly.

The baby is making us stronger? Nora asked, confused, she figured it would weaken her.

I can feel it. Zara said, confirming.

"Ready?...You're dressed like you're ready." Polly's voice said from the doorway.

"Yeah, Let's do this." Nora said, standing and walking to the door.

"Ok quick run down. It's lunch time and the guards are changing so we can sneak it that way. The doctors on the floor all have our backs. Dr. Jones is having the Lobo's moved in two the large exam room saying he wanted to test all their abilities at once. The guards were skeptical but because Lance is overwhelmed with making sure the ceremony is perfect they didn't want to bother him. So they decided to just do it. " Polly said quickly.

"Ok got it. That works perfectly. When we get in there; I want you to get the staff as far from me as possible. I am not exactly sure what I am about to do." Nora said with a half smile.

"Ok. We will enter through the front door. Tater in security and can have the camera glitch for a second, so we need to stay out of view until we get his say so. Same thing when we leave." Polly said, her hand grabbing her other hand and squeezing it as she talked.

"All right, it sounds great. Let's go do this." Nora smiled brightly and walked to the door.

"Ok." Polly said breathily, as she followed Nora.

They made their way down the long windy hall. Polly leading with Nora following closely behind. They were trying their best to walk quickly but not draw any attention to themselves. Polly kept glancing behind them to make sure no one was following them. They made a sharp right, Nora hadn't been this way before. Polly put her finger up against her mouth telling Nora to be quiet. She tapped the wall telling Nora to hug it. Nora pressed her back against it. She then heard the sound of footprints. There were two men having a casual conversation. Polly wrapped her hand around Nora's. Nora glanced at her. She didn't realize until that moment Polly was afraid. Nora nodded to her telling her it will be ok. Polly smiled weakly. The man walked by the hall they were hiding in. They were two very large men. Polly smiled, thankful that they didn't see them.

Polly let out the breath she had been holding in and nodded for Nora to follow her. They made their way back to the main hall they were in. Polly, peeking her head out to see if the men had continued walking and were gone.

"They were the two men that guard the door."
Polly whispered, she tugged on Nora's hand to follow
her.

Nora followed Polly around the corner and then
they were facing the large industrial size door. It just
screamed top secret without saying anything. A sign
hung there saying authorized personnel only.

Authorize this. Zara growled.

Nora went to step forward and Polly's hand cut
in front of her making her stop. Polly pointed up and
then drew a line with her foot, as if to say dont cross.
Nora looked up to where Polly had pointed and there
was a camera. The line Polly had drew was where the
camera would see. Polly held up her finger saying
one minute. Polly's eyes glossed over. Nora's eyes
locked on to the camera. The blinking light on top of it
was blinking green. It switched to red. Polly quickly
tugged Nora.

"We only have twenty seconds to get in." Polly
whispered to her as she dragged Nora to the door.

Polly punched a number into the keypad. The
keypad beeps loudly turning red. Polly looked over
her shoulder at Nora quickly, fear flashing across her
face. Nora was counting in her head. Polly tried again
and the beep got louder.

"That's it, that's the code I have." Polly said the
fear in her face reached her voice.

"1597." Nora said, looking at the camera.

"What?" Polly whispered.

Nora rushed the keypad, her mind counting down 11, 10, 9, 8. She quickly punched the numbers in the key pad. The door let out a loud squeak noise. 7, 6, 5. Nora's mind screams the numbers. Open please open. The door popped open. 4, 3, 2. Nora shoves Polly through the door opening, as the green light of the camera flips back on. The door closed as it did.

"One.' Nora said out loud standing inside the lab.

"Alpha, can we slow the pace a little." Matt's voice chimed in through mindlink.

"No." Jace answered ignoring the plea in Matt's voice.

"Alpha, some of them are struggling." Matt came back again.

"I said No.' Jace growled fiercely.

"Jace no one is going to be able to fight when we get there if we run them like this." Matt said fiercely.

"We need to get there." Jace said frustrated.

"What good is it going to do if we get there and collapse? You can't fight two entire packs alone. What good are we to Nora if we show up like this." Matt said anger coming through his voice.

"Don't fucking tell me what good we are. You adjust the flow of the run. I am still moving the way I am." Jace snapped back.

"You need to slow down." A voice whispered in Cole's ear.

He was racing towards City Lights territory as the chilling feeling hit him. His pack is a good distance behind him. The voice wasn't a mind link. It was as if someone was running next to him.

Did you hear that? That wasn't a mind link. Jace said to Cole.

Yeah, I don't care. Cole growled.

Cole didn't change his pace and kept pushing further. He was creating more and more distance between him and the wolves following him. He had been ignoring Matt's mind links for the past half hour. Sunlight was starting to peek over the horizon and the moonlight trail he was following was fading quickly. He felt his body growing tired but he pushed through it.

As Cole pushed himself faster a cloud of blackness appeared in front of him. A black wall of fog like clouds blocking him from pushing further. He skidded to a halt. He felt his chest burning from trying to catch his breath. Cole paced back and forth in front of the wall of blackness.

What the hell is this? Jace asked Cole aggravated.

The fuck if I know. Cole growled back.

We should-

Go. Cole said, jumping into the black fog.

Jace fell to the ground during the fall he somehow shifted. His body hit the cold hard ground. He let out a loud noise as the air was knocked out of him. He rolled to his side trying to force air back into his lungs as he gasped. A light appeared around him.

"I said slow down!" An angry voice echoed around the dark place he was in, the light seemed to change and move with the way the voice spoke.

Air rushed back into his lungs as he rolled to his side, his eyes straining to see where the voice was coming from. He felt power and he felt anger. He was confused as he stood, his body shaking from being overworked.

"I don't know who you are or what witchcraft this is. I have somewhere to be. You're preventing me from getting there. There will be problems." Jace growled his voice echoing and shaking the room from the power behind it.

"I have too much riding on this! The world has too much riding on you! I can't risk you being reckless and hot headed." The voice came back.

The power in the voice hit him like he had run into a brick wall. He landed on his knees, his body shaking. Cole whimpered in his mind and he submitted willingly.

"Who are you? " Jace asked, confused.

"A friend of your mates." The voice replied.

"I need to get to her." Jace said his tone changed slightly.

"You're in a time out." The voice said back and the light faded.

"What? Wait! No!" Jace yelled trying to go to stand but his legs felt like jello.

"I need to get to her! You don't understand!" Jace screamed.

Jace growled fiercely, his fist coming down on the side of him. His anger and rage shook the darkness he was forced to sit in.

Chapter Fifty Eight
Phase one

"*A*lpha." A voice said panicked to him, he was trying to process who it was.

"Alpha!' The voice said, sounding more demanding and something shook him.

"Jace." Matt's voice pierced through the darkness, as Jace felt his body being shook.

Jace groaned rolling to his side, trying to process what just happened. Sunlight hit his face making his face scrunch up as it hurt his eyes. He let out a groan bringing his hand up to shield his face as he opened his eyes.

"Oh thank god. I was so not ready to be beta." Matt smirked offering his hand to Jace to help him up.

"What? Beta? What the hell happened?" Jace said, pulling on Matt's hand to help himself stand.

His legs were weak. He squeezed Matt's hand hard as he stood. His legs almost collapsed from under him. He took a deep breath and his whole body hurt. He looked around, shaking his head and squinting.

"You collapsed. Fell right down and shifted from Cole. I've never seen something like that happen…except when someone dies. And ya know if you die Dante becomes Alpha, me Beta." Matt said his voice was concerned at first and then turned playful.

"Collapsed?" Jace said his mind was fuzzy, Where were they? He thought as he scanned the forest.

"Yup.."Matt 's voice held a tone saying "I told you so" but he didn't say it out aloud.

He studied Jace how confused he was acting was concerning him. Matt stepped closer to him and reached out going to touch him.

"Alpha are you-

"Nora!" It all rushed back to him, the words your in a time out hit him full force.

He spun on his heels looking behind him, his wolves resting. The pack behind them as well. He spun back to Matt with anger in his eyes. How long has it been? Is she hurt?

"How long?" Jace growled his eyes looking to the sky, the sun saying it was past noon.

Matt stepped back placing distance between him and Jace. The anger makes Ryker whimper inside of him. Matt cleared his throat putting a hand up trying to slow Jace and his anger.

"You've been out for six hours." Matt said his voice just above a whisper.

"Six fucking hours!" Jace yelled, his chest vibrating with anger.

"Why didn't you continue on! Fuck sake Matt Nora! Your Luna is endangered." Jace growled, stepping towards him, his body twitching from the anger.

"Alpha everyone is in position. Logan and the hunters are just outside the City Light's border. Black Sand and Moonlight are in their positions. Red Woods is entering the grounds in an hour. Dark Water is already present and Douglas pack is about an hour out. Nora says she is safe." Matt said calmly, trying to keep Jace's anger down.

"How do you know she is safe!" Jace yells in Matt's face, Matt shut his eyes defensively.

"Asher and Red Woods can still communicate with her. Asher sent a message." Matt said, keeping his response short.

The rest of the pack was cowering behind him. Jace began pacing. The sunlight changed everything. They didn't have the cover of darkness to come in. He backed away from Matt.

"Alpha, we couldn't leave you." Matt said his voice pleaing to Jace's back.

"You should have. This changes everything. We now need to wait for the ceremony to start. Security is going to be heightened until then. Before then we had the darkness." Jace growled.

Jace clenched his teeth together at the word darkness, he didn't know what force that was but he was going to find a way to make whoever it was pay. If Nora is harmed in any way he wouldn't care if they were the goddess herself he would find a way. He had placed a pack member with each group so they could communicate through mind link. He gritted his teeth and looked at Matt.

"Matt send out a message let them know we are moving out and everyone to hold in place until the ceremony." Jace said, shifting his stance and stretching out his body.

"The rest of you, let's move out." Jace said, stepping forward and allowing Cole to push forward.

"That was close." Polly whispered as she looked over at Nora trying to see if she was ok.

"Yeah, let's move quickly." Nora said to her motioning for her to go forward.

Polly nodded and led the way into the hall. The place was mostly empty and it felt wrong. It was the middle of the day and it should have tons of staff. Nora looked around as she was walking by empty exam rooms. The glass windows made for observation. It looked so much like the facility Kip had made beneath his pack house. Chills went up her arms. She never thought she would see a place like this again. This place was bigger, the white long halls turned and weaved through the place. The whole time they hadn't bumps into one person. It was making Nora more nervous. Polly kept looking back at her. She didn't know why but her stomach was knotted up inside of her. Her body is on high alert. Everything was in her scream, something was wrong. She was trying to blame it on the eerie feeling of the hospital setting but she knew it was more.

"It's not too much farther." polly said reassuring her but it didn't make Nora feel any better.

Nora felt her body get defensive. She felt energy rushing through her. It was almost as if her body said it was ready and armed if she needed it. It made her almost smile. Polly halted in front of her. A large steel door was in front of her. It needed a badge to open it. Polly pulled a badge out of her pocket. The action didn't sit well with Nora for some reason. She pressed the badge to the pad and the steel door clinked and released opened.

"Polly, Why do you have a badge?" Nora asked, trying not to sound defensive.

"Oh I work down here. That's why I know everyone. Lucky right." Polly smiled stepping into the door.

"Come on." Polly said to her from inside.

Nora took a deep breath in, her body yelling danger, danger. Everything in her was on edge. She clenched her hands into ist by her side.

You on standby? Nora asked Zara.

Hell yeah, I feel it too. I'll rip her throat out if needed. Zara growled in their mind.

Nora shook her head at Zara but her aggressiveness was what they needed in this life or death situation so she did not blame her. Nora stepped into the room like she was expecting the floor to give out from underneath her. They were in a smaller room that was just a hallway. At the end of the hallway there was another door. The door she had just walked through sealed behind them. Polly walked to the other door and scanned her badge and it popped open.

"So once we go in this room, it's the size of a school gym. The creatures will be chained to the walls. I don't know what your goal is after that." Polly said quietly.

"I'll need you to leave the room while I do it. I'm not sure what will happen either." Nora said, studying her.

Polly nodded and pushed the door open. The door was slow to open. As it swung away, the noise of loud growls and chains rattling flooded Nora's ears. She walked onto the white tile floor and was overwhelmed. Polly wrapped her fingers into Nora's hand nervously. Nora squeezed back as the door was behind them. Nora's eyes surveyed the creatures, it was heartbreaking. These poor people were mutated against their will into an uncontrollable and unrecognizable beast. There was one closest to them, it was the only one quiet he hung his head low. Nora walked slowly over to him and Polly pulled her arm back.

"What are you doing?" Polly asked Nora as she tugged on her.

"This one…What's wrong with him?" Nora asked quietly.

"Nothing, he is just like the rest. We need to hurry, Nora, we don't have much time." Polly said, rushing her.

The quiet one lifted his head and locked eyes with Polly's sadness rushed through them. He knew her. Nora looked at Polly confused, letting go of her hand.

"Polly he or who he used to be knows you. What aren't you telling me?" Nora said, Zara growling beneath her skin.

"He… He's my brother. Can you save him?" Polly whispered, her voice heart breaking.

"Kill me." The creature said, his face half mutated between wolf and human.

"Herny." Polly said, her voice cracking from the tears she was holding back.

"Kill me!!" Henry screamed.

"Oh god." Nora said, putting her hand over her mouth, the rest of the creatures beginning to become more and more restless.

"Polly go." Nora said forcely.

"Please Nora. Please help him." Polly cried begging her.

"Polly I..I can't undo what's been done. I can't reserve it. I…I can just end it." Nora said her voice was sad for her.

"It's my fault. Nora please. Help him." Polly begged, grabbing ahold of Nora's hand.

"The only help is death." Henry said from the wall.

"Henry." Polly cried out, her hand covering her mouth.

"He's right Polly. You need to go." Nora said to her, trying to be kind but stern.

Polly let go of Nora's hand and began walking to Henry. Her body trembling trying to hold back her cries as she approached Henry. Henry locked eyes with her, the one human green looking at her. She went to reach out and touch him.

"Don't! I have very little control." Henry yelled at her his voice breaking as a growl and snarl escaped, his jaws snapping at her hand.

Polly stumbled back. Nora came up behind her and put her hand on her shoulder. She squeezed her shoulder tightly.

"Polly, I need you to go." Nora said, turning her towards the door.

Polly couldn't say anything as she began walking to the door, Her eyes locked on her brother as she exited. Nora took a deep breath looking at the room full of Lobo. She shut her eyes, summoning her power forward. She didn't know where she was pulling the energy from. Normally she had to touch something to pull from it. Her whole body vibrated as she looked around trying to form a plan on how she was going to do this. The Lobo's in the room dropped their heads and became quiet. She realized she was pulling the energy from the room. She was holding it and a light began to radiate out of her. She walked to the middle of the room, her body beginning to shake. She felt like she was going to explode if she didn't let the energy out.

Jace I love you. Nora sent thinking of him hoping that he got the message in case this went south.

She dropped her head forward focusing on the room. She took a deep breath in. Her hand cradling her stomach as she prayed the baby would be safe inside her. She remembered what the Goddess said and she trusted her. She exhaled feeling Zara's strength merge with her hunter side and then released it.

Chapter Fifty Nine
Lobo's

A wave of energy exploded out from her. The force of it made her body float off of the ground. A light radiated out from her filing and blinded the room. The Lobo's didn't even make a sound as it hit them. The room went quiet and as the light faded the Lobo's instantly began to fall against the wall and then sink to the floor. Nora's head shifted back as she was suspended off the ground. Wave after wave of energy pulling out of her. Ensure that the Lobo's are gone. As the last Lobo sank to the floor the energy receded back to Nora. She floated down from the air. Her feet hit the ground and she fell to her knees breathing hard. Her body was shaking from the surge.

"Nora! Nora don't you do anything! You wait for me! Nora! Nora say something! Nora!" Jace's voice flooded her mind, his voice panicking.

She smiled softly, she touched her arm making sure this was real and she had survived. She shut her eyes leaning forward trying to calm breathing.

"Nora! Nora, tell me you're ok!" Jace's voice came again.

"I'm fine. I'm ok." Nora sent back, happy she could hear Jace's voice.

Her hand on her stomach fear and worry ran through her hoping the baby was ok.

"Don't scare me like that." Jace sent back, his voice relieved hearing her message.

"I'm sorry." Nora said, her voice containing a smile.

"I love you too, see you soon." Jace sent back relieved.

The little one is ok. Zara's tired voice came through after Jace's.

Are you sure? Nora asked Zara.

Yes. I…I need to rest. Zara said, exhausted.

*Go ahead. I should be fine for now. I'm sorry.
Nora sent back to Zara as she stood, her legs shaking
as she did so.*

"Nora!" Polly's voice came rushing to her side,
as Polly kneeled down in front of her.

"Polly, I am so sorry." Nora said in reference to
her brother.

"You didn't do anything. It was Bruce and
Lance. Henry was right. That was the only way and
now he is free. Thank you." Polly said, looking to the
ground.

"Polly get up, why are you kneeling? " Nora
said, confused and trying not to sway.

"The power you have, it's goddess-like." Polly
whispered.

"Polly we don't have time for this. Get up and
help me out of here." Nora laughed.

"I..I-

"Do you want us to get caught?" Nora sighed at
Polly stumbling over her words.

"No." Polly said standing slowly, her eyes still
down casted.

Nora became frustrated and grabbed Polly's
hand. She forced her to look at her while trying to
control her frustration.

"Polly, I am not a goddess. I am ..I don't know
exactly what but do not treat me like this. Now we
need to get out of her and back to my room. We need
to get going now." Nora said, tugging Polly's hand
while she spoke.

"Ok…ok." Polly said the tone of Nora's voice
snapping her back into place.

Polly began walking towards the door, her first few steps awkward and then she began walking normally as if still shaken by the events that took place. Nora followed behind her. She watched Polly glance to her brother before crossing the doorway of the gym-like room. Nora wished there was something she could have done for him. Nora slowly closed the door behind them. They quickly made their way to the next door. Polly pushed the large steel door open and froze.

"Hey! What are you, Wait aren't you the soon to be Luna? Does Alpha know-

Nora moved around Polly quickly. She placed her hand to the back of the guard neck and let a jolt of what felt like electricity course through her hand. The man instantly dropped to the floor

"Holy shit." Polly whispered.

"I know, I know." Nora said quickly, grabbing the man's leg.

"Help me." Nora said to Polly who was still standing there looking surprised.

"Right, Right." Polly said, grabbing the other leg of the man.

They dragged him into the hallway they just came out of. Nora dropped his legs and hurried out of the hallway, Polly following behind her. Nora shut the door as Polly exited and the door sealed.

"Can he get out?" Nora asked Polly as she stared at the door.

"Is he alive?" Polly blurted out.

"Yes. I just shocked him ...I think. If he's alive can he get out?" Nora repeated her question.

"No, he needs a badge." Polly said, looking at her and going to poke her hand.

"For the love of god Polly I control it….for the most part." Nora said, swatting her hand away.

"For the most part?" Polly asked, scared.

"Stop, let's go before anyone else comes." Nora said, rolling her eyes and began walking down the hallway.

"Ok." Polly said as they hurried down the halls.

Getting to the main door Polly grabbed Nora's hand, getting her to stop. She had forgotten about the camera. Nora had her hand on the door wanting to get out of the hospital as quickly as they could.

"The camera." Polly said tugging on her hand again.

Nora froze, she shifted impatiently as she watched Polly's eyes gloss over. She felt like she was racing against a clock. She had this overwhelming nervousness telling her that they needed to get back to her room now.

"He's not there!" Polly said quickly.

"What?" Nora asked quickly, her hand still on the door handle.

"He's not at the station to turn the camera off." Polly said, anxious.

"Well we can't stay here all night." Nora blurted out.

"Wait, wait. I got an idea. Stay here." Polly said, running back towards the inner door.

"Where are you going?" Nora said after her.

"I'll be right back." Polly said quickly and disappeared.

Nora began pacing in front of the door, it was a small space and no real room to move. She was getting sick to her stomach each passing minute. It felt like hours. The door to the inside of the hospital finally began to open. A thought suddenly dawned on Nora, what if it wasn't Polly. She pushed back into the wall as if it could hide her.

"Here." Polly said walking through the doorway, in her hand two doctors coats.

"Quickly put it on, when we walk out the door, walk fast and keep your head down. It's the best we can do for now." Polly said, throwing her arm in one side of the coat.

"You're a genius." Nora chuckled, throwing the coat on.

"All right Doctor, Let's get out of here. Remember head down." Polly said, nodding to her to open the door.

Nora opened the door and kept her head down as she walked by the camera. She picked up her pace once out of sight and began moving as quickly as possible down the hallway. She stepped aside letting Polly take the lead.

'We need to ditch the coats." Nora said to Polly.

"There's actually a laundry shoot up ahead we can toss them down there. No one will know the difference." Polly said as they moved.

Polly swung the doctor coat off her shoulders, Nora following suit. She almost giggled as they both tossed the coats down the laundry shoot and rounded the corner. She could see her room up ahead and relief rushed over her. She wouldn't feel completely relieved until they were in the room uncaught. She put her hand on the door knob and pulled the door open. Her and Polly rushed into the room. Nora shut the door laughing, letting out a nervous laugh as she shut the door behind them.

Polly let out a long breath as she began to walk into the room. As soon as they were away from the door, a knock came from it. Nora looked at Polly whose eyes were wide. Nora cleared her throat and turned to the door. She straightened her back and put on her best fake face and opened the door.

'Hello." Nora said, a little confused, staring at the two girls standing at the door.

"Alpha Lance sent us up here to start your hair and make up." The girls said in unisom.

"Um no thank you." Nora said quietly.

"He said to let you know he insisted. He thought you would refuse and he said to go get him if you did after we said this part." The girl with the light brown hair said.

"Fine." Nora groaned letting them in.

---

*J*ace had been pacing the outline of trees that were just beyond the road that lead to City Lights inner city. He could see the big gold gates from his stance.

"Alpha Douglas says he's inside and in position. He's waiting for you and the packs with you to come in. He is currently in the hall waiting for the ceremony to begin." Dalton said quite to Jace as he walked past him.

Jace nodded his response to Dalton but stopped as he watched Matt starting to approach as well. Jace shifted, waiting for Matt to approach him. It was hard for him to sit still. Cole was focused on getting to Nora.

"Alpha, Moonlight has the back of the city. They started moving through the City slowly since they are the farthest. Asher said Red Woods is sitting in the back of the hall. Asher said it's the biggest, brightest building. All other buildings are connected to it. Black Sands are on the other remaining side. The hunters are moving slowly in as it's getting darker." Matt said updating him on every one's location and status.

As Matt was speaking the sun barely stayed up. It had ducked behind the buildings giving the sparkling city a golden glow. Jace let out a breath of relief. He could finally start advancing.

"Let's start moving out." Jace yelled behind him and as if they were waiting on the signal they all instantly started moving.

Chapter Sixty
The Hall

    Nora stared at herself in the floor length mirror. She was staring at a woman she didn't even recognize. She sat like a zombie for almost two hours as the girls attacked her with hair brushes, curling irons, and make up. She was completely numb from the experience. She blinked her eyes trying to adjust to what she was seeing. Her hair was half up, half down in beautiful banana curls. They had placed a large jeweled hair piece on top of her head. The rubies sparkled in the light each time her head moved, standing out beneath its golden frame. Her makeup was done with a smokey eye with a long black eyeliner wing. Her lips were painted the brightest shade of red, making them stand out even more than her honey colored eyes. The girls attempted to take off her onyx and replaced it with yet another ruby but Nora won that argument. She shifted the dress slightly, sending out another broadcast of shimmering light. It was all overwhelming.
    "Ready?" Polly's voice came from behind her.
    "Are the girls from hell gone?" Nora asked with a smirk across her lips.
    "Yes thankfully. They rushed off to get themselves ready." Polly smiled.
    "You looked beautiful." Nora said to Polly.
    Polly looked down confused at herself. She had quickly thrown her hair up into a simple updo and found a dark blue gown. The way her light brown hair curled about her face made Nora smile.
    "You do." Nora said to the face polly was making.
    "Thank you. You..You look-
    "Ridiculous, I know." Nora laughed.

"No over the top but you look like one of those queens you would see in the olden days. You look like royalty." Polly smiled.

"Ri...dic..u.lous. Is what you mean and it's only until Jace gets here." Nora smiled saying his name.

Polly laughed, shaking her head as Nora moved away from the mirror. She walked to the door to her room. She heard noises outside of it and Polly made motion as if to say it was ok.

"Ok here goes nothing." Nora said mostly to herself as she opened the door.

Standing in the hall were two very large men. Nora raised an eyebrow to them as she stepped out into the hall. One man offered her his arm.

"We are to escort you to the hall per Alpha's orders." The very tall one said, holding his arm out to her.

"Ok then." Nora said, slipping her arm in his.

Polly began walking behind them followed by the second man as they walked down the hallway. Nora held her head high and prepared herself to be ready to play the part. She told herself she needed to be excited and happy. She needed to pretend she actually liked Lance. She had been doing well this whole time and this outfit she was sure was going to help her. They reached the doors and the man dropped his arms. Nora's hand fell to her side. The man following behind stepped in front of her. Both men went to the very large doors of the hall. Music began to play that she didn't recognize. The music announced her arrival. The dramatics of it all she tried hard not to roll her eyes at. The men motioned for her to stand in front of the two large gold doors. Nora nodded, stepping forward, putting her game face on. At the sound of the music changing tunes the man pushed the doors open, exposing the room to Nora.

Nora felt her legs stiffen as she looked inside. The room was turned into a long walkway to the throne area. There were church pews lined up where guests were sitting. The church pews were decorated with red and black roses. With white lilies peeking out between them. Hanging from the ceilings were more flowers and along the dark red carpet that led to the throne were white and black flower petals. The room had candles lit about it. Nora's stomach twisted more as the image of Jace, Matt, and Logan setting the hall on fire flooded her mind. She would not let them go down that path.

As the door opened to announce her arrival everyone stood. She felt her chest tighten. Looking down the long aisle Lance was standing at his throne waiting for her. Everything in her head screamed that this was some sick verison of a wedding and her stomach twisted on itself, making her want to empty it. She felt herself starting to panic as best as she tried to pull herself together. She hadn't moved from the doorway.

Come on Nora, you can do this. It's just pretend. She said inside her mind as she took a step forward.

She felt her knee start to buckle and her eyes went to Lance, his face turning to a frown as he saw her hesitate. She needed to get back in character or this could all fail.

"Alpha, we are here. Do not worry. We are with you. You can do this. You are the strongest person I know." Asher voice came through to her in mind link and her eyes scanned the crowd locking with his.

"Alpha we are here." Lyla's voice came into her mind as well, as Nora's eyes looked next to Asher and Lyla was standing there.

Nora instantly felt better. She pulled her shoulders back, placed a fake smile on her face, locked eyes with Lance, and walked like she was walking down the aisle. Reaching the stairs she stopped at the bottom holding out her hand to Lance. He blinked confused for a second and then hurried down the stairs, taking her hand in his and helping her up the stairs. He walked her over to the Luna seat, his hand lingering on her waist. The music died down around them and the hall fell silent.

"You scared me for a second there." Lance whispered to her.

"All the detail and thought you put into this was overwhelming. I had to take it all in for a minute. It is gorgeous." Nora smiled, rubbing his hand that held her waist.

"It's all for you." Lance smiled back, rubbing her hand.

Nora smiled like she was in love with him, her mind thinking of Jace. The way his eyes made her melt, his bright white smile that instantly made her knees weak. How it felt to be wrapped in his strong arms. Lance smiled back at her, touching her cheek lightly before turning to address the crowd.

"Thank you all for coming, please have a seat." Lance said, pausing as he waited for everyone to follow instructions.

"Today we merge three packs into one and form one of the most powerful packs of all time. Today we merge Dark Water, City Lights, and Red Wood." Lance said, pausing once more for dramatics.

"We will also be maintaining the alliance with Silver Mountain." Lance said locking eyes with Douglas, Douglas nodded back in response.

"From there our pack will continue to grow as we move forward with the expansion plan. The new Alpha Council will consist of myself as the one true leader." Lance said, he halted looking around the room, he was waiting for disapproval.

The room was silent.

"Douglas Alpha of Silver Mountain will also be on the council." He said, scanning the room, Nora watched him curiously.

He was wanting a fight, he was looking for that one person to show any signs of disagreement. He watched the guards he had posted alongside on the room shift. They were waiting for Lance to give a command and point the person out. Nora watched Lance's skin begin to twitch and his eyes glow. Nora knew his wolf was just under the surface begging to come out. She looked out over the crowd of people and watched as Dark Water coward and City Lights stared at the ground. What had he done to these people that they are terrified of him? Nora reached forward and touched Lance's arm lightly. He pulled away quickly as if he was ready to fight. Nora ignored it. She looked at him with a sweet smile and she watched him settle down.

"And of course the reason why we all are here. The reason why this merge will happen. The Alpha of Red Wood's pack, the first female Alpha ever. My soon to be marked mate. Nora the Alpha of Red Wood. Her strength, power and beauty will put our pack at the top above all others where it belongs." Lance grinned, speaking of Nora like she was a prize he had won.

At the words "soon to be marked mate." Nora's stomach sank. He held his hand out to her. She smiled and placed her hand in hers. Her eyes scanned the crowd. She was not sure what the next step was in this weird ceremony but something told her it was the part she didn't want to happen.

"Nora my dear, stand in front of me; facing our packs. We will now merge them by marking you." Lance said, giving her instruction.

Nora walked in front of Lance slowly. Her eyes looked over the crowd and she thought that by now Jace would be here with an army large enough to take over. She knew that she had come here to avoid all that. To make sure no one else got hurt. She stood in front of Lance and she felt him come up behind her. Her eyes went to Asher. She saw him about to stand up.

"Asher sit down. It's fine. There's too many of them for our pack to do anything. " Nora ordered him as she felt Lance excitedly pull her against him.

Chapter Sixty One
Onyx

*A*sher gritted his teeth and tried to stay glued to his chair. His mind trying to connect with someone from Cross River, he knew it was impossible but maybe. What the hell was going on? Where the hell was Jace? They were cutting it too close. He glanced at Lyla to his side and saw that her eyes were glossed over. She was mind linking someone. The mind linked ended and she looked to Asher, her face going pale. Asher knew something was instantly wrong. He looked up at the stage. Lance's mouth hovering over Nora's neck inches from marking her.

"Who did you just talk to? What is going on?" Asher sent to her through mind link.

Lyla looked like she was going to be sick, her eyes starting to panic. As she went to stand. Asher pulled her back down to the pew.

"Answer me." Asher demanded.

Nora could feel his breathing on her neck. It made her skin crawl. He tilted her head with his hand exposing more of her neck and giving himself a better angel. Nora shut her eyes trying so hard to remain still. She wanted to run, wanted to scream, to shove Lance away from her and take off. She focused on images of what would come if she didn't do this. If she didn't make this sacrifice everyone she loved died.

The images of what could come kept her feet planted. Her hand went to her stomach remembering the baby growing inside. It gave her strength to remain still. Lance lowered his mouth to her neck and she could feel his teeth grazing her skin. She held her breath, would it hurt? Jace had done it when she was in almost a limbo place between life and death. This was different. Everything was different.

There was a loud commotion coming from outside of the large gold doors. Something was happening right beyond the entrance of the hall. Lance pulled back away from Nora's neck, straightening up. As the golden doors were pushed open.

"Lyla. Who did you talk to damn it!" Asher yelled through mind link to her.

"I had one of the girls from Red Wood go with the hunters so I could be close to Logan." Lyla sent quickly, her voice shaking even though it was a mind link.

"What the hell is going on?" Lance yelled beginning angry that he was being interrupted.

In walked two guards dragging a fighting person. Nora's heart sank as she watched a guard toss the person forward. The blond perfectly shaggy hair flopped forward covering his chocolate brown eyes. He smiled brightly as he looked up, his eyes hitting Nora.

"Logan." Lyla's voice broke as she looked at Logan, her body shaking. Her wolf demanded to shift and save him.

The words no, shattered Nora's brain. Her eyes flickered to Lyla who was shaking almost violently. Her eyes glowing amber as she tried hard to contain herself. Asher placed a hand on her thigh as if he was holding her in place.

"Lyla, keep it together. I won't let Logan get hurt. I order you not to move!" Nora demanded through mindlink at her.

"Alpha, we found this person lurking about." One of the guards said towering over Logan.

Nora looked to Logan, her eyes asking a million questions. Logan would never get caught, something had to have happened..something bad. She held her stomach tightly as it felt she was going to vomit. Pulling the fabric of her dress in her hands. Logan winked at her and that didn't make her feel any better.

"Who are..... Hunter." Lance said, starting to ask who this person was but then Logan's scent hit him.

"How dare you show your face here! You're kind is not welcomed!" Lance bellowed, stepping out from behind Nora.

"Well I heard there was some type of party. And me personally, I love a good party." Logan said, getting to his feet.

"Now this whole thing. I think I'm reconsidering the type of parties I crash. This…this looks like some cult shit right here. Mixed with some weird marriage thing. I don't know about all this. Is the bride willing? Darling, are you ok? Blink once for yes and twice for no." The guard standing behind him hit Logan on the back of the head, his head flopped forward and back, a loud chuckle escaping Logan as it happened.

"You say my kind, like we are the gross ones. But were not the ones playing dress up about to eat your bride to be 's neck in front of everyone. You guys have issues." Logan smirked slowly, raising his head up and locking eyes with Lance.

Nora looked at Logan as she watched Lance begin walking towards him. Nora's eyes begging Logan to stop being a smart ass. It was something she loved about him but Lance will kill him. Lance growled as he walked towards Logan. He ordered the guards through mind link to hold him still. The two guards came up behind him and grabbed Logan.

"Um yeah I am not into this kind of kink either." Logan smirked, seeing Lance fill with anger.

Lance let out a loud growl as he did his wolf claws descended.The guard holding Logan snickered as he forced Logan's head up exposing the front of his throat. Lance grinned getting closer to Logan. Nora's eyes flickered to Lyla who was now shaking so bad the whole section was vibrating. The only thing holding her to her seat was Nora's command and Asher's strength.

"Time to meet your maker Hunter." Lance said, pulling his hand back.

"Wait!" Nora screamed coming down the stairs, the word wait was sent with an energy burst, causing everyone to sway at the force of it.

Nora's feet hit the red carpet of the aisle and Lance turned to her looking confused. He looked like a child that someone told him he couldn't play anymore. It was a mixture of sadness and anger.

"What?' Lance snapped at her, his eyes looking from her to Lance.

"Don't kill him." Nora demanded.

"He's a hunter. Wolf law says to kill hunters on sight." Lance growled at her, turning slightly to look at her full.

"Don't." Nora said calmly.

"Why do you know this hunter?" Lance growled now jealousy coming forward, his body twitched.

"Yes. Stop." Nora said, walking closer but slowly.

"How do you know her?" Lance screamed, turning to look at Logan with a sly smile on his face as he met Lance's gaze.

"We're....friends." Logan said letting the word friends lingered like it was meant to be more, he was playing off the jealousy.

"I will kill you." Lance said bring his hand back.

Nora was almost running down the aisle now trying to get close enough to Lance to touch him. She could make contact, maybe she could do what she did to the guard. Her mind screamed she wasn't going to make it in time. She watched Lance bring his hand back, her heart sinking further into her chest. She needed him to stop, she needed something. Her onyx necklace bounced off her chest swing in front of her eyes. Distraction. The word came to her mind, her hand coming up and capturing the necklace.

"Lance!" Nora screamed, the scream was mind numbing.

Lance stopped never having anyone scream his name like that. It was startling and he was angry as he turned to look at her. Once he turned and locked eyes with her Nora yanked the necklace off her neck. Lance looked at her confused. She held the onyx out away from her and let it drop to the floor. The onyx bounced across the ground away from Nora.

"And that means?" Lance asked, confused.

Nora locked eyes with him and watched as his expression changed. She knew he could smell that she was too a hunter now. He stepped towards her confused. As if he was having trouble registering what his brain was telling him.

"Your..Your a hunter?" Lance said, taking a few more steps towards her.

"Half." Nora smiled, tilting her head to the side as she did.

"But your…you are a wolf?" Lance said, stumbling over his words trying to process everything.

"Yes. Half wolf, half hunter." Nora said quietly, she watched Logan shift slowly putting some distance between him and the guards.

"How? It is not possible." Lance said, stopping a few feet away from her.

"The original hunters were wolves, cursed by humans. They needed something strong enough to kill wolves but also be as close to human as possible." Nora explained quietly.

"You..you're an abomination!" Lance yelled.

"I..I am the abomination. Not what you're doing in that lab. Those poor souls turning into monsters so you can play god. You! You're the abomination." Nora growled her eyes glowing bright amber as she stepped towards him.

"I am going to lock you in a cage and use you for whatever power you have. You will never see the light of day unless I say so." Lance growled.

"Think I was going to make you the Luna of all packs. Who would want you…Like that?" Lance said in disgust.

"Kill the hunter. Lock her up." Lance sent orders quickly as he stared down Nora.

Chapter Sixty Two
Light

*I*n an instant Red Wood packs were on their feet. Lance quickly crossed his way to Nora grabbing her by her hair. Lance began dragging her back towards the throne area. Red Woods moved out from the pew. Asher growled echoed through the hall. City light and Dark water were on their feet ready to fight. Silver mountain remained seated.

"I suggest you tell Red Woods to sit down or watch your pack be slaughtered." Lance growled into Nora's ear.

"In light of the newly found information. I am now selecting myself as Alpha of Red Woods." Lance yelled.

"You are not our Alpha!" Asher yelled, stepping in the aisle.

"Tell them I am the Alpha of all." Lance demanded as he pulled Nora against him.

"Renounce your title and give it to me." Lance said, placing his hand around her throat, his wolf claws digging into her.

Her body isn't reacting. Why did it not think it was in danger? This was one of the most dangerous situations she had been in and she wasn't even getting a tingle. Logan locked eyes with her, he winked again. A loud noise came from behind the golden door. Logan used the opportunity to slam his elbows into the man holding him. The men slumped over to the side. Logan began to advance down the aisle towards Lance and Nora.

Lance backed Nora up the stairs, his head on her throat and dragging her by her hair. Another loud bang and the doors of the hall flew open. Jace stepped into the hall and power radiated through the room. He immediately locked eyes with Nora and she smiled regardless of how much Lance was hurting her. Cross River filtered into the room behind him.

"Jace, how dare you come into my pack lands, uninvited!" Lance growled, he let his Alpha aura pour out from him but it was no match for the anger and strength that Jace was projecting into the room.

"You have my mate." Jace growled walking further into the room.

"I see no mark. She has no mate." Lance growled back, pulling Nora towards the throne.

"Give me my mate!" Jace bellowed, his voice made everyone in the room flinch.

"No." Lance said back, his voice barely a whisper.

"You think you and your one pack can defeat three. Silver mountain, Dark Water, and City Lights. All council packs. All the best of the best." Lance chuckled.

"If you want a blood bath I will give it to you and I will leave her with my mate and my pack." Jace said his voice was so calm and steady that it was eerie.

"Really, that what-

Lance's eyes glossed over as a mind link came through. Nora felt him stiffen behind him, she knew instantly he was receiving bad news. She could feel a low growl rumbling through his chest making her vibrate.

"Any minute love you'll be back in my arms." *Jace's mind linked her.*

"You think Moonlight, Black Sands, and a group of hunters should scare me." Lance said his voice trying not to show he was actually surprised.

"Try again, hot shot." Logan grinned.

"You forgot Red Woods." Asher said, bowing his chest up.

"You are surrounded. How this ends is your choice Lance. All you need to do is let Nora come to me." Jace said calmly.

"Four packs and a group of hunters are still no match for three Alpha councils packs." Lance grinned, tightening his grip on Nora.

"Actually you only have two Alpha council packs," Douglas said standing.

"What did you say, Douglas?" Lance asked genuinely confused about what Douglas had stated.

"Silver Mountain stands with Jace." Douglas announced, immediately the Silver Mountain pack stood and was ready to fight if needed.

"Douglas, you can't be serious!" Lance yelled.

"You and Bruce were made. This whole thing is insane. Corrupt. We need a better way. This, this is not it. Give the girl back to her mate Lance. Save yourself." Douglas said, trying to help Lance.

"That's fine! I still have my creations in the lab. They will wipe you all out." Lance chuckled.

"They're gone." Nora said her voice soft and just above a whisper.

"What? You think I am stupid." Lance laughed at her.

"Check then." Nora shrugged the best she could against Lance.

Lance's eyes glossed over as he mind linked his guards. She felt his grip tighten on her as his body began to shake with anger.

"No!" Lance bellowed, his body shaking.

"No! I don't accept that!" Lance yelled again.

"She came to me!" Lance yelled like a child.

"You came to me! You fucking bitch!" Lance said, shaking her head as he wrapped his hand tighten into her head.

"She came to you to try and save lives." Lyla said from Asher's side.

"The woman you are holding carelessly by force, is who you should be afraid of. She has united packs. Black Sands and Moonlight are in her debit. Red Woods will forever be in her debt because she freed us from a monster like you." Asher growled.

"She is an abomination. Jace, do you know she's a hunter!" Lance yelled to him.

"Watch your mouth or I will rip your fucking tongue out and have you eat it before I kill you." Jace growled, standing next to Logan now.

"She untied hunters and wolves. You best loosen your grip or someone will for you," Logan said.

"Fine..She's so important. So incredible." Lance said, trying to find a way out of this.

Nora can't end in a fight. You must be the one to end this. The words were so hush she barely heard them and she knew instantly what she had to do.

She locked eyes with Jace one last time and took a deep breath in. She placed her hand softly on top of Lance's; it was the gentlest of all touches. She focused on her surroundings around her and focused on herself. Preparing herself to pull energy. She let out a small breath and then began to pull energy slowly from Lance. If she did it slow enough he shouldnt realize it.

"Look at that your perfect angel is touching me." Lance grinned, his hand going around Nora's waist and pulling her closer to him.

Jace instantly knew what Nora was about to do.

"No! Nora don't!" Jace yelled and began running towards the throne.

Lance panicked seeing him coming and then a thought popped in his head. If he finished marking her, he would then be Alpha of Red Wood and he would still control three packs. He still had a chance. Lance yanked Nora's head quickly to the side, his fangs coming down. Logan began rushing the stage as well seeing what was about to happen. Red woods and Silver Mountain blocked City Lights and Dark water in the pews.

She could feel the energy growing inside of her. Zara stirred, finally knowing Nora needed her strength and began helping. Nora could feel it now, it was building and felt like it was consuming her. Lance's mouth came down on Nora, his fangs connecting with her skin. Nora's hand moved to the back of his head forcing his mouth further into her neck. His fangs pierced her skin. As his fangs pushed into mark her Nora released it. The energy sky rocketed into Lance's mouth, vibrating up into his skull. His body was thrown away from Nora as a light blinded everyone in the room. A loud humming noise filled the room.

The light faded away until there was just a glow. The glow was coming from Nora, like a small candle in a darkened room lighting the way. She stood unmoved between the two throne chairs. The room was silent, not a sound was happening. Most were still covering their eyes and trying to see again. Jace was up the stairs in no time. His hands grabbing the sides of her face

"Nora?" Jace said his voice for the first time ever was shaky.

Nora looked straight ahead as if she wasn't there. She was blank. She was standing frozen like a statue. He couldn't even tell if she was breathing. Jace panicked, he reached down touching her wrist. She still had a pulse. He watched her chest rise and fall. She was alive.

"Nora." Jace said again, this time shaking her lightly.

Logan was up the stairs finally recovering from the light blast that made everyone in the room temporarily blind. He looked at Nora and then to Jace concerned.

"What's wrong with her?" Logan asked, going to touch her.

Jace slapped his hand away, not allowing him to touch her. "I don't know, she's alive though."

"Nora, Come on love. Come back to me. Nora." Jace whispered, rubbing her cheek with his thumb.

"Where's Wyatt?" Jace yelled, his voice echoing off the room.

He heard movement behind him, knowing Wyatt was on his way. Jace looked at Nora's face and then something awful entered his mind. She was pregnant, what if. The surge, what could it have done to their baby. His hand went to her stomach. Touching it so gently, afraid to apply any pressure in fear of what damage he would do.

The moment Jace's hand touched her belly Nora's hand came down, capturing his hand with hers. She inhaled like she had been holding her breath and her whole body seemed to want to collapse. Jace quickly put his arms around her and pulled her to his chest.

"Jace?" Nora whispered.

"It's me. I got you." Jace whispered to the top of her head placing a kiss firmly down on it.

Logan let out the breath he was holding it seeing Nora come out of her trance. His eyes wandered to Lance. His body was against the wall, mouth hanging wide open as if he was screaming, and his eyes had gone white. Logan slowly walked over to the body he had never seen anything like that before. He kneeled down and carefully pressed his fingers to the side of Lance's throat. No pulse.

"Logan." Jace asked while still cradling Nora.

"Dead." Logan said quietly.

Nora's head whipped in the direction that Logan's voice had come from and she looked to see what he had meant by dead. She gasped seeing Lance's body.

"I…I.. I did that?" Nora whispered to Jace, her hand going to her neck where Lance had attempted to mark her.

"No, he did that." Jace said firmly.

"Let me see if he hurt you." Jace said quietly, taking Nora's hand off of her neck.

Her skin was perfect, untouched like nothing had ever happened. Nora was still looking at Lance, shocked and horrified. Jace turned her head softly away from it and moved it facing forward. Nora looked out among the crowd confused. Everyone in the hall was kneeling. City Lights, Silver mountain, Dark water, Red Wood and Cross River.

"What's going on?" Nora whispered to Jace.

She felt a wave of power rush through to her. It was so strong she had to grab onto Jace to steady herself. A sea of amber eyes looked up at her from the ground. She looked to Jace confused and baffled, wanting him to explain. She then noticed that his eyes were too glowing amber.

"Jace? Your eyes? Nora whispered, her voice shaky, as she touched his cheek, nervous for him.

"It kind of speaks for itself, Love. You just became Alpha of all Alphas. You are the one true wolf and you have untied all wolves." Jace said, lowering his head to hers.

Chapter Sixty Three
Promise

The words hit her like a ton of bricks. Alpha of all Alphas. She exhaled slowly trying to calm herself. Her immediate response was to yell No. She glanced at Jace who was looking at her like he was so proud. So much love in his eyes. His eyes were glowing amber letting everyone know where his alliance was. She had always thought in the end game he would be the Alpha of all Alpha's not her.

"I need to sit." Nora whispered, overwhelmed by what Jace had just said to her.

Jace scooped her up into his arms, she instantly melted into his chest. He was her safe place and she had missed him. She then tensed up realizing he was making his way towards the throne.

"No, not there." Nora said quickly, realizing Jace was going to put her in one of the throne seats.

Jace laughed, holding on to her tighter. Jace carried her down to the first pew where members of dark water moved out of the way so she could sit. She smiled her thanks as she sat down trying to focus on breathing.

We got this. Zara said in her head, there was a point in time that Nora almost didn't know if she could live with Zara's constant input on things but now she was like a friend and looked for her words.

"Ok." Nora said letting out a breath and then stood.

Jace was surprised at her quick action and went to brace her elbow as she stood. She smiled at him. Logan had come to the pew they were sitting on.

"Nora you ok?" Logan asked concerned.

Nora just winked at him with a silly smile as she stepped out in front of the crowd of packs. Not above them but on the same level. She looked at the door. Zeke and Grayson had made their way in, their eyes also glowing amber. Everyone was so quick to accept her. Everyone looked to her for direction and was awaiting it.

"Ok." She said softly to herself trying to gather herself.

"Nora we can just dismiss everyone and then come up with a plan we don't need to do now." Jace whispered to her.

Nora shook her head no. She could feel everyone's confusion, antipaction, and worry they needed to know they were in good hands.

"Hello. I honestly don't know what to say to all of you. I didn't even lead a club in high school, never mind packs. Anyways, what we need to do at this moment is make sure something like this never happens again. That our future and those of our members in the future don't ever experience the tyranny that we have. There is no such thing as an Alpha of Alphas. Power comes from the people and we can see that here today. You all decided that it should be me. It should not be one person." Nora paused, taking a breath before continuing.

"We need a true council that upholds the standards. We need checks and balances. Every pack brings something different and a different view. So moving forward. Zeke of Moonlight, Chadwick of Black Sands, Asher of Red Wood, Douglas of Silver Mountain, Polly of City Lights, Jace of Cross River, and the ultimate accountable checker Logan from the hunters. This position makes you the person of power in your pack. Do not abuse it. Dark Water will hold a position, but right now it will remain open until I get to know you all better. A council of eight We will no longer be divided and do what is best for our own pack but for our kind as a whole." Nora's voice ran out over the crowd, as she said each person's name she locked eyes with them and at the end of her declarations a loud cheer rang out.

Jace slipped his arm around her and pulled her against him. He nuzzled his face into her neck not being able to help himself; he had been away from her for too long.

"And this is why everyone chose you." Jace whispered.

"Yeah lets hope I don't fuck this up." Nora whispered quietly to Jace.

He laughed behind her, still holding her tightly like he was afraid he would lose her. Nora leaned back into him, she felt his hands go to her stomach and put them there carefully. She smiled knowing what he was doing.

"What do we do now?' Nora whispered to him.

"Whatever you think we should do?" Jace smirked knowing she was hating him for not helping her.

"Home." She whispered as if she was asking, she didn't want to be away from Cross River any longer.

"We will in time love, we got a little bit of a mess here." Jace said, kissing the top of her head.

"Mess, oh!" Nora said, suddenly pulling away from Jace as she scanned the crowd.

"Matt and Logan go down stairs to the lab and destroy everything. All paperwork, all documents, and all computer files. I don't want any trace of what they were doing here to get out to be recreated. Asher, I know you had locked up the stuff at Red Woods from Kip, have someone do the same. This ends here tonight." Nora said her presence turned from the girl wanting to go home to a woman in power.

"I need someone from City Lights to show them the way." Nora said and instantly someone stood up.

"Red Woods go home, Hunters you can as well. Zeke and Chadwick your packs are free to go as well. Douglas, I would like to speak to you before you leave. Nora said locking eyes with Douglas.

"I will leave someone in charge of Dark Water and we will conduct interviews to find someone to represent Dark Water in the council from those interviews. In a week's time we will meet at Cross River to conduct the first council meeting and select from the candidates to pick for Dark Water." The room listened and then began to dismiss themself.

"Lyla, Polly, and Logan should stay back to help with Dark Water." Nora said to Jace who nodded in an agreement.

"Who is Polly?" Jace whispered to her.

"She is part of City Lights, if it wasn't for her I wouldn't have been able to end the Lobo's." Nora whispered back.

"Ok." Jace said as if he had made up his mind, Nora knew he was questioning whether she could be trusted or not.

"Douglas." Nora said, connecting her eyes with him as she tapped Jace, telling him to let go of her.

Jace grumbled and released her from his grip but not letting go of her hand. She began walking down the aisle towards the hall exit. Douglas came out of the pew and began following behind Nora. Everyone shifted out of her way as she walked head held high. She reached the doors and the men by the doors pushed them open for her.

"Where is the office?" Nora paused asking one of the guards.

"First door on the left Alpha." He smiled at her as he bowed his head.

Nora smiled and proceeded to walk down the hall. The members in the hall scooted away from her and bowed their heads. She was confused at why they acted like this. She looked at Jace who shrugged. His pack was more of a family, so yes they did respect him but they didn't scoot away from him like he was some godly being. Nora frowned at their actions as she got to the door. She pushed the door open and walked into Bruce's office. She instantly curled her nose up. The whole office was self absorbed. There was a huge portrait of Bruce behind the desk. Pictures of himself scattered about the room.

"Woe." Nora said out loud looking around.

"Woe is right." Jace cracked up behind her.

"Bruce was a little um self absorbed." Douglas smirked, closing the door behind them.

"That is an understatement." Nora laughed looking around the room.

"So why did you submit to me? Why chose me? Why not you? Were you not part of the Alpha council? Did you not too dream of being the one and only all powerful?" Nora asked her questions rapid fire, her tone becoming very serious.

"Well then, I was expecting more of a threat and not questioning." Dogulas said with a smirk.

"Oh there is a threat in it." Jace said from behind her.

"Like I told the late Lance in the hall. The council downward spiral into something it was not meant to be. It was time for a change but I couldn't do it alone. I wholeheartedly meant that. Which is why I submitted to you." Douglas said his words held value as he said them strongly.

"Ok." Nora said quietly, nodding her head.

"Ok?" Douglas asked, confused.

"Yeah." Nora said quietly.

"Ok." Douglas was kind of put off by the whole conversation, these were not the conversations he was used to having.

"You may remain in the position of council member for your pack. It makes you the point person and in charge of only your pack. However, this is the part that you are used to. Do not attempt to hurt or ruin anything I love. Do not betray my trust. As you can see I do not need a whole army to fight my battles." Nora said, her voice deadly.

"Yes Alpha." Douglas said with a smile.

"Council member Douglas, you and your pack may take your leave. We shall see you in a week's time." Nora smiled back nodding towards the door.

"Alpha, Jace." Douglas nodded the same smile still on his face as he heard out.

Chapter Sixty Four
Reunited

*A*s soon as the door shut behind Douglas, Jace's whole mood changed. Nora felt it in an instant. The fearless, strong warrior that he was melted away and she felt all his fear and anxiety. Jace wrapped his arms around her and buried his face into her shoulder. His body shook lightly, his breathing got caught in his throat. Nora was confused for a second. She squeezed him back and then pulled away slowly.

"Jace?" Nora whispered.

"Damn it, Nora." Jace whispered, holding her tightly, afraid to let her go.

"Are you ok? Is the baby ok?" Jace asked, pulling back looking at her, his eyes searching hers as if looking for some sign.

"We are fine." Nora smiled big, touching his face and her fingers traced his chiseled jawline.

"You need to stop saving everyone. I was so afraid I was going to lose you. Are you sure you and the baby are ok?" Jace said as if he had been holding it together the whole time until they were alone.

"Jace I promise, the baby and I are just fine." Nora said, pulling him for a kiss.

Nora's lips hit Jace's, his hands sliding down her lower back pulling her closer to him. He lifted her slightly letting her ass sit on the desk as he deepened the kiss. She wrapped herself around him. Her hands traveled down his muscle back. She let out a small moan against his lips. She moved against him, her body craving him. Every part of her longing for his touch. Jace lets out a small growl in response and moves to kiss down her neck. Getting to the spot where she used to be marked by him. He lets out a loud growl that made Nora jump and then she started giggling about her reaction.

"You scared me! You just turned a sexy moment into a silly one." Nora laughed, wacking his arm.

"We are going to have to fix this." Jace said firmly as he nipped the spot on her neck.

Nora smiled coy at him and wiggled back away from him. The coy smile turned into a smirk. As his eyes narrowed at her. The smirk always meant she was going to challenge him.

"What?" Jace growled at her.

"Oh nothing." She said her smirk turned into a grin.

Jace braced the sides of the desk with hsi forearms locking her in place.

"It's never nothing when your mouth looks like that." Jace said his voice deep, as he moved forward letting his lips brush against hers.

"I have it on good authority that you like the way my mouth looks." Nora said, biting her lower lip.

"Nora." Jace said her name as if he was making promises of what was to come.

"I was just thinking that maybe ..oh I don't know. Maybe I don't want to be marked." Nora grinned her eyes sparkling with mischief.

"Nora, I swear to god. If you want me to lose my shit then keep going with this conversation." Jace growled, his eyes glowing as Cole pushed forward agreeing with Jace's statement.

Nora started laughing, her hand going to the side of his face. She kissed his nose lightly.

"It was the only way. I..I couldn't reject you. Removing my mark was one of the most heartbreaking things I had to do. You are my other half. I can't wait for you to put it back." Nora whispered to him.

"As you are mine. We need to go home." Jace groaned, pulling off the desk and into his arms.

"I know. I crave home too. We are almost done here." Nora said, running her thumb down his cheek.

Jace pulled back and then his eyes wandered to her belly. He was going to be a father. The thought both excited and terrified him. He kneeled down slowly looking at Nora's belly. Her belly had grown in the short time apart they had been, her small little bump was now showing. He first touched her belly with his hand and then rested his head against it. He stood there frozen just listening. Nora smiled down at him enjoying the moment.

The door swung open to the office and Matt walked in poking Logan in the ribs. Logan was visibly annoyed.

"Touch me again and I swear Matt." Logan said, turning and bowing up at him.

"Calm down hunter boy. I just missed you." Matt smirked, going to poke Logan once more.

Logan grabbed Matt's finger and bent it back. Matt began to buckle under, squirming as Logan grinned.

"Ow,ow ow. Dude." Matt yelled at Logan.

"Boys!" Nora yelled at them, her face frowning in disapproval at them.

"Woe." Matt said seeing Jace on his knees in front of her.

"Are we interrupting?" Logan smirked.

"Shut up." Jace growled standing up and glaring at both of them.

Logan let go of Matt shoving him away. They both straighten up. Matt and Logan shared the same smirk as they both tried to get serious. Jace glared at them as Nora tried to hold back the giggle she had lingering behind her lips. She cleared her throat, trying not to laugh.

"Everything go alright down in the lab?" Nora said a small giggle escaped.

Jace turned and glared at her but she ignored his eyes because if she had looked at him, she would have laughed and they would all be intolerable.

"Yes, everything is gone. No more Lobos ever again." Matt said proudly.

Logan rolled his eyes at Matt and his Lobo's.

"Believe me with a name like that, they don't ever want to come back." Logan said, teasing Matt.

"Hey! It's a good name." Matt yelled at Logan.

"If you say so." Logan snickered.

"I do say so!" Matt growled.

"Enough!" Jace roared.

The two immediately stopped bickering, like they were small children. Nora chuckled, shaking her heads at them. Logan winked at her with a silly grin on his face.

"What now Alpha of all Alpha's? Pretty big title for a girl who had none and stalked me down an alleyway." Logan grinned.

"I want to go home but I have a big favor to ask of you." Nora said to Logan.

"Name it Doll." Logan grinned seeing Jace becoming more and more annoyed with the way he was talking so friendly with Nora.

"Anything for you." Logan added to send Jace over the edge, Jace bounced off the desk and Nora laughed, catching his hand.

Nora pulled Jace back to her and leaned her head against his chest. Her touch instantly calmed him.

"I would like it if you stayed behind with Lyla and helped Polly with the interviews of the Dark Water pack members. I would really like to wrap all this up as quickly as possible." Nora said quietly.

"With Lyla." Logan said out loud, he had a strong connection to her and it was steadily growing.

"Yes, I trust you both completely. You are both good judges of character." Nora said quietly hoping Logan would accept

"Of course. I can run commands here with the hunters and help you with your search." Logan agreed.

"Are you sure?" Nora asked, she for some reason was thinking he wouldn't want to.

"Nora you are on the verge of bring a world of chaos to order. How can I refuse that? My hunters will be safer in the world because you have united us. Wolves will know that not only will hunters hold them accountable but their own kind will as well. Nora, this is ground breaking. Hell yes I want to be a part of this. Besides, we've come too far now for me to tell you no." Logan smiled.

Nora moved away from Jace and wrapped Logan into a hug. He hugged her back fiercely. Jace tried his best to keep his growls to himself but Cole was going crazy inside of him. Nora being unmarked was driving him nuts and making him more possessive.

"You are one of my very best friend." Nora said, hugging him tightly.

"As you are mine. But you might want to let me go before lover boy, wolves out and tries to eat us." Logan chuckled.

Nora laughed and let go of Logan. She walked back to Jace's side and he wrapped his arm around her, making sure to get rid of Logan's smell.

"Jace, you need to chill a little bit." Logan said to him, making a face.

"It's Cole. Nora is no longer marked so it's making Cole become extra possessive." Matt whispered to Logan.

"Ohhh."Logan said, pretending he understood.

"Alright well I am going to get connected with this Polly person and Lyla. Figure out the game plan. The quicker we start dissecting Dark Water the quicker, this will be over and done with." Logan said heading to the door.

"Thank you again Logan." Nora's voice said to his back.

"Yes, Thank you." Jace said to his back as well, his voice solid and meaning it.

"You both are very welcome, my friends." Logan smiled and walked out the door.

"Now what?" Matt asked looking at the door and then back to Nora and jace.

"Home." Nora and Jace said at the same time.

"You don't have to tell me twice." Matt grinned, pulling the door open

Chapter Sixty Five
Phase Two, Happily Ever After

A week flew by in a blink of an eye. There was so much to do and such little time. Just like the time getting away from them Nora's belly was growing and growing. She was surprised how quickly wolf pregnancy advanced. She stood up out of bed grabbing her back, feeling her hips pop. Jace was by her side helping her up fully. Nora smiled gratefully at him. He kissed her forehead and then kneeled.

"Good morning Little one." He whispered sweetly into Nora's belly.

"Little I think is an understatement." Nora chuckled.

"She's going to be strong like her mother." Jace said, kissing her belly before standing.

"She? How do you know it's not a he?" Nora smiled playfully.

"He could be as dashingly handsome as his father…strength I agree will come from his mother." Nora grinned teasing Jace.

"She is going to be as beautiful and strong as you." Jace said as if he had just made it so.

Nora laughed, shaking her head. She waddled over to her closet looking into it. A beautiful champagne colored dress was hanging there. There were soft beautiful sequences that shimmered gold in the light. Jace came over wrapping his hands around her waist and pulling her into him. He kissed down her neck and nipped her marked neck. Nora reached back and ran her hand over his neck, her fingers brushing his mark. Tingles spread through them as they teased each other. Nora leaned further back into him as he held her close.

"Are you ready?" Jace whispered looking up at her gown.

"Yes. This time everything is as it should be.' Nora whispered back to him, her eyes looking at the dress a smile on her lips.

"Well you have two hours, we've spent far too long on our bed sheets." Jace said, kissing her head and pulling away.

"You say that like you were held prisoner." Nora smirked.

"Yes tempertess, you know all my weaknesses, I was at your mercy." Jace said, playing the victim as he walked to the door.

"You like it." Nora grinned.

"Never said I didn't, Love." Jace smirked at her passing to look at her one last time, before pulling the door open.

"Make sure you eat!" Jace yelled over his shoulder as he shut the door.

Nora smiled and ran her hand across her belly. She felt the little flutter inside and it made her feel unbelievably happy. She walked into the closet, standing in front of the dress she hesitated to reach out in touch. The last time she was in a closet with a gown she saw horror. She took a deep breath in and reassured herself this time it would be different. She touched the fabric to her hand and warmth flowed into her.

She was instantly wrapped in a glow and everything felt safe and warm. As the glow subsided she realized she was standing in a garden. The sweet smell of jasmine flooded her nose. It was the most beautiful garden she had ever seen. Jasmine trees lined the opening of the garden one of her most favorite smells in the world, it reminded her of her mother. Across the crush stone path was a wood swing that in the breeze under an arch way of climbing roses. The roses were yellow and the tips were kissed with red. A small brook ran through the center of the garden and it had lily pads and water lilies in it. Everything about this screamed peace and she felt so at home.

"Momma!!" A loud shrieking giggle came from the edge of the garden.

A young girl about the age of four came running, her raven black hair flying behind her. Her bright ice blue eyes squinched up and her nose crinkled as she laughed wildly. Her cheeks were stained with dirt as she ran straight for Nora. The little girl crashed into Nora laughing like crazy.

"He's gonna get me." She laughed and then tried ducking into her skirt.

Nora couldn't help but giggle, who was this little girl talking about. Then her eyes hit him and her heart fluttered like a butterfly who had just found its wings. A slightly older Jace came running across the garden, his hair showing signs of age as it was streaked with the most stunning silver. His eyes had the slightest touch of crows feet as he slowed down and walked towards Nora. He grinned widely as the little girl ducked further into Nora's skirt. It took a second for Nora to realize he was wet.

"Now, now you can't hide behind your mother's skirt forever." Jace grinned, crouching down ready to get the little girl.

"Momma!" The little girl laughed burying herself into Nora.

"Why are you all wet?' She laughed asking Jace.

"Your little heathen tricked me and I fell into the brook." Jace grinned, shaking his head so the water droplets scattered about.

"Well then technique it's not her fault you fell into the brook." Nora chuckled.

"And you can blame her father, he's the heathen." Nora added, narrowing her eyes at him.

"Mhmm birds of a feather." Jace said, stepping close, mischief sparkling in his eyes.

"Alpha, I am sorry to interrupt but your meeting with the council is in just ten minutes." a voice called from behind them.

Nora turned and smiled seeing Dante, a young boy of maybe two clinging to his leg. Nora looked back to Jace and he sighed. He pretended to walk by and then bent down and snatched the little girl up beginning to tickle her. The noise of something behind her drew her attention and suddenly she was pulled back.

"Luna, the council is gathering and we haven't even got you dressed yet. Are you ok?" Sarah said, stepping into the closest with Nora.

"I...I..I am perfect." Nora smiled, thankful for the vision.

"Let's do this!" Lyla's voice came from behind Sarah.

Nora grabbed the dress in one hand and motioned for them to get out of the closet so she could change. She slipped off her bathrobe and let it hit the floor. She was completely naked underneath, when she was with Jace there was no point in going to bed with clothes on. She pulled the dress off the hanger and stepped into it. She pulled the gown up to her chest.

"Hey Sarah, can you come zip me up." Nora called behind her.

Sarah was back inside the closet and before Nora could blink twice she was sitting in front of a mirror as Lyla braid her hair. It was a long braid that went from one side of her head to the other and down her shoulder. She purposely asked for it to not cover her mark on her neck. Sarah then began placing the baby's breath inside the braid. Lastly Lyla came out holding something behind her back.

"I know you don't like over the top but this is a huge deal. You are not only the first female Alpha but you are the Alpha of all Alpha's. The Alpha of all Alpha's is a female! A badass one at that. So we made you a crown." Lyla smiled brightly as she revealed what was behind her back.

"Lyla a crow-

Nora was about to object but when she saw it, she couldn't. It was a simple crown made out of white flowers…white jasmine flowers. Nora's heart swelled. It was like it was telling her everything was finally going to be right. Her vision was not some silly daydream but this confirmed it.

"Thank you." Nora said quietly as Lyla placed it on top of her head.

"Ok…What do we think?" Nora said standing up.

"You are stunning." Sarah said, squeezing her shoulders.

"Breathtaking." Lyla added.

"All right girls, let's get me sworn in and officially appoint everyone into their positions." Nora smiled brightly.

Sarah and Lyla nodded excitedly and walked to the door. As they opened the door Dante was waiting to escort Nora down to the ceremony. Nora looped her arm through Dante's and he began walking her down the hallways to the stairs.

"Dante, what was Jace's mother and sister's name?" Nora asked carefully.

"His mother's name was Mallory. His sister's name was Jennifer but he always called her Lynn. Why?" Dante asked watching the stairs carefully, making sure Nora would not trip.

"Baby names." Nora winked at him.

He grinned and smiled brightly. Reaching the bottom of the stairs Nora went to turn towards the hall. Dante stopped her and shook his head and motioned for her to follow him.

"Dante the hall is that way." Nora said, narrowing her eyebrows at him.

"I know but we're not going to the hall. Just follow me, it's a surprise." Dante chuckled seeing the look on her face.

Dante led her outside and down a crush stone path. There was a row of freshly planted trees and as she stepped into it she realized exactly where she was. Right now it wasn't the garden from her vision but it would be in time. There were flowers scattered about in the most perfect way. She already knew the trees were jasmine saplings and would grow tall and beautiful. She saw the archway with the climbing roses, Jae standing underneath it. She was so taken back she didn't even realize how every pack was gathered there waiting for her. Dante grinned wider seeing her reaction and walked her down the crushed stone path to Jace.

"It's beautiful." Nora whispered to him as she took the hand he held out to her.

"It's not the garden that you loved in Red Woods and it's where it will be but if you can see the vision it will be grand." Jace whispered to her.

"It's going to be absolutely perfect." She whispered back to him.

Jace kissed her cheek as everyone began to rise. Each pack and member would swear their loyalty to her, pack by pack and then Nora would appoint each council member officially. They began starting with Dark Water.

"When this is all over, we should put a wooden swing under this archway." Nora whispered to Jace.

"That sounds perfect actually." Jace whispered back squeezing her.

She felt the intense power rush into her again, each pack member's eyes glowing as the final pack swearing their loyalty. Jace braced Nora as the surge made her shift backwards but she held her own. A cheer went up as the swearing loyalty ended and they were officially one giant pack.

"Zeke from Moonlight, Chadwick From Black Sands, Polly from City Lights, Douglas from Silver Mountain, Shea from Dark Water, Asher from Red Wood, Logan from the Hunters, and Jace from Cross River, you are all my Beta's and Alpha's of your own packs. You all hold a seat on this council, and are the point of command for your pack as we become one united pack! We are now unified!" Nora exclaimed!

A second louder cheer rose up as people clapped and embraced each other. Each council member looked proud and happy. Jace slipped his hand around Nora's waist, his hand touching her pregnant belly. Each council member's eyes glowed the color of their pack but this time an amber rim was outlining their color. Nora smiled seeing Jace's bright ice blue eyes outline in amber. She looked out over the crowd, separate but united. They were all one. The checks and balances would work this time.

"We welcome everyone to join us in the banquet hall for drinks and food….So we can all drink, eat and be merry." Nora grinned silly locking eyes with Asher, who laughed and shook his head at her comment.

Jace and Nora watched the pack filter out of the garden and make their way back inside. Nora looked up at the sky and all of the twinkling stars. The moonlight shining down on them. Thank you she said her comment made to the moon and the Goddess in it.

"Mallory Renee Lynn." Nora said turning into Jace so she could see his face.

Jace looked at her confused trying to process what she was saying, the names hitting his heart but it was like his brain would process.

"Our daughter's name. Mallory Renee Lynn. In honor of your mother, my mother, and your sister." Nora said, touching his cheek.

He nodded, leaning into her hand. He couldn't say anything at that moment. He brought his mouth to hers kissing her deeply. He pulled back looking at this incredible woman and in awe.

"You did it. You made the world a better place and just in time for our child." Jace whispered to her.

"No, we did it." Nora said, kissing him back, the moon seeming to sparkle extraordinarily bright around them; as if it was telling everyone how bright their future would be.